The

The coming

of the first

Europeans

to the Illinois Nation

and the Consequent

War with the Iroquois

An Historical Novel

By

Russell Breighner

ISBN: 1-4107-1071-8 (e-book)
ISBN: 1-4107-1072-6 (Paperback)
ISBN: 1-4107-1073-4 (Hardcover)

This book is printed on acid free paper.

1stBooks - rev. 4/15/03

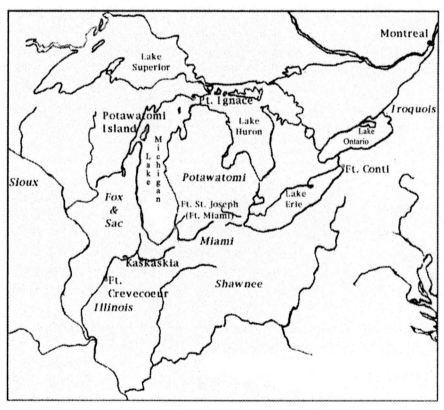

Land of the Noble Free
1680

Chapter 1

The Night of the Ox-Eye

The air was dead calm.

As the large bird continued to circle lazily, the lanky Mohegan watched with interest. Occasionally, the brown bird, whose wings were as wide as a man is tall, would tighten its interest in the clear, still waters below. Though white head would angle menacingly to one side in curiosity, the lazy glide continued.

Admiring the eagle and envying its freedom and spirit, the Indian wondered whether this voyage would bring peace or war. The far-away English colonists would do their utmost to negate French gains among the natives. Raised as one of the 'Praying Indians' in a village near Boston, he was the son of a Mohegan chief. He was well over six and a half feet tall, gaunt, but not ungainly. Squatting on a platform high in the tops of the idle sailing ship, he was one of the two Indian scouts chosen to guide the great French exploration of the lower Mississippi. His dress was simple—a fitted breechclout that was mid-thigh length and single-seamed moccasins with moosehair cuffs. All were stained black with walnut dye. From his earlobes hung black and white wampum pendants. Selflessly generous toward those in need, he was unaware his devoted service would lead to death with his

1

master and with his Shawnee friend in some distant field. From the deck below, he could hear the two white men there discussing some matter of interest.

Standing near the bow of the ship, the speaker, a man of broad knowledge and accustomed to action, was patiently waiting for the rising wind. He was wearing a plumed, French cavalier's hat, as well as boots, all black, as were his flowing, wavy hair and neatly trimmed beard. However, his bleached buckskin shirt was marked with a few, discrete colored bead and quill Indian designs.

Of greater significance, his internal complexities—only partly reflected in his outward appearance—would lead to increasing alienation with his own kind, a dangerous development in a nation where assassination was a common political expedient.

"My enemies? They are not here. I do not fear these natives; I travel freely here, and am always welcome among the Indians."

In the early morning of August 25, 1679, the *Griffin* sat becalmed a mile or so off the eastern shore of Lake Huron. *Griffin,* a two-masted, ketch-rigged brigantine, was the first sailing ship to appear on the upper Great Lakes.

"There's a contrast for you. I am safer in this wilderness than I am in civilized society." René-Robért Cavelier, the Sieur de La Salle, in his mid-thirties and recently elevated to the nobility, was excited by ideas of grand exploration and trade expansion, all to the glory of his idol, the Sun King, Louis XIV. Turning toward his companion, the young La Salle smiled at the irony of his situation.

Nodding understanding, the Italian, Signore Henri de Tonti, was tapping lightly with his gloved left hand on the gunwale. "But there is a report. A Seneca brave was captured and tortured by the *Illiniwek.* He confessed the Iroquois will attack if the French set up trade along the Illinois River."

Tonti was wearing a fine black leather vest over a white blouse. He appreciated his friend better than most and was keenly aware of the obstacles and maneuvers against La Salle, especially by persons of influence in the French court.

Even though he, Tonti, had only recently come to New France, he quickly learned that La Salle was greatly dependent upon his two Indian scouts, Nika and Shadow. Whereas La Salle had the motivation and vision of an explorer, it was these two who would ensure the peaceful passage of this small French party through Indian lands. In spite of their proud and dignified bearing, Tonti knew that beneath a facade of independence, their loyalty to La Salle was unshakable.

"I assure you," LaSalle said, tilting back his head to better penetrate the mists still hovering above Lake Huron, "the Iroquois would never send a large force so far from their lands. A few young braves seeking personal glory, perhaps. But no more than that!"

2

Squinting toward the Bruce Peninsula, obscure beneath the bright, early sunlight, Tonti said, "That opening to the northeast—MacGregor Channel, I believe."

"Quite right. Cape Hurd marks the entrance to Georgian Bay. Tobermory village is just beyond the point. Fur traders cross the bay near here on the river route to Montreal."

Above the two speakers, the rangy Mohegan watched the eagle as it circled idly beyond the bow of the ship.

Squatting in the fighting top—a circular platform on the mainmast from which, in battle, gunners could fire down on the enemy—Shadow preferred to spend his free time there during lax sailing periods, seeking solitude and spiritual nourishment. Big-hearted and generous, the tall Mohegan was competent in languages, diplomacy, and cunning. He was called 'Saget' by La Salle; by all others, remarking on his stealth, 'Shadow.'

On the poop deck, a second Indian also sat in contemplation, gazing over the taffrail at an empty sea and sky. The Shawnee was wearing copper ring-ornaments in pierced ear lobes, a several-strand quill and bead necklace, and a small, tanned-leather breechclout. His moccasins were a soft-soled, one-piece design with quillwork covering the single seam in the front. Stern-faced yet seemingly eternally calm, Nika combined an intellectual toughness with a broad curiosity. His thumb-length hair was a compromise between a shaved head signaling a vengeance lust and the need to appear peaceful to the Nations and tribes on La Salle's itinerary.

The Shawnee and the Mohegan had been captured by Iroquois war parties in separate raids. Taken to the victors' villages, these two ran and survived the gantlet. Later, in Otinowatawa, an Iroquois village at the western extreme of Lake Ontario, in 1669, this energetic Frenchman had ransomed them. But alone this captivity did not animate Nika's hatred. He thought often of his parents and their unhappy end.

Masters of several Indian tongues, both scouts had a good command of French. It had been La Salle's habit to walk together with one or the other, each speaking his native tongue, the other echoing the phrasing, until finally the sounds were mastered and the meaning learned. Eventually, other subjects were exchanged. A former Jesuit and headmaster at the Rouen Latin school—the best school in its class in France at the time—La Salle was at ease in Latin, Greek, astronomy, literature, medicine, mathematics, and geography. From his scouts, he learned Indian languages, customs, and etiquette, while giving both Indians an exposure to European arts and science.

That the Indians had learned French from perhaps the greatest linguist in Canada at the time meant their French was as good as that of most native Canadians. Having twice previously sailed to France with La Salle, these two also had a surpassing knowledge and understanding of European culture.

3

Among Indians, Shadow and Nika were immediately noteworthy for the arms they carried, inspiring both envy and respect. Among peoples whose weapons were based on stone, bone, and sinew, these men carried hatchets and knives made of iron—French iron.

"Nika and Saget—they are my bodyguards. They are my eyes, ears, and tongue," La Salle declared, having noticed Tonti studying Nika. "I trust them far more than many of my own countrymen. As long as they live, I am safe."

La Salle was approaching his thirty-sixth birthday. Five years before, Louis XIV had commissioned him to expand the fur trade to Indian lands beyond the Great Lakes. He also had the monopoly rights to trade in buffalo hides. To protect his frontier-trading zone, La Salle was to build fortifications as he saw the need, but there was no mention of colonization. France at the time needed wealth, not increased responsibilities in Canada.

As the soaring eagle tested the rising currents in the darker, northern sky, Shadow followed its every motion. The eagle's magnificent presence provided a poignant reminder of something in his past, something he could not specifically identify yet strongly felt. He recalled the happy days when he was young and went hunting with his father.

Finally, no longer inquisitive, the eagle resumed regular flight and headed south. As the bird of prey dissolved into the morning mists, Shadow sensed that more than ordinary change was occurring in his world. He sobered at the thought that his tribe, the Mohegans, had ceased to exist. The eagles in his own life were withdrawing.

Eyeing the slack sails, La Salle noted Shadow seated above. He was about to comment to Tonti when the ship's captain, Luc Mignon, walked up muttering, "I'd rather have a light breeze than this worrisome calm."

"In heavy weather, you may need to clear the poles," La Salle observed. "I have heard from Montreal shipwrights that some vessels now have ropes along the yards so sailors can quickly shorten sail."

"Not this crew. I wouldn't want to see these clumsies on any of my yards." Mignon shook his head in disgust. "Footropes are for the new sails with reef points. Furling these sails requires skills and teamwork. We can't work together! No, not that way, we can't. With this ship, it's nearly all or nothing."

Round-built and drawing less than seven feet, *Griffin* carried a blue French oriflamme with three gold fleurs de lis over her transom and from her mast top she showed the royal red banner signifying the king's commission. Engraved on the high transom was the griffin, half-lion and half-eagle, the central figure on the coat of arms of the Governor of New France, Frontenac. Similar in appearance to a galiot, *Griffin* reflected the Dutch design points that had become prevalent since Richelieu began building the French navy in the mid-1620s.

Griffin had been built to transport the fruits of La Salle's trade. Sixty feet long at the deck, she had a beam of sixteen feet and could carry forty-five tons. Her mission was to bring beaver furs, buffalo hides, and other small animal skins from Lake Michigan to the Niagara portage for transfer to Montreal and eventually to France. In return, she would bring supplies, trade goods, weapons, and gunpowder to support La Salle's expeditions.

Griffin carried a square spritsail below the bowsprit; square sails on her main and main topmast yards; and on the mizzen mast, beneath the shrouds, a lateen sail on a long yard, well peaked-up. The mainsail lower third, the bonnet, was attached with lacing—its removal providing a limited means for reducing sail. A singular difference from ships of any period is that in place of the customary long boats lashed to the skid beams on the main deck, *Griffin* carried bark canoes.

* * *

The tools, equipment, and materials—the equipage for *Griffin*—had been manhandled from Lake Ontario up the Niagara River. Against a lack of mechanical support, La Salle's men wrestled anchors, sails, tools, ropes, cordage, hardware, fittings, weapons, guns, cannons, gunpowder, and provisions along the steep-walled canyon and then, just below the falls, they raised this burden two hundred feet to the top of the bluffs.

Construction of *Griffin* had begun at the harshest time of the year—in December 1678, at Fort Conti on Cayuga Creek. Yet within six months, an unlikely assortment of builders, using the design and patterns provided by master shipwright Moise Hillaret, had in fact produced a sound ship. All in all, *Griffin* was a well-behaved sailor, showing little weather helm and having no bad tendencies in a wind.

What the men lacked in fine skills, La Salle supplied. With the adz he dubbed the balks, smoothing the rough frames as though with a plane and with the compass, he laid out stem pieces and futtocks. He coached the men in the process of squaring beams, working in the tapers, rounding off spars, planking and caulking the hull.

The launch of *Griffin* typified the man as much as had her construction. When she sailed from her birthplace on Cayuga Creek, the wind was barely sufficient; she was in immediate danger of drifting toward the falls. Yet La Salle, not unfamiliar with daunting circumstance, brought her away from failure and destruction. *Griffin* escaped the first of her challenges as she entered the waters of Lake Erie.

La Salle's party comprised his lieutenant—an Italian soldier-adventurer, two Indian guides, three Flemish Recollect missionary priests, and a personal servant. The ship's crew consisted of a pilot-captain and six seamen of undetermined worth. La Salle had also hired some twenty others: French artisans and craftsmen—*engagés*—from Montreal and France and a few fur traders and woodsmen—*voyageurs* and *coureurs du bois*—men who preferred to live apart from the European settlements but knew well the arts of Indian barter and wilderness survival.

Unaware that he had focused his attention, Shadow stared absentmindedly at a cloud on the horizon. In an azure sky, a small white top was forming there. As he recalled his Atlantic voyages, the truth of the scene struck him.

"There, to the west, a thunderhead!" Shadow called to a sailor below.

Pitré, working near the anchor cathead, studied the cloud for a few moments, then, beside himself with the import of his sighting, began yelling, "An ox-eye! There. Off the port beam!"

"Ox-eye!" Disgustedly Mignon stamped his foot. Biting his lower lip, he stared at the white knob over the horizon.

La Salle looked up at the slack sails, uselessly shrouding the masts. Annoyed by the captain's apparent anger, he shuffled along the railing to better see this menacing cloud.

"The ox-eye! The ox-eye!" Again came the shouts from Pitré, more agitated than before. "It's growing . . . It isn't moving to either side. We are dead in its path!"

The captain, muttering to himself, slowly shook his head while contemplating some invisible object on the deck.

Unhappy with the captain's lack of response, La Salle asked sharply, "Has something gone amiss?"

His face puffed and dark, Captain Mignon looked up and exploded, "Do you see this inept crew? Everything they do has to be done twice. Their work is not sure, even for basic tasks. They talk, talk, and talk about how to do simple chores. Don't you understand? How can a ship survive when its safety depends upon nincompoops as these!"

La Salle rebuked him, saying, "I'm sure these men are capable of excellent service. They need kind practice, not harsh words. Give them time. I've seen much improvement already. You must inspire each to perform to the best of their ability."

"None of it!" insisted Mignon. "I am sorry I joined your company. I am a salt-water sailor. It is an insult to die in this fresh-water pond!" He spat the words with sarcasm and disdain.

Puzzled, La Salle looked the captain over while pondering the cause for this outburst. He sensed some profound warning in the message from the sailor, but could not gauge its severity. "Just why is this ox-eye such a danger?" he asked.

The captain, turning toward him with anger and exasperation, exclaimed, "Off the coast of Africa, an ox-eye bears a tempest. If such a storm catches this gang, we are finished." He paused, looking meaningfully at his lumpish crew.

Mignon loudly snapped, to no one in particular, "Any salter knows we are in for a heavy blow. An ox-eye spells certain doom for us." He looked sourly around at his stunned audience.

"What can we do? We cannot run until the wind rises. This ship? Ha! Built by woodsmen who carry their tools on their backs! And made of soft pine? Excuse me, but she'll leak and I doubt she'll hold. And this crew? Woodsmen! Outlaws! Priests! And Redskins!" Captain Mignon bitterly chewed off each epithet. "If we do not founder, we will be driven against a weather shore. Or maybe ground against submerged rocks. We do not have enough sea around us. For us there is no hope, there is no safety!"

"You give up too easily," gently chided La Salle. "These woodsmen are as durable as any sailor from Brittany or Poitou. As for the Indians, they know something about rigging, stays, and braces." After a pause, La Salle added, "Our priests are hale and used to punishing work. Do not belittle their help. We can fight this storm. And we shall!"

Sensing La Salle's determination, Mignon shook his head, regained some self-control, and said, "All right, then, as the wind rises we'll head into Georgian Bay. We'll anchor in the lee of some island there."

"If this storm is as strong as you suggest, I doubt that is a good choice," La Salle said slowly, surveying each man on deck. "There are many rocks and islands in the bay. The wind is certain to move round the compass. Our haven will become exposed. If *Griffin* slips her cable, she will founder. This is a sound ship, and watertight. Our safety lies in having sea room.

"There is where we will ride out this storm," La Salle exclaimed, pointing to the expanse of Lake Huron.

Blank-faced as if misapprehending, Duplessis gawked at La Salle. The color of Duplessis' long and tangled beard nearly matched the sandy beige of his buckskins. His close-set eyes seemed to pinch the nose on his long and narrow face. Looking plaintively at the nearby shore, Duplessis felt deprived of its proffered safety, palpable, and within reach. A hard knot formed in Duplessis' stomach, urging him to act, but he could not conceive a rational, sensible deed. Seeing disbelief on the faces of others, Duplessis burst out, "We'll drown out there. All of us! In the bay are lagoons, many places where we can hide. We'll be safe there."

"Those are false havens, death traps. You who have little experience at sea, trust me," La Salle said. "You, all of you, are no longer passengers. Each must pull hard against your harness from here on. Any slack will endanger us all. Whatever Captain Mignon asks, do it quickly and with all your strength. There is no room for even small mistakes; the ox-eye is unforgiving."

"Lake Huron is uncharted water," captain Mignon protested weakly, as if not yet ceding the argument. "There could be shoals and rocks there fatal to our safety."

7

"We have taken soundings since the Detroit Straits. The bottom has shown deep and well-behaved," La Salle rested one hand on the fiferail. Looking toward the ox-eye, he added, "In the end we must face this storm with these ordinary men and they will provide our safety, captain. I am certain of this."

"Death, Mon Sieur, is very ordinary," Mignon winced as he looked at La Salle through narrowed eyes.

"Speak of life, captain," La Salle snapped. "However we come through this storm, life is worth living."

Captain Mignon's black hair continued along his jaw, extending into a short, cropped beard, and as his mustache, it showed sporadic gray. He was a little less than average in height. Not that he stood at his full stretch—he was slightly stooped. And with that, he never held his head erect. In fact, there was really nothing direct about his physique or his manner. His narrowed eyes always looked askance, never ahead. He rarely looked anyone in the eye.

Mignon seemed to be always half-sneering at the thought of someone's misfortune. He took delight in even the smallest failures of those around him. He was not himself a perfectionist, but considered the foibles of others as somehow confirming his superiority. He habitually used condescending nicknames to demean those who served under him. Criticism was his means of asserting dominance, not of helping others. Yet La Salle felt that deep within this self-protective, leathery cynicism, there lurked a human spirit.

"Rustaud! Assemble the topmen!" Captain Mignon waited while the only true sailors aboard, scampering from their various locations about the ship, assembled before him near the main mast. They already sensed the sea change in the captain's demeanor.

"*Mes braves,* standby to furl the sails!" Captain Mignon began, barking his orders. "We are facing a real test. A storm is forming, perhaps a gale. I have been watching the mares' tails drifting since early dawn. We are in for it. There is little time. Bourdon, Pitré—unlace the bonnet from the mains'l. Camus, Rustaud—hand the tops'l to the topmast! With our main we will take the rising wind seaward. Move roundly now! Aloft!"

As Camus and Rustaud scaled the foremast ratlines, they could feel a rising breeze, already rustling over slack sails. From the fighting top, they hauled the clewlines, bringing the lower corners of the main topsail to the mast.

"Foot it in!" came the insistent yell as the sailors got into the chore of securing the heavy sail. Camus and Rustaud lay the material in folds against the mast, reducing unwanted voids and tying gaskets as they worked.

"Amain! Amain!" Mignon continued to yell from below. He shook his head and looked again at the dark gray mass building over the opposite side of the lake. As it extended to nearly half the horizon, opaque blocks broke away, drifting toward *Griffin*.

"Neptune's sheep are grazing!" Mignon bellowed, agitated by the growing white caps on the chop. Long swells already played at *Griffin*, rocking her, making her yards swing wide. Gathering way under a single sail, *Griffin* slowly came about until she had a following sea, carrying her toward the center of Lake Huron, into the path of the storm.

Mignon gauged the sailor's efforts and formed an estimate of the time needed to finish rerigging. "Move smartly! The wind is rising. We'll soon have the first squalls."

La Salle, the priests, the two Indians, and one woodsman toiled in the sail locker, securing loose gear, making room for furled sails. Tonti worked in the galley making biscuits, coffee, and burgoo, an oatmeal porridge that, although not popular, was common fare in rough weather. Two sailors coiled lines for warps and drags, ready for streaming in an emergency. The men below decks, perhaps because of confinement, first felt the pitching of the ship as the growing swells overtook her.

The wind, blowing steadily now as a strong breeze, was singing in the rigging. No one on deck could be heard without yelling. The first squall swept over the ship, soaking Camus and Rustaud as they labored to secure the last topsail gaskets. The deck crew also was drenched as they manned the halyards, easing the bonnet to the deck.

"There's no hurry!" Mignon smirked as a woodsman, enmeshed in a tangle of lines on the deck, working unhurriedly. "Do you not see the white horses running?"

The woodsmen looked blankly at Mignon then realized the captain was focused on the large white breakers chasing each other across the water.

Mignon feared this storm. With so much unseasoned help aboard, he doubted the wisdom of La Salle's stratagem.

The driving rain of another squall thumped against their backs as several artisans struggled to bring the rolled bonnet to the main deck hatchway. The light was now uniformly gray, only the white caps telling water from sky. Already the wind was shearing off their crests, turning the foam into long streaks of spray.

"Brace the mains'l!" Mignon shouted to the deck crew. "Brace her up sharp. We'll run close-hauled."

As the men attempted to turn the mainsail yard, the port brace pendant fouled, leaving the yard askew and the sail luffing.

Responding to shouts from below, Camus worked his way around the fighting top. While reaching toward the suspect sheave, he lost his footing, tumbling over.

On deck, Mignon, attending to another problem, was bellowing, "A Judas tied this cow-hitch! Bourdon, who did this!? Pitré, belay this line!" He called, "All hands! Be on guard! Someone is working *a la diable*. No loose ends! Or we may all end in misery!"

The frantic plea, "Help! Help!" fixed Captain Mignon in his place. Gaping, he looked up to see dangling near the main yard, a desperate Camus, inverted and clinging to a clewline. Only his leg, caught between the brace and the yard, prevented a fatal fall into the dark and frothing sea.

Rustaud, who had been on the opposite side of the fighting top, advanced cautiously past the mast and reached toward Camus.

"His leg! He says his leg is broken!" Rustaud called to the deck as *Griffin*, heaving backward on another cresting wave, violently convulsed the luckless Camus. Nearly losing his own grip on the wet sailor, Rustaud bawled, "I cannot hold him! We need help!"

Instantly the spidery Shadow was clawing his way up the wet ratlines. Rising to the tops as he normally did to find seclusion served him well now. The horizontal rain, intensely pounding his naked back, was like so many pellets testing his skin.

"Shadow's coming, Rustaud. Hang on! The Indian is almost there!" The excited shouts from below matched the deck crew's frantic efforts to control the wanton mainsail.

Rustaud recklessly clung to Camus' convulsing form. Leaning well over the railing, Rustaud clasped Camus by the thigh even though the rain, running into his eyes and nostrils, blinded and choked him.

Meanwhile Shadow, balancing uncertainly on the mainsail yard, advanced quickly beneath the suspended sailor. Holding onto a liftline, Shadow was able to maintain only a precarious balance and could not bring Camus to safety.

"All hands standby by to hand the mizzen lateen! Man the brails! Loose the clew sheet! Start the foot!" Mignon called, ordering the men on the poop deck into action. Clenching his teeth, he looked regretfully at the lateen, for its loss would mean reduced steering control, and in the confused seas he expected, he would not want to lash the helm.

Straining to see the drama in the rigging, the men blinked the rain from their eyes while pulling against the waterlogged, windfilled canvas. The greater their effort, the more resistance the sail made. The ship, too, confounded their labors, rolling and tossing, making footing uncertain on the watery deck.

Drawn by the shouting, La Salle appeared on deck. "Who's the man in the rigging?"

"An unfortunate wretch!" Mignon bawled, squinting at the men above the mainsail. "This crew of inepts should never have left port. If we lose him, good riddance!"

"He is neither unfortunate, nor a wretch. He is one of my men. Remember that!" La Salle snapped. Noticing the hampered sail, he added, "His safety is your first order of business."

"If we cannot outsail this storm," Mignon said through clenched teeth, "there'll be no safety. It's the ship or not one of us'll swim to shore this day."

"May I offer a suggestion?" La Salle insisted against Camus' howls, which sounded more and more like the painful wails of a forlorn bobcat.

An exasperated, silenced Mignon, staring dumbly at the grasping sea, did not answer. The safety of the ship depended upon the timely retrieval of the sails and the battening of the hatches. Delay would imperil them all.

Trying to take his full weight, Shadow clung to the inverted Camus as the heaving ship threatened to toss all careless souls to the rough mercies of Lake Huron.

"In the next trough, place the wind off the port quarter." La Salle, wiping the water from his brow, caught Mignon in a slack moment. "Sail across the face of the next swell, for as long as you can manage."

Looking at La Salle for an instant with unmistakable resentment, Mignon protested, "We're handing the mizzen lateen. The whipstaff won't allow coarse control. On top of that, the wind is moving round; the seas are becoming confused."

Deflecting the captain's objections, La Salle insisted, "We've got to save that man."

Mignon rolled his eyes, pursed his lips, and then in the end acquiescing, began giving orders. He put two of his best men on the whipstaff as he set others to capture the unruly foot of the mizzen lateen, now flapping freely outboard. Listing slightly to starboard, *Griffin* came about to a new course, surfing nicely just below the crest of a following wave.

On Shadow's command, Rustaud released Camus, then called, "He's got him!"

Shadow quickly wrestled his human burden toward the mast where footing and support were more adequate. *Griffin* pitched downward across a crest as Rustaud scampered to assist. With Camus between them, the two began a slow, careful descent.

On the poop three men had secured the foot of the wayward lateen, but were stalled handing the sail to the yard. Startled by their inaction, Mignon eyed the loosely bunched sail and the long yard, swinging back and forth, its topping lift jammed.

Racing toward the base of the mizzenmast, angry at the mutinous sail and contemptuous of his dimwitted crew, Mignon yelled, "Bourdon, aloft! Clear that block. Pitré, ready the gaskets. I want that sail furled and the yard lashed to the deck. Immediately!"

As Bourdon clambered up the mizzen shrouds, Martin abruptly released his brail, freeing a section of the sail once again. Stumbling across the pitching deck, Martin caught up on the taffrail. Retching violently, he fought to maintain his balance as his stomach contents went in one direction, the railing in another. The insensitive wind returned his vomit, liberally seasoning him and the straining men behind.

Recovering, yet nervous and feverish, a rueful Martin resumed his position on the brail, but was able to muster only half his strength. Nevertheless he managed to bring his ballooning sail to the spar by the time Bourdon signaled he had freed the block hanger.

Shaking his head in disbelief, Mignon turned his attention to the rescued Camus. He called down the aft companionway, summoning Tonti to the deck. "We have an injured man here. Take him below for care and treatment. We have enough clutter topside as it is."

"Duplessis, help us!" Tonti yelled as he led a small group bearing Camus toward the forward companionway ladder. "Fetch splints and cloths! We'll take Camus to the mess deck."

Captain Mignon watched as the men assisted Camus down the steep, narrow ladder. He saw that the wayward lateen yard at last had been subdued and that its sail properly gasketed. He was about to go forward when the mainsail snapped.

"She's going to blow out! Ease the garnets! We cannot lose the main course," Mignon cried out, summoning his men again. As they responded, he went looking for La Salle. Finding him on the foc'sle deck, Mignon, out of breath, yelled, "The wind is continuing to rise . . .

"We can no longer sail . . .

"We must clear the poles . . .

"We'll stream drags and warps . . .

"We can do no more."

The wind was now shrieking through the rigging; black clouds, low overhead, seemingly reached down to the masts. The impetuous seas, now mountainous swells, heaved then swallowed the desolate ship. The wind, shearing the wave tops, made long, gray scends of foam and mist.

La Salle, blinking sea water from his eyes, ordered, "Captain, button your ship! And quickly now!"

"As good as done!" Mignon replied. Abruptly, he turned and went aft to where his men were lashing the lateen yard to the deck. Two were leaning over the rail, vomiting. Like some mechanical toy with alternating figures, one would straighten as the other bent over, tasting the burning sourness from yesterday's feast.

"You two!" captain Mignon roared. "Go to the sail locker; bring up the drags. Double quick! Or you'll end up on the wrong side of a battened hatch!"

"Bourdon, Rustaud, aloft! Secure the main course. We must bare all poles, now!" Mignon bellowed, but the men were already moving, the situation obviously critical. La Salle, meanwhile, had gone below to check on the steering and bilge operations.

From the poop deck several worked the main braces, squaring the yard to the mast while others trussed the mainsail by hauling the clew garnets. Slowly the free blowing canvas responded, at first resisting this human effort, but ultimately surrendering, settling snugly around the mainmast. From their perches aloft, two sailors sought quickly to secure their prisoner, the task nevertheless requiring triple time to complete.

The torrential rain gushing over the deck produced an impenetrable, slippery coat. This windswept surface no longer tolerated the presence of ordinary mortals. Movement in any direction was barely possible.

"We must batten down. Everyone alow, at once!" Mignon yelled, hurrying the work aloft while clearing the deck. Standing by the aft companionway, the captain waited anxiously as Bourdon and Rustaud clung to the shrouds. Half expecting to be blown overboard, they descended by fits and starts, unwilling to risk the insecurity of moving to the next rung. As he stood watching these last refugees, the captain was suddenly overcome with fatigue.

* * *

The men had all gathered below—the hatchways were now firmly secured—and Captain Mignon thought all was as well as could be. Nevertheless, a deep anxiety continued to trouble him. In the yellow light of the overhead lantern, he quietly surveyed the hold, seeking a cause for this disquiet. The barrels were snugly wedged; he saw no standing water. Then it struck him. The stays!

"Bourdon, Rustaud! Did you bowse the stays?" Mignon singled out his topmen.

Staring at Bourdon, Rustaud avoided the captain's gaze.

"I reckon we forgot, what with all the other work aloft." Bourdon explained lamely. He knew the stays should have been made extra taut, but time did not allow.

"We could lose a mast," captain Mignon said through clenched teeth. "It can't be corrected now. It's simply impossible."

Tired and disgruntled, the captain made his way aft. He had meant to check on the whipstaff crew, but he stopped short of the after bulkhead, for he heard, rather than saw the water puddling around his feet. It was there, but only when the ship's bow rose.

"Man the brake! Man the brake!" he yelled. "Where's the pump crew?"

There was a stirring in the foc'sle. Mignon watched as two Flemish priests came running. Father Gabriel Ribourde, a hearty, robust man of sixty-four years, caught one of the pump handles. The zealous missionary, Fr. Zenobe Membré, thirty years junior, was on the other. Soon they had an established syncopation, drawing water and expelling it from the ship.

"Who assigned you to the pumps?" Mignon asked angrily.

"La Salle. We've been here over an hour," Fr. Ribourde replied, smiling. "We went forward to, uh, answer nature's call. Too much coffee, you understand."

"Call for a replacement when you need to leave your station," Mignon responded, constraining his impatience. "An hour is long enough. It's time someone else worked these pumps. I'll see to it soon."

"Yes, thank you. Very much," Fr. Ribourde smiled as he curtsied to the rhythm of the bilge pump.

Captain Mignon lingered until the water level began to recede. Satisfied this was hatchway water and not a leak, he asked to be notified of any increase, then went further aft.

Finding La Salle near the steering area, Mignon reported tiredly, "The swells are fifteen feet and growing. If a surging wave catches *Griffin* broadside, she'll capsize. It is extremely important for the helm to keep her bow to the seas. The drags and warps we streamed will help a bit, but the wind is moving round again."

La Salle nodded and waited as the captain scurried off to his cabin. Yelling above the storm, La Salle asked the whipstaff crew, "How can you steer? You can't see what is going on outside."

"We w-w-watch the lantern," answered Chapelle, a round-faced, stocky man of average height and one of the *voyageurs* that would have been much more at ease in a canoe. "When it s-s-seems to hang to one side, we steer in that direction. This heads the bow to the trough."

"That seems to be the best we can do. Carry on with your good work. And let me know what I can do to help."

"W-w-we've been here for quite some time," Chapelle complained.

"I'll go forward and send a replacement crew," La Salle said and stepped out of the orange-yellow light into the darkened hold.

Griffin continued her serpentine wallowing, laboring down into another trough, only to be lifted and raised again into the dark, full fury of the gale. Pitching and yawing in the tumultuous seas, *Griffin* heeled hard over as she fought to save her human cargo.

Huddled in the hold, the crew of the *Griffin* knew they no longer controlled their own destinies. Listening to the shrieking wind and the drumming rain, they wondered what fate awaited them.

The men had been confined for several hours. From all signs, they knew the storm had continued to increase. The normal dankness of their restless wooden dungeon, the aroma of the fresh-worked oak timbers and pinepitch, the odors of sweaty clothing and buckskin succumbed to the sour smell of frequent vomit, all blending into a suffocating atmosphere. Some, finding no comfort, were overcome with nauseous disorientation.

"Lord, let me die!" Martin gasped between heaves. He had emptied his stomach some time ago yet he was allowed no respite, no recovery. Feebly bracing himself against the bulkhead, he nearly fell over as the ship rolled away. "I'm so sick. I want to die! O Lord, I cannot take this."

No one responded to Martin's lament. A few stared blankly as they tried to focus on some distant, unreachable refuge.

"I need air. A bit of fresh air," Martin wailed, rolling fitfully on his side. "Is that asking so much?"

Unable to offer any aid, La Salle made his way to the captain's cabin, and was surprised to find Mignon there. "How much longer will this storm last?" he asked.

"Hours, maybe forever. This storm, he is worse than the Bayamo, even worse than the Black Squall of the Caribbean." Lying prostrate in his bunk, the captain, under the weight of his dejection, trailed off toward other thoughts. "And this crew isn't worth much, even in fair weather."

"Perhaps you need to forgive," La Salle said after observing Mignon for a minute. "But first, you must forgive yourself. Forgiving is hard."

"Forgiveness! Have you noticed? We are all going to die!" Mignon spoke despondently. "Soon we'll be caught, caught in a cross sea, I tell you. We will roll onto our beam-ends. Or a following surge will drive the stern under. Take your choice—we shall not escape."

"The worst death is to die unforgiving," La Salle said in a conciliatory tone. "Martyrs forgave even their executioners."

"You talk of noble acts, now?" Mignon grunted. "Only ignoble death waits for us."

"In forgiving, we are all noble. To be free of guilt is the only true freedom," La Salle said. After an interrupting surge, he added, "Even the lowliest criminal should not die unforgiven."

"Outlaws deserve to rot and die!" The captain scowled as he stared at the cabin door. "Prisons, galleys, and gallows! These are the gods of the strong. None of your sentimental rubbish."

La Salle stood, half-turned, prepared to leave, but said, "Your atheism is a denial of your own spirit. Your logic has brought you to utter defeat."

"Your God is implausible. It is too easy to deny His existence." Mignon rolled onto his side, his back to La Salle.

"Our hope is no less than reliance on the improbable." La Salle paused, waiting for a response, but none came.

"You may be right. Our survival is improbable," La Salle said at last. "Do you have any recommendations for my ship?"

"No. No one can survive topside in this gale and there is little we can do below. We can only wait for the end." Mignon felt some comfort as he watched La Salle retreat from his cabin.

Dejected, La Salle retraced his way forward. Passing the bilge pump watch, he was startled to see the priests Membré and Ribourde still working the brake.

"How long have you been here?" he asked.

15

"Does it matter? Anyway, the captain is sending replacements," Fr. Ribourde responded politely. "To die idle is painful, don't you think?"

"Enough of that!" ordered La Salle. Combating Mignon's pessimism helped raise his own spirits, but he was dismayed by this callous oversight—relief on the bilge pumps was long overdue.

"Are you keeping ahead of the water?"

"In fact, no."

"What do you mean?" demanded La Salle.

"It is not much, but the level is rising."

Upset with this new discovery, La Salle went forward and quickly returned with two others. "Here, Messier and Chapelle will take your places," he announced. As the new team took over the bilge pump, the priests flexed their cramped hands. In the dim light, La Salle noted a dark patchiness in their coloration. He grasped Ribourde's hand and turning it, saw the red, pulpy mass where blisters had formed, burst, and peeled.

"Go up with the men. Keep them calm. And do not permit negative talk. Wrap those hands in cloth." La Salle spoke sternly with the old priest.

"Tonti! Make short watches on the bilge. These priests have been there too long. Their hands are useless now." La Salle met Tonti near the main mast, where it passed through the hold, as Tonti was returning from an inspection forward. "We also need to set a new watch on the whipstaff."

"Where's Mignon?" Tonti was puzzled by the captain's absence.

"He is wallowing in the irons of his despondency," La Salle replied. "He has given up, I'm sorry to say."

As *Griffin* heeled under a fresh gust, La Salle nervously surveyed the cargo tie downs. Everything seemed to have been properly secured, but his concerns were growing. More and more he worried he had led his men into a lethal trap.

On entering the crew's quarters, La Salle snapped, "Duplessis, Martin, Fr. Hennepin, Saget, and Bourdon, man the whipstaff! Be careful. The force on the rudder can knock you off your feet. Bourdon, you are the lead helmsman."

Watching the men go aft, La Salle turned and demanded, "Henri! You have a musical talent, isn't that so?"

"Yes, I used to play the tiorba," Tonti replied, remembering the days when he played a twelve-string lute and sang with his men. The son of the Governor of Gaeta held up his gloved, mechanical hand, and shrugged. "The siege of Milano. That is where my playing ended."

"But you still sing?" La Salle was speaking louder than necessary, compelling the crew's attention.

Tonti glanced at the men. Their fear was palpable, but he saw that, over the noise of the storm, they were listening.

"Yes, I do," Tonti said, returning to the question. He braced himself as the bow of the *Griffin* plunged downward, the ship sliding down the crest of yet another swell. Smiling, he added, "Perhaps I could provide a little melody now?"

"Do you know any French songs?"

"Oh, yes, of course. I know the music of several French composers. Viscount Conti provided many excellent entertainments." Tonti looked at the anxious faces around him and strained to maintain a conversational mood. "I was his guest."

Remembering La Salle's nearly fifteen-year absence from France, Tonti added, "Perhaps you have heard of Camberfort, Guédon, or Boësset? These are the leading composers in France." Beaming with a touch of patriotic pride, Tonti looked around, trying to encourage the anxious audience. "And it is because they have studied the Italian opera style."

Tonti paused as the ship once again yawed on the roiling sea.

"Perhaps you know the works of Moulinié?" he called, uncomfortable at distracting the men and not quite able to distract himself.

"Antoine, or his brother Etienne?" La Salle shot back, offended at the suggestion his tastes had become outmoded and provincial.

It was the inactivity that most bothered La Salle. He felt choked by the inability to take any action. In spite of that, he replied, "I prefer the younger man's music."

Smiling at the response, Tonti rubbed his chin. Recalling a popular song, he was about to begin when a surging wave sent hundreds of pounding fingers probing along the deck.

It wasn't the thunder above that commanded sudden silence. Concentrating with suspended breathing, each person listened attentively for the least sound of water penetrating the ship. After some moments, almost by agreement, the men relaxed, again looking at the other for a reassurance that was temporary.

"I have just the song for us," Tonti exclaimed. "It is called 'Come My Betrothed.'"

As another wave thundered onto the deck, Tonti was glad for the opportunity to sing as it helped him control his own apprehension.

Mentally La Salle was counting the waves as they played against the ship. He knew periods of large waves would be followed by a series of smaller ones. Hoping for a reprieve in the smooths, he nevertheless feared the rogue monster waves that he knew roamed Lake Huron that night.

The words of the *air de coeur* floated on the Italian tenor's voice, resounding through the crew's quarters.

> *Veni, Sponsa Mea*
> *Veni, de Libano*
> *Veni, coronaberis.*

Tonti was beginning the first stanza, "*O gloriosa Domine—*" when muffled shouting erupted from the rear of the ship. Hardly had he realized something was amiss when *Griffin* abruptly listed heavily to port. Amazed,

Tonti watched as the storm lantern, suspended from the deck beam, frenziedly threw its unstable light athwart unseen crannies—the lantern swinging crazily as the ship continued its rapid roll. Tonti and most of the others slid briskly down the tilting deck; one or two men, quick-witted, grasped the stanchions, now nearly horizontal.

Thunder deafened those inside as the breaking wave struck the ship broadside, the roar resonating from all directions, stunning in its proclamation of doom.

"The ship is sinking! We're going to drown!"

Wildly climbing the uptilted deck, several made futile attempts to grasp some firm structure, to do something more than passively await their fate.

A budge barrel broke loose in the forward hold. Slipping its bonds, the hundredweight cask caromed across cargo and deck, crashing over its obstacles, climbing the bulkhead to be deflected by the upper deck knee, threatening to crush the less-than-nimble in its descent.

"The ship is going to break up!"

"No! She's holding! The *Griffin* is a good ship. Don't give up hope!" La Salle yelled despite his own terror. His eyes probed each seam in the planking, seeking the slightest indication of intruding seawater. "Don't be frightened! We're still watertight. We will ride it out!"

Ice-cold fear flooded the men in the hold. Choking down the seductive impulse to madly rush to the false freedom of the open deck, several nevertheless succumbed to the fear that held them prisoners to a frozen numbness.

The ship, contorted in her wallows, creaked and groaned as timber worked against timber, she straining to right herself when a resounding crack, sharp as a thunderbolt, came from the mainmast.

"Chafing! The mast is chafing against the wedges," Rustaud called out. "Nothing's broken. It's all right!"

"Nothing's broke, he says," LeBlanc clucked, breaking into a broad, sheepish grin. A black-bearded fur trader used to long hours in a bark canoe, LeBlanc had never before been aboard a sailing ship. Tears welling in his eyes, he exclaimed, "My God! He says nothing's broke! Ain't that amazing!"

"Yeah! That's right! Nothing's broke!" Pitré chimed in, slapping his thigh in a display of false courage. Denying his own convictions, he lied, *"Heu!* This ship's got some life in her. We may just make it yet!"

The budge barrel lay suspended against the near-vertical upper deck. Having exhausted its spite, as the ship righted itself, the barrel tamely rolled down from the ceiling, landing gently, but with a decided lack of sympathy on top of Camus' legs.

Shrieking at his latest misfortune, Camus sat pinned beneath the gunpowder keg. A trembling heap, Camus weakly pushed against the oaken bulk.

Someone cursed.

Instantaneously, he was struck, the blow knocking him crashing over the cask, onto several men beyond. Tonti, startled, turned to see La Salle looming in the doorway, livid.

"There'll be no blasphemy on my ship!" La Salle roared. "Tonti, see that this barrel is secured."

At Tonti's command Rustaud struggled to remove the barrel. Camus bit his lips, sobbing at his pain.

"You have a knack for accidents, do you not, *Mon Ami?*" Rustaud grimaced as he raised one end of the barrel, then winked over his shoulder as he and Tonti lifted the keg into the cargo area. "Maybe today you should take up fishing, eh?"

In the dim cabin light, La Salle braced as the ship careened into another trough.

Tonti, who had inspected Camus' injuries, rose to announce his findings. "Good news! Camus' leg is not broken. Badly battered perhaps. But not broken!"

Noting Tonti's feeble encouragement, La Salle surveyed each of the men. He noted their fear-bleached faces peering out from sweat-matted hair and beards. He challenged them to show courage, "We are being tested. We shall not fail; we are not made of base metal!"

"The rudder! The rudder!" Someone yelled from the whipstaff room. "The rudder is jammed! God help us!"

"Henri! Keep order here," La Salle shouted as he stood awkwardly in the 'tween-deck waterway, bracing himself against the unsteady, rolling deck. "I must go aft to see what has happened.

"Nika, Rustaud, follow me!" La Salle ordered and they scrambled aft over the ship's tilted furniture and loose cargo. The whipstaff crew could be heard bawling in the after hold.

As La Salle came into the steering room, he was dismayed to see the men crumpled together in a low corner of the deck, the whipstaff frozen in position.

"O God! We're all going to die!" Duplessis was moaning. Wild-eyed, he was sitting more or less on top of the heap, his knees up to his chin and his arms hugging his legs.

La Salle was struck immediately by the stench of fresh vomit, then saw it on the deck and on some of the prostrate men. "What . . . Why are you . . . ? What has happened?

"Bourdon! Answer me!"

"The whipstaff—it's jammed!" Bourdon stammered from his nook. "Duplessis threw up! It's all over the floor. We lost our footing, couldn't stand. Lost control . . . Whipstaff's useless. Rudder's fouled . . . We're finished!"

"Nonsense!" La Salle screamed at Bourdon. "We're still watertight!

"Rustaud, what can we do for the rudder?" La Salle turned, jabbing his hand against the chest of the man behind him.

"I'm not sure," Rustaud stammered, unable to come up with a solution. "Could be fouled. Could be we backed over our drags."

La Salle stared hard at the man.

Rustaud shook his head. Hoping to convince La Salle of his folly, he blurted out, "No one can survive topside in this gale."

"Can we can steer if the lines are cut?" La Salle demanded.

"Dunno," Rustaud looked away from La Salle. It was not a difficult choice; Rustaud knew certain death waited on deck. He preferred the small comfort of remaining inside the ship. "Who could do it?"

Griffin heeled, again rolling nearly onto her side as she fell off the coming sea. As the ship shuddered upright, the mainmast, like a giant tuning fork, vibrated down to the keel, grinding down the men's resolve with another fiendish boom.

"Lord, pardon us our offenses," Fr. Hennepin implored from his dark corner.

"No, no, no! It's impossible, I can't do it," Rustaud objected to La Salle's silent, insistent demand. "It's pitch black. There's nothing to see. Anyone topside'll be carried away. Anyone!"

"Lord, for our safety—a chapel for St. Anthony!" Fr. Hennepin pleaded, propped against the sloping bulkhead.

La Salle became increasingly frantic. Overwhelmed with constant reversals, he succumbed to the idea of failure, feeling for the first time hollow and weak, unable to conceive an escape to safety for him and his men.

"O Lord! Deliver us in this hour of need!" Fr. Hennepin continued.

Stung by the priest's prayers, La Salle retreated from his surrender and, rising to his full stature, roared, "No! No! This ship is not my tomb!"

A low grunt from behind arrested his attention.

Turning swiftly toward Nika, LaSalle immediately understood and bawled, "Can you do it?"

La Salle studied the Indian intently.

Sniffing at the stagnant, stench-filled room, Nika declared, *"Ici cela sent le renfermé. Je prends l'air."*

"Ce n'est pas facile à faire," La Salle objected.

Ignoring the comment, Nika drew out his hatchet and checked his scabbard.

Gratefully, La Salle accepted the offer. *"Prennez soin de vous-même."*

"Je m'arrangerai!" Nika said and went to the companionway ladder. He stood there for a moment taking in several deep breaths.

Those nearby watched with mixed feelings. Some doubted his chance for success; others didn't care. Nika stood waiting beneath the hatch.

La Salle unfastened the cover and stood ready. Finally, as a wave made a clean breach, La Salle flung open the exit and yelled "Now!"

Nika lunged onto the deck, which was still awash with chilling water. Losing his footing, he slid down to the bulwark. Gathering his bearings, he noted the hatch had closed, no helpful light escaped. He felt only the sloping deck, otherwise there was no up or down, front or back; there were only the unseen, angry rain stabbing his skin and a wailing, impatient wind forcing suffocating, mist-filled air into his lungs.

In a moment, Nika recovered from his initial shock. He felt the ship rolling broadside onto another swell. He hurried across the deck to the upper railing and, bracing against the coming wash, placed his feet against a hatch coaming and grasped the free end of a fiferail line.

The overpowering force that struck knocked him free, sluicing him around the deck. Jumping up as the water receded, Nika ran along the railing onto the poop deck, frantically seeking the after pinrail.

Coming upon a tangle of ropes, he furiously tested one after another. Most were slack or led to the upper rigging. Finally he found one that led over the side and was taut. Holding onto the free end of a tackle line, he began awkwardly chopping at the dragline with his hatchet.

A surging wave, smashing Nika mercilessly against the bulwark, totally engulfed him. The relentless current pulled him, submerged, away from the railing, and slammed him against the deck again and again. Abruptly he washed against the lateen yard, the furled sail cushioning the impact. Gasping as he emerged from the receding tide, he realized his hatchet was gone.

Nika struggled back to the railing, searching for the miscreant rope. He came upon it just as the ship rolled away from another swell. Grasping the rope tightly, under the thundering cascade Nika twisted violently, pounding against the deck and the bulwark. Bruised and aching, he kept his grip.

Slowly, as the water receded, he brought his knife from the scabbard, his arms leaden. He sawed at the rope once more. This time it parted.

The watery onslaughts continued. There was no letup in the wind and driving rain, yet *Griffin's* behavior improved noticeably. She was rolling less as she sluggishly brought her bow to the seas.

Nika was exhausted.

Somehow he located the main mast. He was relieved just to be away from the punishing after-bulwark. He settled around the mast—his temporary refuge—hugging it with his arms and legs.

As he rested, an icy tiredness suffused him. Each wave now seemed colder than the preceding. A growing drowsiness begged him to sleep. He began to shiver.

Once more the water embraced him, lifted him, bore him from his seat. He could neither resist, nor cling to the mast. Incomprehensibly, he was on his feet. From the depths of his confusion, he vaguely began to sense someone standing near him.

Then Nika realized that not the sea, but a human held him. Shadow! Shadow had found him. Together they braced once more against the mast, waiting as the vessel yawed into a rising swell. As the ship righted itself, Shadow dragged Nika from the mast, the two tumbling through an open, lit hatchway.

Someone offered a blanket. Nika's sore body welcomed the comfort. Dazed, he sat transfixed while he slowly regained his strength. At length he gazed tiredly at Shadow and, smiling weakly, teased his friend. "And what brings a Wolf from his den on a night like this?"

Shadow snorted. "As you said, it is stuffy in here. Since when are you the only one who can go out for air?"

"But how did you find me? There is no night darker than this."

"Ha! You are noisier than a thumping rabbit in heat. How can we rest with a graceless Shawnee scuffing about the deck?" As Shadow gazed at his friend, the glint in his eyes betrayed his true feelings.

"So you knew I was sitting by the mast?"

"I brought you back only because, as I said, you'll be quiet and I can rest."

"You worthless Mohegan! If ever I have the chance, I'll throw you to the fishes," Nika said, grinning as Shadow broke into a broad smile.

"Do that! Until then, let us have a smoke. I have kinnickinnick." With an air of anticipation, Shadow rummaged in his tobacco pouch. He savored the prospect of sharing his private mixture, a special blend that included willow bark and sage.

He was delighted his friend was safe.

Chapter 2

Dance of the Calumet

Her sails billowing brightly with the fresh morning breeze, *Griffin* cocked her yards toward the playful, rolling swells. Racing ahead, the waters splashed against the far, sandy collars of the three islands posting the exit from Lake Huron. Where these lands rose above the mist-draped waters, the finer colors of rock and foliage brilliantly reflected the dawning. Choosing her way and careful to preserve a clean wind during the passage, *Griffin* headed between the small, low island in the middle and the towering one to the north.

Crisp in the new light, high crags proudly saluted the passing adventurers with the sound and clatter of wakening wildlife. As hawks and eagles wheeled and dove in the higher air, a heron skimmed over the water, making a deep, croaking sound as it gracefully swept the air with its wings. The plashing surf sparkled beneath the dark pines and hemlocks shielding the shoreline.

Nika enjoyed the opening of this day, as he did most days. As he inhaled nature's vitality, he noticed Tonti nearby, similarly absorbed in studying the quiet drama.

"Mish-ili-mach-in-naw," Nika said quietly, and, without turning, listened attentively for Tonti's response.

Tonti repeated the word slowly, carefully. He knew Nika had meant it for him. Confident of his pronunciation, he turned an inquisitive eye toward the Indian.

Nodding approval, but still observing the island, Nika said, "It is, you see, the 'Great Turtle.' Do you feel its spirit?"

Tonti looked obliquely at the Indian, then again faced Michilimackinac Island. Part of the eastern wall rose over one hundred and fifty feet before rolling back from view. The ship was now slipping swiftly past the island.

"When you feel the life around you and know that you are a part, but only a part of this life, then you will begin to see things as the Indian does. And you will come to better understand the Indian." Nika said, searching among the trees and towering bluffs.

Tonti recoiled, feeling a slight challenge in this remark. "Ahh, yes! I see now what you are saying. Europeans see the world as too abstract, inanimate."

"It is, after all, essential to your culture, isn't it?" Nika asserted. "By denying the spirit, you are free to destroy the gifts of nature."

"I do not think we are destroying as much as building. Europe represents one of the finest civilizations the world has known," Tonti replied.

Declining the argument, Nika instead smiled politely and said, "Have you traveled much? Do you find travel easier in Europe than here?"

"With *him*, one never travels easy," Tonti said, wagging his head toward La Salle. "I do not believe he rises from the same spot in the morning where he lay down to sleep the evening before. He is always on the move."

Tonti sized up the Shawnee, then shaking his head, exclaimed, "That storm! I have this feeling I have come through some kind of doorway, you know, as though I may never go back, never return to the settlements."

Smiling, Nika said, "That may not be as bad as you think. It is a sign: Your worst storms are behind you. You are going to spend a long and peaceful life among the Indians! In fact, the things of your past will remain forever a memory."

"Oh, you mean my hand?" Tonti stretched his gloved hand then gazed wistfully at the looming cliffs above. "I've gotten used to it. I hardly remember the use of my fingers. But I agree with you on one thing—I have seen enough of war."

As the *Griffin* passed close by a brushy dead tree in the water, four geese, their black necks stretched stiff, flew quickly away, their wingtips grazing the morning surf as they sought fresh solitude.

"What of Europe? Do you long to return there someday?" Following the flight of the geese, Nika spotted a large osprey nest high in a dead pine. The nest appeared empty.

"No, it is too confining. Too many petty interests there competing for power, influence, and wealth. Here in Canada freedom flowers on the very trees, it leaps from the earth; it flows on every stream. This is invigorating!"

"Then you will be happy on this journey with La Salle. You will meet many peoples, all free. Freer than your countrymen, in many ways, you'll see."

"I recall La Salle said you had been to France—What? —Twice now, I believe." Tonti rested his gaze on Nika.

The Shawnee shrugged indifference. He watched the flight of the four geese as they made large, sweeping circles offshore.

After a pause, Tonti mused, "Yes, that door is closed. I am never going back. I accept that without regret. After all, there is nothing for me to return to."

"Brave words! Especially since you know little of what lies ahead." Nika nodded approval. "That is the mark of great courage—to sail into the unknown and not look back."

After a pause, he added, "Where you go, I go too!"

Tonti, somewhat surprised, said, "I should say the same for you! You have shown more loyalty to La Salle than many white men. And for how long? Ten years or more?! I appreciate such dedication. Indeed! What could he have achieved without you and Shadow?"

"Do you see those geese? They are alarmed," Nika directed Tonti's attention to the circling birds. "Yet there is nothing for them to be frightened of."

"How do you know they are frightened?" Tonti asked. "I had noticed them."

"When they fly in circles, they wish to return to their nesting area, but won't," Nika observed. "They fear exposing its location. Do you see they do not fly in their usual formation? None is leading. And listen to their calls. Two are making rapid yaps like a dog barking. At the same time one is making long, slow *gronnk, gronnk, gronnk* sounds. If you listen, you can hear the worry in their song."

Concentrating on the geese, Tonti grimaced, then turning, looked at Nika for a moment as if making a new assessment of his companion.

"Many white people fear the Indian. They call us savage," Nika stood erect. "But you will find hospitality and generosity, if you do not act as the goose."

Noting Tonti's grimace, Nika smiled, and turning from the receding island, he noticed a low, green bar growing along the western horizon. Point Ignace lay at the southern tip of this new landmass, a flat landscape without drama. Nika wondered whether the human reception would be emotionally unmoving as well.

* * *

News of *Griffin's* coming had thrilled the mission populace for some time. For months, Iroquois runners had reported the construction of a huge wooden canoe near Niagara Falls. Later, canoeists from Lake Huron brought amazing stories of a fantastic floating island, one with bears climbing in its trees. But no one had fully appreciated the significance of these reports. Ottawas, Hurons, and Ojibwas gathered along the pebbly beach to study this amazing vessel as it approached, its white sails shining against the bright, eastern sky. Wiping their hands across their faces, several sought to dispel the incredible chimera.

The woodsmen, missionaries, and traders alike were equally incredulous.

"A large sailing vessel on the upper lakes!"

"Pure fantasy!"

"He's brazen, all right. Looky what he's brought beyond Niagara."

"So he's got determination. Who needs these noble bluebloods here? Ain't we got intelligence and courage enough ourselves? Mark me, no good'll come of this."

"You're right. He's out to change things. And it won't be to the good for you and me."

Nika and Shadow watched from the bow as many Indians launched their canoes into the chilly waters. Soon a fleet of birchbarks loaded with howling and gesticulating Indians fairly blocked the progress of the floating fort. Some fired muskets in exuberance, while not a few of the animated warriors fell recklessly into the water.

Some of the Europeans on shore were renegades from the law, a few even fugitive agents of La Salle. Among these, trepidation, not welcome, was a common reaction. La Salle had been expected, but his arrival doubted. Now before them, his presence and authority loomed large. Flying the royal pennant and carrying the Canadian Governor's engraved coat of arms—this was no ordinary trade ship. *Griffin* was at one and the same time an armed merchantman and the French-Canadian Navy of the upper Great Lakes.

The Jesuits, too, were apprehensive. La Salle had left their order after ten year's service and now seemed more loyal to the king than to the pope. Louis XIV desired to subordinate ecclesiastic appointments in the Gallican church to his own will and satisfaction. The Jesuits, sworn to defend the pope, enjoyed less standing in the court now than when they first came to New France.

Yet the Jesuits had an established legal right to trade with the Indians in mission lands adjoining the Great Lakes. La Salle's charter granted him no exemption to this. The Jesuits were guaranteed that any new enterprise would lay well beyond their frontier. Their control of the missions as well as communications on the trade routes further ensured their authority.

Sails furled and losing way, *Griffin* drifted over the crystal shallows. At last the cable played out as the anchor fell from the cathead and splashed to the bottom. A swivel gun boomed a salute; the concussion sweeping the crowding canoeists; from the trees an answering roar echoed across the waters. Some of the Indians delighted in this display of power; others were aghast at this awesome, unexpected blast.

Nika, Shadow, Tonti, and La Salle clambered over the side into a waiting canoe. On a staff at its stern, a fluttering oriflamme—three gold fleur-de-lis on a blue field—demanded respect for the king's agent. In his best ceremonial style, La Salle wore a plumed, black flat brim; a crimson cape edged with gold; knee boots; and the sword and scabbard of a nobleman.

Ashore, La Salle assembled his company in parade order. At its head, he marched to greet the mission Father Superior and persons of rank from the Ottawa, Potawatami, and Ojibwa Nations. After the ritual greetings, La Salle marched his men to the Ottawa mission chapel. Stacking their weapons, the men entered for a Mass of thanksgiving.

After the ceremony, La Salle approached a group of waiting, uneasy woodsmen. On questioning, they admitted that they had squandered his funds, had failed to pursue his interests, and were—without apology—using his resources purely for their own profit. They further indicated others had deserted to the north, and some to Green Bay. These four, whom he had sent a year before as part of an advance trading party, he arrested.

As the sergeant of the guard placed the prisoners in irons and led them away, La Salle turned toward Tonti and said, "Henri, I want you to arrest those men at Sault Ste. Marie. Take twenty of my men with you and bring those rascals to justice."

"May I have Nika to guide?" Tonti said, looking warily toward several traders lolling near their huts.

La Salle followed his observation. "Of course, you must watch your back. Those criminals have no wish to see you. Nika is a truth-seeker. They will not easily deceive him, nor will they be able to elude him using false trails."

"Did you notice two Iroquois braves sulking in the Jesuit's enclosure?" Tonti asked with pointed concern.

"Yes, but there is no surprise in that. The Jesuits use Indian runners as messengers. Jesuit missions are centers for information outside the settlements. Any message to Montreal passes through the Jesuits and their Iroquois couriers.

"This is why the Jesuits trouble me. They are jealous of my work. Their influence at court has waned. And they see me as another obstacle. Yet I must maintain good relations with them. But I doubt they would openly interfere with my affairs," La Salle said, noticing the two Iroquois had turned away from the unwanted attention.

La Salle considered the Indians, wondering whether they were merely casual visitors or indeed spies sent to chart his progress. The reason for their presence didn't matter, though, for within a short time, he was convinced, the news of his passage to Lake Michigan would be known throughout the Iroquois Confederacy. While he delighted in the enthusiasm shown by most of the local Indians at the coming of the *Griffin*, he was a bit annoyed by the sullen attitude of these bystanders.

"Well, then, we must proceed," Tonti said. "I am resolved to quickly end this business at Sault Ste. Marie. I shall leave in the morning."

As they strolled along the lakeside, La Salle caught sight of the *Griffin* and was amused by the antics of the curious Indians crowded aboard. Several had scaled the ratlines and were clambering precariously along the upper yards as the ship rolled gently. To their great amusement, the Indians had discovered the thrill of riding in the tops of this large canoe, even though one or two had already been tossed into the water.

Mignon desperately tried to control the crowd, fearful for the safety of the ship. Vainly he yelled at the cavorting warriors, who, not understanding a word, became even more amused by his frantic gestures.

"Why are you smiling?" Tonti asked La Salle, "Aren't you concerned she may capsize?"

"No, I don't think there is any danger of that. But our captain Mignon, you see. He is having an excellent time! Don't you agree?" La Salle was chuckling at the spectacle.

"Hmmph!" Tonti shrugged. Accepting La Salle's carefree attitude, he tried another course. "What do you think of his seamanship? I wonder whether our stormy passage could have been better managed."

"He is mediocre at best. But in Montreal . . . What is available?" La Salle said nonchalantly. "He knows his ropes and can sail well enough in fair weather, as you know. But in any difficulty, the man has little enough courage."

"Can he be trusted? Do you think your rivals can sway him against you?" Tonti glanced again toward the mission enclosure.

"No, I do not trust him. Nor do I trust many of these men, for that matter, where there is no stiff authority." La Salle said, a hint of censure in his voice. "I must tell you, though. I had hoped to return to Montreal from here. I do have urgent business there. My rivals, as you call them, constantly press their case against me. I had wanted you to take charge of the expedition to the Illinois lands. But now you must set matters straight at the Sault and I must go with Mignon on the *Griffin*."

As they were speaking, they came to the entrance to the palisaded Huron village. Shadow and Nika were engrossed in conversation with several braves.

As La Salle announced his change of plans, Nika remarked, "We should be able to go to Sault St. Marie and return in a few days. It is not far, the weather is fair, and we shall be here before you sail to the Bay of Stinking Waters."

"No, I must go to the *Baye des Puants* now!" La Salle declared. "If I delay here, those rogues there will disappear into the woods. Unfortunately, I cannot delay."

"What about Fr. Hennepin?" Tonti nodded toward the Huron gate. Fr. Hennepin was sharing coffee with a Jesuit and a few Indians.

"He's reliable and courageous. But you must be careful of his vanity. Where his pride is not involved, he is honest. Otherwise, I am afraid he sometimes tells things more as he feels they should be rather than as they are."

La Salle glanced sideways toward Tonti, then added, "He is young, and a good priest. In France, he was in several battles, where—heedless of the enemy—he worked to save the wounded."

"So he has had an taste of military life?" Tonti mused.

"In a way, of course. But the principal skills needed here are the ones that keep you out of war," La Salle said firmly. "Too much courage can be as harmful as too little."

"There is another matter," La Salle spoke in an unexpectedly serious tone. "Earlier at the mission, I saw several Potawatami braves flaunting Seneca scalps. They bragged how they had ambushed an Iroquois hunting party near the Miami River. Several braves from a Mohawk trading party saw this display and were outraged. Wisely they contained their anger. The Iroquois will avenge this murder. Saget has heard rumors of an Iroquois war dance, but the Iroquois runners will not discuss where or when a war will occur."

"I have learned the Iroquois are influenced by English interests to prevent an alliance of the French and the Illinois. There could be a war simply due to your presence in Illinois country. If this happens, whose side do you take? If the French support the Illinois, the Iroquois will destroy your missions and trading posts. And if you side with the Iroquois? In either case, you are in the wrong camp," Tonti observed. "Your enemies—whoever they are—are clever, very clever, indeed!"

"The important matter is to avoid such a war. I must hurry to the Illinois to ensure peace." La Salle grimly considered the choices before him. "I cannot return to Montreal. That business must be delayed."

La Salle studied the sand for a moment, then impatiently shoving some aside with his boot, he said, "When you have brought those criminals here, have them bound over to the colonial prison in Montreal. Then bring your men to the mouth of the Miami River. I will await you there. Nika will guide—come south along the eastern shore of the lake."

The decisions made, Tonti went off to gather Nika and the men for the trip north. La Salle ordered the remainder to prepare to sail to Green Bay. An eagerness infused the two groups as new horizons bedecked with adventure beckoned.

* * *

"It is a fair wind that drives us. This is a magnificent day!" Deeply inhaling the fine morning air, the blacksmith was speaking to no one in particular even though a cluster of men crowded the nearby foc'sle, several enjoying the sensation of sailing over the clear waters of a new day.

"Yes, truly it is, *Mes Amis*," Messier responded from the crowd. A short, stout, solidly built habitué of the rivers, Messier's black and white skunk skin hat marked him a *voyageur,* a fur trader inured to long treks in birchbark canoes laden with pelts. Ambling along the gunnel, Messier pointed his index finger at the blacksmith and said, "But stand ready, *Monsieur La Forge*, we will not have the luxury of this sailing ship for long. You will soon learn the craft of the *voyageur*."

"I would have thought you just paddle away. Do you mean there is some special skill to canoeing?" interrupted Martin, a small statured man, whose large, rolling eyes seemed perpetually incredulous, or as some would put it, inquisitive without end, a blank question mark never answered.

"There you have it!" Messier exclaimed, looking around, noting the gleam in the eyes of the woodsmen and the expectant curiosity on the faces of the *engagés*, artisans hired by La Salle but who had had however little experience outside settled areas. "You see these sails? The wind is doing the work. But, in the canoe—it is a different story altogether."

La Forge guffawed. He too sported a skin hat, a tight buckskin shirt emphasizing his ample chest and upper arms. "Don't tell them, Messier. I don't think they will be too happy to hear about all this toil, do you suppose, eh?"

"No, no. Tell us," one of the sawyers insisted. "We are used to hard work. What do you think? Are you treating us as children, or what?"

"But this is different work. When the day is done, there is no warm meal on the table, there is no warm cabin, and there is no wife to bring slippers and tobacco. One league is enough to blister your hands if they're not already callused, and we manage up to twenty leagues in a day. That can mean 50,000 or 60,000 strokes. A league is roughly three thousand strokes. You must always count your strokes so that you know your distance.

"The most important questions are How far to the end of this leg? And how long will it take?" Messier paused to emphasize the gravity of his warning. "Wrong answers mean death. Then there is tomorrow—you cannot portage around tomorrow. Whatever happens today, you must sail straight into tomorrow."

"But surely you do not travel without resting?" La Forge asked, his thick neck covered with a red neckerchief.

"Of course not! We are still French, aren't we?" Messier beamed. "Did you not bring your smokes? *Voyageurs* take pipe breaks—about every hour and a half. A normal journey is a four-pipe day. But a long trip, well now, that's a six piper."

"Well, then, that's not so bad," Martin said, his eyes gleaming. "So then, we make camp in the evening and sleep till dawn, no?"

"Not so fast, Tete-Platte!" Messier bawled, causing several to laugh at the flathead sobriquet. "There are several important matters to be attended to, even when out of the water."

Another woodsman, hearing the discussion, came over to join the group. Duplessis was rather thin but of average height, about five foot, eight inches tall. His long narrow face and close-set eyes created an unusual symmetry which was further emphasized by the manner in which he center-parted his long, brown hair. Duplessis was one of the few *coureurs de bois* that La Salle had hired. Generally regarded as outlaws, or at least renegades, they abjured white civilization for the comfort of the forests and usually married into Indian society. They excelled at primitive living and in Indian languages, and in other skills, not normally commended.

"Well, it's not just strokes, you know." Messier was saying. "Travel on the river can be treacherous. You must be able to read the surface and the current."

"One submerged log . . . an unseen rock . . . a sudden waterfall, and you'll be lucky if all you have to do is mend your canoe," La Forge cut in.

"If not build a new one," Messier insisted. "You townsmen have much to learn if you are to live and survive in the wild."

"Lord, would you just look them!" La Forge suddenly teased. "They're still wearing socks!"

"Hosiery, fine shirts, and underwear are for gentlemen. There are no luxuries here." Messier smiled. "Even for La Salle. He has taken the native ways, you'll see. And in the canoe, he is an excellent *avant*.

"Everything depends upon the *avant*," Messier sat back. "The man in the bow, he sets the pace. A good *avant* is the jewel of the river. He selects the route through rapids, he must see the obstacles and avoid them, and he must know when the men are tiring. And he chants. His songs help the men paddle in rhythm."

"And Messier is one of the best," La Forge exclaimed.

"But we were hired to build a sailing ship. It's your business to bring us to the great river," one of the sawyers grumbled. He was wearing a black workman's blouse, a gray vest, black woolen trousers, and boots.

"What I am saying to you, *Monsieur*, is that even before you arrive, it may be necessary to build a canoe—with simple tools—from the raw forest. Do you need an adz, a froe, a two-man saw, or a forge? No, not here. The most important tools are the ones you keep in the toolbox between your ears. If you don't have it there, you will not survive," Messier said, tapping a finger to his head.

"We probably won't survive long anyway," the sawyer harrumphed. "I've heard many tales of savage attacks."

"Perhaps, but many of those raids were probably provoked. Do you see how freely La Salle, the *voyageurs*, and the *coureurs du bois* travel among the Indians? You show them respect and they respect you. M. La Salle does not travel with an army, nor does he threaten the natives. Do not fear the Indians and do not show fear," Messier said.

Sighing in the morning air, La Forge said, "I think I'll have some of Tonti's coffee."

"So, Tete-Platte, what do you think now?" Messier smiled at Martin. "Think you can manage a *voyageur's* camp?"

"What do you mean?" Martin suddenly became serious, reasserting his dignity without directly responding to Messier's fillips. "There can't be many special concerns to camping, can there?"

"In the first place, the canoes must be unloaded each evening. This means all our baggage, weapons, gear, furs, food, yes, even the portable forge," Messier responded with a certain detachment.

"Why not leave the canoes on the beach? Why bother with all this work?" The sawyer, seeming unable to comprehend Messier's suggestion, joined the discussion again.

"The canoe is our shelter. It is a lean-to. You prop the boat with the bottom toward the wind and you sleep with your head beneath the boat. You'll see. It will all make sense once you've done it. Believe me, *voyageurs* do nothing that is not necessary. We have long practice," Messier said. Then from his pouch he pulled a white, clay pipe, then tamped it full of tobacco.

"Well, if you can do it, I don't see how I would have any trouble." Duplessis shrugged.

"One last thing. Perhaps more important than anything else," Messier said, squinting at Duplessis while bringing out a flint and stone. "You will not go very far without fire."

"Now what's the problem?" Duplessis asked. "Surely we have flints, and there's plenty of fresh tinder about."

"And when it rains? And what about the times you are soaked and freezing? Not the time to be looking for dry wood, eh?" Messier started to suck on his pipe, faint wisps of white smoke curling from his mouth.

"I'll tell you this." Frowning at the reluctant glow in the bowl, Messier looked at Duplessis and resumed. "You must be very careful to be always able to have a fire. There are times your life may depend on it. In the wild, fire is as necessary as water."

"Not too many years ago, a friend of mine fell through the thin ice over a small stream and froze to death." Messier was speaking slowly again. "He froze because he could neither walk on his frozen legs nor build a fire. I found his body, barely a hundred yards from his cabin, six months later.

"Char cloth. That's the secret." Messier resumed after taking several long, thoughtful pulls on his pipe. "If you have a good supply of char cloth, you can always start a quick fire."

At least one other passenger went for his own pipe, intent on blending the cheering aroma of fresh tobacco with the pleasant morning air.

"Well, I don't have any. And I don't see where we can get this char cloth in the forest. Do the Indians trade it?" Martin fidgeted, kicking his toe into a scupper.

"Land Ho!" A sailor yelled, aloft in the rigging. He was pointing excitedly. "A few points off the starboard bow!"

"Is it land? Or are these islands?" Luc Mignon called from the stern.

"Could be either," the sailor called back. "I see only scattered tree tops."

"Well, you'll soon find out the Indians don't have cloth at all. If they're lucky enough to get cloth through trade, they won't use it making fires. That's for sure," Messier said, returning to the subject of the *voyageur's* arts. He noted Luc coming to the front of the ship. Most of the men were scanning the indicated horizon, anxious to see this new land. "You must make char cloth as you go."

His jaw agape in uncomprehending puzzlement, Martin turned toward Messier.

Noticing Martin's curiosity, Messier smiled reassuringly. "It's actually very easy. I will show you these little secrets when we're on land."

Martin screwed up his eyes and scratched his behind. He was uncertain that Messier was teasing again.

"Islands! There is a large island and several other islands!" the lookout called from the crow's nest on the mainmast.

"Then we are on course!" Luc seemed pleased, but not wishing anyone to understand that, kept shading his eyes with his hand, peering at the far horizon. "We shall be passing the northern entrance to *la Baye des Puants* in a few hours."

* * *

By the afternoon that day, the fifteenth of September 1679, *Griffin* lay at anchor near a large island at the mouth of Green Bay. An Indian canoe flotilla scurried to greet the ship. After shouts of peace and friendship were exchanged, a Potawatami delegation boarded.

"Our Chief, Onanghisse, welcomes you," announced one of the Indians. "Members of our tribe visited Montreal some summers past. We have great friendship for the French." The speaker paused while Shadow translated for La Salle.

Gazing slowly about the men and the ship, the man added, in a tone of approval, "The French are as brothers to the *Po-te-wa-tami*. We are happy the great French chief has come to honor us with a visit."

La Salle ceremoniously presented the messenger with a hatchet and, through Shadow, asked to be brought to Chief Onanghisse. Then La Salle, Shadow, and Messier climbed into a waiting canoe and were escorted away.

As the canoe advanced toward shore, La Salle confided with Messier, who was squatting in the mid position. "The *Po-te-wa-tami* may make good trade partners for us, but be alert. They are not so happy with us as they appear. They know the profit to be made as agents for tribes farther west. When they first visited Montreal in '74, they received good prices for their skins. But lately they have brought too many and they are not satisfied with the lower rates. They do not yet understand our market. The *Po-te-wa-tami* suspect the French are cheating them."

Messier fidgeted a bit, looking around at the accompanying canoes. He worried their welcome might not last.

"So we must be careful to be fair," La Salle asserted. "But we must not be overgenerous." He was already anticipating business negotiations with the tribal council.

Messier nodded understanding. His sense of excitement and pleasure was increasing as the boats neared the waiting crowd of Indians on the shore.

"Shadow, explain the Indian names for me," Messier asked.

"Onanghisse means 'Shimmering Light,'" Shadow responded after a brief hesitation.

"I have heard these people referred to as *la Nation du Feu*." Messier was intently studying the waiting crowd on shore. Men wore breechclouts and leggings while the women wore leggings and knee-length dresses comprising two pieces of doeskin joined at the shoulders and at the sides. Deerskin belts with quillwork added modest decorations.

"Many years ago, the three tribes that came to this area were one great nation. The *Adawe*, *Anishshina-pe*, and *Po-te-wa-tami* settled in different areas. The *Po-te-wa-tami*—the People of the Fire—became the guardians of the tribal flame."

Shadow had some years before befriended Potawatami braves and learned their tribal history. The reason La Salle found his service excellent was due to this strong interest in tribal lore and etiquette. A European with Shadow's sagacity and linguistic skills would have been considered a promising diplomat.

"You know the Ottawa as excellent traders. *Adawe* means 'to buy, to sell.'" Shadow continued, since he perceived La Salle was also listening. "The third tribe, the Ojibway call themselves *Anishshina-pe*, the Human Beings."

La Salle stepped ashore, straightened his cape and, with his party, followed the escort to the tribal reception. Along the way, astonished but inquisitive Indians lined the path, many running ahead time and again to catch another glimpse of the bearded Frenchmen and the tall Mohegan.

Wide-eyed children bursting with curiosity clasped their hands over their mouths while some adults bit their lips in silent wonder at the strangeness of these explorers.

Standing before the council, the aristocrat assumed his usual ceremonial dignity. His demeanor was formal, yet his face expressed warmth and humor, the intelligent eyes and aquiline nose emphasizing his confident authority. Great care had been exercised in his appearance and dress. His coal-black hair was neatly brushed, his fine mustache properly clipped, and his chin beard freshly trimmed.

Chief Onanghisse, too, expressed a regal dignity as he received his guests. From beneath a cloth turban—prized goods so far from the French colony—his hair fell over the shoulders, copper ornaments hung from his ear lobes while a raccoon tail was secured at the nape of his neck. Decorated with colored quillwork designs honoring the bounty of the earth, a tanned deerskin breechclout reached to the knees in both the front and rear, a broad blue sash edged with red covered his waist. Leggings seamed along the sides went from his thighs to the tops of his ornate moccasins. A small leather medicine pouch hung from a thong around his neck.

Speaking through Shadow, as he always did on formal occasions, La Salle announced his mission of exploration and discovery. After discussing trade with the western tribes, La Salle added, "I am looking for men that I sent to this area a year ago. They came to trade but I have not heard from them since."

"Your men are nearby. They are good traders. You will be pleased with the pelts they have gathered. They are in the French village. We will take you there."

La Salle was pleasantly surprised; he had not expected a favorable outcome. It seemed that not only had these men remained loyal to him, they had accumulated valuable goods for his profit. The generosity of Onanghisse, too, augured well for his business affairs—a rare event for La Salle—a pleasant, positive outcome.

"Stay with us some days. In two days, we shall have a feast and dancing in your honor." Onanghisse graciously offered the hospitality of the village. "My people will be pleased to entertain you with the Dance of the Calumet."

To Messier La Salle expressed his pleasure over the recent events, to Shadow he said, "Tell the Chief we are happy to accept his hospitality. But in a few days we must continue our journey to the Illinois country. The year is growing late. He will understand."

On the following morning several guides led La Salle and several of his men, including Fr. Membré, to the French encampment. One of the nine loyal agents, on meeting La Salle at the gateway, brought him to the inside of the small palisade. While the others proudly observed, La Salle surveyed the several shacks and also the storehouse. The latter contained a large collection of cured beaver, badger, deer, and other skins. A few choice buffalo hides lay in one corner. La Salle quickly apprised the quality of these, and turning to Fr. Membré, exclaimed, "At least 10,000 *livres*, perhaps more. This should appease a few of my creditors."

"Oh, of course," exclaimed the priest, rubbing his hand over a martin pelt. "But how can we bring these skins to Montreal? Surely this shipment is too large to send by canoe!"

"Yes, you are correct," La Salle said, delighted with this treasure. "We are the ones who must travel by canoe. We will send this cargo on the *Griffin*."

Returning to the outside area, La Salle addressed the assembled traders. "Men, you have done well. Very well, indeed. I sincerely appreciate both your loyalty and your enterprise. Tomorrow we shall begin lading these furs on *Griffin*."

Many were disappointed. "*Sieur*, we had hoped to go with you to the Illinois country," one of the traders began pleading. "We could collect these skins on our return. They are quite safe here. The Potawatami will guard them for us."

"I am sorry, too, that you cannot come with me," La Salle spoke deliberately. "I will need all hands on this voyage. But these furs must be brought to market as soon as possible. My creditors must be paid or I must cease exploring. And from these profits, you will receive the year's wages that I now owe you."

"Perhaps some of us could accompany you," a husky woodsman protested, uncomfortable at the thought of returning to the confining etiquette of civilization. "Having a *sou* in Montreal is never so rich as being penniless among the natives."

"I have already considered the course of your employment. Again, I am sorry. *Griffin* has a crew of only six. That is not adequate. And the portaging of these furs around the falls at *Nyàgarah* will be difficult, even for all of you." La Salle said, looking straight at the men. "As you see, there is no question of where your duty lies."

Disappointment lingering, the men accepted their assignment.

"After you have delivered this cargo, I want the *Griffin* to bring supplies and trade goods to the mouth of the Miami River. I shall await you there. Then we shall see who may journey with me to the *Golfe de Mexique*."

The evening closed with a sumptuous banquet, the Potawatami providing venison, lake fish, waterfowl, corn, and beans. Dancing and chanting began near sunset and lasted late into the night.

Shadow had been particularly heartened by the celebrations. After the festivities ended, he sat alone for a while outside his teepee, reminiscing about the days of his joy-filled youth, spent in a Mohegan village near Boston. He recalled too, that in spite of many years of amicable relations with the white people, in subtle ways their regard for the native had gradually degenerated, and this in spite of the fact that the Mohegans had fought alongside the colonists, subduing other tribes. Eventually even the elders despaired of reestablishing the tribal dignity in the eyes of the colonists. Over time many Mohegans migrated away from the colony. Those that remained vainly sought to adjust to the new culture, but too much had changed and the Mohegans ceased to exist as a tribe.

Shadow accepted that he would never again recapture the happiness of his early years. And he wondered about the differences between the French and the English. There were contradictions in the attitudes of each, but the French held the Indian in a higher regard. Perhaps, he thought, alliances among the Indian nations and the French would confine the English excesses to the colonial area. As his melancholy deepened, he realized how weary he had become and retired.

* * *

The next afternoon an honor guard of several Potawatami warriors escorted La Salle, the three priests, Shadow, most of the crew of the *Griffin*, many of La Salle's explorers, and the nine agents to the ceremonial ground. Wearing his crimson cape, La Salle strode into the presence of the tribal council as all stood waiting for the preliminary ceremonies to begin.

Chief Onanghisse had selected a glade where all could sit in the shade of the branches of the surrounding trees. A rush mat painted with various designs was placed in the central spot. On this mat, Onanghisse arranged his private manitou—his personal medicine—a replica of a serpent he had once seen in a dream, the talisman in which he placed full confidence for success in war, fishing, or hunting.

Igniting the tobacco in his calumet, Chief Onanghisse slowly inhaled, then satisfied it was well lit, offered it, stem first, to the sun, then to each of the four winds, that each in turn could partake. Solemnly he placed the calumet to the right of the manitou, resting the stem on a branched stick. Having thus established the two most honored totems for the celebration, Chief Onanghisse withdrew from the central area.

Turning to his men, La Salle explained, "Less honor is given to the crowns and scepters of kings than these nations bestow on the calumet. It is their god of peace and of war. Display it, and you can walk through the midst of your enemies. In the hottest fight, they will lay down their arms when the calumet is shown."

"I should hope I will never find myself in such circumstance," Fr. Membré said thoughtfully. "Holding only a pipe, reasonable men do not attempt to walk among their enemies in the midst of battle."

"What may seem reasonable to a European does not apply here," La Salle replied. "Learn and trust the ways of these people, for your greater safety, Father."

Several warriors now approached the manitou, formally setting their bows and arrows, quivers, war-hatchets, and clubs around it.

Adding to La Salle's comments, Shadow spoke to the French, "The calumet dance is performed only on important occasions. Only the color of the feathers distinguishes the calumet for war from the one for peace. Red is the color for war."

"How does this pipe get such an importance?" Fr. Membré asked.

"The stone comes from a sacred place where no one may war. Even blood enemies may not fight there," Shadow replied. "Notice the bowl—it is fashioned from a soft red stone. When fresh from the earth, the stone may be carved with a knife. After a while, the bowl becomes hard as stone and can be polished."

Duplessis turned to Martin, who was seated next to him, and winking, said, "Pay attention, Martin. Snakes and tobacco, these'll save your skin, someday. Mark my words."

"I don't see the need for magic charms," Martin said, shaking his head.

"Oh, come now." Duplessis recoiled. "Surely your musket is your totem. I've seen how you take care of it."

"That's for hunting. I hope I never see the day when I have to shoot another man." Martin grumbled.

Next the appointed singers—men and women with the most gifted voices and the best harmony—entered the ceremonial area. These proceeded to the most honorable place under the branches. Immediately they began a ceremonial chant.

The remaining tribal members, as well as visitors, all settled into their places around the circle. But each brave, on arriving, first saluted the manitou by taking the calumet in a respectful manner, inhaling the smoke, and blowing it from his mouth upon the manitou, as if offering incense. Then, supporting it with both hands, the brave danced with it in cadence, keeping good time to the rhythm of the chant. Around the manitou, he executed many differing figures, and sometimes, turning from one side to the other, he showed the calumet to the whole assembly.

"Tobacco was among the first gifts of the spirits to the people. It too is sacred." Shadow made further interpretive remarks for the French. "We make offerings of tobacco to renew the relationship between men and the spirits. The smoke from the sacred pipe carries your words and thoughts to the spirits."

"Extraordinary!" Fr. Ribourde burst out. "This scene resembles the performance of the Ballet."

"Well, I've never been to the 'Ballet,'" Duplessis smiled at Martin. "How about you?"

"Is that something the King's Regiment does on horses?" Martin looked blankly at Duplessis.

"You Bumpkin!" Messier burst out. "It's theater. It's done on the stage." Then he rolled his eyes and shook his head.

At that moment, Wind-in-the-Pines, a celebrated Potawatami warrior, stepped to the middle of the display and, without breaking cadence, took up the calumet, smoked, and then offered it to the sun. His tanned leather breechclout had quillwork bands along the bottom of the flaps, which extended to the knees, both front and back. The upper face was painted black with red circles around his eyes. His exposed torso was also colored red and black. Behind his shoulder he carried a skin pouch for fire-making equipment, tobacco, and personal sacred objects. The very large cuffs of his soft-soled, one-piece moccasins almost touched the ground and each displayed a symmetrically opposite design.

Dancing, Wind-in-the-Pines inclined toward the earth and spreading the feathers of the calumet, he bounded around the circle, offering the pipe in turn to several, that they too might smoke.

"His name comes from his battle skill," Shadow explained in French. "His attack is swift and silent. The only sound the enemy hears before he strikes is the noise of a gentle breeze."

The beat of a drum intruded, and harmonizing with the chanting, announced a new phase of the ceremony.

Taking his cue, Wind-in-the-Pines made a signal to the audience, inviting a mock combat. A warrior rose, came forward, and, choosing a lance and war-hatchet from the mat, prepared to fight. With slow and measured steps in the cadence of the drum, the latter thrust and jabbed, while Wind-in-the-Pines, protected solely with the calumet, dodged and parried the fanciful blows being rained upon him. Wind-in-the-Pines retreated, pursued constantly. Then, braving the lance and whirling tomahawk, Wind-in-the-Pines counterattacked. With the calumet he forced his adversary to flee at last.

"An excellent ballet," Fr. Ribourde beamed, enjoying the spectacle immensely. "People who have such art cannot be evil. Such craft is the opposite of evil."

"Well, now, that was a nice show," Martin volunteered.

"And what would you know about such fancy things?" Duplessis grumped.

"Why don't you leave him alone?" Messier interrupted. "How is it you're such a critic, Duplessis? Are you so much better than the rest of us? Why don't you just shut up."

Duplessis stared hard at Messier, but made no response.

Wind-in-the-Pines, victorious in this bloodless duel, now began chanting an account of his victories in battle. In several fights, he had defeated Iroquois warriors in the hunting lands beyond the big lake, *Michigami*.

The audience approved and encouraged his narration, thereby prolonging the account.

Finally, Wind-in-the-Pines recounted his rescue of a number of Miami women from the land below Lake Erie.

When he had finished, Chief Onanghisse presented Wind-in-the-Pines with a fine robe of beaver skins as a token of the tribe's respect for his bravery.

Motioning to La Salle, Chief Onanghisse invited him to the center of the circle. After a ritual smoke, the chief presented the peace pipe to La Salle. "This is our gift to you. Take it with you to the Illinois nation. Show it to them as a token of the everlasting peace and friendship between the French and the *Po-te-wa-tami*."

Impressed with the gravity of the present, La Salle responded by offering gifts to the chiefs and their wives: blankets, kettles, guns, and beads.

* * *

In four days *Griffin* was ready for the return voyage to Fort Conti. La Salle and several Potawatami held a final conference with Mignon, his crew, and the fur traders.

"I expect to see you in a few months. You have my orders for the men at Fort Conti. They are to take your cargo to Montreal so that you and my men may return quickly here." La Salle handed Mignon a sealed packet, then said, "These Indians have some further advice for you. Do not head for the middle of the lake on your departure, but follow the coast. In high wind, there are sand bars directly offshore which could strand your ship."

Mignon took the packet, looked disdainfully toward the Indians, grimaced once more, then turned and walked to the canoe that would take him to his ship. On deck and—for the first time—in total command of *Griffin*, Mignon began barking his orders. As the crew hoisted the ship's canoe aboard and lashed it on the hatch, others loosed the main and topsails, hauled up the lateen boom, and readied the sheets. As the anchor came free, the *Griffin* began a slow drift, gaining control with the rudder as she gathered way. A salute was fired from one of her swivel mounts. The westerly breeze, lazily carrying the gun smoke toward the middle of the lake, stiffened her sails and straightened the pennants. As their various tasks were completed, some on board gathered on the poop deck, taking a last, parting look at the island of the Potawatami.

On the shore, La Salle noted with not a little chagrin that Mignon was sailing directly toward the sandbars, in spite of the Indian's warnings. Shaking his head, he was bemused by the thought that that would after all be the expectable response to authority from any person as obstinate as Mignon. Waving his plumed hat in farewell, La Salle was suddenly overcome by an inexplicable, melancholy foreboding. But he quickly fought off the feeling as somehow arising from sentimentality. He assured himself that it was an irrational, therefore, false notion that the ship and all aboard would never be seen again.

* * *

Several days later, La Salle was ready to resume his journey to the Mississippi. He had obtained four canoes for his party of fourteen. These canoes had been decorated with Potawatami icons of good fortune and happiness. And the weather remained pleasant. Good omens, he told Shadow, while watching the western sky where drifted occasional sprays of gray and white against a deep blue.

It had gotten to a late hour in the afternoon. Wind-in-the-Pines, with his family and others, had departed earlier to go to their winter villages. The departure of a number of other Indians from the island only increased La Salle's restlessness.

Chief Onanghisse, sensing La Salle's impatience, said, "It is better to wait for the fresh hours of a new day. The passage is not long for those who know the waters. But there is not much sun remaining if you should have any difficulty."

"Yes, thank you for your concern," La Salle replied. "But regardless of the hour, I am anxious to resume my journey."

Turning to the priests and Messier, La Salle said, "The crossing of the mouth of *le Baye des Puants* will take several hours. I am concerned that we now have a longer, more dangerous journey to the Illinois country. As you know, this is not how I had planned to go."

"The evening wind is from the land. In the morning, the breeze will help carry your canoes toward the shore," Chief Onanghisse observed.

"True enough," La Salle smiled. "We are thankful for your hospitality. The *Po-te-wa-tami* have been gracious in our behalf. But I am now concerned we have little time to spare if we are to find a safe shelter for winter."

"You have a difficult task," Chief Onanghisse rejoined. "It is dangerous traveling along the lake in a canoe. We have some sad experience with this. You have much equipment with you; I wonder that you have room for adequate food supplies."

Nodding somberly, La Salle said, "The Chief understands well my problems."

"I must return to my village," Chief Onanghisse said. "We look forward to your return. We shall have a great business together, you and I. *Adieu!*"

Russell Breighner

Chapter 3

Michigami

The lake had a glassy, calm surface. Having observed the weather for most of the day, La Salle gauged that the best prospects were presently before him. With neither wind nor waves to impede them, a fast crossing could be made. Screwing up his determination as he swept the late afternoon sky one last time, La Salle ignored the collection of Frenchmen, Indians, and priests on the beach expectantly waiting among the laden canoes.

Shadow and Fr. Ribourde watched as La Salle, deep in reflection, alternately pawed at the sand, or squinted toward the western sky. Anticipating the direction of La Salle's thoughts, Shadow looked at Fr. Ribourde and both locked glances. A smile began to work around the corners of Ribourde's mouth. Shadow then noticed the subtle change as La Salle's eyes sparkled and his back stiffened. Before La Salle could announce his decision, his men knew it, both breaking into broad grins.

"We go now!" La Salle proclaimed, walking toward his friends. Seeing they had anticipated his intention, he too smiled broadly. Caught in the emotion of the moment, all laughed.

After a moment, La Salle recovered a more serious mien. Abruptly, he barked, "Prepare the men. It is late, but we begin our journey on *Michigami!"*

The men below gave a cheer, for they too were anxious to begin. Fr. Ribourde went down to the beach, giving orders as he went. The canoes were laden with the usual cargo of exploration—foodstuffs, tools, gunpowder, trade goods, and the blacksmith's portable forge. In addition, La Salle's fragile fleet carried what few other explorers had dared: the ironware and tools necessary for building a sailing ship in the wilderness. Variously the men scrambled about, re-checking their packs, taking slack out of the oilskin wraps, and tightening the tie-downs.

"We will not see land for a while, as we cross the mouth of the bay," La Salle advised the travelers. "We must be careful to maintain a true course. This will not be easy. Without a fixed point to guide us, we may wander." He paused to emphasize the seriousness of the situation. "It should be an easy voyage, but keep together. Let no one lag."

Within minutes the cumbered flotilla sat in the water, gently rocking as wavelets played against the boats. Messier—as the avant, La Salle, Shadow, and Fr. Ribourde in one canoe took the lead, the other three boats following in a loose trail formation.

For several hours the men stroked in a steady pattern, beating time with Messier's chants, as they coursed south along the eastern coast of Washington Island. The canoes were not too close together, but then none was in danger of losing contact. As the fleet passed through the lee of Detroit Island, it caught the wind from Green Bay. Beneath dark clouds now scudding low overhead, La Salle ordered his men to bring their sluggish canoes to a more southwesterly course. Resolutely the men labored against the salt-air gusts seeking to drive them toward the center of Lake Michigan. The first smattering of a mist brought on a chill that was mental as well as physical.

The horizon decreased noticeably in scale and definition, quickly becoming a dull, blue-green curtain not far distant. In spite of their efforts, it now seemed to the men they were in a futile situation, vainly paddling in the center of a dark, watery bowl, going nowhere. Of itself, it wasn't disconcerting—these men were inured to stiff demands. But increasingly, the disorientation brought on by the absence of a sensible reference gnawed at their confidence. They felt suspended between the gray sky and the dark waters, endlessly seeking a non-existent haven. Not a few began to suspect that a safe crossing was beyond achievement.

The monotony deepened as into the evening, signs of fatigue began to show. Several men seemed to be forcing their effort, no longer rhythmic and natural. Messier had ceased chanting.

Abruptly, Shadow called out as he noticed one of the trailing canoes stopped dead in the water. Signaling to Messier to hold, La Salle watched the stalled craft, then waved and yelled at the lagging boat, but could raise no response. Reluctantly, La Salle ordered Messier to bring his canoe to the derelict.

On approach, La Salle discerned one of the crew sitting on the gunwale with his exposed buttocks overboard.

"He has the shits!" came the explanation as La Salle's boat came within hailing distance.

"He must have eaten something green," yelled a man in the bow.

"Does he have a fever?" queried La Salle.

"I don't think so. We'll be all right in a moment," Duplessis replied. No one in the canoe appeared willing to resume their previous effort.

"Here," La Salle said as he pulled out a flask. As the two canoes closed, he passed it over. "Have a drink of this."

"Merci, merci!" Chapelle responded, finishing a long draught of brandy. Then, tottering in the unstable craft, he rose to re-arrange his trousers, clumsily restoring them to about their normal position. Duplessis looked severely at La Salle, resentful that he had once again rashly led his people into unnecessary danger.

Slowly the two canoes went to rejoin the others. The sky had become the darkest gray, the sea beneath black. Only occasional whitecaps told one from the other.

La Salle re-assessed the situation—with the interruption and the closing sky, it would be all too easy to assume a false course. He guessed at a direction toward land. Considering the direction of the wind and the waves before the halt, he gave Messier a heading, then watched as the other canoes fell in behind.

A slow rain began to fall. Steady at first, it soon increased in intensity. Soaked and sullen, the men continued their mechanical paddling. It had become difficult to distinguish the other canoes even though they were now well bunched.

"Hennepin! Keep up the pace!" Fighting against his rising fears, La Salle was now becoming more concerned that he would miss landfall.

Shadow lit a small lantern and placed it on a pole extending over the bow of his canoe. Through the yellow sphere of light, crowding raindrops made silver streaks while orange-gold flashes reflected from the lake. This beacon for awhile made it easier for the canoes to stay together.

"The *Po-te-wa-tami* use such lanterns for spear-fishing at night," Shadow explained to Fr. Ribourde, who nodded appreciation.

La Salle continued to yell out to Hennepin—in the only boat with two paddlers—and to the other lagging canoe. It was becoming more difficult to pick them out in the darkness. Yet from the darkness came reassuring calls that Shadow's lantern was visible.

With a sputter and a pop, the light suddenly vanished as the rain at last triumphed. With a cold chill the men realized that all reference had been lost. The hoped-for night sky and stars were smothered. Only instinct and luck remained for a safe landfall. Trusting to his remembered course, La Salle prayed that in spite of the rising wind, he could bring his flotilla to shore.

"How are you doing, Fr. Hennepin?" La Salle yelled hoarsely into the darkness once again. The rain had long since soaked his clothing, water running freely under his buckskin shirt. A full-blown downpour all but blinded the other paddlers.

"Heu!" Someone shouted weakly from somewhere. "We are taking on water."

"Are you bailing?" La Salle called back, signaling his crew to halt again.

"Yes, we are. But we cannot last much longer. Is it far to land?" The plaintive voice carried a tone of desperation.

"It is toward our right! I can hear the surf," Shadow announced loudly. "And I can no longer smell the Bay of Stinking Waters."

Encouraged, the party redoubled their efforts. Soon all could hear the welcome, though menacing surf.

Messier's canoe was the first to land. The four men aboard pulled hard as the craft jetted through the breakers. Within an instant, the men were into the surf, dragging the heavy canoe far up on the beach. The second canoe came in, then the third.

Fr. Hennepin and La Forge were in the last, the most heavily laden canoe. Unable to gain sufficient speed to course through the breakers, the canoe began to slew about and founder.

"We're lost! The boat is out of control!" Hennepin shouted into the dark as he dropped his paddle and grabbed the gunwales, expecting the canoe to swamp. Miraculously, the canoe bumped against some obstacle, stabilized, and seemed to come to rest in the shallow water.

"Well! What have we here?" came the robust shouts of Fr. Ribourde. He and two others had waded out and caught Hennepin's canoe, a black shape among the dim whitecaps. The waders steadied the craft, then dragged it onto the beach. The old priest helped the younger one disembark. With a hearty yell, Ribourde led as the two straggled away through the surf.

Shadow had already begun the process of starting a fire under the small lean-to he had erected. La Salle was busy organizing the men and the gear, and preparing other shelters against the pouring rain. The small flame struggling amidst the wet tinder provided more promise than warmth.

Duplessis was complaining again. For five days the men had remained on the headland, waiting for a clearing in the weather. "Why did we leave the Potawatami village? There we would have had warm food."

"And f-f-friendship," Chapelle leered, tossing his head with a suggestive emphasis.

"If you are only interested in Indian women, why do you travel with this man? And these priests?" Duplessis was perplexed. "We've been days in this camp. I am tired of pumpkins and corn. And the rain . . . ."

"We can't carry much food. You know that. There's no room. Too many tools and trade goods. Farther on, suppose we visit some friendly village, eh?" Chapelle entertained visions of a hospitality not to be found in Montreal.

"Not La Salle. He is not interested in your belly or your dreams. Twice he has nearly killed us. Do you not think, maybe next time, he will succeed?" Duplessis fumed.

"Then why do you stay with him?" Chapelle tossed a stone at the water.

"He's taking us south. Where it's warmer. Maybe I'll find me a place there where I can hunt and trap."

"This is surely no place for me. I'm with you. Besides, just think of the pretty maidens we'll meet along the way." Chapelle could not be shaken from his expectations.

Abruptly Duplessis changed direction, "I do not expect him to live forever." His voice, suddenly tinged with anger, startled Chapelle. Not wishing to provoke his friend, Chapelle dropped the conversation, hunkering down under his oilskin. One of the priests was approaching along the beach.

Restless with the forced layover, Fr. Membré paced about, sometimes praying his daily office, sometimes wondering about his future missionary work. As he passed, he nodded toward Duplessis and Chapelle who appeared as two wet, angry hens squatting under a dripping pine tree. A little farther he came upon Messier sitting under a small lean-to, heating a closed metal can over a low fire.

"So, what is this?" he asked, pointing to the curious container. "Are you making some special meal?"

"Ha! No, Father. This is char-cloth I'm making." The stocky Canadian motioned the priest to sit. "It's rainy days as this when a traveler most needs char-cloth."

"I'm afraid I don't understand," Fr. Membré replied. "What is char-cloth?"

"Nothing, really," Messier said, moving the can about on the coals. "Just bits of cotton rag. After it's been heated in a closed can, it is a great fire-starter. One or two sparks, and poof, the flames are snapping at your tinder."

"Just one more trick of the *coureurs!*" Fr. Membré smiled.

"Please, Father. There are a few of us who prefer to be called *voyageurs,*" Messier scowled. "The *coureurs de bois* are more renegades and outlaws. But there are those who conduct legitimate trade with the Indians. We are the ones who bring their furs to Montreal."

"By very long, tiring canoe journeys, I hear," Fr. Membré mused. "It's a very long distance from Sault Ste. Marie."

Messier removed the can from the fire and placed it on the earth, where it sizzled as cooling raindrops danced fitfully across its lid. He looked up as Martin and Duplessis walked up behind the priest. Martin was staring dumbly at the blackened tin.

"So, then, it doesn't bother you, travelling by canoe along this great lake?" Fr. Membré squinted at the sky, privately doubting the rain would ever cease.

"A good crew could travel to the Gulf of Mexico by canoe," Fr. Membré surmised, "and not be too much the worse for wear."

"Well, now! La Salle has his picked men. He has placed the best according to their skill." Rummaging under his jacket, Messier pulled out a clay pipe and a pouch and momentarily began tamping tobacco into the bowl. Screwing his eyes, he glanced sideways to Duplessis and said, "Be thankful we are not all ragtag, vagabond woodsmen."

"Enjoy your smoke," Fr. Membré said, rising to go. "I will see what entertainment the other priests have found."

* * *

The storm abated—the spell of rain that had kept the expedition immobile finally broke. The small flotilla resumed its journey and for two days advanced along the coast. The men then camped again, on a rocky island, when another squall broke upon them. The following day, the first of October, dawned clear and calm. Once more the explorers went to sea.

"Fr. Gabriel, we are doing well today," La Salle was speaking to the old priest in the lead canoe. "We've come a good ten leagues already."

"I'm sorry to say this, but those clouds look ominous. Perhaps another storm," Fr. Gabriel Ribourde grumbled. "There is already a bit of spit in the air. Perhaps we should bivouac early."

"Have you been watching the tree line?" La Salle had been concentrating his attention there for some time. "We are being watched, I think, by a large body of Indians."

"*Po-te-wa-tami*," Shadow said, reassuringly. "There is a village nearby. They will welcome us."

"No, I will not land here," La Salle said, surprising those in his canoe. "Our trade goods are for the Illinois peoples. I am afraid the men may use up our wares obtaining personal favors. We must go farther."

His words and the misting rain numbed the men's spirits. Hungry and tired, they gazed with longing at the passing trees, seeking some sign of hospitality.

In his own canoe, Duplessis mechanically applied the paddle while chasing some dark thought. So far it had eluded him. Nevertheless, he continued to encourage his darker mood, hoping thereby to find solace, if not the path to retribution.

For another hour or two, La Salle stubbornly kept his party moving southward even as the storm mustered its opposition. A hard wind rose and mercilessly drove a constant rain against the men while the now maddened surf thrashed endlessly on the nearby shore.

"Time to land!" A paddler in one of the trailing canoes insisted.

Momentarily taken aback by the impertinence, La Salle pondered the alternatives, then reluctantly, gave the signal to halt.

"Be alert!" La Salle ordered. "The beach is low and shallow. The rollers rise quickly near the shore. You must be quick to avoid sinking. Follow my example."

Taking the lead while the other crews watched, La Salle's canoe raced through the surf. The men paddled with redoubled vigor, trying to catch the crest of a breaker. But they did not succeed. Sliding backward into a trough, they were overtaken by a large comber. The heavily laden canoe, swept from stern to stem, rose and fell sluggishly, foundering in the surf. As the canoe swamped, La Salle jumped into the water, grabbing the gunwale.

"It's deep here, but not too deep," he yelled, his head just above water. The others followed his example, obeying the implied command.

Barely afloat, the canoe bucked again as another wave sloshed over it. Struggling to maintain their footing, the men pushed the reluctant boat forward.

"She's sinking. I don't think the canoe will make it," Fr. Membré bawled.

"Get under the canoe! Lift!" La Salle commanded as the men fought to save the boat.

"Watch out for the under-tow!" La Salle called out as a strong, outgoing surge sucked his feet from beneath him.

"He's gone!" From an offshore canoe, someone shouted above the roar of the surf, "La Salle's been carried off!"

For a panicky instant, those struggling with the water-filled canoe were paralyzed. Scarcely maintaining their own footing, they were gripped by the fear of drowning as once again a comber slapped them across the shoulders.

Suddenly La Salle appeared out of the turbulent waters. Rising above the wash, he stood taller than before. "The bottom is coming up!" he rejoiced as he emerged in the waist-deep surf.

Relieved, the men made one final effort that released them and the canoe from the grasp of *Michigami*.

"Fr. Gabriel, what a sorry fish you are." La Salle teased Ribourde as he half-carried the old priest from the water.

"At least I don't yet smell like a fish. Thank you very much, indeed." Fr. Ribourde sat on the sand, breathing heavily.

Offshore, Fr. Hennepin and Chapelle were aligning their canoe—the only one with a two-man crew—for the next run-in, when Duplessis brought his canoe alongside. Speaking to Chapelle, he said, "You see? La Salle is trying to kill us again. He will not stop till he has done us in. Mark my words."

Staring at Duplessis, Chapelle signaled readiness to Fr. Hennepin and the second boat lunged toward the breakers. Coming through the white water, Chapelle howled uproariously. Waders caught the bow and propelled the craft onto the beach as Chapelle continued his yelling. But as to whether he was expressing fear or exuberance, none could tell.

The third and fourth boats followed. When all were ashore, the men secured the boats and gear, then built shelters and a fire.

"I want guards posted," La Salle bawled above the noise of the storm, surprising the men by his seemingly unnecessary caution.

"The *Po-te-wa-tami* are friendly," Shadow protested. "Their village is far. We do not threaten them."

"They have seen us. They are probably in the woods here now," La Salle said, convinced of his suspicions. "All of you, check your guns. Make sure they are dry and have fresh powder."

Disgruntled, the men proceeded with tasks they felt unnecessary. Two water-soaked sentinels climbed the high embankment to take their stations. About an hour later one of the priests came along, serving them a brisk tea against their inner chill.

After a small cooked meal the next morning, La Salle and Fr. Membré went strolling along the now quiet beach. Rising above the rim of the lake, the benevolent sun painted the spreading clouds in crimsons and pinks. A friendly breeze blew gently from the northwest. Confident the coming day would be prosperous, La Salle relaxed a bit, walking briskly.

"Fr. Zenobe, I need a small favor. Would you go back to the village for me? We do need provisions, you know," La Salle said in an even tone.

Sensing La Salle's relaxed mood and rare candor, Fr. Membré prodded, "Why did you not stop there yesterday? These are friendly Indians, you know."

"There is no danger from them. It is my own men that concern me. The few goods we have, we need for trade with the Illinois tribes. Without goods, we have only words. And the Indians find words alone cheap."

"You mean you think your men would steal from you?" Fr. Membré frowned, but stopped short of further comment.

"I have no doubt of it," La Salle asserted. "These men can give good service. Better than they might admit, or even that they might think themselves capable of. But all the same, we must guard against their weaker natures. If I do not control them in all respects, if I should loosen my grip in the slightest—they become as useless as pebbles. Perhaps worse."

"I shall take the Mohegan and the voyageur, M. Accau. 'Le Picard' is a good man around the Indians. He has studied their language," Fr. Membré advised, glancing toward the men busy about the campsite.

"Good! Then good luck! And return before sundown," La Salle smiled as they parted. Returning to the campsite, he watched as the three gathered weapons, food pouches, and a few trade articles. They then set off, marching at a brisk pace to the north.

"Indians! Indians hiding in the trees," shouted one of the sentinels. Hardly an hour had passed since the departure of the priest and his escort. There had been an increase in suspicious activities beyond the outposts and the sentinels had become increasingly agitated.

"But they do not attack," La Salle said, calmly eyeing the woods. "Perhaps they are merely curious."

Some men nervously checked their muskets and powder horns. They peered into the surrounding brush, armed and alert.

"We are less than a dozen," Chapelle whined. Looking around, he noted their exposed position, standing in the open, their backs to the lake.

La Salle sternly warned his party against rash action. "Do not start a battle we cannot win! Do not shoot unless you fear for your life."

Carefully he unfolded a deerskin parfleche, took out the calumet given him by Chief Onanghisse, and began walking slowly toward the woods. Holding high the peace pipe, La Salle shouted Algonquian words of peace and friendship.

In ones and twos, the Indians came out of hiding. Over twenty presented themselves. The sacred protection of the calumet had overcome their reserve. Relaxed, the visitors explained their caution: When La Salle did not stop at their village, they assumed his purpose was hostile.

Satisfied, but not fully convinced by this apology, La Salle indicated his need for provisions. The Indians promised to bring a supply of venison the next day.

That afternoon, Fr. Membré's mission returned, the three bearers well burdened with corn. "Well, the village was deserted." Fr. Membré smiled. "But we found the corn cache! We left trade goods in payment for what we took."

Shadow and Leblanc unshouldered their bundles.

"I hear you have had visitors," Fr. Membré said distractedly as he remembered to remove his own backpack.

"Some of the men from the village had followed our boats," La Salle observed flatly, content that nothing untoward had developed. "Tomorrow they will bring meat. This has been a good day."

"I will help them," the Mohegan said, then departed, following the Indians' trail. Anticipating the hospitality of the camp, he looked forward to an evening of games. "I shall return in the morning."

Early the next day, as the October sun coaxed glistening reflections from the slumberous, turquoise lake, a small group of Indians burst from the woods. Shadow and several Potawatami came forward carrying packs of dried meat.

Shadow beamed as he greeted La Salle and the priests. "I have won these," he said, proudly unfolding a deerskin wrap containing several pairs of moccasins.

"The workmanship is very good and the designs show the maker is quite skilled," Fr. Ribourde said, admiring the booty. He added, in a more serious tone, "Surely, you weren't gambling?"

"Indians love to gamble, and I am good at throwing sticks." Shadow replied insouciantly.

"These are fine specimens," La Salle, too, was drawn to the workmanship of the porcupine quill and bead designs. "Do these marking have a special meaning?"

"They show appreciation for the beauty of the earth. The Indian shows this by displaying comeliness on his feet. These moccasins express thankfulness for all that is around us." Shadow was pleased to explain. "The Indian is careful to preserve what is not needed for his use. Where the Indian walks, little is disturbed."

"Just so, just so. And are you going to wear these yourself?" Fr. Ribourde asked for no apparent reason.

"To wear the shoes of another tribe is to walk in their ways. No, these I will give to the French." Shadow grinned. "The *Po-te-wa-tami* will be glad to see French in their moccasins."

Wind-in-the-Pines, who understood French, grunted. He had helped with the negotiations on provisions the day before. He turned to La Salle, "How do you plan to come to the Illinois lands?"

"We shall follow the shore to the lower end of *Michigami*, then ascend the *Rivière des Miamis*," La Salle said without interest, but welcomed the change in the discussion.

"You are wrong." Wind-in-the-Pines stared at La Salle for a moment. "*Michigami* has no river at its lower end. Who has told you this?"

"French explorers," La Salle said, remembering the travels of Fr. Jacques Marquette and Louis Jolliet on the Mississippi and Illinois rivers in 1673. Jolliet had lost his original maps in an accident, but his redrawn example placed the Miami River clearly at the foot of Lake Michigan.

"Then you should know the river of the Miamis is on the other side of the lake." Wind-in-the-Pines insisted, "You must cross *Michigami* here."

"Perhaps. But a crossing is extremely dangerous." As La Salle scrutinized Wind-in-the-Pines, he began to suspect that the Indian intended to endanger the venture. He began to wonder that Wind-in-the-Pines could be an agent, perhaps for the Jesuits. The Indian's command of French indicated some association with the missionaries.

"I have heard that not many years ago, Potawatami warriors, more than a hundred, were drowned making a crossing," La Salle continued. "They were caught in a storm. We have already seen many sudden storms in just these few weeks."

"Wind-in-the-Pines has crossed *Michigami*." The Indian shrugged, ostensibly disinterested.

"Chief Onanghisse has advised us not to cross the big lake." La Salle replied coldly.

"We must go." Wind-in-the-Pines abruptly ended the conversation, turned and quickly walked away.

La Salle watched the Indian disappear into the forest, then, leaving Shadow and the priest, walked alone to the top of a dune overlooking the lake. Pondering the dangers ahead, he was concerned how he would meet new challenges. The expedition was about to enter the lands of the Sac and Fox, fiercely independent tribes, not disposed to be friendly with the French. And it seemed his enemies had already peopled his path with agents of defeat.

* * *

"Tomorrow we leave Potawatami lands." La Salle addressed the men after the evening meal. "Despite the little food we have, we must go far and fast. We must hurry for the Sac are found in these areas. They are one of the most dangerous tribes around the Great Lakes. Avoid contact. Sound the alarm at the first sign of trouble. You must be ready to fight at all times."

While the cook fire glowed brightly against the thickening twilight, the last muskets were cleaned and reloaded, the bundles and packs tied and retied, all in readiness for an early start.

Beneath the false dawn, the canoes on the beach reflected the dark orange-red radiance of dying embers amid the gray campfire ashes. Before many were aware that more than half the night had passed, Fr. Ribourde began rousing the men. After a meager meal, the men assembled near their boats, stowed the last gear and baggage, and arrayed the canoes on the beach.

"If these Sac Indians find us, you may see more pretty maidens than you care to." Duplessis began tease Chapelle again. "I understand the women torture the captives here. And they are good at what they do. One fast slash—*Zut!* —And your manhood is gone!"

Chapelle, more than a little disgusted with his friend, replied, "Let's see how good you are with a paddle. Maybe, if you keep you mouth shut and work hard, there won't be any Indian threats to w-w-worry about." Chapelle's stutter showed that he was at least a little upset by the taunts.

Aiming toward the one bright area on the horizon, the men splashed through the gentle surf, pushing their canoes onto the next stage of their trek.

For days the adventurers pressed on. The monotony of their effort fortunately was unbroken by any encounters with Indians.

Over a month had passed since the explorers had departed Green Bay. By late October, they had passed beneath unnamed, high, insurmountable cliffs, passed by the Chicago river, and came finally to the lower end of Lake Michigan. Provisions had been stretched, then rationed, then consumed. Fatigue and a constant diet of hawthorn berries had diminished the will and depleted the energy of the band.

"Here. We'll camp here." La Salle landed to investigate an animal carcass on the beach, watched the others come ashore, then strode off into the woods with Shadow. "There's game in the area. We'll make a short reconnaissance to see what is active."

Shadow stalked ahead, attentive to the sounds of the woodland as he went. He listened to the songs of the birds, heard the squirrels barking warnings. Occasionally, some unseen large bird, suddenly rustling the autumn leaves, would take flight as the two approached. Shadow had noticed ground scrapings that a buck had cleared and marked with its scent in mating preliminaries. The stags were in rut. Farther on, Shadow had found deer droppings that contained undigested persimmon seeds. All signs pointed to a large deer presence and good hunting prospects.

"A few days brings much venison." Walking on a bit, Shadow pointed to a black mess on the ground. "See? Bear droppings." Testing the soft, still warm manure with his finger, Shadow said quietly, "He is near. This is not very old."

"Good, let us return now. I want to see how well the camp is organized." La Salle looked carefully around. "We will remain at this site for a while. The men need their rest. Meanwhile, you can take one or two on a hunt."

As they returned to the beach, Fr. Hennepin came running up. "Well? How does it look? Do you think we should stay here? If I have to spend another day in that canoe, you will not be able to pry me out with a bear claw."

"Walk, if you wish. The river of the Miamis is only a few days. The beach does not continue, and there are high sand dunes. But you can do it." La Salle was pleasantly informative and surprisingly permissive.

"By the way. We found an excellent natural vineyard among the trees. Try some of these white grapes. They are sweet and fruity, like the grapes near Niagara," La Salle said, offering a cluster to the priest.

"Mmmm . . . Yes . . . Delightful!" Fr. Hennepin consumed the bunch with a discerning attention to each grape. "You know, we do need sacramental wine." He turned to one of the workmen, "Leblanc, bring a bucket and an axe. Help me gather grapes."

"Could we have a few days for the fermentation?" The priest turned again to La Salle.

"Ferment as long as you wish," La Salle chuckled. "I have already decided to stay here for a few days. But do not forget. We must rendezvous with M. Tonti. He may already be there, on the *Miami* River."

"Tonti! . . . On the *Miami*? If I don't eat some meat soon, I will not be able to leave this place." Duplessis grumbled. He and Chapelle were dragging a canoe to the tree line and had overheard the comments of the men.

"S-s-sure. That's true for all of us. We are all weak and tired. So why should you complain? What makes you special? Help me move this gear." Chapelle was pleased to gain an advantage on his manipulative friend.

La Salle inspected the camp as the men erected pole shelters, roofed the lean-tos with bark sheaths, and floored them with brush and leaves. Beneath the trees, unloaded and overturned canoes shielded the cargo from the rain. The men knew the routine well, but one immediate need remained.

"Saget, do you think you can bring in some venison soon?" La Salle called. "And who do you want to hunt with?"

"I am ready now." Shadow replied from the edge of the settlement. "'LePicard' wants to come too. We will return as soon as we have a kill."

"M. Accau is a good shot. I have seen him practice." La Salle said. "Have some tea before you go. And good hunting!"

After checking their weapons and knives, the two hunters disappeared into the woods.

Somewhat later in the afternoon, a heavy drizzle began and continued for the remainder of the dull evening. As darkness came, the adventurers sprawled about, seeking sanctuary for their benumbed bodies. They were long inured to fasting, but this spell of meager rations had become prolonged. Exhausted, they looked toward the morrow, hoping for some reprieve.

Shadow and Accau reappeared at the camp early in the morning. They were carrying a deer carcass suspended from a pole across their shoulders. Shadow announced he had also killed a bear.

"We'll bring out the bear meat after we've skinned out this fellow," Accau said. A pouch hanging from his belt held the heart, liver, and kidneys from the gutted deer. By the convention of the forest, the hunter making a kill had first call for the choice organs and marrowbones of the prey.

Yesterday's rain continued through the following day. By afternoon, the slow drizzle had increased to a steady downpour. The men, having dined on roast venison, were huddled under their shelters when a shout rang out.

"*Heu!* There's an Indian at the boats. He's stealing from us . . . C-c-catch him!" Chapelle had spotted the intruder, but could not intercept the thief who successfully escaped.

"It's Shadow's jacket. He s-s-stole Shadow's jacket!" Chapelle whooped.

"You say an Indian stole a jacket?" La Salle had joined the perplexed crowd staring at the trees. "There must be others about. Have your weapons ready. This may be difficult."

For hours the rain continued, the low rumble of thunder sometimes reverberating off the griseous lake. Crouching in their shelters, fighting the chill, damp tedium dripping upon them, the men were nevertheless tense and alert.

Once more an Indian was seen sneaking around the boats. This time he was captured. The thief was a boy, about seventeen.

La Salle took charge of the prisoner. "Tie this man to a tree! Guard him well. And fortify the camp! I will go to his people to retrieve everything that was stolen. Saget, come along. You will explain that if they do not return our goods, I will kill the boy."

Taking a pistol, La Salle marched off, the lanky Mohegan easily keeping pace with the shorter Frenchman.

A group of Indian scouts, wearing otter-skin turbans and bark rain capes, were surprised when they espied a bearded man with a tall, gracile Indian—both apparently indifferent to the weather—storming toward their camp. Even from a distance the Fox could see the men were determined. Word quickly spread. With ready weapons, additional warriors emerged from their wickiups. They watched with sullen interest as the unexpected visitors descended the sand ridge.

"Frenchman! We are the *Meshkwahki-haki*. Do you wish to die today? Or do you come in peace?" The leader of the band advanced, menacing La Salle with his lance.

"We come in peace to all Indians." Shadow used sign language and Algonquian words to convey La Salle's demand. "To the Red Earth People, La Salle says only that the jacket stolen from him must be returned. Otherwise, the prisoner will die."

"You have great courage to say these words to us. We are the Oshkosh—the bravest of the *Meshkwaki*. If you kill the boy, you will all die. Without mercy. Do you not fear death?" With a haughty coldness, the speaker stared at La Salle as his words were translated. Their faces dark with anger, Fox warriors crowded the visitors.

"I have heard of the Red Earth peoples. They have great courage and power in war. Their enemies show them much respect. But the Red Earths are also just." La Salle held up the boy's medicine pouch, confirming his capture. "You may kill us, but our father in Canada will send soldiers to avenge our deaths. I do not believe you want war with the French over a stolen jacket."

"We cannot return your jacket. It has been cut into pieces." The Indian paused, choosing his words. "Let us propose a fair trade. Return to your camp. You will have an answer when the new day begins. Fights-Bear-with-Knife speaks."

56

Satisfied with this pledge, La Salle glanced at Shadow and the two headed toward the beach.

"A thief is not worth killing," Shadow suggested, as they walked along.

"It is not the jacket that is important." La Salle did not once look back as they headed again up the sand ridge. "If we had not reacted, *les Renards* would have thought us weak and cowardly. They would surely have killed us for that. Indians kill the spineless and the stupid; in France, we sometimes give them positions in the government."

That evening La Salle ordered the camp moved to a wooded peninsula. Chevaux-de-frise were erected, and the men took turns standing watch through the night, which passed without incident.

By dawn, the rain had stopped and a cool lakefront breeze fanned the soggy company. As daylight spread, the sentinels became convinced of a presence in the woods. They alerted the others who, grabbing weapons, slid quietly into position behind the barricades.

"Watch the shadows. If you see movement, sound the alarm," La Salle whispered loudly. He had expected Indians would be posted to watch his encampment, but he remained uncertain of their intentions. "Fr. Hennepin, these Indians know the 'Gray Robes' are men of peace. They will not shoot a priest. Show them you are fearless," he commanded.

"O Lord! I place my life in your hands!" Fr. Hennepin crossed himself, looked once more at La Salle, then slowly rose to full height. Holding his rosary with both hands, he cautiously advanced into the open. About ten paces beyond the enclosure, he halted. Not certain of his next move, he held up his hands, showing he was unarmed.

Intent on retrieving the boy, by force if necessary, Fox warriors came from the woods. Impatiently brandishing weapons and giving out war whoops, they formed a large semicircle around the barricade. Over a hundred and twenty armed men stood in war paint. Several had hands painted on their bodies, signifying the killing of an enemy in combat; some wore grizzly bear-claw necklaces, others had stripes painted on their faces. Red designs were predominant, but black and blue markings also appeared.

"How many guns do you count?" La Salle shouted to Hennepin.

"Only seven!"

"Good! We have the advantage," La Salle commented.

"An advantage?" Duplessis was stunned. He looked at Leblanc laying next to him behind the abatis. "Do you see all those Indians?"

"Yes, but we have La Salle. He will get us out of this, you watch." Leblanc grinned back.

Messier, lying behind a log, took his knife from its sheath and placed it on the ground next to his musket.

"What should I do now? Shall I come back?" Fr. Hennepin wanted to return to the relative comfort of the enclosure.

"Just show them your fortitude!" La Salle ordered. "Many Indians use the musket to frighten those enemies who aren't accustomed to it. Unlike the Iroquois, most have not yet learned the art of accurate shooting. You are safe where you are."

"Good God in heaven above! I see your purpose. I am to help them improve their aim," Fr. Hennepin protested, taking a step to one side.

"No, do not move in this direction. If you do, they may suspect a trap. Stay where you are. I do not think they really want to fight. But you do make a splendid target."

La Salle soon identified the war chief. "The chief is to your right. Walk slowly toward him."

Duplessis followed Hennepin's movement with his musket. Soon he had the chief in his sights. "Shoot the leader, and the others will run away," he glowered.

"Don't shoot, Duplessis! You trigger-happy fool!" Alarmed, La Salle yelled out, "Men, rest your guns. Point your muskets over their heads."

"Duplessis, you take your command from me. If you wish to exercise your ignorance, go back to Montreal," La Salle fumed. "Your reckless attitude is a danger to us all."

Seeing La Salle's men relax their stance, Fights-Bear-with-Knife signaled his force. Others began calling loudly to settle the warriors.

"One day Sieur de La Salle will learn who's smart," Duplessis spit the words. "I am not stupid!"

Leblanc grunted.

Messier stared at Duplessis for some moments, his thumb slowly caressing the breech of his musket. At length, the stocky woodsman called out, "Duplessis, provoke a fight, and I promise you, I'll save you a kiss from my sweet 'Antoinette.'"

Duplessis rolled his eyes, gritted his teeth, and hunched down behind his barrier.

Fights-Bear-with-Knife walked toward Hennepin and demanded, "Where is our brave? Bring him that we may see he is unharmed."

"He is here. He is safe." Fr. Hennepin said, displaying his growing skill with the Algonquian language.

The boy, his hands tied and his feet hobbled, came into view. A parley ensued. And since both sides wanted a peaceful outcome, the war party offered full compensation for the stolen jacket.

"Since you have acted in good faith, and have pledged your friendship, the boy is free!" La Salle signaled his men who released the prisoner.

"We give you these gifts." Fights-Bear-with-Knife had a brave present some beaver skins. "Bring your men to my village and honor me today as my guest. You may stay in my *wi-kiya-pi*."

La Salle agreed and he and his men followed the chief to the Fox camp. A meal of waterfowl and venison was prepared that afternoon. Indian dancing and singing lasted well past evening as the hosts expressed their happiness and hospitality.

"But you cannot go to the Illinois," Fights-Bear-with-Knife insisted, after having dined with La Salle. "They are angry with the French. They will kill all of you. They have learned the French arm the Iroquois to attack them." He and La Salle were now seated in the open, watching the men and women stamp in the rhythm of their harvest dance, a ritual of thanksgiving and a prayer for plentiful game.

"This is not true. The French do not urge the Iroquois to attack anyone. The Iroquois have felt the sting of French weapons. We are not allies." La Salle suspected his rivals were inciting the Illinois. "Did the Illinois learn this from the Jesuits, or from traders?"

"They captured an Iroquois scout. They tortured him to death. Before he died he told them of this plan. The Illinois are sure of this. You must not go there." Fights-Bear-with-Knife impassively studied La Salle while he considered this situation.

Chagrined, La Salle nevertheless grew more determined to continue, sensitive to the injustice done to his mission and to his reputation.

Learning too, that the mouth of the Miami River lay to the east of Lake Michigan, he realized that Wind-in-the-Pines had been truthful and that the map drawn from memory by Louis Jolliet was inaccurate. He resolved to discuss these issues later with the men.

"As a pledge of our friendship, we have a gift for you." The chief raised his arm in signal and three middle-aged women came forward.

The women sat down, their legs folded beneath them, before La Salle and Fights-Bear-with-Knife. One had a small deerskin bundle.

"These are members of our senior women's society. They are the best clothing makers. They offer these leggings to you." Fights-Bear-with-Knife announced as the leader formally presented the package to La Salle.

Carefully unfolding each legging, La Salle ran his fingers over the stitching, admiring the quality of the handwork. The red-dyed deerskin was seamed down the front and fringed on the sides, below the knees. Each ended with a fringe hem. In front was a pointed flap, large enough to extend to the toe of the moccasin. Separate fur-strip ties would serve as garters, normally worn just below the knees.

"Among our friends, these leggings will speak of the friendship of the French and *Meshkwaki*. You are as a brother to us."

"I will wear these with pride." La Salle respectfully refolded the leggings. Looking at the women, La Salle could see in their dark eyes twinkling reflections of the council fire. Smiles brightened their cordial faces. As they stood to leave, La Salle rose and thanked them all, bowing and kissing each on the hand in turn.

When the feted men returned to camp that night, they were happy. The good humor and graciousness of their hosts, and a plentiful feast, combined to make them feel their fortunes had greatly improved. More importantly, their confidence had increased and the sense of risk declined. They realized contact with the natives, even in strained circumstances, was not dangerous so long as tact, diplomacy, and above all, respect, were employed.

* * *

As they were strolling along the beach the next morning, Fr. Membré asked La Salle, "Weren't you afraid yesterday when the Indians faced us?" It was an idle question—the priest already knew his leader was a man of strong character—but he remained fascinated with the turn of events.

"As you saw, they are not hostile. In fact, they are very hospitable, considering we are intruding on their hunting lands," La Salle replied, pleasantly surprised by the question.

"I do not think of fear in these circumstances." La Salle reflected for a few moments, then resumed, "I trust to God's will and grace. If it is His will I should die today—then so be it. My hope is that I am in fact doing His will in all that I do. The difficult part is in knowing what is God's will."

"How is that difficult? Many people are confident they know God's will." Fr. Membré remembered his choice as a seminarian. He enjoyed theological studies and had hoped to continue, yet felt a strong calling to become a missionary.

"Do they? I am skeptical of those who claim God has given them specific guidance." La Salle glanced at his companion. "I am convinced that at the most important times in our lives, God does not intervene. It is an especially powerful independence He gives us when He allows us to act, bravely using our own free will. It is His way of showing His trust in us. What higher honor can a Creator bestow on His creatures? It is when He is silent that we mature most. God speaks loudest when He says nothing."

"I think I follow your meaning," Fr. Membré said on reflection. "It's similar to a parent assisting a child. If the parent does not let go, the child is hindered. Even though there is some risk for the child, the parent must nevertheless let the child have the experience. In spite of the danger—or perhaps because of it—it is a moment of growth. For all!"

"Yes, it is precisely when God has not shown us His will that we must do no less than act with the greatest boldness and courage." La Salle tossed a stone toward the lake. "Consider Jean d'Arc, for example."

"You refer to her campaign against the English?" Fr. Membré observed absently, staring at the ground, trying to anticipate La Salle's point.

"Correct. She was captured and brought to trial—in Rouen, my hometown, nearly two hundred and fifty years ago. She was accused of heresy and given a choice of accepting the false charges or death. Agonizing in her cell for days, feeling abandoned by God, in the end she made the most courageous decision of her life."

"And so they burned her at the stake," Fr. Membré said, fidgeting with his rosary.

La Salle watched as several swallows darted about in the morning sky over the lake. After a moment, he said, "You know, the English, they have no class, no finesse."

"But of course! What Frenchman does not know this?" The priest screwed up his eyes, caught by this sudden thought.

"You know, when the English burn transgressors, they build huge bonfires, but the heated air kills the victim instantly. *Hélas!* They are dead. It is not pretty, but it is mercifully quick."

"I had not thought about that. You mean the victims are not killed by the flames?" Fr. Membré said with not a little distaste, his face pale and empty. "This is not something one normally reflects on."

"No, but compare this with the Indian way. They have made an art of death by fire. They roast their victims slowly, starting at the feet. They cook them for hours, sometimes for half a day. They use a small fire so as to extend the victim's agony. And they add other tortures in order to measure the victim's courage. The more fortitude the victim displays, the more they honor him with torment. For the victim, defiance is not just a matter of personal honor, but it is the honor of his tribe and race that is at issue."

"This is too gruesome. Such stories I have heard—I had hoped they were exaggerations, wild stories to frighten enemies." Fr. Membré vacillated between fascination and disgust. In the end he was unable to drop the subject. "You seem to have gained intimate knowledge of this Indian torture."

"No, the stories are not exaggerations." La Salle stared absently over the water. "The Senecas once burned an eighteen-year-old prisoner just to entertain me . . . It was a horror. I shall never forget that lad and his great courage.

"They despise the cowardly, you know. And they are always ready to measure the brave. And those who are truly brave, they honor."

For a long time, the two walked along in silence.

"By the way, I have heard you refer to the Fox Indians as *Outagamis*, as does Fr. Hennepin," La Salle said, coming out of his reverie.

"But it is a good name. I learned it from Indians near Green Bay," Fr. Membré protested, happy though to have a lighter subject for discussion.

"Precisely. They are the Chippewa, deadly enemies of the Fox. If you wish to live in peace here, avoid using their Ojibwa language."

La Salle smiled at the weathered priest, whose beard framed a round, red face. "I think you are a good missionary. But you can see there is always much to learn about the natives."

After a few days rest, the men once again loaded the canoes, once again launched them through the surf, and once again settled into routine, rhythmic paddling. The course was east by north, becoming more northerly where the high sand dunes rose directly from the water's edge. The last leg of the long journey to the river of the Miamis was drawing to a close.

Chapter 4

Son of Walks in Thunder

A timid morning sun glared through hazy cloud stretching lazily above the horizon. The indolent lake sent indifferent wavelets sloshing against the beach. And an uncertain breeze provoked soft gusts of chill air. Stretching aching limbs, the men gradually emerged from under their lean-to canoe shelters and variously greeted the day.

La Salle and Shadow immediately went to the top of a nearby ridge, hoping to find evidence of Tonti and the others.

"You're certain no one has been here?" La Salle asked Shadow.

"I see no trace of white men or Indians. No, M. Tonti has not arrived. Nika would have left a marker. There is none."

La Salle squinted at the neutral sky, then said, "Let's discuss this with the men. I'm concerned. Tonti has had adequate time. Let us see how the others feel about this."

Meanwhile back on the beach, someone had already made a small cooking fire. Others who had been busy about the camp watched expectantly as La Salle and Shadow approached.

"They have not been here. There is no trace," La Salle informed them. "I don't know what this means. Perhaps there has been an accident. We do not have adequate supplies for travel to the Illinois country. But I owe you this much. Tell me your feelings. Do you think we should go on, or should we winter here?"

Messier, one of the *voyageurs*, spoke up. "We hired on to explore the *Fleuve Colbert*. I want to go on. But without guns and powder, we are safer here. And what about this route? Louis Jolliet made maps when he and Fr. Marquette explored the area. But surely, Jolliet's maps are wrong."

"Jolliet lost his original drawings and made new sketches from memory. It is likely he has misplaced the mouth of the *Rivière des Miamis*. Many Indians recommend we ascend the Miami to its Great Bend. There is a portage there to a connecting river that flows into the Illinois. This will prove an easy journey, they say." La Salle was glad for the question, as he was not fully confident of the alternatives. "Jolliet and Marquette returned from the Illinois country by ascending the *Rivière des Plaines* to the *Rivière Chikagou*. But there is much portaging on Des Plaines."

"All the more reason we should wait till next spring. We could winter over at Point Ignace." Fr. Hennepin said, uncomfortable at the prospect of wintering in the open.

"He's right! We could go north along the eastern shore now, before the lake ices over. It would be nice to live in a warm cabin for a spell," Le Picard said, agreeing with the priest's implicit suggestion.

La Salle kicked at the sand. Returning to the Jesuit mission was not what he wanted to do, but it would not be a total retreat.

"What if we winter here?" he asked. "How would that suit you? Perhaps by spring we will have news of Tonti."

"Yes, yes. That would be fine," Fr. Ribourde spoke up. "Even with the little we have, we could approach the Illinois sooner and build a base for our missions."

"That's fine," replied Leblanc, "But we will have to sleep under the stars—"

"Not if you can swing an ax," Fr. Ribourde chided. "And I've seen you in action—at Fort Conti!"

"So what do you say?" La Salle interjected. "Who would return to Michilimackinac, and who stay?"

A few voted to return; the majority preferred to remain.

"Well, then, let's do it. We shall build a stockade and a storehouse. There, on that ridge." La Salle was heartened by the men's decision to go on with his project. "At the head of the ridge line is a large basin where two rivers join. This would make a suitable harbor for *Griffin*. Marquette reports this area is well supplied with game—moorhens, geese and ducks. Even buffalo graze not far from here."

"Break out the axes and saws! In a few days we will all be sleeping under roof," Fr. Ribourde boomed.

As the men sharpened their tools or organized into teams, La Salle addressed his scout. "Saget, I want you to hunt. Bring us enough venison for the winter. We will remain here for some months."

Shadow nodded, then went off to gather his hunting gear.

La Salle then went to the ridge top where he began laying out the outlines for the buildings and the stockade. He marked an area thirty by forty feet. This was to be protected by a twenty-foot high palisade with earthworks.

Many of the workmen began felling and trimming the trees needed for the fortification.

* * *

As the autumn weather continued crisp and frosty, Shadow headed north along the twisting Paw Paw River. With a fair breeze rising, low clouds splayed across the eastern sky. Winter would soon bare the landscape and whiten it with snow.

Hiding his canoe, Shadow approached the forest. In the field and along the edge of the clearing, he set several traps for small game or birds. Coming upon a well-trod deer trail, he followed it into the woods where a cold, white sun reflected off branches and twigs rimed with frozen dew. Along the way, he studied thickets of rhododendron and wild azalea—good nesting areas. His chilled breath floated on the still air. Bright yellow leaves hanging on an old hickory tree signaled a good mast, while purple-ripe persimmons provided another delicacy for the creatures. In fact, he had already seen fresh droppings full of undigested persimmon pits, confirming the recent presence of deer.

Shadow sat on a mossy log, listening to the forest, waiting for the return of his prey. He felt elated, happy just to be among the trees, most now scantily dressed with the last dead leaves of autumn. He quickened at the musty odor from those leaves moldering on the ground. Occasionally he heard the snap of a twig, the scurrying of chipmunks, the occasional whisper of a breeze. The squirrels barking, the birds singing, the crows cawing–all bespoke a harmony and purpose Shadow strongly felt and was thankful for.

Shadow was at peace. He was one with this world. It was one with him, inseparable. As he slowly scanned near and far, he breathed a sigh of contentment. He watched as slow, watery crystals of time dripped from frosty branches warmed by the rising sun.

At length, he decided to move to another location.

As he quietly rose, a low, quick motion caught his attention. He studied the trees ahead. Barely visible, a small furry bulge could be seen extending along the trunk of one. The black knob located above the fur exhaled a small breath into the chilly air. Shadow knew then that the deer had been observing him. Hidden by the tree, the deer stood, facing away, his head turned just enough to keep Shadow in view. Shadow smiled, as noiselessly, the deer disappeared. The chase was on, and the prey had the advantage.

Calmly checking his nocked arrow, Shadow advanced to where the deer had been standing. Only an old deer trail showed where the prey might have gone. There were no fresh tracks. Nonetheless, he stalked silently on. His keen eye probed the ground and each bush he passed. No tracks showed, no broken twigs. Yet he felt he was on the correct trail. Presently he came to a junction—the path he had been following curved to the left, but directly ahead a faint track led into a more open expanse under tall hardwoods. Although it had been nearly an hour since that first, tenuous encounter, Shadow instinctively decided to venture into the more trackless area, away from the obvious trail.

He began to doubt that he might again see this deer. But his intuition proved more accurate than his skepticism. Halfway through the stand, he found a single imprint of a deer's cloven hoof. Just one. But it was recent. The deer was not running. It was not alarmed. And it was not far ahead. The deer had been toying with him, leading him, staying just out of sight. The deer was curious and Shadow appreciated its playful attitude.

After a while Shadow came to a deep gully. He hesitated, concerned that he might expose himself crossing the high ground. He waited for awhile behind a sheltering tree, listening. As he shifted his position, the slight motion caused the deer to break cover. The deer had been lying in the gully and now bounded leisurely away. Shadow saw only its bobbing head and antlers as it followed the narrow ravine.

Deciding that further direct pursuit would be fruitless, Shadow rested for a few moments. He expected the deer would stop again, especially if not chased. Now that he had a rough idea as to where his adversary might be headed, he circled swiftly back through the hardwood, returning to the same gully but beyond the point where he expected the deer. He had guessed correctly.

As Shadow came marching loudly through the brush from an unexpected direction, the deer stood mesmerized. The deliberate noise Shadow made imitated that of other deer coming through the woods. The prey stood transfixed, watching Shadow march over the rise. Shadow stopped, an arrow-shot away. Hunter and hunted gazed at each other, without hatred, without fear.

The deer stood broadside to Shadow, facing his right. Shadow gradually raised his bow to the shooting position.

Spirit of Deer. I am sorry that I must kill you. My people are hungry. Do not be angry with me. Shadow had the bow at full tension as he sighted over the arrow. The deer had not blinked, had not stirred.

The arrow burst into the air. At the snap of the bow, the waiting deer had leaped, high and forward. The arrow cracked through its ribs, all the same. Shadow had anticipated the deer's move, knowing he had to make a killing shot. He watched as the wounded deer bounded into a small copse of mountain laurel.

As he walked slowly toward the thicket, he nocked another arrow. As he neared the laurels, Shadow could discern the deer's face within the dark green foliage. Again the deer was motionless, but its eyes were glazed. The deer had died where it stood—a large splatter of blood wetting the forest floor beneath it.

Shadow continued his hunt, finding only an owl and a porcupine in the traps he had earlier set. He winced with disdain as the owl offered only tough and chewy meat, but he was pleased with the porcupine as its liver was considered a delicacy. After appeasing the spirits of his prey, he carried his meager yield to a cache near the Paw Paw River. Finally, he settled into the task of field dressing the deer. At the end of his day's work, Shadow placed his harvest into the canoe for transport to the fort.

Returning to the camp, Shadow was amazed at the progress made during his absence. Living quarters and a storehouse were complete, the palisade nearly so.

Several *coureurs de bois* aided Shadow in the care and storage of the game, preparing it by bleeding and hanging the carcasses to dry and age, setting aside the soft organs and marrow bones for immediate use.

Surveying the poor results of Shadow's hunt, La Salle sighed a reluctant approval. Turning to the Indian, he announced a new assignment.

"Saget, I want you to scout the Miami River, but only as far as the portage at the great bend. Be alert for Iroquois bands. But otherwise find out what Indians may be camped along the way. Ask about the Illinois country." La Salle eagerly anticipated the next stage of his voyage. "Take Duplessis and Messier. Do not stay longer than two weeks. With Tonti and Nika absent, I cannot come looking for you too. You are my eyes and my tongue."

Shadow looked around at the men in the room. Messier he trusted, but the thin and pale Duplessis had shown an increasingly sour attitude. Shadow suspected La Salle was sending Duplessis on this mission because, in the fort, he would simply become more of a nuisance.

Messier responded enthusiastically—he was pleased to travel but Duplessis masked his acquiescence under a cloak of grousing.

"I should like to go along," Fr. Membré burst out, surprising La Salle. "There is not much employment for me here, and I can help with the canoe."

Raising his eyebrows, La Salle looked toward Shadow who remained inscrutable. Sensing that the Indian had no objection, La Salle approved the request.

"What we need is more guns. If there's a fight, a priest won't be much help," Duplessis whined.

"This is a peaceful venture. Don't provoke hostility. Be gone!" La Salle commanded, ignoring Duplessis' discontent. He watched wistfully as the men gathered their weapons and gear. In other circumstances, he would have led the reconnaissance, leaving someone else in charge of the fort, but as there was no one present who could control the men, he resignedly remained behind.

Near the harbor basin, the four slid a canoe into the river, steadied the craft as each boarded, then began the ascent of the Miami.

About six hours later the canoeists entered a distinctive area where the river was marked by low banks and a shallow channel—an ideal crossing point. Shadow decided to investigate. While Messier, Duplessis, and Fr. Membré hid the canoe, Shadow searched the terrain along both banks. Beneath a huge willow sheltering one bank, he found a well-marked trail bearing to the west and followed it for a short distance.

Doubling back to the river, Shadow surprised a file of Indians wading toward him. Startled at each other's presence, both parties halted.

One of the Indians in the river yelled, *"Waigonain ewinain maundun?"*

"I am a scout, these men are French," Shadow responded, also in Algonquian, and pointed to his colleagues under some nearby trees.

"Waigonain wau iayun?"

"We are seeking the trail to the Illinois country. We come in peace. Who arc you?" Shadow asked.

"We are *Asa-ki-waki,* the People of the Yellow Earth. We have a winter camp nearby. Come, share our evening meal." The leader of the Sac band motioned for his group to resume their advance. Coming out of the water, the Sac warriors eyed Shadow's companions, and silently continued walking toward their village.

Shadow walked with his Sac hosts for a while, discussing several items of interest. He then dropped back to rejoin the three Frenchmen, trailing the rear of the column.

"Why are we going with these Indians?" Duplessis, slightly vexed and uncomfortable, grumbled. "I thought we were to reconnoiter the upper river."

"They are a Sac hunting party returning to their village. The father of one of the braves is dying," Shadow explained. "Their camp is not far."

Duplessis felt trapped. He resented the detour and he felt particularly alarmed at being isolated among people he considered primitive.

"It is an Indian custom to assist the dying and his family," Fr. Membré remarked. "No civilized person does as much to comfort the dying as these people. Look smart, Duplessis, here is an opportunity for you to display your more noble qualities."

Duplessis ignored the priest's admonishment. "Nonsense. These people are savage. They have no 'qualities,' as you say. Just look how backward they are, living in the forest like wild creatures."

Towering over Duplessis, Shadow stiffened as he stared at the man, but said nothing.

"I'm for it!" Messier interjected. "Let's go to the village. Perhaps there we'll learn the new route to the Illinois River."

"Women, you mean," Duplessis smiled cunningly, his eyes slanting evasively as he suddenly realized an unanticipated aspect of the visit. "Uh, excuse me, Father," he said, catching himself in a rare, self-conscious reflection.

"Remember, Duplessis, you are a representative of La Salle and of the king, and for that matter, you are a Christian," the priest reproached him.

For several hours they marched toward the southwest. Coming to a faint side trail, the party turned to the south and within another hour or so, came to the Sac village.

Whistling Elk sat there, near the base of a huge willow oak. The dying man was dressed in his finest costume, his face washed and his graying hair neatly combed. He wore his finest shirt with hair fringes and red-beaded strips. He also wore bright bead necklaces around his throat, ear and nose rings, and new, highly decorated moccasins. Braced against the tree, he sat with his waist and legs covered by a fine, white buffalo robe, his personal weapons arranged by his side. Near his feet, mourners placed gifts. Two women daubed his face with vermilion paint, intermixing blue and black markings into the design.

Occasionally, the man would open his pain-filled eyes and moan. To his concerned attendants, he signaled dismissively that they were not the cause of his discomfort.

Some women were kneeling close by, watching Whistling Elk intently. Whenever his suffering increased, they would accompany his moans with mournful chants, ceasing only when he seemed to recover.

Feeling certain the end was at hand, the family of the dying man showed him the funeral gifts. With an approving nod, he signaled satisfaction with each of the presents. His eyes glistened as Shadow stepped forward, placing his iron knife and leather sheath by the man's side.

At times, Whistling Elk seemed to lapse into a semiconscious state, his limited arm motions suggesting he was reenacting ancient fights and combats.

"I have heard the Indians have great regard for the dying," Fr. Membré said to Messier. The two were observing from a discrete distance. "Now I understand a little better the early missionaries. It is difficult to speak to our people about death and dying, but these people show little fear. They see the spiritual, after life as simply a continuation of their earthly existence. This magnificent act of faith is impressive.

"Too many Europeans have difficulty admitting even that there is a spiritual aspect to man's nature."

"You priests! You go on about these 'spiritual' matters. You waste your lives waiting for the 'Happy Ever After' but it's how one lives that matters.

How one lives is the only thing that matters," Duplessis snorted, his flinty, narrowed eyes flashing as they danced about.

"But that's the choice you ultimately make, isn't it?" Fr. Membré rejoined. "How you live—whether you satisfy only your selfish interests or whether you serve a higher authority. Those whose lives fully embrace ethical principles are the ones who find true inner peace.

"These Indians will go nearly naked in the winter cold, if only to preserve their best clothes and robes for their funeral. Their everyday existence is focused on one goal—and they are happy when they face that threshold. It is a lesson you should consider, my friend."

"Can we go now?" Duplessis was looking around the camp area, eyeing the women as they passed near. "Don't you think we should finish scouting?"

"It is evening and we are guests. We should not leave as long as Whistling Elk lives." Shadow looked askance at Duplessis. "La Salle would not leave."

Duplessis beckoned to Messier and stomped off with him to go wandering in search of amusement.

Watching the men leave, Shadow turned to the priest and commented, "The spirits of the unburied roam the earth in an unhappy state. This is why the Indian will fight to recover the dead from a battlefield—to ease their journey to happiness. The graves of the dead are a sacred responsibility. The living affect the spirit life of the dead through the treatment of their remains. To the Indian, body and spirit are linked, even after death."

* * *

Throughout the evening and into the night, the death vigil continued. At the first gray light, dawn restored the true colors to all things. On meeting his final sunrise, Whistling Elk rolled his eyes, grimaced, and then unable to breathe at last, slumped his head onto his motionless chest.

Immediately, his oldest son, naked but covered with fire ash, ran howling and dancing throughout the camp. On hearing the news, some women were overcome, crying hot tears while the men fought to conceal their grief. Foods, mats, and other gifts were brought to the newly bereaved family.

Bark sheathes were prepared for the interment. The body was arranged in the fetal position while a small pit was dug. The exquisitely dressed body of Whistling Elk was carefully placed in the grave and surrounded with his weapons and other personal belongings.

"It is a good day," Shadow said to Fr. Membré as the two witnessed the funeral. "The spirit of Whistling Elk is happy."

"Now we must finish our assignment," Fr. Membré said. "I saw Messier and Duplessis wandering from the camp a short while ago. Before you retrieve them, though, I should offer a few prayers for Whistling Elk and his family."

"The family has indicated they are pleased to accept your prayers," Shadow reported after a brief discussion with the bereaved.

Fr. Membré composed himself, then said, "Very well then, I shall recite Psalm 130, our usual prayer for the dead."

Raising his arms and eyes to heaven, Fr. Membré intoned, *"Out of the depths, I cry to You, O Lord! . . . ."* Ending the Psalm, he made the sign of the cross over the grave. Looking up, he noticed several grinning Indians.

"Why are they smiling?" Fr. Membré asked Shadow.

"They are amused that when you pray, you do not chant and dance as is the Indian custom," Shadow replied.

For an instant, Fr. Membré thought he detected a twinkle in Shadow's eye. "Very well, I shall remember that next time."

"We must return now to La Salle," Shadow declared. "I shall find Messier and Duplessis."

"What about our reconnaissance? There is much to explore yet," Fr. Membré countered. "We have seen only a small section of the Miami River."

"Sac braves have told me all we need to know. Better to save time and return to La Salle than to follow an empty trail."

Shadow left the priest at the graveside, among the other mourners. Within a half-hour he had returned with the two other Frenchmen. Together the four marched back to the river, recovered their canoe, and began the easy voyage to the fort.

As they beached the canoe on the riverside, Messier noticed that many of the men were down on the lakeshore, excitedly watching some activity.

"It looks as though something is happening on the lake. Perhaps the *Griffin* has arrived," Fr. Membré observed.

Jogging over to the group, Fr. Membré was soon disappointed. He detected not a sailing craft but several canoes coming from the north. "Indian or French?" he asked as he entered the knot of observers.

"Difficult to say," said one. "There are not as many as might be in Tonti's crew. Must be an Indian party."

Energetically waving his hat at the canoeists, a lookout roared from a knoll across the river's mouth, "It is Tonti!" He turned, ran down the hill, jumped into his canoe, and paddled across the estuary. "I can recognize that Italian anywhere," he beamed, clambering ashore.

The approaching canoes, bobbing among the lake swells, began a sweeping turn into the mouth of the Miami. Hello-ing back and forth, both groups began greeting each other with unchecked joy and excitement.

"Where is Nika? Where are the rest of your men?" La Salle cried out as Tonti's canoe beached. With some concern, La Salle nevertheless clasped his arms around Tonti in greeting.

"They are not far behind. Nika and the others are hunting; they will come in a few days. We ran out of food . . . we have been living on acorns." Tonti looked around at each of the men, glad to be among familiar company. "It's been, what? Nearly three months since Pt. Ignace. Lord, are we happy to see you."

"As soon as you have eaten, I want you to take a few men and go back for Nika and the others." La Salle said sternly. "We have some provision here. I am concerned about their condition, you understand."

"Yes, of course," Tonti replied, momentarily taken aback. "We shall be underway within the hour. But where is *Griffin*? I thought that you were bringing her here."

"*Griffin*? You mean you didn't see her at Pt. Ignace? I found some of my men at Green Bay. I sent them with a shipload of furs to Ft. Conti, in mid-September. Did you not hear of her?"

"No, not a word. Nothing! I came through the mission much later—it was October. If she had passed there, I would have known," Tonti said with some exasperation. "So what do we do now? With no equipment or supplies, you cannot explore the *Fleuve Colbert*."

"On the contrary. *Griffin* may still be afloat somewhere on *Michigami*." La Salle said with an abstraction that Tonti recognized as signaling the beginning of an idea.

"I had planned to remain here at Fort St. Joseph. But the fort is not adequate for all these men. We shall gather what resources we have and move to the Illinois country. We must go before the hard days of winter set in."

Tonti laughed. Shaking his head, he said, "You are too unpredictable! You change your plans at every step. Just when there is a difficulty and you should retreat, you advance. *Heu!* But there is one thing I know for a certainty. You never stand still. I like this. Let us go on, then. To the Illinois Indians! May they spit in your eye!"

"They may do more than spit, I'm afraid." Smiling, La Salle attempted to temper his friend's zeal. "They have been told we are allies of the Iroquois. Their welcome may be of a different warmth than you would prefer."

"When do we go?" Tonti brushed aside the caution.

"I admire your enthusiasm. You may think me endlessly restless, but I find you equally optimistic," La Salle said, studying his lieutenant. "It is now the twentieth of November. I think we should depart by the first of next month. Two weeks should be adequate for you to bring in Nika and the others, don't you think?"

"Of course! Let me go now," Tonti rubbed his hand on his sleeve.

"Take your men to the fort. First you should have a good meal." La Salle signaled the newcomers to follow Tonti while his own men unloaded the canoes and moved the equipment from the beach.

After dining, Tonti departed with two *voyageurs*, once again paddling north across the swells of *Michigami*.

A few days later, during the early afternoon, La Salle ran to the beach, having heard news of his returning crew. Once again a convoy approached the river's mouth, ascended the channel, and coming to shore, disgorged a tired and hungry band.

"Nika!" La Salle beamed, embracing his guide. "It is good to see you again."

Nika smiled, straightened, and said, "It is good to be here. M. Tonti says we are going soon to the *Illiniwek*."

"Yes, in a few days," La Salle responded, feeling elated that he now had all his explorers together. "But for now you must eat. Shadow has some turkey, corn, and paw paws. You men have starved too long."

* * *

In the evening dusk, after their meal, Fr. Membré, Nika, and La Salle went for a stroll along the lakeshore. Nika had surveyed the fort and the harbor and was pleased with the arrangements.

"I am happy you have been able to rejoin our company. I miss the walking talks we shared," La Salle said to Nika.

Turning to the priest, La Salle explained, "We walk and exchange information. Nika is an excellent student. He has a great curiosity. I have offered to school him in France, but he will have none of it."

Fr. Membré eyed Nika searchingly, as though appreciating a quality that was somehow contrary to his expectations.

Fr. Membré spoke abruptly, as though suddenly reminded of La Salle's presence. "So why did you name your fort in honor of St. Joseph?"

"He represents persistence in the face of disappointment," La Salle replied. "He and I are alike in several respects—we are exiles, wanderers. The authorities pursued him, an outcast among his own people. Even when forced to shelter among animals, he was not brokenhearted. I like these similarities, even though they are not exact."

"So then, he has become a guide for you?" Fr. Membré said, raising an eyebrow.

"When he set out on his ventures, he did not know the route or the outcome in advance. When I first came to New France, I burned with the desire to find a passage to China; I even named my first estate *La Chine*. But those early reports of a westward waterway proved inaccurate. The Ojibwa speak of the *misi-sipi* which they say flows south, south into the Gulf of Mexico. I know now I will never find a direct route to China, but here I am and so I shall explore this 'Big River.'"

"Progress!" Fr. Membré beamed. "This is the great movement of our times. I am delighted to be here, to bring civilization to these wild people."

"Your 'progress' is a strange concept. In the English colonies, it has had unhappy results," Nika warned.

"I don't follow you," Fr. Membré looked toward La Salle for support.

"As I have told you, Nika is an excellent student," La Salle said wryly. "We have had rare discourses on these matters."

"But how is progress dangerous?" Fr. Membré looked puzzled.

"Less-developed peoples are inferior when they show no progress or do not adapt to the culture of the superior people," Nika explained.

Nika looked at the priest, then chopping his words, said. "The Massachusetts colonists force the natives to adopt their ways, or face extermination."

"Extermination?" Fr. Membré thought for a moment. "I have heard of wars there, but extermination?"

"How is it a war when whole peoples disappear? When peaceful nations are not allowed to have the weapons or lands needed for hunting and survival?" Nika stopped to consider the priest for a moment. "This is your progress. Pequot, Nipmuc, Wampanoag, and Narraganset. These tribes are no more forever."

"How did it happen that the Indian civilization was pronounced inferior?" Nika resumed after a pause. "It is unfortunate Europeans tend to look on the Indian as less intelligent because we did not invent the wheel. But they are wrong."

"Oh? I am puzzled. Do you mean to say the Indian did invent the wheel?" La Salle looked keenly at his protégé.

"Of course not! We saw that the wheel is evil. Just look at your country." Nika spoke gravely. "Roads run like ugly scars across the face of your earth mother. The wheel crushes all that comes in its way; it is the enemy of the flowers and the grasses, of things that give beauty to life."

"So you are saying the Indian invented the wheel, but then discarded the idea?" La Salle teased, a small grin playing at the corners of his mouth.

"We did not as you say, 'discard' the wheel: We banished it! We decreed that the wheel should disappear from our lands forever." Nika continued in his serious mood, a suspicious sparkle in his eye.

"And how did you do this?" La Salle asked, enjoying the exchange.

"We gave the wheel to the Great Hare and told him to take it as far away as possible. But he gave the wheel to the most ignorant people he could find," Nika retorted.

"Very interesting," La Salle said, seemingly bedeviled. "And why do you claim these people are ignorant?"

"They made a god of the wheel and credit themselves as genius for having discovered it. Yet they do not understand their idol destroys Spirit and Beauty. Europeans do not see what the Indian sees. The Sun-wheel leaves no tracks. It crosses the heavens without trace; it leaves no record of its passing, no blemish on the loveliness of the sky.

"This is the challenge. Let your people devise a trackless wheel, then we shall decide who is ignorant and who is genius." Nika finished with a dignified, solemn tone.

"Very interesting. But the two civilizations are not really comparable on the same level, as I see it," Fr. Membré spoke pensively. "One culture fosters a person's inner life and soul, ignoring material development beyond the essentials for living. The other emphasizes the sum total of intellectual, philosophical, ethical, and aesthetic achievements, but measures its achievements largely in material terms. Our claim to superiority is based on the sensual. We quantify but true greatness demands quality, a quality that is not occasional or peripheral. Our civilization must dedicate itself to moral and ethical principles in all aspects of life and government."

"And how does it happen that only a priest can understand these differences? Is there no one else capable of respecting the native culture?" Nika asked pointedly. "Will there be peace and brotherhood among nations, or will the arrogant dominate?"

"You are concerned the white man will kill more Indians?" La Salle asked, turning toward Nika.

"The Indian does not fear death. That is for the white race," Nika said. "We love this beautiful land and we shall be here forever. In the silence of the night, when the white man's children's children think the shops, the streets, the fields, and the pathless woods are deserted, we will be there. For the Indian there is no death, only a change of worlds. No matter how many Indians he may kill, the white man will never be alone. This land will swarm with the invisible dead, and the dead are not powerless."

The men walked along, for a few moments in silence.

"So tell me, Nika," Fr. Membré asked, "Where do you come from? I mean, where did you live before you were hired by La Salle?"

"I was not hired. I was a prisoner of the Iroquois. La Salle purchased my freedom," Nika replied, looking toward the receding daylight above the lake.

"I understand you are from Shawnee Nation," Fr. Membré prodded.

"I am from the Piqua tribe," Nika said. "The Piqua are the religious leaders of the Shawnee."

"Aha! Now I am less than surprised you are among La Salle's company," the priest smiled. "Tell me about your family."

After a pause, the Indian continued. "My father was a chief, before an Iroquois band killed him."

"I am sorry to hear that. Was there a war?" Tonti asked.

"I was young. He took me on a hunt, with other braves. Some wives came to skin and dress the dead animals." Nika's face hardened noticeably.

Fr. Membré reflected on Nika's tone, then asked quietly, "And your mother . . .?"

Nika stared severely at the empty sunset sky over the lake.

After a while, Tonti said, "Now I understand. The Iroquois call you 'War-hatchet' because they have heard of your vow of vengeance."

"You have spoken with the Mohawk at *Nyàgarah*," Nika said flatly. "There is one, Limping Wolf . . . my father's blood is on his hands."

Testing a nettle bush with his foot, Fr. Membré continued, "And what sort of man was he, your father?"

"Fearless. He is called Walks-in-Thunder." Nika watched an osprey gliding beneath an orange-crimson cloud hanging in the graying sky. "Renegade Lenapes captured my mother—before I was born. For three days, my father tracked them through the forests and mountains. He caught up with them early one morning, before they broke camp. It was raining. Yelling his war cry, he charged down the side of a hill, his tomahawk his only weapon."

"How many were against him?" Fr. Membré asked, becoming more interested.

"Six. They saw him coming and prepared to fight." Nika paused, watching as the fish hawk plunged into the lake. Looking at the priest, he continued, "As my father came on, a lightning bolt exploded in a tree above him. He did not stop; he did not falter. Halfway down the hill, a second bolt hit the ground between him and the enemy—a ball of blue fire shimmering on the ground, burning the grass and leaves. It was too much. When the air cleared, the Lenapes were gone."

Fr. Membré studied Nika, who had turned again to look at the lake. "So your mother was recovered safely?"

"Happily so," Nika said. Looking over the water, he saw the osprey skimming toward the shore, the silver prize glistening in its talons. "When the Shawnee sing of my father, they say he had much courage and great medicine."

"Medicine has a special meaning for the Indian," Fr. Membré mused. "Both a spiritual and a medical sense, I believe."

"It is private," Nika replied. "I cannot share my personal medicine with you. I will not even tell you what it is, for that would weaken it."

"From what I have seen," Fr. Membré observed, "Indian medical practice is on a par with that of the French barber-surgeons. I am amazed at your use of plants and roots to treat illnesses and wounds."

"Your medicine men care only for the body. Indian medicine treats both body and spirit." Nika looked at the last remnants of the setting sun. "If the spirit is not well, the body cannot heal itself. It is because of the white man's concern with the physical world that it is difficult for him to understand Indian ways."

"It is time to return to the fort," La Salle interjected. "Tomorrow we depart for the Illinois country, the first stage of our exploration of the *Fleuve Colbert*."

* * *

76

Under a propitious sunrise, La Salle and his men canoed up the Miami River. After a journey of two days, they came to a large bend where they disembarked for the portage to the Kankakee. Only Nika was absent, hunting and scouting along the way.

"We cannot wait here; we must move on," La Salle announced, prompting the men to organize for the overland trip. "This trail will not be difficult for Nika to find. The *Theakikee* is several leagues overland. It will take us a day to portage there."

"*Theakikee?*" La Forge, the blacksmith, mused. "That's a new one. Why are we going on this river?"

"It's an Indian name, 'Slow River Flowing in a Big Swamp,'" Messier replied. "You should be happy. With this forge to portage, there'll be less work here than coming down the rocky Des Plaines. Not many swamps have white water, do they?"

Messier and La Forge carried the portable forge and tools, L'Esperance shouldered a kettle and other cooking utensils, others saws, hammers, as well as carpenters and shipwright's tools. When all were burdened, La Salle led the way, setting the pace down the faint trail.

Immediately behind La Salle, Duplessis stepped off, an extra food pack strapped to his back. He carried his musket at the ready, as did several others.

La Salle set a brisk pace at first, pulling ahead of the file which became increasingly strung out. Coming up a slight rise, Duplessis turned and noticed that Messier, the next closest person, was some thirty yards back. Duplessis yelled, "What we need is rest and food. A fire. And women! This is work for a farmer, not for the likes of us."

"Duplessis, stop grumbling. Nothing pleases you. Perhaps you should have remained in the north woods." Messier turned to La Forge. "This man is tiresome and protests endlessly."

"I agree. Travel at this time of year may not be comfortable. But then, can you imagine the hordes of insects this place must breed in summer?" Messier yelled back at Duplessis.

"All the same. It's not the cold or the insects. It's our leader. He's lost half the time and then he's rushing into hostile country. Sometimes, I think he cares more for the Indians than for his own kind. I'll take your gnats anytime. It's the arrows that'll be stinging, you'll see." Duplessis wiped his mouth with his sleeve. Glancing round he noticed that the group behind was lagging, that La Salle was not far ahead, just disappearing over a knoll.

As Duplessis passed over the rise, he quickly pulled to one side, into the crowding bull rushes, and began playing with his pack straps. "I'll be just a minute. I'll catch up with you shortly," he said as Messier and La Forge passed by.

Glancing back, Duplessis assured himself that it would be moments before the next person approached. All the while watching La Salle, he quickly lowered his pack, and, carefully raising his musket, took aim. A slight click registered the cocking of the weapon.

Staring down the long barrel, Duplessis was perfecting his aim on the distant image of La Salle's back when suddenly the face of a scowling, angry Indian appeared above the end of the gun barrel. For an uncomprehending instant, Duplessis stared at Nika, who waited, a trigger-pull away from death. Duplessis' determination to shoot La Salle melted into confusion. Before he was able to resolve his dilemma, a sharp blow knocked the musket from his hands. A second kick to the legs collapsed Duplessis to the ground. Nika was immediately on top of the man, a cold knife against his throat.

The two glared at each other.

Swishing grass signaled the approach of others. Suddenly Nika was gone, replaced by two *voyageurs* standing by the trail.

"Are you all right?" one of the men asked.

"I'm fine," Duplessis snarled. "I must have stumbled. Just thought I'd catch my breath," he muttered. Rising to his feet and pulling his collar over the fresh bruise on his throat, he gathered his musket and gear, then rejoined the march.

Plodding down the hillock, through the saw grass and bull rushes, the men noticed that the ground was becoming spongy. Not far ahead lay the headwaters of the Kankakee.

La Salle was standing by a small marshy creek, his feet sinking into the yielding ground. He had found a suitable spot for launching the canoes. Looking back along the strung-out column, he yelled, "Be careful! This swamp may swallow you whole!"

He's right about that, Duplessis swore to himself. *One of us is not coming out of here alive.*

Chapter 5

Plenty Fish

Under a mid-morning grayness, the eight canoes followed the leisurely current, drifting slowly beneath the overhanging trees of the lee shore. Ahead, the curving bank merged with a high prominence, its sheer cliffs signaling the narrowed waist of Lake Peoria.

As they glided beneath the cliffs, the men listened to the occasional calls and rattle of the wildlife concealed above. La Salle felt reassured as the random activities indicated no human trespass, no ambuscade, and no threat to the safety of his men.

A few miles beyond the cliffs, the highland gradually receded, dwindling to a small ridge that followed the course of the river draining the lake.

On the left, prominent, highly fissured bluffs approached the waterway. These steep ravines and gullies formed by the runoff from the tableland formed staircases to the summit.

"Smoke! I see smoke ahead." Shadow whispered, pointing to a lazy wisp of gray smoke laying above the tree line. La Salle's flotilla had by now descended about three miles beyond the end of the lake.

La Salle squinted. Against the gray overcast, the nearly motionless smoke seemed illusory. "What is it? A hunting camp, or a village? What do you think?"

"I see many fires. The people are careless. It is a village," Shadow replied in a whisper.

"They have no lookouts," La Salle mused. "They don't seem to know we are here."

"Bring out the calumet," Fr. Hennepin suggested. "They will respect a peaceful approach."

"No! Not at all," La Salle replied sternly. "If we first display the calumet, they will think we are cowards. No, we must show courage through bold action."

La Salle considered his position. After a moment, he ordered, "Form the canoes line-abreast. Lash the thwarts together. Tonti, take the right flank. I will hold the left. Men, prepare your muskets. Stand ready to fight!"

The flotilla formed into a floating blockhouse, palisaded with bearded men, and bristling with leveled muskets.

"War? Or peace?" La Salle shouted as his fortress drifted into the view of the villagers. "Do you want to fight? Do you want peace?"

Startled natives began running away from the riverside. Panicked women shouted for their children, men hastily grabbed convenient weapons. Others ran about, yelling warnings. A few armed men guardedly approached, halting at a discrete distance.

"Peace or war?" La Salle continued calling in Algonquian. Turning to his own, he said, "At least no one has fired on us. A good sign. We will land over there, near their canoe park. Then we shall see what develops."

The explorers disembarked, secured their canoes, formed a battle line and faced the settlement. Several old men came forward, three holding peace pipes.

"Peace!" said one, a Kaskaskian of medium stature, his thumb-length hair streaked with gray, his weathered face deeply lined, his nose and ears pierced. "Welcome to our village."

La Salle responded by extending the calumet given him by Chief Onanghisse. Recognition of the Potawatami pipe prompted smiles and a noticeable relaxation. The villagers, now inquisitive, came forward and began to crowd the novel visitors.

"We are French explorers," La Salle announced. "We are on a mission for the great French king. We intend to travel down the *Fleuve Colbert*. For your hospitality, friendship, and assistance we bring you the word of the true God, we offer French help in your defense, and we bring you weapons and trade goods.

"We stopped at an Indian town upriver, across from the standing rock. We were hungry; we had not found game in many days. We raided the corn cache there. But we will pay the owners for what we took."

The old Kaskaskian nodded slowly, attentive to La Salle's speech. "We know of the French. Our brothers, the Miamis, bring us news of French fur traders in the north country. We have heard, too, of the French God. We are pleased to see the Gray Robes. We will listen to their words. We are happy the French are our friends."

Speaking for La Salle, Nika asked about the course and conditions of the Mississippi River.

"The Father of Waters is broad and quiet," the old man replied. "It will take no more than twenty days journey to its end. On its banks you will find the Tula, Casquin, and Daminioa tribes. The Cicasa dwell on the morning side. All will give you a warm and friendly welcome."

The old man led La Salle and his men to the council area where the elders welcomed them. One of the tribal leaders addressed La Salle. "You offer peace and friendship and we are happy because the Illinois shall prosper with French trade. You pay for the food you have taken and we see that too as a good sign.

"Our people can use iron kettles for our cook fires. Your knives and hatchets, too, we welcome. We will impress our friends with buckles, buttons, and gold braid on our clothing.

"We have heard the Iroquois are preparing to attack the Illinois Nation. The Iroquois carry English muskets. Our warriors have no guns; we need French weapons." The speaker paused, slightly longer than usual, signaling a response would not be considered a rude interruption.

"Muskets and gunpowder we will bring in a few months. We do not have extra weapons with us. Within a year, my agents will bring the goods you have requested. We will trade these for the skins of the buffalo and other animals," La Salle replied, feeling a certain satisfaction with this exchange.

The speaker resumed his speech. "This is a an auspicious moment. Come, let us feast and celebrate our new friendship," he concluded by inviting La Salle and his party to prepare for eating.

As La Salle and his men took places of honor, the hosts brought forth a meal of bear meat, corn, and beans. Chiefs Nicanope and Omawaha led the celebration, explaining that the Principal Chief, Chassagoac, was absent on a hunt.

Nicanope, a tall, thin warrior with a serious disposition, studied La Salle with a fixed, penetrating gaze. In spite of the cold, he was wearing a simple deerskin shirt, breechclout, and moccasins. With his hunting knife, he motioned toward the main course, "One of our hunters killed this bear only yesterday. Crooked Arrow, a Moingwena, went into the bear's cave and slew it."

Crooked Arrow stiffened with pride as the French silently admired his obvious courage and applauded his hospitality.

"This is delightful." Fr. Hennepin said, relishing a mouthful of roast bear loin. "It tastes much like fresh pork," he said, reaching for second serving.

La Salle addressed the council and spoke of his plans to go to the Gulf of Mexico. He indicated he would sail there on a ship he intended to build nearby.

"You wish to journey to the great sea beyond the Father of Waters, to see the land and the peoples there," Nicanope responded as La Salle finished. "There are some things we must say to you. Far to the southwest, where the land is a desert, Spanish armies from Mexico invade Indian lands. It is the same as in the time of our grandfathers' grandfather. Then a great Spanish war chief came through our neighbors' lands. He took what he wanted without asking; his soldiers abused the people as they pleased. The memory of the Spanish lingers as the odor of rotted flesh. Are the French the friends of the Spanish, or of the Indians?"

"Yes, I do understand your concern. I have read of De Soto's journey," La Salle said, gazing intently at Nicanope. "The French are also concerned over these Spanish expansions. The ways of the Spanish are not the ways of the French. We respect and honor the tribes that meet us in friendship. Even the Iroquois understand this about the French."

Even though Nicanope had not expected a different response, he was satisfied with La Salle's attitude.

The speeches continued and eventually transmuted into stories of cultural and local interest. Meanwhile the feasting continued unabated. As the last fires dwindled, the hosts led the feted guests to their lodgings. What had begun as a dull January day in the winter of 1680 was drawing to a handsome close, the stillness of the night filled with pleasant memories.

* * *

Nicanope had just lain in his bed when a runner appeared at the lodge entrance. "We have new visitors. They have urgent matters to discuss. They ask to meet with you now. They say they know of French plans against the Illinois."

"Summon Chief Omawaha and the council elders. We will speak with these men. Bring them here." Nicanope asked his wife and the others to spend the remainder of the night with friends. Meanwhile he revived the small fire and seated himself at the head position.

The visitors waited outside as the chiefs and council elders assembled. Finally, a Mascoutin chief known as 'the Deer' entered. Six Miami warriors accompanied him.

"I am Mousoa," the chief announced while affecting the dignity of an important embassy. "I bring news of the true intentions of the French. You are being deceived. The men who are now sleeping in your camp will bring great harm to you. Hear my words."

"Tell us of these dangers," Chief Omawaha commanded, his voice dry with skeptical indifference. He was of a rather stocky, medium build and, due to the late hour, was not wearing his usual ornaments. Absently he toyed with the iron knife La Salle had given him that evening.

"La Salle is a spy for the Iroquois. The French are arming the Iroquois for an attack on the Illinois Nation. La Salle seeks to put you off-guard so that he may pass through your country to your enemy, the *Wazhazhe*. He will arm the Osage against you. Then you will be crushed between attacks from the east and the west."

"How is it that you know these things?" Chief Omawaha asked, slowly pulling his knife from the scabbard and shoving it back again.

"I know La Salle. I have seen how he treats the Indians near his Fort Frontenac. Some Black Robes, too, talk of his empty plans."

"And why do you come here in the night? You have been following him?"

"Yes, we followed. We thought if they attack immediately, we would cut off their escape. But now we see that you must be warned of the danger."

"How are we to prevent this treachery?" Omawaha looked mistrustfully to Chief Nicanope who had so far followed the discussion without comment.

"You must stop La Salle now. His promises of support and friendship are false. His men are not brave. Frighten them. They will run like rabbits." Mousoa motioned to his escort. Two Miamis went out of the lodge, returning within a few moments carrying several parfleche bundles.

"To mark the truth of our words, we place these gifts before you," Mousoa said, sweeping his arm over the goods his men had spread before the chiefs.

Looking over an array of kettles, knives, and hatchets, Nicanope nodded satisfaction.

"Very well, We have heard your words," Nicanope concluded. "We will consider the proper course. It has been a long night; the sun is rising in the east. We must all rest a bit. Go in peace."

Mousoa and the six braves hastened out of the lodge. Within minutes, they had departed, returning to the north.

As the council broke, several exited Nicanope's lodge, squinting as they encountered the weak, early morning sun. Omawaha came out, grunting as he surveyed the dry, leafless trees scratching against the dull gray overcast. The gnawing sensation that truth was absent caused him some anxiety.

Impelled by his disquiet, Omawaha set out to determine who was lying, who telling the truth, and indeed, who and where was the true enemy of the Illinois. Vexed by these questions, he resolved on a direct course of action.

Approaching the lodge where La Salle was sleeping, Chief Omawaha discovered Nika already up and about. "I have come to speak with La Salle," he announced.

Nika, recognizing the gravity in the chief's bearing, nodded, and saying, "I'll fetch him," disappeared through the entrance.

"We must talk," Chief Omawaha said as La Salle emerged, straightening his tunic. La Salle looked quizzically at Nika, but seeing his impassive face, concluded nevertheless that something unusual and urgent had occurred.

"Certain visitors came to us last night. They claim to know your true intentions. I wish to discuss their words with you."

"By all means. I, too, want to hear what they said," La Salle said lightly, noticing meanwhile that passing villagers regarded him coldly.

The three strolled along the riverbank, Omawaha narrating, Nika interpreting, and La Salle becoming noticeably agitated.

"It is not true! None of this is correct," La Salle said grimly at the conclusion of Omawaha's tale. "There are many who do not wish to see me succeed. Someone has sent these men to you. I do not yet know how, but I will prove the falsehood of their words. Thank you for giving me the opportunity to defend myself."

Chief Omawaha studied the man. This was precisely the situation he had hoped for. He had wanted to see La Salle's reactions, to probe the man's character. Here was a brave man, an explorer, but was he honest? Omawaha held a reserved respect for the man, but the grave charges weighed heavily and could not be easily dismissed.

Looking long at the sullen, steel gray river quietly flowing, La Salle said, "I shall speak with Chief Nicanope. I will tell him where these lies come from."

"It is better for you to speak to the council. I will arrange for it, this evening, after the men have rested. We will all hear you then." Chief Omawaha turned abruptly and walked away.

"The people who welcomed us yesterday have a changed attitude," La Salle remarked to Nika as they watched Omawaha return to the village. "Mousoa's fantasies have spread far."

"Lies travel faster than truth," Nika replied. "Robèrt, let us hope the council hears you as openly as it did Mousoa."

* * *

La Salle remained troubled throughout the afternoon, his melancholy intensified by the sullen attitude of the villagers. La Salle pondered how readily the night had devoured yesterday's welcome. He was perturbed by a frigid aloofness that now walked among the lodges, suspicions that lurked behind the trees.

Toward evening, La Salle learned that the principal men were gathering. La Salle, with Shadow and a few Illinois-speaking *coureurs du bois*, went to Nicanope's lodge.

"Yesterday we were full of joy at your coming to our village. But we were too eager for your success. Some of our speakers have made your journey on the Father of Waters seem too easy." Speaking slowly, Nicanope began in a most solemn tone. "Today we must warn you of the dangers. Since you face almost certain destruction, you may wish to reconsider building your large canoe." Nicanope spoke with his head tilted back, his expression spoke nothing less than utter condemnation.

"You will never return from this journey on the great river. Besides our friends that we told you of yesterday, there are other tribes along its banks who have no desire for French friendship. They do not want your goods or your weapons. They will devour you and your men.

"Without local people to guide you, you cannot survive. There are monsters, alligators, and serpents hiding in the rushes and under the trees. The river is full of treacherous currents and whirlpools; you will find sudden waterfalls and endless cascades. Your canoe will be demolished in these waters.

"The river ends in an abyss where it disappears into the earth. No one can escape. You may thrust my words, I speak for your safety." As Nicanope ended his portentous dissuasion, he assumed a pose of rectitude before the hushed, stone-faced, and disapproving audience.

Several of La Salle's men had understood the Illinois harangue well enough to realize their peril. Their resolve mingled with the lodge smoke and drifted into the cold January air. They had been convinced the only safe course lie in returning to the north, back to Canada.

La Salle, outwardly calm but seething at Nicanope's dissembling, said, "I thank you for warning us of these terrible dangers. But danger does not frighten the French. We welcome these challenges; the greater the enemy, the greater the glory."

Shadow interpreted while La Salle groped for a telling response. "The monsters you describe, we shall meet and defeat. We have sailed in many treacherous waters. We know how to avoid these sudden, silent precipices you warn of."

La Salle studied each face in turn as Shadow finished translating. None had blinked, no one winced, and not a change had registered.

Infuriated, La Salle burst out, "It is not the dangers of the river that concern you. You had a visitor last night who fed you with the poison of my enemies. Mousoa lies! If the Chief of the Muscoutin were speaking the truth, why does he come in the night? Let him say his words in the daylight. I will speak to his face. Bring him back that I may show you whose words are truth."

La Salle stomped on the earth before him "Here are his gifts to you. You have buried them beneath this lodge. These are French goods he has given you. But who gave them to Mousoa? And why? Bring Mousoa to me. We shall learn the truth of his words."

A few of the audience were clearly taken aback, surprised that La Salle had learned of the nocturnal messengers.

"Mousoa is gone. We cannot bring him back. We have no way of learning who speaks the truth." Nicanope said dryly as several nodded agreement.

"Why do the French need the Iroquois, or others, to do what we can do on our own? When we came to your village, you were unarmed, disorganized. We could have killed many of the Illinois then. If we mean to kill you, why do we bring you French muskets? If we have plans against the Illinois, why do we not give these guns to your enemy?"

La Salle felt he was making an impact, but knew argument alone would not erase the damage. "You do not have to judge between the words of Mousoa and La Salle. Compare our actions. We have already pledged much for the defense of the Illinois. How can you believe the words of Mousoa? The French have words, too, and deeds to reinforce these words."

La Salle's eyes glistened as he glanced around the room. His speech had produced an effect, but suspicions still burdened his audience. La Salle knew Mousoa's dramatic exchange had produced the stronger effect, that his men were dispirited, and that his own authority had suffered. Worst of all, La Salle could see fear on the faces of his men.

Nicanope remained silent. At length, satisfied there would be no further response to La Salle, the chief signed to some attendants for food. Several women brought pots of buffalo meat and corn boiled in bear fat and placed these before the guests.

After his men had eaten, La Salle—who had eaten only enough to satisfy courtesy—expressed thankfulness for Nicanope's hospitality, then led his men into the outer darkness. Looking back from the lodge entrance, he noticed Nicanope, still seated near the fire, darkly engrossed in thought.

A light snow was beginning to fall as, on the way to their lodge, La Salle attempted to alleviate the men's fears. At the least, he seemed to achieve a partial success. But he also knew the men, especially the artisans new to the open life, were naturally fearful of the Indians.

Concerned that some further treachery might yet occur, La Salle ordered six guards posted. Then he retired, expecting to deal further with his men in the morning.

* * *

"Gone! They're gone!" Tonti burst into La Salle's lodge. "The guards have deserted. There is no sign of them anywhere."

86

La Salle blinked the sleep from his eyes; an ache in the pit of his stomach registered once more his opponent's success. A heavy mental fatigue labored his efforts to regain full consciousness. "I hope your are mistaken," he muttered as he slipped into his moccasins. "We are just too far from the settlements . . . ."

Nika and Shadow were waiting outside as Tonti and La Salle emerged into the frosty morning air. "They have taken a bag of maize, their guns, and some gunpowder," Nika reported.

"They were the best craftsmen," Tonti lamented. "Two master ship's carpenters and two of the best pit sawyers—gone."

"Saget and Nika. If any of the villagers ask, tell them I have sent these men on a mission. Do not allow the Illinois to know my workers are deserting," La Salle pleaded earnestly, blinking against the glare of reality.

"Tonti, assemble the men after breakfast. We must adjust to this new situation."

La Salle, clearly saddened, watched as Tonti went off to gather the remaining workers. He resolved to separate the French from the Indians, to build a fort for their residence and protection.

"We are going forward with our journey!" La Salle exclaimed despite a nagging, inner hollowness. "Do not be concerned that the Illinois are reluctant to support our explorations. They feel a French presence here contributes to their safety. So I have decided to build a fort, there, on that bluff across the river. That site is ideal for defense."

La Salle paused while the men appraised the crevasses steeply rising to the headlands above. "On the flats near the river, we will build our ship.

"Today we will move our equipment to the work site. You workmen stay clear of the villagers. The priests may go about their missionary work." La Salle paused. He knew these steps were necessary, but a vague sense of futility continued to gnaw within.

"Keep a lively eye about you. There may be further mischief about. Take especial care that your guns and tools are not stolen." La Salle finished, wondering if his plans held any more promise than the empty smoke drifting over barren trees.

By late that afternoon the first logs had been prepared, ready for the erection of the palisade. While the workers dragged the heavy timbers into position, La Salle and Tonti marked off the course of the stockade wall, the disposition of the fort's buildings.

"The men seem to welcome the work," Tonti observed. "I think our months of travel have produced soft muscles. This task will soon cure that."

"Tomorrow I will begin construction of my ship," La Salle said, anxious for tangible confirmation of his original goal. "I need two good men to train as pit sawyers. I will work with them until they are skilled. Do you have two to recommend?"

Etienne Boisrondet and Jean D'Autray had begun their day well before breakfast. Tonti went to inform them that they would be apprenticed to La Salle. As they came to the ravine they found La Salle already at the intended construction site.

"This is an ideal location," La Salle proclaimed in welcome. "We will build the ship next to this creek. She'll launch directly from here with very little run. The mouth of the creek is wide and deep enough to serve as an anchorage."

"I can see this shelf will serve nicely. The ways will be here," Boisrondet said, testing the firmness of the snow-skimmed soil with his boot. "But, where shall we dig the saw pit? This low land doesn't seem adequate."

"Good for you!" La Salle smiled. "The saw pit will be atop the bluff, near the fort. We will rig tackle for lowering the finished timbers. Let's go up there now. Tonti already has some men working the pit."

The three quickly returned to the headland. There, near the planned eastern wall of the fort, Tonti had outlined a pit nearly five feet wide and about forty long. At one end, excavation to a depth of three feet had begun. A carpenter was building trestles for assembly over either end of the pit.

"Very nice!" Tonti beamed. "Here we are, thousands of leagues from French shipyards and we are going to build a magnificent brig! In a few months the *fleur-de-lis* will be snapping to the breezes on the *Fleuve Colbert*. This will be a glorious achievement, no!"

"All you have done so far is dig a hole in the ground." La Salle smiled at his enthusiastic assistant. "Just keep the men working, then we shall see about your romantic visions."

"With you it is always reason. You conceive an objective and you move the heavens to reach your goal—no matter the obstacles. Don't you ever dream?" Tonti chided.

"My goals are neither romantic, nor impossible. These 'obstacles' make our path less direct perhaps, but they only stop those who cannot imagine the valley on the other side of the mountain." La Salle replied.

"There, you see, you are dreaming. Who told you there is a valley ahead?" Tonti slapped La Salle on the shoulder. "There is no valley! This is only a trick of yours. You do this to make us climb the mountain. We will never see this valley of yours. I am sure of it. It is all in your mind."

"Perhaps there is no valley. But there will be no pit either, unless you get cracking," La Salle said, his frosty breath drifting on the chill air. "The weather may not long remain favorable."

Motioning to Boisrondet and D'Autray, La Salle drew them aside. "It is time to begin your training. In order to square timbers, you need to saw to the line. The top man must balance on the log while following the scribe mark. This ensures a true cut."

Boisrondet, small framed and intelligent, began examining the two-man saw. Jean D'Autray looked on as La Salle began to explain the process in detail.

"First we shall saw a few sleepers. This will give us a bit of practice. We'll place the sleepers on the ground and use them for dry stacking the cut timbers."

Turning to D'Autray, La Salle continued, "You will be the pit man first. You follow the top man, making sure the cut is vertical. Once you've got the knack the two of you should be able to begin producing straight timbers in about a week."

"So I walk the log following a true line while Jean keeps the blade plumb," Boisrondet mused. "It seems easy enough."

"This is how we will cut squared timbers. Most of the wood for the keel and keelsons will be squared. We will use flitch cuts for futtocks, stems and planking. Tonti will select the proper wood for these parts and mark it for the needed shapes," La Salle said.

Several men using sling harnesses were dragging a large pine bole toward the pit, now about half excavated.

"What about the curved pieces—frames, knees, things like that? Surely we can't make these things," D'Autray said, screwing up his eyes.

Pointing to a limb crotch on an oak tree, La Salle continued, "If we could find local hackmatack, we could fashion knees by bending its roots into shape. Unfortunately for us, this tree grows only in the north. Crooked timber we will find in the lower ends of oak. I will match the bentwood to the patterns for the knees and frame pieces. We want the grain to follow these curves as closely as possible."

Boisrondet walked over and examined the limb joint on a nearby oak. Running his hand over the area, he said, "This will not be as easy as sawing long runs. It's likely to be heavy and too short to handle."

"If we cannot saw these pieces, we will have to beat out the curved pieces with axes and then dubb them smooth with adzes. Otherwise, we will need to rig a press for steam bending straight timber. And that may be a bit more difficult." La Salle grimly watched as the loggers levered the first bole into position alongside the pit. "I think we shall have a strong ship. There are plenty of fine trees here, even some walnut."

Later that day, when the pit had been fully excavated and the trestles erected, several men aligned a large pine bole alongside the pit. They then levered one end of the log onto a trestle. Securing it in place, the men then raised the other end into position.

"Very well," La Salle said, eyeing the log. "Let's begin the work of sawyers." The men walked slowly along the pit, scrutinizing the pine spar that had been stripped of its branches and most of its bark.

"A keel made from pine or oak is good for eight or nine years. A keel of East India teak will last for sixteen years. Using these local oak and pine woods, our ship should last at least a good four years," La Salle said, continuing his instructions. "We will duplicate the *Griffin*, but this ship will have higher gunwales as a protection against arrows. The keel you are to fashion will be 42 feet long; the ship's beam, 16 feet. Collect your tools now while I prepare the work."

Tonti meanwhile had been directing woodsmen felling trees that he had marked earlier for marine timbers. Others continued to build the stockade and housing.

With their saw honed and oiled, Etienne and Jean watched as La Salle finished his inspection of the pine bole, satisfied it was securely chocked and tied. La Salle then scribed a straight line following a taught cord stretched along its length. "This will be our first cut," he said. "Jean, perhaps you may start in the pit. I will begin on top. Etienne, you will watch for now."

Balancing atop the log, La Salle swung the two-man saw into position, setting the blade against the end mark. D'Autray firmly grasped the free end. Slowly and carefully, La Salle began sawing, keenly following the scribed mark, walking backward as the kerf advanced.

Duplessis stopped chopping. He looked at Martin, and ignoring his expression of constant amazement, said, "Would you look at that? I'd say 'Lord Tender Paws' is going to have a few blisters by evening. What do you think?"

"I don't know. He seems to handle a paddle or an axe fairly well. Maybe you think too little of him, huh?" Martin looked at his own callused hands. "Did you ever see an Indian with hands tough as these? I expect they'd blister up pretty quick, too, working as we do."

"Those Indians will blister up pretty quick anyway when they see all these stumps. Trees is sacred to them."

"I'll grant they'll be none to happy to see this stubby field," Duplessis said, rubbing his chin.

"Hey, Duplessis!" Messier called out from nearby. "Did you see your Lordship squaring timber? I never expected to see a blue blood working like us."

"Well, you're not exactly an artisan yourself, you know," Duplessis responded curtly. "You look just a mite uncomfortable, next to an axe."

"Time to get back to work, don't you think?" Messier smirked as he swung the axhandle over his shoulder.

* * *

Not long after the evening meal La Salle experienced abdominal pains, followed by nausea and vomiting. Trying to walk, he could only stagger. Someone helped him to his cot, where he collapsed in a feverish sweat.

"He's having trouble breathing." Fr. Membré called out, noting the long, slow breaths. Tonti and Fr. Hennepin came to La Salle's side. Within an hour La Salle began to complain of double vision. Speaking only with difficulty, he said he was extremely weak and dizzy.

"Poison!" Fr. Hennepin reasoned. "I'm sure he has been poisoned. Find the antidote he carries in his pouch."

Fr. Membré ruffled through La Salle's parfleche, finally coming up with a small packet of powder. Taking a measure, he mixed it into a small amount of water. "Be careful with this potion. He may have difficulty swallowing. Here's some water. Let's see if we can get enough down to help."

One of the priests raised La Salle while Tonti held the cup to his lips. After a series of sips, La Salle lay back on his cot.

"Try this as well," Nika said, collecting black scrapings from dead embers. "The charcoal will neutralize the poison and cleanse the system. Give him more water."

After about an hour, La Salle seemed to be resting. At least, his symptoms did not worsen. Pensively, the priests and Tonti watched La Salle closely, attentive to his slightest discomfort.

After a few moments, Fr. Hennepin spoke softly, "I'm afraid he's dying."

"Nonsense!" Shaking his head, Tonti insisted, "Perhaps it's his Jesuit discipline, perhaps his birthright. Have you noticed? He does not do the ordinary. That would be too common. Have you ever seen such spirit?"

Fr. Membré pleaded, "He should have quit, he should have gone back. So many things have not worked out on this voyage."

Tonti looked at the priest in disbelief. "No! He may stop, but he will never retreat."

Fr. Ribourde put another pot of water on the fire, rubbed his hands for warmth, blinked against the heat, then turned and solemnly observed, "Yes, I believe you are correct! M. La Salle is not likely to die in bed. That is not his fate."

Tonti nodded toward the priest then bent over again to check La Salle's breathing.

"There is a paid assassin in our camp," Fr. Hennepin said, looking at the other two. "I fear someone desperately wants La Salle to fail."

"But who?" Tonti asked, shaking his head. "Do you suspect the Jesuits? They certainly stand to lose mission territory and trade."

"That possibility is not worthy of mention. Assassination is not their style. No, it is more likely a trader in Montreal." Fr. Hennepin replied.

"Or a political interest! Poisoning has become de rigueur in certain Paris circles. Just four years ago Brinvilliers was burned for the practice. And LaVoisin! I'm afraid poisoning and politics are a too common mixture in

France." Fr. Membré adjusted the firewood on the grate, then added another log.

"If this is true, then someone in Montreal arranged the death of La Salle long before we departed," Fr. Hennepin speculated.

"There is a traitor among us. Keep your eyes open," Tonti cautioned. "We'll be waiting when the wretch next shows his hand. M. La Salle takes his meals separately, so we'll be watchful there."

Throughout the night, La Salle remained weak and nauseated. Only toward dawn did he begin to recover, falling finally into a deep and restful sleep.

After breakfast, the men at the work site discussed the news of La Salle's illness.

"Martin, you see, I told you 'Lord Tender Paws' wasn't fit for hard work." Duplessis squinted, his eyes darting back and forth as he swirled the coffee in his half-empty cup.

Martin looked wide-eyed at Duplessis. "You know, that's the second time he's been sick. If he dies here, what will become of us?"

"I really hadn't thought of that," Duplessis said, smiling. "But don't you worry none about it. Duplessis will get us both back to the north woods. No, don't worry at all." His eyes glittered as he looked at Martin. Picking up his ax, Duplessis walked over to join the others, already at work cutting palisade posts.

In the afternoon, La Salle, still weak and abed, called in his personal servant, the priests, and Tonti. When they were assembled, La Salle addressed the servant, "I do not blame you, L'Esperance, for what has happened. I know you too well, I trust you and I know you love me. However, from now on I will no longer take a separate meal. I will eat from the common pot. Whoever has done this will not have such an easy target next time."

"Your mountain has gotten a bit steeper, wouldn't you say?" Tonti observed. "One of you own is trying to kill you."

"A coward! We shall not be stopped by a coward; we will finish this voyage," La Salle spoke weakly, but waved a stern finger. "Remember the important thing: Don't quit! Don't give in!"

"I wish just once you would quit! Here you are, flat on your back, and you talk of going on. You advance when you should stop. The men complain that you drive them too hard, too far. There are times I think they fear you and your ambition more than an Indian attack," Tonti remonstrated with La Salle. "Sometimes they are not certain you are human. Perhaps, if you quit just once you could convince them—and me—that you do have some normal limits."

"I know you are made of sterner stuff than that!" La Salle responded. "You are not one to let woodsmen and riffraff do your thinking for you."

"Of course not! But look at your circumstances. You are thousands of leagues from the sources of your support. You do not have the equipment necessary to build another ship. There are untold hazards on this great river. The Indians may be hostile. And you have a traitor in your crew!" Tonti said, sweeping his arm at the innumerable threats.

"Don't loose your clouds on my horizon!" La Salle exploded. "I can see clearly what must be done as well as what will be needed. Some of your woodsmen cannot see beyond the length of an axe handle."

Taken aback, Tonti protested, "It doesn't take a woodsman to say 'Enough!' And, in any case, I credit these woodsmen with great sense."

"So, what are your intentions?" La Salle looked coldly at Tonti. "Do you intend to stay? Or do you wish to return to the settlements?"

"Stay. What else?" Tonti shrugged.

"Ha! As I expected!" La Salle beamed at his friend. "Sometimes, I think you are only testing me. You may not like to admit it, but you and I—we are both of the same mind, sons, if you will, of the finest civilization."

"Civilization?" Fr. Membré exclaimed. "We have an assassin in our company who also represents that civilization. I am uncertain what this means."

La Salle, ever the schoolmaster, smiled at the student-priest. "An interesting observation. Perhaps you could pursue this point?"

"What I mean to say is that I wonder sometimes that civilization is nothing more than a veneer," the priest replied, chewing his lips. "It is all too easy to call these Indians 'savage,' but is that not itself a conceit? I am only beginning to learn their customs, but I have already discovered their basic nature is good and generous."

"And Europeans are less civilized because we harbor assassins?" Tonti asked without interest.

"No, of course, not. No, it's not the individual that's the core problem. It's interests within the government that all too readily turn to assassins to effect their goals."

"That may be true, but it doesn't seem to reflect on our level of civilization," La Salle prodded.

"It does when you consider that the personal characteristics we deem savage exist in our governments. We have transferred personal evil to an impersonal structure. What is loosely called civilization is in some cases merely a sophisticated use of state power to take someone's property, freedom, or life. We use this power as a screen, a mask, for our own greed."

"Yes, I do indeed see where you are going with this," La Salle nodded. "And I am not surprised you oppose violence in the name of the state. But do you suppose a government built on religious principles can last?"

"The true measure of any authority is how it behaves in the absence of any other power. There is a marked difference between actions based upon morality, integrity, and responsibility and those based upon purely human

93

standards," Fr. Ribourde observed. "How much of our heritage is marked by violence and greed? Are not despoiled landscapes the marks of our passage? Treeless wastes evidence our growth, yet we condescend to those who harmonize with nature."

"The only true civilization is the one inspired by and founded upon the eternal principles of religion," Fr. Membré replied. "Until we have achieved that level of progress, we have not distanced ourselves greatly from our savage ancestors."

"So your claim is that civilization has masked a lack of moral development," Tonti observed. "Well, this is something to think about."

"It started with the Romans," La Salle said, needling Tonti. "They built roads throughout the empire and gave measured plots of land to citizens and conquered alike. In this way the masters reduced the governed by replacing their freedom with property."

"And the man who has much, has much to defend," Fr. Membré added. "As the man who has nothing is truly free, these natives have based their society on spiritual ideals."

"Good!" La Salle agreed. "You see now they lack the concepts of power and property that lead to corruption and decay."

"Remarkable," Tonti said. "I am beginning to see our friends differently."

Turning to a new subject, La Salle said to Fr. Membré, "I have heard you have taken lodging in the village."

"Yes, I have. But there is a certain unpleasantness." Fr. Membré grimaced. "The Indians reek of bear grease. They rub it into their hair, they cover their face with it as a protection against the cold."

"My dear colleague is young. He will adjust in time. I think he misses his homeland. In Flanders polite people wear powdered wigs, sew spices into their cloaks, and douse themselves with perfumes—to disguise their poor hygiene, I do believe," Fr. Ribourde said, smiling under his beard. "But I must point out Louis has already been 'adopted' by several children."

"Well, that's another story." Fr. Membré hesitated.

"No, please do go on. I would like to hear about these children," La Salle insisted.

"It wasn't exactly welcome at first sight. Three boys followed me everywhere. They have these pieces of wood attached to a stick." Fr. Membré made a serious face. "They were constantly buzzing me with these 'roarers'— to chase away evil spirits, you see."

"So now you are cleansed of all your evil?" Fr. Ribourde chuckled.

"Oh, of course! But eventually their curiosity got the best of them. We are now fast friends. Come with me to the village soon. I think you would enjoy meeting them."

"Yes, I should like to do that," La Salle said, laying back on his cot. "I also have some business with Nicanope. He persists in trying to frighten my men with tales of monsters and disaster on the *Fleuve Colbert*. Some find it hard enough living as we do among the natives. I cannot afford any further desertions."

Toward midmorning of the following day, La Salle, feeling well enough for a moderate sortie, went with Nika and Frs. Ribourde and Membré to the village. They were casually strolling about when Fr. Membré spotted his boys, busy developing their hunting and fighting skills.

The oldest boy, Buffalo Calf, appeared to be about 17 years old. He was extremely accurate with the bow. Another Illinois boy, Muskrat, about a year younger, impressed the French with his quick arrow barrages. Starting with ten arrows in one hand, he would be firing the last before the first came to ground.

The smallest, Milkweed, aged ten, retrieved the arrows and spears for the older boys.

"Milkweed, come here," Fr. Ribourde requested.

Carrying a few of Muskrat's arrows, the boy approached the visitors.

"Nika, ask him how he got this name," Fr. Ribourde suggested.

"He says that each summer he collects milkweed leaves for the old men," Nika translated. "They use the white juice as a treatment for warts and moles."

"Aha! If that's the cure, I know a court minister who should cover his face with milkweed sap!" Fr. Ribourde burst out laughing.

The French all roared at this comedy, but Milkweed stood there deeply embarrassed since he did not understand the source of the humor.

Seeing the boy's plight, La Salle said, "Nika, tell him I am pleased to know him. I am impressed with these boys. In fact, if they would like to earn a French knife, have them come to the fort. I could use their help on small chores."

Eager to impress their new benefactors, the boys resumed their weapons practice with a renewed enthusiasm. The French party observed for awhile, then returned to the fort.

That afternoon, Fr. Membré went for a stroll and meditative prayer. Passing through the work area, he came upon some men truing a felled tree.

"Father, I hear the missionary work is not going well," Messier remarked, taking a break from his woodcutting.

"It's not discouraging. It's the same everywhere with the Indians," Fr. Membré replied. "They are curious and, sometimes, even excited with our faith. But most are reluctant to fully accept our precepts."

"They live for their warrior code, their cult of courage. They have an undying need for enemies—to prove their manhood." Messier said, shaking his head.

"But that's just the problem," Fr. Membré protested. "This 'cult of courage' as you call it, is also a barrier to higher unity among the Indians," Fr. Membré remarked. "There is a great need for forgiveness, forgiveness among tribes. Only through such forgiveness will the natives be able to create the kind of unity that will ensure their survival. In the English colonies, there are wars of extinction, whole tribes disappearing as they are outlawed and destroyed piecemeal, one at a time."

"Well, I see your point," Messier said, scratching his beard. "But this would mean a change in culture. This goes against the basic character of the Indian."

"In case you haven't noticed, the message we priests carry goes against everyone's basic nature." Fr. Membré grinned, his eyes sparkling. "Unfortunately, too many who hear Christ's message do not understand that it is a call for all of us to change our lives."

Duplessis, working nearby, caught Martin's attention with a jerk of his head, and the two ambled over to join the discussion.

"Now, I've seen my share of people sprinkled with holy water. I tell you I don't see much change in the world," Duplessis said, testing the priest. "God hasn't give me anything I haven't taken with my own two hands."

Seeing the downturn in the discussion, Messier winked at the priest then went off to get a drink of water.

"Look at those Indians. They act as if they were some kind of nobility." Duplessis gestured toward the village. "If you ask me, they are just plain lazy. Did you ever see one do real work?"

"I think they behave like our nobles," Martin replied, staring blankly at Duplessis. "They're free, don't you understand? They don't owe their labor to any one. They have no debts. You and me—we always owe somebody something."

Duplessis spat on the ground. "Yeah, sure, noble and free all right. Don't make me laugh!"

"You're wrong, you know," Fr. Membré interjected. "The Indians feel a great debt to their Creator. They are always thankful for even the least blessings. To me it is a striking combination. This deep spiritual humility on the one hand and a great sense of personal worth and dignity on the other."

"But that is just for the men. The women do the real work. I've never seen a man working in the fields." Duplessis shrugged.

"The women are happy with their share of the labor. They do not rank lower than men. And it is the women who own the fields, the lodgings, and the food supplies. In some tribes the women elect the chiefs," Fr. Membré asserted.

"Did you ever see an Indian yell at a child? Or spank a child? They don't. It's amazing. The worst they will do is throw water in a willful child's face. They teach their infants not to cry. By pinching the child's nose." Pointedly, Fr. Membré added, "And they treat everyone with respect, even those who seem least deserving."

Fr. Membré studied Duplessis and Martin, then, receiving no response, resumed his walk, seeking again solitude and silence among the trees.

"I'll be free, just you wait and watch," Duplessis muttered at length, directing his words at the back of the now distant cleric.

"No. You can only run away from your responsibilities—and that is not freedom," Martin mused as he whet the blade of his ax.

"So you say. Ha! I could leave this expedition tomorrow. And don't you worry; I'd not fret at all. It's them that owes me. We've done our fair share. And what have we received? Not a sou!" Duplessis grabbed a small pine branch, wrenching it from the tree.

"You and I shall never be free," Martin objected. "You see who lives within the stockade, and who doesn't, don't you?"

"Prison, you mean," Duplessis bit off the words, looking toward the fort. "You talk of responsibilities. Consider this. The government has been laying 'responsibilities' on you from long before you were ever born. The *coureurs du bois*, now they understand true freedom."

"Yes, I know what you mean. Even La Salle—he owes everything to the king and his creditors. I hear he is paying as much as 40 percent interest on his loans." Martin looked at the distracted Duplessis.

"Martin, you are a silly goose!" Duplessis smirked, watching absently as the fleur-de-lis scratched at the sky above the palisade. "This place can't hold a man such as me."

"But our contract—you can't just leave!" Martin protested.

"Maybe, maybe not. But don't tell me I'm not free. I'm as free as those buzzards in their stick houses." Duplessis waved an arm in the direction of the village. He shrugged, picked up his ax, and prepared to chop down another tree.

* * *

A few days later, while hunting on a February morning, La Salle had shot a turkey, Shadow three. The hunters had caught the birds returning to their roosts following a night of foraging.

While awaiting further prey, Shadow abruptly pointed to a solitary canoe making its way up the lower river. From their ambuscade on the bluff, La Salle and Shadow watched as the lone Illinois scout came slowly upstream. Intrigued by the large wooden structure on the riverside, the man diverged from his intended course, coming ashore near La Salle's half-built ship.

In wonder the scout walked around the hull, running his hand over the curve of the frames, feeling the smoothed surface of the wood. With his fingernail, he attempted to pry out a few nail heads. While studying this novel framework, the scout was startled by a bearded man and a strange, tall Indian stepping out of the brush.

"Peace!" Shadow saluted. "I am Shadow, Mohegan. And this is M. La Salle. He has built this big canoe."

"I am Plenty Fish," the man responded. "This is my village. I have been traveling many months. Others who are with me will come along soon."

"Where did you voyage?" Shadow asked.

"On the Father of Waters," Plenty Fish replied without emphasis. "I have traveled to the large sea at its mouth."

Enlivened by the import of the man's information, Shadow quickly translated for La Salle.

At once interested, La Salle studied the man. Plenty Fish was of medium height, and was as physically developed an Indian as he had ever met. Plenty Fish appeared to be about thirty years old.

"Ask him to describe the Gulf of Mexico," La Salle demanded, intrigued by the possibilities of this development.

"Yes," Plenty Fish replied, "There are big canoes there, much bigger than this. They carry white sails and fire guns with the noise of thunder."

"Spanish war ships!" La Salle exclaimed. "Ask him if there are any white colonies."

"No, there are none. Otherwise we would trade for their goods." Plenty Fish indicated his equipment was all native made.

"And he went there by canoe?" La Salle was beside himself at this point.

"It is an easy, many days ride. And there are no obstacles," Plenty Fish said reassuringly.

"Tell him we have heard of monsters, waterfalls, and whirlpools blocking this great river," La Salle insisted, anxious to hear an encouraging response.

Plenty Fish burst into laughter. After his amusement receded, Plenty Fish said, "Someone has been telling you fancy tales. There are no such hazards. I will draw you a map."

Using a piece of bark and a charcoal, Plenty Fish sketched the path of the Mississippi from the mouth of the Illinois River to the Gulf of Mexico.

Immensely satisfied with Plenty Fish's report, La Salle invited the Indian to feast with himself and Shadow.

After a meal of fresh-killed turkey, La Salle presented Plenty Fish with an iron knife. He also gave him a hatchet as a pledge to secrecy on their meeting and conversation.

"My lips are sealed," Plenty Fish pledged as he ran a finger along the knife, wincing as he cut himself on the unexpectedly sharp blade.

La Salle smiled slightly as the Indian smarted then sucked on his wound. "This has been a great day for me. There is much I owe you, Plenty Fish. I will be forever in your debt."

La Salle was elated. He was beside himself with the news Plenty Fish had given him. "Yes, yes. Let us visit Nicanope," he said. "Please, go now, Saget, bring Etienne and Jean. I'll find Fr. Hennepin. We have allowed ourselves too much credence in the fairly tales of Chief Nicanope. It is time to let him know we are no longer deluded."

La Salle, Fr. Hennepin, Shadow, Boisrondet, and D'Autray trooped into the village, and on learning where the principal elders were gathered, went to that lodge. Seated in a circle, the Indians, who had been feasting on bear meat, graciously invited the unexpected guests to join them. La Salle was given a central place of honor. Observing the French delegation as it moved onto the rush mat, Nicanope and several others noted an animation in La Salle's bearing.

"The Maker of All Things takes especial care of the French," Shadow began, after all were seated. "M. La Salle has learned the true nature of the Father of Waters, its peoples, and their customs. He knows there are no monsters, no waterfalls, and no whirlpools. The truth of this is shown by this map."

La Salle, using a large piece of bark, drew a charcoal outline of the Illinois and Mississippi Rivers. The accuracy of the sketch map impressed many. Several expressed astonishment that La Salle had gained such accurate information.

"Surely your chief has great medicine!" one of the elders exclaimed. Turning to his own chief, he added, "Nicanope, what is your opinion of this French magic?"

Slowly at first, as if searching for the words, Nicanope replied, "The French words have truth. We told you of monsters because we are greedy. We do not want the French to trade with other tribes. We want your Gray Robes and your goods for the Illinois people."

Nicanope, somewhat relieved that La Salle had learned the truth, looked slowly around the assembly. Most seemed pleased with the outcome of events; none felt compelled to speak further on the matter.

La Salle noted his own men now appeared calm. He, too, relaxed, feeling the prospects for success were growing stronger.

"For the Illinois we offer these tokens of our deep friendship," La Salle announced, opening a small pouch. "These needles and awls will help with your leather work," he said, displaying the sharp tools. He also produced a few 'Jesuit' rings, which carried the image of the cross and the letters IHS. One of the chiefs placed a ring on his finger and proudly showed it to those nearby.

"You will sail to the great river soon?" Nicanope asked with a lighthearted nonchalance.

"No, I do not have the equipment I need to finish the ship," La Salle answered. "If I wait, it may be a year before all the necessary gear arrives. I cannot wait. I must soon go to speed up this delivery. The sails and rigging I need are on my other ship, the *Griffin*."

Late that evening a buoyant La Salle led his party back to the stockade. "Plenty Fish was a God-send, wouldn't you say?" he asked Fr. Hennepin.

"God does work in mysterious ways," the priest mused. "What's truly surprising is whom He chooses as His agent at times. In the end, all things work out to the good."

"I'm sure of it," La Salle said, gazing across the river at the last twilight of the day. As he entered the fort, La Salle felt a surging sense of confidence, a renewal of purpose, and an increasing capacity to overcome all obstacles on the path to the top of his mountain.

As if to underscore the sudden change in fortune, several visitors arrived the next day. A Quapaw from near the mouth of the Arkansas river, a Wazhazhe, and a Chickasaw spent some time giving Shadow detailed descriptions of the lower Mississippi River and its peoples.

Stinker, excited at the prospect of French trade, extended to La Salle the welcome of his tribe and the offer of Quapaw guides for the journey to the Gulf of Mexico.

Pleased with this welcome news, La Salle thanked his guests. Curious, he asked Shadow about the Quapaw Stinker.

"He is an adopted Natchez," Shadow explained. "He has married a Quapaw woman and lives with her family. But his people are numerous and inhabit the banks of the lower river. He would make an excellent guide."

"And his name? How did he come by this?" La Salle nodded toward the distant guest.

"Among the Natchez, there are the nobles and the common people." Shadow's eyes glistened, "And the commoners are known as 'stinkers.' The nobles may not marry among themselves, but must marry a stinker. Do you not think it is also a good idea for French nobility to marry stinkers?"

La Salle looked long at his guide.

* * *

Increasingly, La Salle felt the need to return to action. Yet it was still winter, mid-February, and not an appropriate time for travel.

Yet a fourth visitor arrived. La Salle was seated in his cabin discussing with Tonti the slow pace of construction for the ship's hull when a exceptional Indian appeared at the door.

"I am Slow Walker. I come from the Dakota lands," the handsome young man announced. His buckskins and robe were all bright white. He wore white porcupine quill armbands with deer fur and weasel skin pendants. "The Dakota nation has heard of the traveler La Salle. I have come many days to speak with him."

"I am La Salle, please come in," replied the bearded man in buckskins. "I have heard of the Dakota people. But the Seven Tribes of the Council are over a hundred leagues from here, to the northwest. You have made a long journey. Make yourself comfortable and tell me your business."

"I come on a mission of peace and brotherhood," Slow Walker said, squatting on the floor of the cabin. "Justice and peace are inborn in the heart of every person. Individuals, families, tribes, peoples, nations—all are called to live in justice and to work for peace. The Dakota have heard of your missions and your desire to journey south on the Father of Waters. But we desire that you come north to our lands."

"I am pleased with this request. I will see what I can do for you," La Salle replied. After studying the man's dress, he asked, "Tell, me, that object hanging from your belt—isn't that a horse hoof?"

"Horse hoof? Yes, horses are new in Dakota lands. The Dakota people much admire the horse for it has great strength—and spirit." Slow Walker smiled.

"This is truly amazing," La Salle said, turning to Tonti, Nika, and Fr. Membré. "In all my travels, I have not previously seen evidence of horses anywhere beyond the settlements. Yet here they are on the plains."

"The wild ponies come from Spanish lands in Mexico," Slow Walker remarked. "But we ask you, send us a Gray Robe if you cannot come. The Dakota wish to hear the words of your God."

"Yes, Slow Walker, I will do this. I am much interested in having a mission among the Dakota peoples," La Salle said. "And we must discuss trade in buffalo hides."

"Tomorrow we talk trade," Slow Walker agreed. "It is said you have great respect for the people of this land. It is very important that you secure peace for the Dakota with the white man."

"I assure you—I give you my word—I will do all I can," La Salle said solemnly. "But first, I must continue my exploration. When I return from the *Fleuve Colbert*, my missionaries will tell me what they have learned and what I must do."

"This is good." Slow Walker nodded. Laying a pouch containing the bowl and stem of a calumet before him, he said, "Let us now smoke for peace and brotherhood."

All took new places on the floor, flanking Slow Walker who had been sitting opposite the entrance. La Salle and Nika sat near the south wall with Tonti and Fr. Membré opposite.

Nika rose and taking a braid of prairie sweet grass, lit it. As the aromatic smoke drifted upward, Nika carried the burning wand around the circle, passing over each person in turn, then waved it ceremoniously over the pipe bundle. After snuffing the grass, Nika solemnly unwrapped the pouch. First he removed the pipe bowl, an intricately carved red catlinite stone, itself a sacred object among many tribes. The stem, the lower leg bone of a buffalo calf, was decorated with colored feathers, bird skins, and bits of hair. Lifting the stem with his right hand and the bowl with his left, he carefully assembled the pipe and reverently passed it to Slow Walker.

As Slow Walker filled the bowl, he prayed over each pinch of tobacco and passed the pipe through the sweet smoke drifting over him. Intoning a chant for peace, Slow Walker lit the tobacco, offering the smoke to the spirits by pointing the stem in order to the east, to the south, to the west, to the north, skyward, and finally earthward. Nika then took the pipe clockwise around the circle, allowing each in turn to smoke or to waft the smoke over their heads. La Salle was the last. The pipe was then returned to Slow Walker.

The ceremony finished, Slow Walker ritually cleaned and rebundled the pipe. Silently he then rose and went out of the lodge.

* * *

"Don't you think when things are going against you, maybe that is a sign you are trying to do the wrong thing?" Tonti asked, looking askance at La Salle. It was early the next day and the two were strolling near the ship. A light snow covered the frozen earth.

"Perhaps. But here we are, not far from the *Fleuve Colbert*. Therefore, too many things have not gone amiss. It is not yet time to think of failure," La Salle said wistfully, gently running his hand over the ships planking.

"I was not thinking of failure. It is merely the idea that you could do much for the Indians here, even without your voyage of discovery," Tonti said, scuffing his foot in the fresh snow.

"Yes, I know what you mean. But you do not always accept fate so easily either," La Salle said, smiling at his friend.

La Salle thought for a moment, then admitted, "I am blessed to have you with me. We have a large challenge before us. But we are not stopped."

"No, I wouldn't say we are stopped," Tonti said. "I was trying to suggest that we should stay here, that perhaps we can produce a greater benefit working with the Indians we know. It seems your voyage of discovery is filled with setbacks."

"Yes, it seems we have had reverses, true enough. But there is no reason to change our plans," La Salle said. "We must continue—I must go on."

"I did not expect otherwise," Tonti said.

Chapter 6

Chassagoac

The icy wind whistled over the palisade, a howling daemon—pounding fists thudding against the log walls of the cabin, probing fingers rattling the bark roof—hissed curses through chinks in the door. Receding slowly, it waited, waited, then again and again it rose, in relentless gusts assaulting the crude hut.

In the fireplace amid gray-white smoke clouds, fire-talons squeezed sap-filled logs, forcing flame-devils to emerge, dancing and leaping, eager to greet their howling master. Frustrated in this, they retreated, spitting spitefilled sparks about the room.

"Useless! If this pitiful fire is an example, Hell is not a very warm place," Fr. Membré exclaimed, shaking his head in disgust at the sputtering green wood. The priest threw another pine log onto the grate, poured himself a cup of half-warm coffee, and then rejoined the conversation.

The small group was seated in a circle on a buffalo-skin rug on the hard-packed, frozen earth floor. After nearly two frustrating months of shipbuilding, fortification, and peace, La Salle had become impatient to continue his quest.

"Henri," he announced, "I am placing you in command. I must go to Fort Saint Joseph. *Griffin* should be there by now. With her supplies, we can arm the *Illiniwek*, and we can go on to explore the *Fleuve Colbert*."

"As long as the game is plentiful, we should be able to fend for ourselves. I would be happy, though, if Nika remained with us; he is welcome among the *Illiniwek*." Tonti had been slowly turning his coffee mug, warming his hand against its fading comfort.

"How long will you be gone?" Tonti asked abruptly.

"I should return within two or three months," La Salle said calmly, absently staring at the contrary hearth. "If you're thinking about the Iroquois threat, don't concern yourself. They will not attack as long as the French are here."

Impish flames bellied outward once more, flickering briefly under a crackling cloud of thick smoke as a gusting downdraft sucked at the only warmth in the room.

"I shall be glad when we resume our voyage down river," Fr. Hennepin said. Pulling his wrap close against his throat, he anticipated the more pleasant circumstances farther south.

"You are too restless," La Salle chided, a large grin spreading across his face. "You are going to be travelling soon, sooner than you probably expect."

Fr. Hennepin, appearing mildly surprised, said, "But the river is still icebound. Where shall I be going?"

"You shall explore the upper *Colbert*. You are to establish a mission among the Dakota. I am sending you because you alone have the courage for this expedition. Accau and L'Esperance will assist you. They will prepare my trading posts. It is important that I exercise my franchise in this area. I am the only Frenchman with a patent for trade with the Dakota. You must also tell them the French king offers his protection and that we bring peace and brotherhood."

"You mean you want me to go there? Now?" Fr. Hennepin's eyes shone as two small moons surrounded by his weathered face and glistening black beard. For a moment he continued to stare at La Salle, slowly absorbing his message. "Surely it will be easier to travel in a few months."

"Travel is easier on ice than in mud. If you delay, your journey will become more difficult." La Salle was amused at the priest's reaction. He knew though, that Fr. Hennepin's sense of disappointment at not participating in the larger exploration would yield to the realization of the importance of leading his own path-breaking venture.

Observing that the priest was shivering, La Salle added, "Besides, it is more comfortable being active outdoors, than sitting idle inside a cold hut. Don't you agree?"

"I think the problem is, no matter the weather or the time of year, you are never comfortable in one place for long," the priest countered. Gradually he awakened to the possibilities of his new assignment. So far, only one or two explorations had been carried out in this territory. Here lay beckoning the prospect of new missions, new discoveries, and perhaps even recognition as an explorer of the first rank. "Nevertheless, I will do as you wish."

"M. Accau will help you with the Indians. He has trained in several of their tongues. M. L'Esperance has good skill as a woodsman. He will guide and hunt, so you shouldn't lack for provisions."

"And just where do we go? The *Colbert* reaches almost as far to the north as it does to the south of the Illinois river. At least, that is the impression I receive from discussion with the Indians."

"To the mouth of the *Rivière Ouisconsin*. I shall meet you there no later than August. Louis Jolliet and Fr. Marquette have explored this and the Fox River as far as *la Baye des Puants*. These rivers will serve as principal trade routes in that area. Be sure you inform the Dakota Indians of my exclusive trade rights."

"And these Dakota Indians—are they pacific?" Fr. Hennepin had heard stories, but doubted their truth. "I have heard Chippewa refer to the Dakota as 'the Enemies from the South.'"

"Remember to treat them as you would the Iroquois." La Salle smiled as he looked around the circle of men.

"And you are sending a priest with only two armed men to these people?"

"Do not show fear and they will respect you. Courage is your best defense. And remember this. They have requested your visit. So you should be received with the usual hospitality given strangers." La Salle concluded the discussion of Fr. Hennepin's charge.

"Well, then. I'd better get the men ready. By early tomorrow, we shall be on our way." Fr. Hennepin went out to inform Accau and L'Esperance of their imminent mission to the Sioux lands.

* * *

"And how many are to remain with me and Nika?" Tonti had been lapping his knife with a stone. Interrupting his sharpening, he tested the blade against a stick.

"I will take only Messieurs Hunaut, La Violette, Collin, and D'Autray. They are hardy travelers and will help bring back the gear and supplies from the *Griffin*. Saget will provide us with wild game so we may travel with few provisions. Therefore you will be able to use such stores as we have here, plus whatever Nika kills."

La Salle rubbed his chin. He was torn between the need to go to Ft. Saint Joseph for supplies and weapons and the need to stay at Ft.

Crèvecoeur for defense. How could he best ensure the safety of his men and the Illinois Indians against the Iroquois?

"The Illinois been generous on our behalf. They have allowed us to hunt freely in their lands. I do not think they will betray us after you have gone," Nika said, as though reading La Salle's thoughts. "The Iroquois will not attack if there are French here. They do not want a war with Canada. We will be safe."

Agreeing with Nika's assessment, La Salle relaxed and fell quiet.

"There is an Indian maiden here that is a delight!" Fr. Ribourde spoke up. "She wants to become a convert."

"Do you speak the Illinois tongue?" Nika was puzzled.

"No, not well. But she and I are working on both French and Indian expressions. So far I have succeeded in narrating several stories from the Bible. She is a quick student, and a very intelligent young lady."

"Well, I am glad to hear our missionary effort is having some success." La Salle smiled at the interruption.

"Because of language difficulties, it will take some time to fully prepare her for baptism. And there are others who are curious, but remain distant. We shall see these later, I am sure."

"She has selected a Christian name," Fr. Ribourde said, smiling broadly. "She calls herself 'Elizabeth' after the mother of John the Baptist. She was impressed that when Elizabeth became pregnant, it was said of her: 'All things are possible with God.'"

"This is the essence of faith: a total reliance on God. How beautiful to see," he observed, pleased with this small success.

Fr. Membré was absentmindedly sifting cold earth from the floor through his fingers. "Chassagoac and I have had several conversations. He too is interested in our faith. It would be a great success for us to convert the principal chief of the Illinois."

Fr. Ribourde walked over to the fire. He poked at the embers, pulling them close together, then placed a log on them. "It is always so rewarding to find natives eager to learn," he said.

Fr. Membré, too, was glad of this early achievement. "I have come to understand some of their beliefs as well. There are many similarities between Indian and Christian spirituality. They believe strongly in a spirit world where they distinguish good and evil. To the Indian all life has great value. They have strong family loyalties and they do not abandon nor neglect the poor, orphans, or widows. And they honor a Great Spirit Who is a Supreme Being. This is admirable."

"The Indian sees the spirit world in everything around him. It is not remote. The white man's spirits are far away in the sky or locked in stone buildings. For many, the spirit does not exist," Nika coldly interjected.

All were silent for a moment. La Salle spoke first to the priests. "Well, continue your good work with the Indians. And also with our men. See that you make better Christians of them as well. Their example is very important to your effort."

To Tonti, he continued, "You know I detest blasphemy. I do not tolerate tawdry and uncivilized behavior. Please remind my men of this. You have my authority to punish any such behavior as you see fit. It is necessary for their own good as well as for the success of the mission.

"I shall want to give Fr. Hennepin some further guidance for his venture." La Salle said, rising and looking around the room. "After his departure tomorrow, I shall prepare my own team. We will leave the following day."

La Salle went out of the hut and finding the priest and men spent some time in detailed discussion with them.

* * *

The day opened cold and clear as La Salle and his men shoved their laden canoes down the slope to the frozen Lake Peoria. It was the First of March 1680, and the sun had risen weak and pale. A chill breeze carried the sharp scent of ice.

"We'll have to drag the canoes," La Salle mused. After inspecting the cargo lashings, he assessed the frozen river. "Stay on the shore. This ice may be false."

Placing the canoes on sledges, the men shouldered the hitch ropes and began the trek north. Within a few hours, Fort Crèvecoeur had fallen below the bleak horizon behind.

Before mid-morning a uniform gray overcast spread across the sky, snuffing the promise of a warm sun. The air too seemed to have become more chilling.

"Fortunately, the wind has swept most of the snow from the ice." D'Autray attempted to be optimistic against the meager pace. He was on the second team and yet the soft snow of the broken trail remained knee-deep.

"We'll do fine," La Salle said, looking askance at the lake ice. He was leading the team pulling the first canoe, his usual position whenever a trail was to be broken.

"He will always 'do fine,' as long as he is travelling," Collin muttered to D'Autray. "Just look at him. I don't think he knows the difference between pulling a canoe over ice and paddling across a summer lake. It's all the same to him. But to stay in the same place for two nights. Ah, now that's a torture."

"Maybe it's people he doesn't like. Anytime there's a town, a fort, or an enclosure, he is eager to leave."

"He was not meant to be confined—by man, or by a woman." Collin's foot slipped on a patch of ice beneath the snow.

"What do you mean?" D'Autray paused as his friend regained his balance.

"Well, you've heard . . . there are rumors."

"Do you mean the woman in Canada?"

"Precisely," Collin affirmed. "A mademoiselle Madeleine de Roybon d'Allonne. I've been told she is living on his seigneury at Fort Frontenac."

"Yes, her. What do you think? I imagine she is quite attractive in her lacy gowns, yet they say he hardly seems to notice her feminine qualities. It is said she has loaned him money for his ventures. The rumor is she came from France just to pursue him."

The party had reached the head of Lake Peoria.

By noon of the next day, as the men were edging along the still frozen river, pleasant drizzle began to fall. Due to their earlier exertions, many had removed some of their outer clothing. Their overheated bodies at first absorbed the cooling drizzle but then the rain came in torrents. All were quickly soaked and suddenly chilled.

"This rain will help us. See, it is melting the snow. By tomorrow, the ice should be breaking." La Salle continued high stepping into the wet snow. "Perhaps we will soon be able to canoe. Let's hope so."

Before daybreak on the third day, the men heard the river growling. Whereas previously, an unnatural, deep silence had covered the landscape, the unmistakable crunch and swirl of newly broken ice announced the early return of spring. Launching the canoes into the swollen current, the men battled the drift ice with clubs and hatchets. But the effort was futile.

"Back to shore!" La Salle commanded. "We are not making any progress. We will only exhaust ourselves."

By early afternoon, a freezing rain began which further slowed the teams, now dragging their canoes through the forest parallel to the river. Later the rain turned into a moist snow.

"I am tired and disappointed. Let's camp here for the night. It seems the weather is against us anyhow." Chilled, D'Autray felt a desperate need for a fire.

"We will have a better time of it after this storm passes," La Salle promised, agreeing to the early halt. "We'll camp near those cedars. They'll make a good wind break."

Within minutes, the men had cleared an area of snow, erected lean-to shelters, and built a small fire. In a suspended kettle, some venison stew was cooking. Some dried their shirts or jackets on sticks near the fire.

"Our first days have been marked with little advance, but at least we have a beginning," La Salle said as he dipped a second helping from the pot. "We'll make an early start tomorrow."

In the morning, the men awoke to find several feet of fresh snow on the ground.

"Do you ever notice how silent it seems with new snow?" Hunaut was testing the snow depth outside the camp perimeter. "There is no more peaceful or quiet time than after a fresh snowfall. Even the animals are still."

Collin was knocking the snow from his overturned canoe. "It's grand! Unless you have to travel," he said, without enthusiasm.

Shadow had already risen and made coffee. Returning from a short reconnaissance, he announced, "We will not go far today. This snow is soft and dry, in places nearly waist deep, and there is an ice crust in open areas. We will need snowshoes."

Under a clearing sky, the trek resumed. La Salle was again leading. For hours, the only sound was the crunch of ice underfoot and the swishing of canoes sliding across the snow.

Towards evening, the familiar shape of Plum Island rose from the snow-covered river. Beyond, on the far shore, the rock later known as Starved Rock towered to over a hundred feet. The caravan had reached Kaskaskia, the summer town of the Illinois.

"Saget, would you scout the area? It appears deserted, but look for signs of wild life. We shall stay here as guests of the Illinois for a few days. We'll use their abandoned lodges." La Salle had already begun unpacking his canoe.

"I have seen wolf tracks. And I smell buffalo. There is one close by," Shadow said as he checked his musket. Slinging his powder flask over his shoulder, he added, "I shall be back by dark." He disappeared into the silence of the frozen woods beyond the Indian town.

"Footprints!" D'Autray cried out. "Over here. Several Indians have been here recently; maybe an Iroquois scouting party."

La Salle and La Violette ran over to where D'Autray stood.

"These are not Iroquois tracks," La Salle said, squatting near the marks. Examining their characteristics, he announced, "These impressions were made by moccasins with large flaps. *Illiniwek!* They may still be in the area."

D'Autray and La Salle walked slowly back to the camp. On the way they studied the snow for further evidence of the Indians' whereabouts.

"Build a large fire this evening. Perhaps they will see it." La Salle was anxious to meet with the visitors. "I would like to learn from them whether the Iroquois have come beyond the Great Lakes."

The sound of a distant shot echoed against the far ridge and reverberated through the trees. After a short span, a second report was heard. The men listened, straining against the evening stillness, seeking a clue to the meaning of the shooting.

"Saget has found his buffalo," La Salle announced after a few moments of silence. "Our fire shall be a beacon for him. He will return soon."

As the twilight turned from dark gray to black, the roaring fire released orange-red fingers toward the leafless trees towering over the campsite.

Later than he had promised, Shadow appeared, carrying the choice parts of the slain buffalo.

"There is a ridge beyond the village. The buffalo go to its base to escape the winter wind." Shadow gestured toward the north. "Tomorrow, we will have a feast."

"We have seen Indian tracks," La Violette said with a little excitement. "A small party. We hope they are not hostile."

"I, too, have seen their tracks." Shadow poured a small cup of hot tea for himself. "They are friendly. The Iroquois may come, but it is too early. Their war scouts would not leave such an open trail. Sometimes they wear animal feet to imitate deer or bear."

The next morning, while the men were finishing a small breakfast, La Salle and Shadow went to tour the town.

A few hours had passed when the men in the camp noticed a silent file coming from the snow-decked town. Shadow was leading, followed by three Indians and La Salle.

"That's Chassagoac, principal chief of the Illinois," Collin said, recognizing one of the approaching Indians. "I recognize his hair. He keeps it cut short, except for those locks hanging down around his ears."

"Men!" La Salle exclaimed as the party gathered around the fire. "Let us share a meal with our friends.

"La Violette and Collin, take your axes and see that we have plenty of wood. Hunaut and Saget will prepare the buffalo steaks."

"Chief Chassagoac," La Salle addressed the man dressed in a long buffalo robe. "My men are tired from the difficult journey from Fort Crèvecoeur. We are going to Michigami for supplies and trade goods. We wish to rest for a few days here in the Illinois lodges."

"I have spoken many times with the Gray Robe, Membré," Chassagoac said, squatting on a bark mat. "He is a good man. I trust what he says. He tells me you are a friend of the Illinois. Yet you are leaving us while the Iroquois are beating their war drums."

"We do not have enough guns, men, and powder here to defend the Illinois. I must go to Ft. Saint Joseph to bring muskets and gunpowder."

"We will move here soon for summer. Your fort Crèvecoeur is far down the river. It will not protect us against the Rattlesnakes."

"I have seen the stone column across the river. *Le Rocher* is suitable for fortification. On the river side, it has a vertical cliff, unscaleable," La Salle said, drawing a rough sketch in the snow. "We could build a palisade on the top of this rock. With falconets and muskets, we control the river. No enemy of the Illinois shall pass."

Chief Chassagoac grunted. For a while he considered the prospects. Finally, he said, "This is good. And you will build this fort when you return?"

Bringing forth a red blanket, La Salle said, "Here is a gift to seal my promise.

"There is another matter of concern to me." La Salle said after the chief had examined and approved the gift. "My men at Fort Crèvecoeur are poorly provisioned. Would the Illinois help them obtain food while I am away?"

Chief Chassagoac gladly agreed to extend the tribal hospitality to the French. A smoke of the calumet was proposed to seal this understanding. Chief Chassagoac was particularly thoughtful as he drew long and slow, the kinnickinnick glowing orange-red in response. As he studied the glowing tobacco he worried that an Iroquois war party would be little deterred by the French fort. He watched the rising smoke carrying his thoughts to the Great Spirit.

The smell of roasting buffalo meat aroused the men's anticipation of a pleasant evening. It was not long before the choice and delicate meats had disappeared. Muscle meats were roasted and packed, stores for the journey ahead.

The next morning, the Illinois Indians departed, silently disappearing into a gray mist hanging over the snowy landscape.

After the men had spent a few days recuperating, La Salle was again eager to resume the journey to Lake Michigan. "Tomorrow is the fifteenth. We have already spent two weeks. We need to hurry. Clear water is showing. I think we shall be able to use our canoes at last."

Collin walked gingerly over the shoreside ice, testing its strength. A muffled cracking radiated from beneath his last step. "Here," he called out. "Here it begins to thin." With that, he knelt nearby and began hacking with his hatchet.

The men slid the canoes to Collin's newly made launch basin, fast filling with loose, broken ice.

"Be careful," Hunaut called from the lead canoe as it broke through to the main current. "This free ice is heavy. It could punch holes in our birchbarks."

The two canoes began slowly to advance. Two men paddled while the third in the bow used either a pole or an axe to gain safe passage. Occasionally the surging current spilled onto the shelf ice, leaving a muddy discoloration to mark the edge of the channel. In spite of the men's effort, La Salle found it difficult to claim progress.

"This is impossible. We are not making much headway. We'll have to portage again. Let's try the north shore," La Salle said, gauging the extent of a small rapid ahead. "The going will be easier there."

The men were passing a long narrow island at the time. There was a series of riffles on either side, but those on the north seemed shortest.

"The next portage is just before the bluffs at the head of the Illinois river. We should be there by tomorrow afternoon," La Salle advised, hoping to encourage the men with the prospect of more open waters.

The following day, the canoes were coasting easily beneath those bluffs, having made the final portage. To the east the Des Plaines joined the Kankakee River forming the mighty Illinois.

With a renewed energy Hunaut headed his canoe toward the mouth of the Kankakee as he sensed the overland passages were finished.

"No, no. Not that way! The Kankakee will be ice-bound in its upper reaches." La Salle assumed the stronger current of the Des Plaines would have cleared the ice there. "We will ascend the *Rivière Des Plaines*."

* * *

"Well, so much for ice-free rivers," La Violette carped as he helped drag the canoe over the riverbank. La Salle's party had managed only a few hours' travel on the Des Plaines before finding it impassable. Fatigued at the thought, La Violette said, "It will be difficult to chop our way through this."

"It's not just the ice," La Salle explained. "It's been more than five years since Marquette and Jolliet opened this route, but I recall Jolliet mentioned that mound you see in the plain. From here the rapids extend four leagues upriver. This ice merely forces us to choose between portaging north to the *Rivière Chikagou* and walking to the east.

"The snow-cover is not deep, and since the northern route is less direct, we'd do better to strike out cross-country now. We'll travel faster if we leave the canoes. We'll hide them and carry our provisions. It is already the 18th of March. We could arrive at the fort in a few days," La Salle said. Then looking at Shadow, he added, "Find us a trail."

"I will scout from the top of the mound," Shadow said, indicating the only hill in the area, about two thousand feet from the river. Rising only about thirty feet, it dominated the plain. It measured two hundred by six hundred feet and was barren except for a lone tree. "I know of this place. It is sacred to the Indian.

"The Illinois and Miami peoples call it *Missouratenouy*—the Earthen Vessel," Shadow explained, responding to the unspoken curiosity of the travelers. "It was made to save mankind. As the waters of the Great Flood receded, the boat came to rest here. Later it rolled over and turned into earth."

Shadow shouldered his gear and nestled his musket in the crook of his arm. He remarked pointedly, "It is not mentioned that your Noah had room for the Red man, but we too have special care by the Maker of All Things," and hiked toward the mound.

From its peak he surveyed the surrounding plain, making note of landmarks on the horizon and estimating the most direct line to the lake. Momentarily he descended and rejoined the others. Walking in trail, the company set off in an easterly direction.

The snow cover was indeed thin; the thawing mess beneath was nearly liquid. Moccasins became quickly soaked with chill water. Walking was an uncertain exercise, pushing against the yielding ooze could result in a slip, a fall, or a sprain. A long, dark brown line stretched slowly across the white plain, marking the resolute advance toward Michigami and to the fort.

* * *

"Get busy with the axes. We'll have to build a raft. Do you see those sand ridges? They mark the shore of *Michigami*. We are nearly there."

La Salle looked at the rain-swollen, Little Calumet River blocking the way. "This is our last crossing," he affirmed.

Collin and D'Autray began felling trees while Hunaut and La Violette trimmed branches and assembled the raft. Shadow in the meantime prepared a meal while La Salle scouted along the riverbank, seeking a favorable launch site. From that point La Salle estimated a probable landing based on the width of the stream and the force of the current. The river was several hundred yards wide and swollen with the runoff of melting snow. Satisfied with his calculations, he returned to the camp.

"I think this will do just fine," he said, appraising the raft and its workmanship on his return to the work site. "We will also need six long, stout poles. The river may have a deep channel."

"I will be happy when we arrive at the fort," Hunaut grumbled as he and Shadow wove slender cedar roots to make lashings for the raft-beams. "There have been too many cold nights and snow for me. I feel as though I have a permanent chill. I can't shake it."

"The spring sun will soon grow strong. There will be warm days and your moccasins will dry." Shadow made a tea from the dried sassafras roots he carried. "Try this, it will chase the dampness."

* * *

Having crossed the river, the men marched off and crossed the distant dunes. Beyond the dunes they followed the shore of Lake Michigan until, late in the afternoon of the twenty-fourth of March, they saw the jut of land and the wide, sandy beach that marked the mouth of the Saint Joseph River.

Anxiously peering into the deepening dusk, La Salle strained to discern the outline of a ship. "Where is *Griffin*? My ship is not here!" he exclaimed. His great hope, the object of the journey, the rescue of the Illinois, was nowhere in sight.

In spite of his tiredness, arching his back erect, he quickened his pace. Only Shadow kept up with him, the others straggling behind. La Salle's eyes probed the river beyond the beach where the Saint Joseph empties into Lake Michigan. His eyes, tracing the small sand spit extending along the north side of the current, detected the small, round knoll guarding the inlet, and looking inland, he also saw the small stockade on the hill.

Against the darkening sky, the upper branches of the riverside trees cruelly mocked him—seemingly so many bare masts. Thus taunted by ghost ships, La Salle began running toward the inlet, his anxiety deepening. Shadow loped along, his long legs easily crossing the soft, nettle-strewn expanse.

"The harbor!" La Salle yelled to Shadow, "The ship could be in the harbor."

The two were racing along the riverbank now, having dropped their packs and weapons. As they skirted the north end of the rise that hosted Ft. Saint Joseph, they came to the basin formed by the confluence of the Paw Paw and Saint Joseph Rivers.

La Salle stopped abruptly, staring across the waters. Unconvinced, he stood for some moments, probing every shadow, every shape. Gradually, he came to accept the truth.

"There is a light in the fort," Shadow spoke gently, almost in a whisper. "The men may have news of *Griffin*. Your 'big canoe' may be sailing on *Michigami*."

"I gave orders for Mignon to wait here!" La Salle bit off the words, being careful to direct his anger away from the Indian. Glancing back, he noticed the remainder of his party coming off the beach.

Turning to Shadow, he said apologetically, "You are probably correct. Although I cannot imagine why Mignon would go out to brave the spring storms. Nor would I expect any harbors north of here to be ice-free. That man will not entertain unnecessary risks."

Making one last hopeful sweep of the darkened waterside, La Salle turned and exclaimed, "No, no, no! He is not sailing. Something is amiss. Let's see what they know at the fort."

Spinning around, La Salle hurried off. Charging up the hill, he ran through the open gate and, finding an occupied building, burst into the room, startling the occupants.

Chapelle and LeBlanc were sitting at the table mending clothing.

"You left the gate unfastened," La Salle accused as he seated himself opposite Chapelle.

"T-t-the Indians here are friendly," Chapelle responded as he hastily gathered his sewing instruments. "Besides, we have nothing for them to s-steal."

"Exactly! And just where are my goods? . . . My ship . . . and my crew?" La Salle looked sternly at the two caretakers. Shadow had entered and was standing nearby, in a darkened corner of the room. The other men filed in, dropping their packs and baggage in a pile. Then they collapsed onto the bench or otherwise squatted on the floor.

Chapelle and LeBlanc both rose from their seats, surprised and puzzled by the sudden appearance of La Salle and his men. "We are glad to see you. But how did you come here in this season?" Chapelle temporarily ignored La Salle's first questions as he helped stow the packs near the cabin walls. After he closed the door on the outer darkness, he turned to face La Salle and said bluntly, *"Griffin* has disappeared. There is no word."

After a pause, he continued, "Leblanc and I have gone to Pt. Ignace as you requested. The missionaries there have not seen *Griffin* since she left for Green Bay in September."

"Not only that, but we also cruised around the west side of the lake. No one has seen either the ship or her crew," Leblanc insisted.

Sighing, La Salle wiped his face. "I cannot believe she could disappear that easily," he said, drumming his fingers on the table.

"Mignon!" La Salle suddenly slammed his fist onto the table, gritting his teeth. "No, I do not think she is lost. She will turn up. Somehow you must have missed her. Let us have a meal. Tomorrow we will decide what needs to be done."

Chapelle was one of the earliest risers the next morning. As he turned in his cot, he noticed candlelight in the room. In a far corner, working with paper and ink, La Salle sat at the desk, rapidly writing.

"Would you care for coffee?" Chapelle quietly asked as he pulled on his moccasins. He stood up, stretched, and—rubbing his hands against the chill—walked over to the hearth.

"Please. And when you've rebuilt the fire, would you start a breakfast for the men? We are going to have an early start today." With a flourish, La Salle signed, folded, and then sealed the letter with candle wax.

Chapelle placed a pine log in the pit then filled a pot with water and coffee beans. Soon the other men woke to the smell of coffee brewing and greasy meat frying.

While the men breakfasted, La Salle paced about the room. Confronted with the unexpected setback of *Griffin's* absence, he carefully considered his options. There were no immediate or simple alternatives. To return to Fort Crèvecoeur gained nothing—Tonti represented the French interest there and had a score of men for fighting, if it came to that. Nowhere around Lake Michigan, including the Pt. Ignace mission, was there an ample supply of weapons for the Illinois. Besides, without the furs on *Griffin*, La Salle had nothing to offer in trade.

Montreal held the only prospect for help. In addition to his assets at Fort Frontenac, La Salle was expecting a shipment of equipment and men from France. The unavoidable cost of this solution was time. If he simply waited at Fort Saint Joseph, he would lose at least a year and his loans would come due. By going to Montreal, he could get help in less time and renegotiate his credit. Reluctantly, he resolved to make the journey.

As he paced about, the men at table noted the tightened fists, the tense jowls, and the pinched corners of the eyes. Several ate quietly, severely refusing to direct their eyes away from their plates or food. An unknowable struggle that they could not influence was coming to a conclusion. Whatever the outcome, they would soon know their own roles. They were after all, eager to serve. The discomfort they dreaded most was that of standing still at the crossroads of indecision.

"Chapelle and Leblanc, you two are to go immediately to M. Tonti. Take this letter to him. Tell him he is to fortify *Le Rocher*." La Salle had stopped pacing and stood in the middle of the room, facing the seated men.

"The rivers are not yet free of ice. It will take some time to go there," Leblanc observed. "And we will need a canoe."

"Saget will give you a route. You will not have to walk the whole distance. We have hidden canoes near the *Rivière Des Plaines*. You will avoid the usual route on the Kankakee."

"There is not much food here and we will need to carry at least a week's supply. The spring hunt has not yet begun." Chapelle said as he collected the men's plates and forks. He welcomed the thought of leaving the confinement of the fort. He and Leblanc had been stationed here for five months; he anticipated the pleasant hospitality of a large Indian settlement.

"The faster you travel, the less food you will need. You must make all possible speed." La Salle had approached the table and was now looking intently at his messengers. "I had expected *Griffin* and its weapons. Now we have nothing to offer for the defense of the Illinois.

"Tonti must begin to fortify *Le Rocher* as soon as possible. He will need the tools and guns from Fort Crèvecoeur. It is all we can do at this time. You must go quickly if we are to have any success."

The two agents quickly gathered their gear and came to the table for a last cup of coffee.

"Tell us about Signore Tonti," LeBlanc suddenly asked La Salle. "Did he fight in the Sicilian wars?"

"He is the son of the governor of Gaeta. He lost his hand in battle. He has also served as a French captain." La Salle paused fondly remembering his friend. "He is one of the most honest and trustworthy men I know."

"Is it true what they say? That when a grenade wrecked his hand, he cut off the damaged bone and flesh, bandaged the stump, and resumed the charge?" Collin asked in fascination.

"I have not asked him about that. I do not know," La Salle replied, a smile playing at the corners of his mouth. "But I do know this—never underestimate him or doubt his courage."

With an end to the questions, La Salle sensed the men were reassured on Tonti's leadership. La Salle was pleased with the inquiries because it conveyed awareness that they might have to follow the man in battle. And that might become more than a possibility.

116

Addressing Chapelle and Leblanc, La Salle said, "I think you will find M. Tonti dedicated to helping the Indians. You must do your part to help him."

With that the messengers departed.

* * *

Shadow had been squatting on the bare earth, his cold eyes following La Salle's every movement as he paced about, discussing his plans, directing LeBlanc and Chapelle. Slowly Shadow drew a stone back and forth on the edge of his tomahawk. It was his habit, almost an obsession, to keep his weapons immaculate and sharp.

"And?"

It was the simplest question, yet La Salle immediately understood the point of Shadow's question.

"I have no choice. The rest of us must go on to the settlements. And we, too, have little time. We must acquire guns, powder, and men. And we must return before the Iroquois arrive. It is because of my enterprises this war has come about. I must do all I can to stop it."

La Salle stood at full height before the door, impatient to depart. He opened the door a bit, peered briefly out at the weather, then reclosed the door.

"The *Illiniwek* were suspicious of the French. We have won their trust and I cannot betray their faith in me. I must do all in my power now, for them and for the king. And you, you all must make every effort for success. We depart immediately."

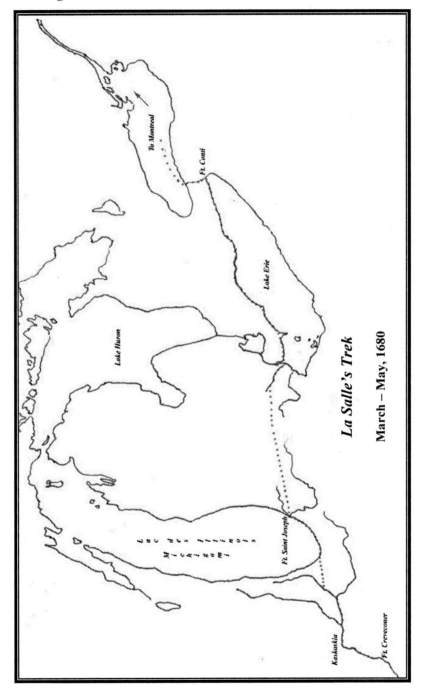

La Salle's Trek

March – May, 1680

Chapter 7

White Lace

"There is an Indian crossing, a *pawa-ting*, several leagues upriver," Shadow reminded La Salle. Squatting on the floor, he was busy with his weapons. From La Salle's restive state, Shadow felt he might soon need their use. Holding his tomahawk edgewise, he studied the keen blade. "A Sac trail leads toward the Raisin and Huron rivers. We should make good time to Lake Erie."

"Or we could fail completely. It is the wrong time of year for travel. We will see more snows, the ground will be thawing, and ice may block the rivers." La Salle winced as he resumed his pacing. "Worse than this, if Iroquois scouts are out, they will be on that trail!"

"There is no other way. It is impossible to canoe on the lakes. At this time of year, we would not survive." Shadow's face was grim as he finished honing his knife. Yet he cocked an expectant eyebrow toward La Salle for he was confident he was not to be daunted by inhospitable nature or by hostile Indians.

"We will make our own trail!" La Salle replied, surprising Shadow not in the least. But in fact, he thought he detected a twinkle in the Indian's eye.

"It is the only safe choice we have. We will go through the Indian hunting lands. At this season, there will not be many hunting parties about."

La Salle looked at the men as they readied their packs. At that moment, the nagging thought returned that an agent had infiltrated his entourage. He quickly dismissed the suspicion, reassuring himself that these men had shown themselves dedicated and loyal.

"I need your support," La Salle announced. "We have come a long way, only to find disappointment. We have before us another long journey. We must go on to Montreal. We must get weapons for the Illinois Indians. Their very lives may be at stake. We must go quickly, or else we fail."

Shadow grunted as he pricked a finger, testing his knifepoint. Satisfied with its sharpness, he sheathed the knife, got up and went to the cabin door where he studied the early dawn. After a moment, he closed the door, put on his packs, and said to La Salle, "You will not rest until we are back with the Illinois tribes. Neither will I. I go now to scout a trail."

Shadow quickly disappeared down the hill to the St. Joseph River. Collin ferried him across, then returned to bring the others with their heavy gear. Shadow had about an hour's lead by the time the main party had crossed to the eastern bank.

Hardly another hour had passed before Shadow returned to report. He found La Salle and the men following his blaze marks.

"A forest of vines blocks our way. It goes far to either side. There is no easy passage," he said. "And there is not much game in this area, only a few birds and squirrels."

"I would not expect much game in the vines," La Salle mused. "The better for us in a way. The Iroquois will certainly scout the main trails. We will go through the vine forest."

"Ah, well. You weren't really in a hurry to get to Montreal, were you?" Hunaut smirked toward D'Autray, raising his eyebrows and tilting his head.

D'Autray shrugged, then smiled. "I shall be happy anytime we come to Montreal. I may buy new clothing. These 'skins badly need repair. With the pay La Salle owes me, I shall be able to dress with the finest and have a very good time. You'll see."

"*Heu!* These brambles are an endless torture," La Violette bawled, pulling at the thorns piercing his sleeve. He was walking a little behind La Salle who, in the lead, with each step cut away at the brambles. Even as the vines were severed, loose ends snapped back, entangling and gashing the men behind.

La Violette looked around at the green wall of impenetrable, spiny vines. Thick mats rose to the chest; occasional clusters were twice the height of a man. Pockets of snow lay in shaded nooks, and the air had a sharp, cold feel. La Violette continued his struggle, but felt his efforts increasingly futile.

"At this rate, we won't reach Montreal before late summer," Collin said, pulling at the barbs ensnaring his pants.

"Be patient," La Salle called out, grimacing as the free end of a freshly cut vine slapped his face, leaving a short, red gash. In the freezing March air, the sting was doubly intense. "If you go too swiftly, these brambles work against you. They do not go on forever, though. Soon we will be free."

* * *

"In two days, we have not come far." Collin was third in line. "Even following someone is no advantage. Cut vines are even harder to manage. You can't push them away and you need two hands to cut them again."

"We will rest in the next open area," La Salle said as he continued working with his knife against the vines. "We need to make a few repairs."

"A few repairs?" La Violette turned toward D'Autray, and smiled. "Our clothes are torn, our faces scratched, our hands a bloody pulp. I am glad we only need to make a few repairs!"

D'Autray grunted acknowledgement. "At least we do not have the Iroquois to add to our wounds. Perhaps you prefer their gantlet. Think of that before your complain too much."

Shadow continually eyed the crowns of the trees ahead as he walked. He sought a break in the canopy, a telltale patch of blue. "There is a clearing ahead. To the left," he announced finally.

"Yes, I see it." La Salle said, changing direction slightly. After two and a half days struggling against the vines, the chilled men broke into a clearing where they immediately began setting up camp.

"Do you see signs of game?" La Salle asked, following Shadow's probing eyes.

"A few deer are watching us from the woods on the far side of this field. They are curious. We shall eat venison today." Shadow grimaced. Not taking his gaze off the concealed deer, he readied his musket. He set off, silently skirting the open field.

"Rest awhile. And be quiet." Turning to the other men, La Salle spoke softly. "Saget is on a hunt. Don't startle the game with noise or motion. He will have a better chance if we don't interfere."

Silently, the men spread their robes on the snow and sprawled in the mid-day sun, glad for the respite. Sheltered from the snappish breeze, the men gratefully absorbed the sun's warmth, one or two falling into a deep sleep.

They had not rested long before their attention was arrested by a distant shot. Not much later a second shot confirmed Shadow's presence among the deer.

"Collin and Hunaut, go help bring in the kill," La Salle called as he resumed trimming saplings. He was making a tripod for the cooking kettle.

The first carcass was brought in. Soon the snow near the firepit was bespeckled with blood, deer hair, and tallow as La Violette and D'Autray skinned out the first buck.

Shadow stood watching the men, dismayed at their apparent unconcern for the spirit of the animal, for its strength, for its speed. After a moment's reflection, he went off to his own cot to rest.

* * *

Shadow was busy cleaning his musket when a twig snap caught his attention. The noise, barely audible to the others, was too near to be a feral animal. Quickly he replaced his unloaded musket with his bow and slowly turned to the threat, ever searching the nearby shrubs. He made a silent signal to D'Autray, nocked an arrow, and crouched in readiness.

Seeing Shadow's alarm, La Violette grabbed his musket, raised it to his waist, and strained to discover the enemy. Fearful, Hunaut rolled his heavy body on his bedding, tensely watching the others. Collin, too, sensing danger, had stopped his work. He glanced from one to the other, wondering what had caused the alert. Slowly he lowered his skinning knife to the ground and casually walked toward his musket, which was leaning against a large, shagbark pine.

D'Autray, squatting near the fire, checked his knife and hatchet. He did not know whether to feign unconcern for the benefit of the unseen observers or to go for his musket, some distance away.

Shadow was about to step forward, when La Salle loudly yelled, surprising his men, "*Ahwanian e-mah ai-aud?*"

"*Po-te-wa-tami! Ahwanian iau we yun?*" From the tall grass, the Potawatami hunter responded, also in Algonquian.

"*Nous sommes Française,*" La Salle answered.

"*Anuneende azhauyun?*" The hidden Indian continued to question.

"To Montreal," La Salle responded, raising aloft the calumet of Chief Onanghisse. He added, "Come forward in peace."

"We heard shots. We thought you were Iroquois." One of the newcomers smiled, apparently delighted to have been in error.

"Have you seen Iroquois sign?" La Salle quickly became serious.

"Words fly like clouds," the Potawatami said, waving his arm broadly over his head. "Their war drums are calling. But we have not seen their tracks."

"Thank you for this information," La Salle said, a little relieved. "Please share our camp this evening. We have food for our friends."

* * *

Early the next morning, the six Potawatami went off to resume their hunt. La Salle's party also prepared to break camp.

"Today, we are an Iroquois war party," La Salle announced with a particular emphasis. He was studying the unenthusiastic gray edge of the day. Turning to the men, he said, "We will have fewer visitors if we seem dangerous."

"How do we do that?" D'Autray paused as he assembled his belongings.

"Saget will mark trees in the Iroquois manner," La Salle said. "We will walk Indian file. Be careful not to break branches or twigs; do not leave debris on the trail. Carelessness could mean your life."

Shadow cut the bark on one or two trees. Using charcoal he drew several images, including bearded and bound men. "Hunaut walks like a French farm horse. No brave could mistake his footprints for an Indian's. So we have French prisoners." He smiled as he finished, "And we have scalps!"

La Violette grinned, imagining himself an Iroquois warrior.

La Salle's eyes gleamed with reassurance. "It is not yet April. We must move quickly to the settlements," he said and resumed marching energetically to Montreal.

The six men walked for most of the day, halting only for short rests. The countryside was slightly rolling, the forest becoming broken, finally yielding to wide, grassy fields.

"Our trail is too obvious," La Salle observed. He had stopped on a rise and, watching his men, saw the trace of their passing. He scanned the expanse of waist-high grass searching for a new stratagem.

"The grass is dry," Shadow answered the unspoken question. He was running his hand over the sun-drenched saw grass rising through occasional patches of melting snow. "It will burn."

"Excellent! Go back on our trail, about half a league. A small fire will cover our tracks." La Salle took over some of Shadow's baggage. "This breeze should help. We will wait for you in that copse ahead."

About an hour later the men watched as a low cloud of blue smoke began drifting along the western horizon. Soon Shadow came loping through the grass.

"Time for tea," La Salle said, motioning to a boiling pot tended by D'Autray. Shadow strolled over and squatted near the fire. After a few moments he began sipping from a cup of the hot beverage.

"We'll camp here today. It's a bit early, but we can use the extra rest." La Salle had noticed a certain sluggishness among his travelers. "Tomorrow we may have wet going. There is a wetland beyond these trees, and I see no way around. We must cross directly."

Considering the difficulties of walking through the marsh, La Salle thought it better to wait for an early attempt. While the group waited for Shadow, La Salle had gone scouting. Having surveyed the area ahead, he had rejoined the men just as the Indian returned.

On the following day, after obliterating the evidence of the campsite, the party plunged into the spongy, sucking ground of the marsh. For hours they sloshed among scattered cat-o-nine tail clusters until at last the ground again became firm.

It was early afternoon when Shadow silently signaled a halt. "Fresh tracks," he whispered, squatting to study the impressions in the mud. "Another hunting party . . . Potawatami . . . They may still be in the area."

"Be alert, men." La Salle, too, was observing the moccasin prints. "If we can find their trail, they may find ours. We will have no fires tonight."

* * *

For the next three days the men continued their march, apprehensive, tired, and sullen. They crossed fresh Indian trails almost daily. From the ardor of their effort, the men's buckskin shirts had become thoroughly soaked with sweat. At night, the men would hang these shirts on sticks to dry.

"We sweat all day and freeze at night. I do not think I will last much longer." Hunaut was chewing dried venison. Bare-chested, he was wrapped in his buffalo robe as he strolled among his still–bedded companions.

"Merde alors! Look at these shirts. They are frozen stiff," Hunaut exclaimed as he shook his rigid buckskin. "There is no way we can wear them. We will need to thaw them over a fire."

"All right, go ahead," La Salle agreed as he stroked the unyielding cold stiffness of one. "But let us work quickly; a fire will likely attract unwanted attention."

Soon the men, still bare-chested, were fanning two small fires with their frozen shirts.

"You are shivering!" La Salle suddenly noticed that Hunaut's face was unusually flushed. "Do you feel ill?"

"I don't feel well or ill. I couldn't sleep. The ache has returned in my gut. I've had two bloody stools since last evening," Hunaut said, impatiently pressing his hand on the fire-warmed shirt. "I'm afraid the drying is going to take some time."

With growing concern La Salle studied the man for a moment. He feared that his condition would worsen with travel. The early spring weather was uncertain; a sudden cold spell could intensify Hunaut's illness. Sighing, La Salle turned to go when an Indian rose from not far away in the grass, startling him.

The man stood in the field, a Potawatami hunter, La Salle judged by his lack of war paint, long hair, and bearskin robe. The thirty-year-old man was wearing a beaver-fur turban—a symbol of his importance—and a tanned leather breechclout with the flaps hanging to the knees in front and back. The breechclout was decorated with quillwork bands along the bottom.

Deerskin leggings seamed down the sides were gartered below the knees. The moccasins had the very large cuffs favored by the Prairie Indians.

"Frenchmen! Do not shoot. We are friends," The leader announced as three more hunters rose from the grassy field. As these approached the camp, another four emerged from other hiding places.

"Welcome, brothers," La Salle exclaimed, raising his arm in salute. The hunting party came in, friendly but quizzical.

"We are friends," the leader repeated. "We saw your smoke and your Iroquois marks."

"We are not Iroquois but Frenchmen with frozen shirts. It was freezing last night." La Salle examined the coffeepot to see that enough remained.

The Indian visitors mingled with the campers, amused at their predicament. "You make much smoke. Too much for Iroquois." One of the visitors smiled and took some hot coffee.

"This is good. We have heard of the French coffee. It warms the insides. Do you have beans?"

As the guests finished drinking, La Salle produced a small pouch. "Take these. Now tell me, is there a river nearby? We are travelling toward Lake Erie."

One of the hunters pointed. "Three days. You will find a river going to your lake."

Rising from his squat, the leader said, "We must go. Be careful with your smoke. The Iroquois drink blood, not coffee."

La Salle watched as the hunters melted into the frosty morning. His own men were still drying their clothing.

"Hunaut, you are trembling," La Salle said with chagrin. He reproached himself for not taking action sooner. Handing the man's drying stick to La Violette, he exclaimed, "Hunaut, go lie down! Cover yourself with your robe, and keep warm."

"Saget, tend to Hunaut. I think he needs medicine," La Salle said, resigning himself to another delay.

Shadow took a hot stone from the fire, wrapped it in deerskin, and placed it against Hunaut's stomach. He then carved a strip from the outer bark of a young white pine. Carefully, with his knife, he pried out the inner bark, placing the pulp in a pot of water.

"Soon Hunaut will have hot tea. This will stop the shits," he said. After he prepared the brew, Shadow helped the patient drink.

He then went to a nearby stand of cattail where he began digging. He returned with several rhizomes covered with dormant sprouts and young shoots.

"Hunaut eats too much meat, but this will help. Eat these," Shadow said as he gave him the raw shoots. He then put the peeled rhizome into a pot; the sprouts he steamed over the boiling water.

While tending the cookpot, Shadow observed Hunaut. He was skeptical that Hunaut held an awareness of the spirit world above any minimal level. He resented Hunaut for his self-indulgence, his indifference to the harmony of nature, and his failure to appreciate nature's gifts. His present illness seemed to the Indian nothing less than a reflection of Hunaut's neglectful spiritual attitude.

"This is tasty, no? You should eat more green, stay healthy." Shadow jabbed Hunaut roughly in the ribs, then stared hard-faced as Hunaut grunted, rolled his eyes, and struggled to come to a comfortable position.

* * *

"This flat land may be a watershed," La Salle announced. For two days the group had traveled—the plains, freshly bright with new snow had dazzled them. "All the streams we have crossed so far flow to the west or south. We must be nearing the divide. Soon we shall find the easterly rivers."

"I've got to stop again." Hunaut, having another fit of cramps, scampered behind some bushes for privacy.

"That's the second time in two hours," La Violette commented. "Do you need more of Shadow's tea?"

From behind the bushes, Hunaut moaned acknowledgement.

La Salle looked wistfully ahead, tempering his frustration. The Huron River must be near, yet he felt it was receding from his reach, even as he stood there. He knew any task, once interrupted, requires more effort to rejoin.

"Collin, you look pale. Are you well?" La Salle exclaimed, and becoming alarmed, inspected all the men's faces. "Do not hide your illness. It is better to care for a small fever than to continue in this weather and end up in worse conditions."

"It is not just a fever this time." Collin was glancing about, seeking a privy site. "I too have the cramps. I must go now."

"Perhaps we should camp near here for the remainder of the day," La Salle said resignedly. "La Violette, make sure Hunaut's mess is well-buried."

La Salle watched dourly as Collin hobbled toward a grassy spot. To the others he said, "There is a tree line about half a league ahead. I see the silver mark of a sycamore, a sure sign of water. You men start the camp while I go to see whether that is a river or a pond."

Scanning the horizon touched by a dark afternoon sky, La Salle took his bearings, then struck out.

An hour or so later he returned. "What *is* this?" he asked, looking surprised. Both Hunaut and Collin were prostrate. "Is it that bad?"

"Dysentery." La Violette was cooking a meal. "Both have bloody stools. We all need rest and good food."

"Tomorrow, while these two recuperate, we will build a canoe. We have come to the Huron river. I am sure of it." La Salle seemed pleased, in spite of the unfortunate circumstances.

The next morning while D'Autray kept the kettle boiling, La Violette and Shadow used hot water to loosen the bark of an elm tree. When they had an adequate supply of bark sheaths, they began driving short, framing sticks into the ground, outlining in this way the form of the canoe. Then they spread the elm bark over the shape on the ground and placed the keel piece upon the bark. Shadow set ribs to the keel, and finally brought the bark against the ribs, shaping the sides. La Violette helped Shadow tie-in the bow and stern pieces to complete the basic assembly. They forced thwarts between the gunwales, strengthening the hull.

While the final assembly progressed, Shadow went searching for a hackmatack tree. Quickly he found a stand of the reddish brown, straight-trunked wood in a peat bog. Retrieving an adequate supply of the slender roots, he returned to the work site and sewed the bark covering pieces to each other and to the ribs and gunwales.

By evening, the canoe was nearly finished. La Salle, returning from another scouting sally, came to the work area.

"It is ready for pitch," Shadow said, stepping back to appraise the canoe's alignment.

"Good! Let that be enough for today," La Salle said, satisfied with the progress.

When the four returned to the camp, La Salle asked. "How are our invalids doing?"

"As you can see, we are still alive," Collin answered. "I am afraid Hunaut is not able to stand. But Shadow's blackberry-root tea has at least stopped the cramps."

Hunaut lay on a bed of cedar boughs. His face was extremely pale, his drowsy eyes half-focused on the makeshift shelter over him. He seemed to be neither asleep nor awake. It was difficult to tell whether Hunaut's health was improving or deteriorating.

"Do you need anything?" La Salle addressed Hunaut. "We will have a meal in a short while. Would you like a warm drink in the meantime?"

Hunaut rolled his head, his lips moved, but no sound emerged.

"Don't worry. You will be fine in a few days." La Salle pressed the young man's cheeks and forehead. "You're very clammy. But by tomorrow you should be able to sit up. Look at Collin. See, he is already recovering."

The next morning, while the others finished a breakfast of jerked venison and coffee, Shadow dug a small pit near the canoe. In it he mixed heated pine resin and deer tallow.

"It is ready," he announced as he added charcoal ash to blacken the pitch.

La Violette and D'Autray removed the canoe from the framing and brought it closer to the pitch pit where they placed it inverted on the ground. Using a stick ladle, Shadow carefully treated all seams and lashing holes with the hot pitch. He quit when he felt the craft was indeed watertight.

La Salle had remained at the camp with the convalescing men. He was carving the broad, wooden blades needed for canoeing in shallow waters. These he would fasten to peeled sapling trunks to make paddles.

"Hunaut, how do you feel today?" he asked as Hunaut rolled fitfully on his side, waking from yet another restless nap.

"My gut is burning . . . I feel very weak . . . dizzy." Hunaut was staring at the firestones.

"Can you sit up?"

"Maybe . . . in a while." Hunaut chewed on a small bit of dried venison. He had been struggling to hold his food since early in the morning but still could tolerate no more than a mouthful. "I am sorry for causing this delay . . . I know you need to go quickly."

"There is no need to apologize. Do not embarrass yourself on my account. Such things cannot be hurried." La Salle pursed his lips as he shaved the bark from the paddle handles. "We will come to Montreal with God's good speed."

Hunaut rose to a half-sitting position, bracing himself on an elbow. Smiling wanly, he said, "I feel dizzier."

"This will pass," La Salle said, interrupting his knife work. "Do not force yourself. You will only cause a relapse."

"The canoe is ready," D'Autray announced as he sauntered in from the work site.

"Bring the others," La Salle ordered. "We have plenty of daylight. We will pack now and leave at daybreak. I think Collin and Hunaut are well enough to travel. We'll help them to the river. But first have La Violette prepare us some hot food."

Early the next morning, the men awoke to find a light, wet snow had fallen. "Everything is so bright!" Hunaut observed, his eyes pained by the brilliant light. "See how the snow clings to each and every branch. These trees—they remind me of white lace—a ruffle along the river!"

"Well, you seem to be recovering," La Salle smiled, then gazed across the snow-clad landscape, in the direction of the watercourse. After a moment, he turned and commented, "Be careful around white lace. It is often deceptive, like the bait in a trap. In the wilderness this 'white lace' is often deadly for those who become too enchanted with its 'charm.' Likewise, beware of people in white lace, for they can be especially treacherous, even fatal."

"I wonder whether he means government officials, the King and his court, or women," La Violette grunted. "I expect he means all of these. From what I hear he is never comfortable around any of them."

D'Autray scratched his backside. "For sure, he can not abide the Minister or the King's Courtiers. Otherwise he would not be here in the wilderness. Or perhaps they can not abide him. Who knows?"

"Women! Why do you think he fears them? Do you think he has had a bad experience?"

"Ha! No, I do not think he has had any experience." D'Autray smiled. "But you know there is a certain Lady staying at his estate. Maybe she is waiting for him, no? Perhaps he has just not met the right one, you never know."

"*Cela se peut.* Perhaps he is too demanding. Many women would not be attracted by his 'style.'" La Violette shrugged as he pulled on his pack straps.

"You know, he is too reserved, *désintéressé.* I think he does not know how to relax around women." D'Autray tilted his head, looking questioningly at La Violette.

"He is too religious. His Jesuit training has taken his *joie de vivre.*" La Violette smugly nodded. "His brother, Jean, still wears the lace surplice. These two do not see eye-to-eye at all. And do not forget he himself has worn the 'white lace.' He has never told anyone why he left the priesthood. Never!"

Carefully the semi-invalids took positions in the canoe, amid food packets and cooking gear. The remaining four boarded then, pushing off, began the downriver journey to Lake Erie.

La Salle was happy to be under way again. The river was shallow and slow moving; occasional clumps of marsh grass broke the surface. The snowy banks drifted easily by, blending into the white background. The going was undemanding. La Salle and his men relaxed and were glad for the opportunity to travel by water.

Hunaut still felt weak. In spite of the bearskin wrap, he felt a chill. D'Autray, too, had recovered some strength, but still felt uncomfortable.

"Look, look!" La Violette yelled as the canoe rounded a bend. "The river is blocked."

Several trees had blown down, closing the river. Much deadwood, carried down in floods, had become enmeshed with these.

The canoe was beached where the bank seemed scaleable. La Salle disembarked, saying, "Rest here while I scout ahead. La Violette, make a small fire and heat some food for the men, but do not make smoke."

La Salle and Shadow stomped off through the snow.

Soon Hunaut was warming his hands around a hot cup of nettle tea while La Violette cooked venison and sagamite.

After about an hour, the two scouts were seen hurrying back to the camp.

"I am afraid the river is choked with debris and deadwood for some distance. And beyond that, it is shallow and broken by islets in many places," La Salle said, surveying the housekeeping.

"If we must walk, I'm up to it," Hunaut bravely volunteered. He was surprised he had spoken that way because he really wasn't confident that he could walk very far at all. He was simply willing to try anything that held promise of bringing him closer to rescue and comfort. All the same, he had not the faintest notion of where the nearest dwelling might be or when he might arrive there. He sensed that somehow not knowing the certainty of his rescue was a large factor in deepening his misery.

"We shall walk to Lake Erie." La Salle announced with that finality that he used when he felt there were no serious alternatives. "The Huron river goes a bit to the southeast. We shall bear off to the Detroit Straits where a shorter lake crossing can be made. I estimate that we will be there in a day at most."

The men shouldered their gear and marched in silence under a dull, pressing gray sky. The snowy, marshy land sucked at their moccasins; the canoe they were towing slid freely over the muck.

"Hunaut, how are you holding up?" La Salle was genuinely concerned. "It is not much farther. We will stop and have a fire soon."

"My feet are cold, my leggings are wet to the knees, and I have a constant chill. But I can manage." Hunaut gamely tried to sound optimistic, but his voice betrayed the aching struggle within. He sensed a growing, solidifying reluctance to further travel. He felt his will and determination were draining into some unseen, irretrievable catchment beneath the soggy ground.

Hunaut knew that the price for stopping would be the forfeit of his precious life. Once stopped, he would never again be able to move, he would never reach shelter. Having come however feebly to that realization, Hunaut fought a growing numbness, an indifference to his fate. His motions had become perfunctory. He became as if detached from himself, suspended between the bright snow and the dull overcast. He became more depressed as the thought of the comforts and delights of town were no longer entertaining. He could feel his heart beating—fast and weak.

Someone ahead was shouting and pointing. The lake was in sight! But Hunaut did not respond. He stumbled along, dragging his water flask by the strap, mechanically following those ahead.

"We have dragged our canoes over half the distance from *Lac Pimitou* to the *Lac des Eries*." La Violette was speaking to D'Autray. The two of them, bringing up the rear of the column, were towing the canoe laden with gear and the few remaining provisions. "It is time to end this portaging and take to the water like proper *voyageurs*."

"You are probably exaggerating," D'Autray said with chagrin. "Nevertheless, tomorrow you shall get your wish for we cross the Straits. It is not too many days to Montreal now, *Mon Ami.*"

As the men spread along the shore, gazing over the water, Shadow gathered kindling, intent on starting a fire. La Salle went to scout as La Violette and D'Autray began to set up shelters. Hunaut was helped onto a mat of fresh-cut branches. Collin readied the cooking gear and started a meal.

Throughout the evening, Shadow tended Hunaut, giving him occasional small feedings. The Indian made a mush of corn and beans mixed with local herbs and roots. Shadow was encouraged that Hunaut managed to keep this food down.

Eventually the patient fell into another fitful sleep, tossing frequently. All color had drained from his face. A cold, clammy sweat appeared from time to time. The other men, also exhausted, nevertheless stood watch in turns during the night.

Morning came. Beneath a partly cloudy sky Hunaut slept on. La Salle observed the man for a while, then declared, "He has passed the crisis. He is resting well. I think he will recover."

Distantly contemplative, La Salle poured himself a hot brew and looked once more across the lake. Breaking his thoughts, he turned suddenly to Hunaut, who was now awake. "You have regained some of your strength, but I do not think you can endure the journey to Montreal. I have a plan to bring you to shelter as soon as possible."

"Do you mean to leave him at some Indian village?" Collin was busy cleaning the cooking utensils.

"No, that would be risky. If the Iroquois find him, they may learn that I am not at Fort Crèvecoeur. La Violette is strong." La Salle said, turning to Hunaut. "He will take you to Point Ignace. A few days voyage, then you can enjoy a well-earned rest.

"La Violette, if you think you can't do this, we can make another arrangement," La Salle said, looking intently at him.

"Do not worry on my account. This little journey will be a holiday for my friend and me. Eh, Hunaut?" La Violette grinned, jerking his head back.

"When you arrive at Pt. Ignace, I want you to learn what you can there about the *Griffin.*" La Salle had been pawing at the snowy earth with his foot. He frowned briefly as the bared earth changed to mud, then continued, "Go north through the straits. On Lake Huron, keep the coast close on your left. Take good care of M. Hunaut. Do you feel up to this voyage?"

La Salle began restlessly pacing, waiting for La Violette's response. "I expect to find both of you in good health when I return."

"We shall come to the mission whether Hunaut is able to paddle. This I guarantee," La Violette said, winking toward the patient. He put down his coffee cup and began gathering the necessaries for his assignment.

The other men began construction of a raft for the lake crossing. Shadow gathered cedar roots and vines for the lashings while Collin and D'Autray cut down trees and dressed logs. While La Salle was busy fashioning oars, he noted that the sky was closing.

From behind a few, rose-rimmed purple clouds, the rising light of dawn cheered the men. A gentle breeze heralding the new day grew. It moved slowly around to the east while thickening dark clouds gathered in the southern sky. The lake, too, assumed an ominous mood. Small waves stiffened as occasional white caps dotted the dull expanse.

Several times La Salle interrupted his work to look across the lake, gauging the distance to the gray bar that marked the opposite shore. "An hour, maybe two," he announced. "After we cross, we'll raft along the north shore."

When La Violette and Hunaut were finally ready to depart on their journey north, La Salle and the others came over to make their farewells. Hunaut sat warmly bundled in the bottom of the canoe, his back resting against the middle thwart. Although he was weak, he felt elated at the prospect of coming to a safe haven. He smiled gamely, waving an arm as D'Autray and Collin pushed the canoe through the surf. La Violette set the craft on course, and the two voyagers soon blended into the murky seascape.

Not long thereafter, Shadow, D'Autray, and Collin dragged the new-built raft into the chilling water. Testing that the baggage was firmly secured, La Salle made one last estimate of the wind and the weather. Grimly he surveyed the darkening sky but considered the worse dangers were those suspended over Montreal and Fort Crèvecoeur.

"I am tired and I know you men are exhausted. This crossing will not be easy, but it is our last voyage on open water. There is bad weather approaching. If we do not cross now, we may have to delay here several days. Needless to say, we must push on." La Salle had made his decision; it was not the best of circumstances, but it was the only choice.

The weary men accepted the unavoidable. They too were anxious for shelter and rest. Shadow alone seemed indifferent to the hardship and said nothing. It was his usual response, an unspoken willingness to accept events as they came. His service to La Salle was never tempered by personal considerations.

The first half of the crossing had been dull, mechanical, and monotonous. The rising wind, which continued to move, was now settled in the northeast, almost directly ahead.

"Harder! We must pull harder!" La Salle insisted. The men were flagging; he could see their uneven rhythm, the unmistakable telltale of approaching exhaustion. The air blowing over them carried the chill bite of snow and the sweet smell of pine. A stinging rain began its assault in heavy, semi-frozen drops.

"Ashore! Ashore, head for that point!" La Salle, yelling above the wind and crashing surf, pointed to the nearest landfall. Shivering, Collin had ceased rowing. The effort from the other three was barely adequate. "We'll beach here for a rest. It is impossible to do more in this weather. We cannot follow the coast, it is too exposed."

Pulling the raft from the beach near a stand of pine, La Salle and D'Autray tied off a painter to a tree. Collin, who had collapsed, was wrapped in a bearskin and placed on the raft. D'Autray went stumbling among the trees, digging through debris piles, seeking dry tinder.

Puzzled by rawness in his chest, Shadow leaned against a tree, recovering his strength. The rain continued, water dripping on the men through the pine overcast. Only La Salle seemed to have an energy reserve, as he set up shelters and arranged a fire pit.

Eventually D'Autray returned, having gathered ample pinecones and dry branches for a fire.

Brewing a hot tea, La Salle said, "I had hoped we could raft as far as Fort Conti. Now I see that is impossible against this wind. We'll rest here for a while and when you are up to it, we shall walk. But first, we must destroy the raft. It is a marker the Iroquois would not miss."

Collin and D'Autray set to work, knocking the raft apart, casting the logs adrift on the lake. Watching the flotsam wash away on the choppy waters, La Salle reminded his men, "We must make the best progress we can. It will soon be May. There is yet a possibility we can bring help to the Illinois. A few more days and our journey is nearly over. What do you say? Can we make this last stage? Eh?"

Hope feeds at the breast of misery. D'Autray stirred, rising slowly on rubbery legs. Like an infant, the man took tentative steps, his lower limbs seemingly independent. Shadow watched as Collin, grinning sheepishly, clung to a tree for support as he gamely exercised unwilling muscles.

La Salle, tired and aching himself, slowly gathered his weapons and pack. There had been other, similar situations when he had been unable to overcome inertia. But that was not the case this time. Looking over the lake he saw only gray doom hanging above the land of the Illinois. It was this recurring image that most restored his determination.

As Collin and D'Autray went about adjusting their packs, Shadow finished drinking a special brew he had made from young green needles of the white pine—Indian medicine for a sore throat. Slowly he rose to his feet, replaced the cup in his pack, and slung his gear over his shoulder, the pain in his chest increasing from the effort. Again weakened, he sat on a mossy log.

"Aren't you coming?" Collin goaded Shadow. In anguish the Indian had slumped against a tree. He looked at Collin, then at the others, then stiffly stood again and began walking.

"Shadow will come," he intoned monotonously, disinterestedly. The pain in his chest seemed sharp, like a cramp. It had also spread, no longer confined to a single point.

"We will not go far today," La Salle said, watching the men make final adjustments to their loads. He studied Shadow, concerned that his difficulty might reflect more than simple tiredness, but also understanding the Indian would never admit as much. "We will stop in a few hours to rest and eat."

"Eat what?" Collin grumbled at D'Autray. "We haven't got much. Soon it'll be moccasin stew, you'll see." Collin suddenly felt hungry, but satisfied himself with a sip of water.

"Try the inner bark of the pine. Grind acorns, too, but wash the flour—many times," Shadow said. "Red cedar berries, if you can find any, have good oil, but do not eat anything bitter. Indian hunters go many days without food, with only sarsaparilla root to chew on."

Following the Indian's instructions, D'Autray and Collin found several sources of nourishment in the barren surroundings.

Gradually the men walked off their tiredness and apathy. The noticeable wobble in their gait slowly disappeared. Soon the party was again marching at a fair pace.

For some time they traveled through a conifer forest, past pockets of snow, over silent beds of rust-red pine needles. Even though exhausted, they generally resisted the urge to halt, but on coming to a large glade, they decided on an early end for the day. With little preparation and with no evening meal, the men collapsed onto fresh-cut bough mats. One by one they quickly lapsed into a deep sleep where they remained for a solid night's rest.

* * *

"Saget! What is the matter? Why are you not up?" D'Autray shook Shadow. La Salle had risen but Collin was still sluggishly tossing about in his bed. Uncharacteristically, Shadow—habitually the first to arise—lay quiet. D'Autray motioned toward the hot pot on the fire.

"No, no coffee," Shadow stirred as he responded. He rummaged about in his medicine pouch and brought forth some wild cherry bark. Handing the bark to D'Autray, he said, "Here, make a tea from this."

La Salle watched intently as the Indian laboriously rose to take the tea. At first, he drank profusely, the infusion producing a mild sweat. It was obvious the Indian was still experiencing chest pain. And his breathing was shallow. Shadow sat on a fallen log and nursed the last sips of the hot beverage, occasionally holding the warm mug against his chest.

Shadow finished the tea, placed the cup beside him, and said groggily, "I am ready, let us go."

La Salle went over, concerned for his friend. "Are you ill?"

"I ache," the Indian whispered, making an unusual admission. Staring vacantly before him, Shadow tugged at his robe, tapping his chest with his fingertips. Then he lay down again on his cot.

La Salle bent over to feel the man's forehead. "You are running a fever, you should not be hiking today," he observed. With a pang of dismay, La Salle saw the blood that had dripped from Shadow's nose. An icy coldness gripped La Salle as he studied the prostrate form. Shocked with a sudden feeling of helplessness, he realized he had assumed the Indian to be indestructible. La Salle's sense of futility gradually turned to melancholy with the conviction that Shadow was seriously ill.

"Rest, my friend," La Salle said as he placed a reassuring hand on Shadow's shoulder. "I am feeling tired myself. Do you feel you can sit?"

La Salle did not mention the blood. He preferred to encourage the Indian, withholding judgment until he knew more about the seriousness of his condition.

"The tacamahac has leaf buds that do not freeze in winter," Shadow whispered, motioning to the nearby trees. "You will find this tree near running water."

Placing a hand on Shadow's shoulder, La Salle said, "I shall return with your medicine shortly. Is there anything else I should look for?"

"No, the sap that runs in these buds is enough," Shadow replied, breathing slowly and deeply.

La Salle set off into the woods, following several streams, seeking the balsam poplar. As he walked, his frustration mounted. The feeling grew that Montreal had suddenly become more remote, the rescue of the Illinois Indians an unattainable goal. He began to reproach himself: Have we come too far? Have we tried to achieve too much? Is this mission even possible?

An increasing skepticism dragged him inexorably into the dark swamp of doubt. The little recriminations that had bubbled so slightly on the surface in the beginning soon became a whirlpool of dread. Before him swirled all the unfortunate affairs that had plagued his endeavors—the petty court intrigues, the rivalries of the Montreal fur traders, the lurking resentment of the Jesuits, the opposition of his brother, and the attempts on his life. Plodding through the woods, La Salle struggled against a leaden cast, his limbs becoming heavy, reluctant. His spirits low, he felt all was futility—his exploration stymied, his ship overdue, an Indian war on the horizon, and his men—driven to the limits of their endurance—facing annihilation.

Coming upon a balsam poplar, La Salle felt deliverance both for himself and for Shadow. Pulling down a lower branch, he collected a cupful of the resinous buds. With some increased hope he headed back to the camp with this promising medication.

When he peered through the trees, La Salle caught sight of his men and the Indian. The realization that they were dependent upon him snapped at him. Casting off the mantle of despair, he resolved to go on. Feeling shame for his loss of composure, he reassured himself that he had had no other choice: he must follow the path to which he was now committed. He must follow it to the end, whatever end that might be. Someone else might have stopped, might have given up. But somewhere deep within his psyche only one solution blazed: Montreal!

Walking back into the camp, La Salle felt increased confidence. Now determined, his fears receded once more into bad memories. Seeing Shadow near the campfire, La Salle went over to him and handed him the sticky balsam poplar buds.

Shadow quickly made a salve, mixing it with a small amount of bear fat. He pressed this ointment into his nostrils and inhaled, the balsam aroma providing immediate relief for his bronchitis.

"Fort Conti is not far," La Salle spoke encouragingly as Shadow continued inhaling. He hesitated to say more, hoping the Indian would recover enough to resume the trek.

"Let us go," Shadow said, but remained seated.

"I am not sure you should, just yet" La Salle placed a hand on the Indian's shoulder. "We are all tired. We may rest a bit more before going on."

The Indian stood, drew himself up, and started pacing in a circle. As he walked, his tread became firmer.

"I am ready, let us be going." he again insisted.

"All right, then. Let us go on," La Salle replied as Shadow continued walking about. "I can see your medicine tea has helped."

A morning breeze had risen. Gently sweeping the pine tops, it freshened the gray day. La Salle studied the swaying trees. An east wind was rising; he expected another storm. He looked around at the three men. They were completing their preparations for marching, but were taking longer than usual. La Salle sensed that Collin's fever had returned and he was trying to hide that fact.

"Jean, help me build a canoe." La Salle spoke, turning to D'Autray. "These men pretend they can walk, but I doubt they can make three leagues. We must hurry. I fear this will be quite a storm."

As the two began gathering bark, Collin and Shadow assisted as best they could—maintaining the boiling water, preparing hot food, and readying the lashings and pitch.

* * *

The next day the first snows came to Point Pelee as a consistent, wet, wind-driven nuisance. Blowing into the men's clothing, covering the construction, obliterating the shelters, smothering the timid fire. Despite the increasing difficulties, D'Autray and La Salle worked persistently.

In short order the canoe was finished, the voyagers embarked and were once again afloat on Lake Erie. Only two were capable of propelling the

136

canoe. Collin and Shadow, feverish in spite of extra robes, suffered in silence.

"This storm is a blessing," La Salle said, hoping to encourage Collin. "The wind has moved again, giving us a lee shore. We'll have smooth waters as long as the wind lays in the north."

Shadow grunted. La Salle studied the man from his position in the rear of the canoe. It was difficult to determine whether the Indian had indicated acknowledgement or some new physical discomfort.

Under a sullen sky as the canoe continued skirting along the ghostly coast, heavy white snowflakes drove through the gray monotony, clinging to the men's beards, mustaches, and eyebrows, stinging their exposed skin. La Salle's band traveled in this weather for hours at a time, only resting occasionally.

On the second day, La Salle ordered the canoe toward the lakeshore. Nearly two months since departing Fort Crèvecoeur, he saw ahead, on a rise above the sparkling blue water, the welcoming palisade of Fort Conti.

It was Easter Monday, the Fifth of May, 1680. In the afternoon, one of the men at the fort, returning from an errand, was about to enter when he saw four strangers, quite some distance away, disembarking from a canoe on the lake shore. As he studied the newcomers, he noted that three were bearded. One seemed to be half-carrying a tall Indian, who was limping badly. Their gait was weary, their buckskins tattered, and they carried almost no provisions. They had the appearance of shipwreck survivors.

"Armin! DesLoges! We have visitors!" Martin Chartier, a robust woodsman, called to the compound. The other four defenders of Fort Conti came running, stopping just outside the gate, guardedly watching as the distant group slowly picked its way through the brush and fallen trees.

"Who can they be?" Armin wondered aloud. "They seem harmless. Suppose they are *coureurs*? *Coureurs* should be farther north. Maybe *voyageurs*. But, no, *Mes Amis*, they have no trade furs."

Chartier studied the approaching men. "La Salle! It is La Salle himself. I recognize him. And that is his Indian, Shadow. The other two, I am not so sure . . . . Wait! . . . . Yes! That one is my old friend Jean D'Autray!"

Hailing his comrades, Chartier ran down the slope, embraced them excitedly, and began jumping about with exuberant joy.

"Oh, you men do not look so good," Chartier said, after greeting La Salle. Their appearance, their sunken eyes, and the slow, difficult speech shocked him. "What is the matter with the Indian? He is very ill, no?"

"Exhaustion. We are all very tired," La Salle smiled stiffly. "Help us to the fort. We need rest."

"Where have you come from? And why do you travel so early in the season? Were you in that storm yesterday?"

"Later, we'll talk later. We have other important matters to discuss first." La Salle eased Shadow's arm from his shoulder onto that of Desloges and they walked, faltering, to the fort.

Once inside, the weary men slumped onto the primitive bunks. All except La Salle. First he assisted Armin who was tending to Shadow's comfort, then when he saw that Collin and D'Autray were fed and resting, he called the men of Fort Conti to a conference.

"These men are unfit for further travel. I must go on to the settlements. I have supplies and men coming from France—"

"Oh, no!" Armin interrupted. "Your supplies are gone. The ship has been lost . . . caught in a storm . . . off Gaspé."

La Salle was stunned. Molten lead began flowing again through his arms and legs. He looked dully at the speaker, fighting to deny the significance of this announcement. The putrescent jester, Dismal Failure— invisible to the others—sitting across the table from him, howled with mocking, derisive laughter. *Do not quit, do not give up*, La Salle reminded himself, his knuckles whitening as he clamped the table's edge.

Shaking off this miasma of defeat, La Salle focused on the immediate problems. The loss of these supplies could mean a considerable drain on his credit and a probable further setback to his schedule. But he could not tolerate further delays.

Armin paused, then added, "Twenty men came on another boat. They were 'detained' by the Governor. All but three have since returned to France."

"Is there more?" La Salle asked dryly, sensing that Armin was holding something back.

"Your creditors in Montreal are claiming your properties. They have seized Fort Frontenac. It is said you and your enterprise are bankrupt." Armin sighed, finally relieved of his burden.

La Salle hesitated. The muscles in his jaws were working incessantly. After a moment, he too sighed, "All right, so my supplies have been lost at sea, the men I hired have gone, and my assets seized. I still have the *Griffin*." La Salle's face displayed his determination.

No! Collin thought to himself, *La Salle still has not accepted the loss of his ship.* With a grimace, he glanced at D'Autray who nodded understanding. The two convalescents sank deeper into their cots.

Chartier squirmed, uncomfortable at having to convey further disappointment. "I am sorry but *Griffin* has not returned since she sailed ten months ago."

Armin spoke softly, nervously looking around the assembly. "The Jesuits at Point Ignace have seen *Griffin* only once, sailing west to Green Bay."

La Salle stared at Armin. Suddenly he felt extremely tired. "The Jesuits! They should be happy not to see *Griffin* again."

138

All his efforts had come to naught, seemingly there were no avenues of relief available. Unable to penetrate the thick curtain of failure falling across the stage of his destiny, he suddenly recognized the principal actors—his creditors, the bureaucracy—were all fools and buffoons, even less human than the satirical characters of Moliere, witless, arrogant harlequins intent only on their myopic self-interest and pleasure.

Drumming his fingers on the table, La Salle shook off the shades of defeat. Consumed with physical and emotional exhaustion, he struggled to rationally consider his options.

"Tomorrow, in the morning, we depart. I want three of you to come with me; two will remain to nurse these men. I had hoped to spend a day or two here. But I see now I must go quickly. I am afraid, more than ever, that a greater disaster waits on the Illinois. I must repair my finances and bring all possible aid to Tonti and the Indians."

Having decided his agenda, La Salle rose from the table and went over to the recuperating travelers.

"You men are to stay here and rest. I am going on to Fort Frontenac, then to Montreal. In a few weeks, I shall come back and we will return to the Illinois."

Turning to the Indian, he said, "Saget, I am especially sorry to have to leave you. You have served me well. Take care that you may get well. I will soon need your skills and woodsmanship."

"I am not dying," the Indian responded in a dry voice, then coughed, a few glistening drops of blood appearing beneath his nose. "I will wait here until you return. Go to the White Lace. Tell them the Children of Onontio are in great danger. The Great Mountain will help us, I am certain."

"You are brave," La Salle said, placing a hand on the Indian's shoulder. "Rest well. I hope, too, that you are fit by the time of my return. I will see the Governor. How much help he will give us is another question. *Au revoir, Mon Ami,*" La Salle said, and bending over, kissed the Indian on the forehead. Turning, he went to his own cot and lay down.

Russell Breighner

Chapter 8

Fort Heartbreak

Whipping over the bluffs at Fort Crèvecoeur, the April breezes snapped the skirts of the priest's gray cassock. Holding his beret with one hand, Fr. Ribourde stood facing the wind, squinting to watch the activity below.

"It will soon be Easter," Fr. Ribourde said to the Italian next to him.

"Yes, good fighting weather, to be sure."

"I understand our men are becoming edgy. A scout reported the Iroquois war drums have been sounding for some time now."

"LaSalle said that would happen. We shouldn't be concerned," Tonti replied dryly. "He says the Iroquois make war preparations mainly to scare their neighbors. I think some of our hired men feel a bit . . . exposed."

Standing outside the palisade, the two were observing the operation on the riverbank below. Fr. Membré had gone to the Indian town earlier to arrange for a supply of Indian corn and meat.

"We will soon have an adequate larder again," Fr. Ribourde said approvingly.

"Yes, it's been nearly six weeks since La Salle departed," Henri de Tonti said and glanced wistfully at the wind-rippled surface of Lake Peoria. "I think it is time for his return. Surely some trade goods from the *Griffin* would seal our friendship with these people. I expect he is also eager to begin his exploration of the Mississippi."

"Plenty Fish has told me that in another month the weather becomes very warm in the river's lower reaches." Fr. Ribourde winced as another gust pushed against him. "I understand the climate in summer can be most uncomfortable there. Too many mosquitoes and alligators, I hear."

Tonti squinted at a solitary white cloud drifting leisurely across the bright sky. "And how is your work with the Indian conversions coming?"

"It is slow, but there is progress. It takes a certain amount of time to master their language. It is difficult to convey Christian concepts, although the spiritual vitality of the Indians does provide a common base."

"You seem to enjoy the challenge. Can you accept that your work may come to naught?" Tonti raised a quizzical eyebrow toward the priest.

"But of course I enjoy this work—tremendously. It is an extraordinary privilege just to know these people. I hope I may yet live long enough to write about their customs and manners. They are quite admirable," Fr. Ribourde beamed. "But even without converts, one's work never comes to naught."

"I see." Tonti's serious demeanor reflected the sincerity of his own desires. "It will not be easy, but we must do all we can to maintain peace and to bring brotherhood to these people."

"We have a simple concept for that. It is called 'forgiveness.' Their warfare continues endlessly because they do not recognize—do not allow—forgiveness among tribes. Many tribes live in a state of continual war with their neighbors. So long as one brave must avenge the death of a brother, a father, or a friend, there can be no peace. Never has a greater need for the Christian message been more apparent."

"But your progress with conversions is so slow. There are those who claim your effort is futile." Tonti said. Shading eyes with his hand, he peered more intently at the action below.

"We are growing sturdy oaks from small acorns. We do not simply sprinkle water and call the people 'Christian.'" Fr. Ribourde inhaled deeply, enjoying the invigorating fresh air. "We must guard against superficiality and we accept only genuine conversions."

"True, but I have heard of other missionary areas where there has been a return to native practices." Tonti was studying the transport effort below. Several canoes with supplies had come up the river and French workers were already piling food bundles on the grassy shore.

"Yes, sometimes we do suffer disappointment, but in the end, we will succeed." Fr. Ribourde turned toward Tonti and smiled.

"Do you really think the tribes will accept Christian concept of forgiveness in order to form a larger nation?" Tonti looked askance at the priest. "Do you think they see this as needed for their survival?"

"It is difficult to say. If they do not unite, then the destruction of each tribe and nation will occur in turn," Fr. Ribourde said sourly. "The Indians all too readily fight ancient enemies and do not fully recognize the new."

"What does La Salle think of this? Surely he sees more than trade and missionary posts in his plans," Tonti said with some pique.

"I'm sure he does, but Indian unity is not his principal concern. Not yet! He is still animated with the spirit of exploration. Did you know that some years ago he actually sought a route to China through Canada! Now he wishes to discover the mouth of the *Fleuve Colbert*."

"Do you see those men?" Fr. Ribourde directed Tonti's attention inside the compound to three braves intently watching the blacksmith. "It is the warrior code that is a major obstacle to conversion. The warrior seeks power, personal power, the courage and strength to overcome his enemies. Where religion fails to increase his power, he is no longer interested. The warrior sees the 'Praying Indian' as weak.

"It is this absence of brotherly love that is most dangerous for the Indian Nation. While brother fights brother, the trespasser takes their lands." Fr. Ribourde continued with some heat, "In the Massachusetts colony, the English settlers use one tribe against the other in just this way. Already Pequots, Narragansetts, and others have disappeared. Shadow's Mohegans, once an ally of the English, may soon be no more."

"Does La Salle understand this?" Tonti spoke in a half tone, as though speaking more to himself.

"No, he sees the problem of the colonies. He does not think that that malice extends to these lands," Fr. Ribourde insisted. "With English arms and support the Iroquois have so far destroyed the Hurons, exterminated the Eries, and crushed the Neutrals and the Tobaccos—all gone! The Iroquois continue to terrorize all Algonkian tribes."

Tonti looked searchingly into the face of the priest. "And M. La Salle with twenty Frenchmen intends to stop such an army?"

"Plus one Italian," Fr. Ribourde chided.

"Oh, of course, I had forgotten. There is the difference!" Tonti smiled at the sarcasm. "Besides, this is an Italian with only one hand," he said, raising his gloved fist.

"I seem to recall reading something about 'love your neighbor as yourself.' Isn't this soulless assault on our neighbor a disguised form of savagery? Do we not delude ourselves by reserving the label 'savage' for those who must resort to cruder forms of plunder?" Fr. Ribourde observed. "If we use the instruments of society to take our neighbor's goods, his land, and his life—Are we really civilized? Or are we simply exercising an organized form of barbarity?"

"So you are saying abstract ideals can become pagan gods demanding offerings and sacrifice?" Tonti said, cocking his head.

"Perhaps. But I would insist that any general principle that embodies even the least evil means must be questioned as to its real good." Fr. Ribourde crossed his arms against the chill air and began pacing slowly back and forth. "If nothing else, acceptable societal evil encourages the growth of other forms until full-blown corruption results."

Tonti watched the Flemish priest for a moment, then turned his attention to the file of men bringing supplies up the difficult trail.

"The Iroquois hate the French, you know." Fr. Ribourde said as he stopped to watch the approaching men. "French arms have stopped Iroquois raids along the St. Lawrence. The French control the fur trade to the west. To the south there are no furs, only unfriendly Catawbas and Cherokees."

"So the Iroquois are boxed in, so to speak, and the French are part of this barrier?" Tonti turned as he spoke.

"But this is pure nonsense, don't you see?" Fr. Ribourde said with irritation. "It is the argument the Iroquois are concerned with their economic survival based on the fur trade. It suggests the Iroquois are blithely ignorant of the growing threat to their cultural survival in the English colonies. No, I do not credit the Iroquois with stupidity.

"As it happens the Iroquois have an unquenchable love of war. They believe themselves the master race. So it is not at all clear which circumstances they consider obstacles," Fr. Ribourde said, facing Tonti.

Tonti smiled. "I admire the Iroquois. They have a certain spirit, indomitable. They do not color their horizons with the dark palisades of confinement, but with the bright red blood of glory. They are, after all, magnificent fighters."

Satisfied that the orderly efforts below were coming to a successful conclusion, Tonti turned to enter the compound.

Fr. Ribourde followed.

Inside the fort, three intently curious Indians followed every motion of the blacksmith as he worked at his portable forge, making a new hatchet. Pumping the bellows in a steady rhythm, he concentrated on the color of the red-hot metal, gauging the proper temperature by the change to a dull, blood red hue. Satisfied, he hammered the edge to a fine line, reheated the shape and quickly annealed it in a vat of suddenly hissing, popping water.

As the blacksmith withdrew the now iron-gray hatchet head, the youngest brave, Barking Squirrel, a Moingwena, nodded satisfaction as he glanced at his friends.

"This is good. Iron knives, axes, and guns give power to the Indian. We must learn to take the red earth and make weapons, as the French do," Barking Squirrel said, animated by the imagined feel and balance of his new hatchet.

"No! This is not work for an Indian," Crooked Arrow, a Kaskaskian and a veteran of several wars, exclaimed. "Let the French make our weapons.

144

We will give them furs and corn. They will give us strength against our enemies."

"But the French do not respect the harmony of the land. They tear the earth for the red powder. They do not thank the great Manitou for these gifts. We must appease the earth spirits for their offense. Then we may use their iron." Swift Fox, a short and spare Peoria, considered extremely intelligent by his peers, sternly reproached his companions.

Crooked Arrow agreed. "The French have a strong faith. They honor many of the same spirits as we do. But they do not fully understand the spirit world. They do not understand that all things exist together, that Our Grandfather has placed all these things here for our good."

Barking Squirrel studied the blacksmith, fully absorbed in his work. "He does not speak our tongue. He has not heard a thing. It is the same with spirits. They speak and the French do not hear."

A few Frenchmen entered the compound, each carrying food packs to the storage hut. With them was Fr. Membré who paused, panting, at the gate, then came across the yard to join Fr. Ribourde and Tonti.

"Well! We've had a good start to the day. Corn, dried fish, venison, and some buffalo meat." Fr. Membré was pleased with his success. "The villagers were generous as usual."

"I understand the Indians will soon have their corn planting ceremony," Tonti responded, scrutinizing each load as the men came into the enclosure. "Do you deal with one of the chiefs?"

"Oh, no. Nothing like that. The women do all the planting and harvesting. The corn belongs to them. I negotiate through Elizabeth with her mother, Dawn Bird. She has a good sense for barter. She is firm but fair. Dawn Bird treats the corn in the field as if each plant were one of her children. She sings to the spirits in the growing plants to ensure a good harvest."

"Aren't these plant spirits a pagan concept?" Tonti raised an eyebrow toward Fr. Ribourde.

"The Indians have identified several kinds of spirits. By praying to these spirits the Indian is thanking the Creator for the good things He has given us."

"I have heard the Indian frequently referred to as pagan. You make them sound less primitive." Tonti noted the last of the supply loads being carried to the storehouse.

"A pagan idolizes a stone or a tree and believes in the magical power of inanimate objects," Fr. Ribourde said, pulling at his beard. "The Indians have sacred places—stones, mountains, trees—where the spirit world interacts with that of man."

"And have miracles occurred at these sacred places?" Tonti looked quizzically at the priest.

"I do not know that miracles have happened. But to the Indian, these are places where he may go to meditate, to seek spiritual guidance and reinforcement." Fr. Ribourde said, recalling some of the missionary descriptions he had studied in Montreal. "The violation of a sacred place is as great an offense to the Indian as is the violation of a consecrated church to the Christian."

"I am always happy to learn more of the Indian customs," Tonti replied. "I hope to master their language so I may discuss these matters directly. The Illinois are a pleasant and peaceful people. I should enjoy living among them."

"You are not at all like La Salle. He is restless, while you wish to put down roots." Fr. Ribourde smiled to himself.

"All of us, sooner or later, tire of travel and adventure. There is much to be said for the pacific life."

"There is a more serious matter you should attend to," Fr. Membré broke in, still panting. "Some of our men are becoming lax in their morals."

"What are you saying?" Tonti snapped his eyes toward the newcomer.

"It seems one or two are, well, 'pursuing' some local women. The Illinois have a strong code on adultery. They are especially hard on unfaithful wives. An embarrassing incident would not help our cause, nor would it forward La Salle's."

"The women will be punished?" Tonti asked, sizing up the workers as he spoke.

"Yes. According to custom, they may be severely beaten, or worse." Fr. Membré said.

"And which of the men are guilty? Do you know?" Tonti demanded, his anger growing. He knew the men needed female companionship, but he expected them to act with moral integrity and respect.

"No, the Indians will not say. Nevertheless we may need to make amends to satisfy Indian justice." Fr. Ribourde's solemn reserve reflected his sense of the severity of the situation.

"We must satisfy our own justice," Tonti said, glaring at the men busy in the courtyard.

"All right, you men," he called out. "Gather round. We need to talk."

Slowly the men assembled near the smithy. Several expressed casual disinterest, anticipating another lecture on proper conduct. La Salle and Tonti continuously reminded the men to respect the Indian customs and to behave in a 'gentlemanly' fashion. For a few, especially Duplessis and his friends, this nonsense remained within the compound.

"There is a report that Frenchmen are having affairs with Indian wives. These women will be beaten for their infidelity. The Indians are also seeking justice for the guilty men. Step forward now! Otherwise it will be much harder for you later, I promise."

Tonti's eyes flashed as he paced back and forth. The men were haphazardly arranged in three rows. Tonti studied each face intently. A few blinked, some looked away, several seemed indifferent.

"We are strangers in this land. The Indians have been hospitable, indeed generous. Do not wreck our efforts here to satisfy your base desires." Tonti paused, hoping for some show of responsibility, or at least understanding, from these woodsmen and laborers.

Someone farted loudly, prompting an unguarded snicker. But the latter quickly recovered a more serious expression. A few, turning in the direction of the outburst, fought to restrain impulsive grins.

Pursing his lips in disgust, Tonti continued, "It is only because you are French the Indians have not acted."

Nika came into the compound. Seeing the assembly, he quickly surmised that a subject of import was being discussed. He sauntered over to join the three Illinois Indians who were observing Tonti's parade.

"Ha! It is not my skin that saves me. It's my brains," Duplessis muttered, leering at Martin standing beside him. "Those Indians aren't smart enough for a sly dog as me."

Grinning, Martin looked toward Tonti who was at the other end of the formation.

Nika, having overheard Duplessis, turned toward him, looking him hard in the face.

Duplessis raised his gaze in feigned tedium.

Catching the silent exchange, Crooked Arrow memorized Duplessis' features. Although his understanding of the French discussion had been spotty, he knew the Shawnee had identified the adulterer.

"If you do not come forward, we shall leave your punishment to the Indians. I have no choice," Tonti said, hoping this threat would bring forth the culprit.

After a continuing period of pretended ignorance by the men, Tonti concluded. "All right. You will all lose privileges until the matter is settled. Except for those on hunts, all French must be in the stockade by dusk. There will be no more 'social evenings.'"

"Lovely!" Duplessis grinned to himself, his eyes narrow slits through which he followed Tonti's pacing. "We've built this fort. We've done as much as can be for La Salle's boat. We have nothing to do but sit on our hands! Might as well be in prison. There's no adventure here. That's for sure."

As Tonti had again passed beyond earshot, Duplessis whispered triumphantly to Martin, "Just watch this old dog skinny over the fence. You'll see. This is no place for me at night. Excepting your ugly puss, I'd rather be elsewhere, thank you very much. If'n you know what I mean." Duplessis ended with a certain emphasis.

"Suppose I go with you?" Martin raised his eyebrows, grinning broadly, distracted to the point of forgetting Tonti's presence.

"Any man caught in adultery will receive twenty lashes. Behave like gentlemen. All of you! Now return to your tasks," Tonti regretfully added this final admonition, his anger not abated.

"Français!" Barking Squirrel yelled. Standing near the gate, he was pointing north, toward a speck on Lake Pimitou.

"A canoe!" Fr. Ribourde exclaimed, running to the gate, shielding his eyes against the sun. "Two men! I see one canoe with two men. How do you know they are French?"

"They wear the hats and the beards," Barking Squirrel replied. "They do not have—how do the French say it? —Graceful motion. They paddle with too much muscle."

"I see," Fr. Ribourde said, grinning at the ambiguous answer. Nevertheless, he saw that the men were making a determined effort.

Tonti had joined the onlookers. "Is it La Salle? Can you tell who they are?" He strained to identify the canoeists.

"No, it is not your chief," Barking Squirrel answered. "I know him. These two I have not seen before."

"Then bad news approaches," Tonti grimly assessed the import of the swift messengers. "Let us go down to meet them. We may have serious affairs to attend to."

A file of men stretched out along the trail down the ravine to the landing as Tonti, the priests, Nika, the Illinois, and several French rushed to the landing.

On the opposite shore, several curious braves had gathered, intent on La Salle's return with the promised weapons.

Approaching the shore, Chapelle ceased paddling. Waving his hat, he yelled "Hallos" to those waiting to meet him. As the canoe touched the embankment, outstretched hands steadied the boat while he and LeBlanc jumped ashore.

The Indians on the far shore, disappointed that La Salle had not returned, began to disperse.

Tonti, recognizing the canoeists as the men he had last seen some six months before, at Fort Saint Joseph, pushed through the onlookers and approached the messengers.

"What news? Where is La Salle?" Tonti asked, expecting bad news. "Will he be coming soon with supplies?"

"N-n-no, Sir! *Griffin* has not arrived at Fort Saint Joseph. M. La Salle has gone on to Montreal. He will bring men and weapons. But much later. He sends you this letter, S-s-signore Tonti." Chapelle opened an oilskin package and handed the sealed page to Tonti.

Tonti eagerly took the document, opened it, and scanned the brief note. "All right," he announced, "we have work to do!

"M. La Salle is not returning soon. He orders us to build a fort near the Illinois summer town. I will go there immediately to survey the site."

Pausing, Tonti surveyed the expressionless, bearded faces around him. "I remind you that you are to be on your best behavior with the local Indians. All bad example on your part weakens and destroys the good relations between them and France. All immorality will be punished. You are civilized men. Do not let your selfish interests interfere with the interests of your king. I shall return in a few days."

He looked to the priests, hoping that the queasy foreboding he felt was not apparent.

Fr. Ribourde stood there, robust and healthy in the early sunlight. He, too, exhibited no external uncertainty, but his unusually stolid demeanor conveyed apprehension.

"Very well, then," Tonti resumed, resigned to the circumstances. "I am on my way." Commanding Boisrondet and Renault to accompany him, he marched to the fort to gather the few necessities for the short trip.

Barking Squirrel turned to Nika. "How is it that the words of La Salle speak from this paper?"

"It is called 'writing' by the French," Nika's eyes twinkled.

"I do not understand how the paper speaks," Barking Squirrel explained as Crooked Arrow, Swift Fox, and Sleeping Crow crowded Nika.

"I will make words come from the paper," Nika said.

"Fr. Ribourde. Do you have paper that I may demonstrate writing for our friends?"

"Why, of course, Nika." The priest pulled a folded sheet of parchment from his breviary. "Write on this and I will read your message."

Nika drew Crooked Arrow some distance from the others. "Tell me something about yourself that no one here knows."

"My brother, Sleeping Crow, lives with his wife's family in the Tamaroa village. She is expecting a child before the corn ripens." Crooked Arrow spoke solemnly.

"Good!" Nika used a piece of charcoal to scribble a short line on the paper, then with Crooked Arrow walked back to the others and gave the note to the priest.

As Fr. Ribourde intoned the announcement, the Indians gaped in amazement as Crooked Arrow affirmed its accuracy.

Swift Fox placed both hands over his mouth. "This cannot be!" he exclaimed.

Glaring at the priest, Sleeping Crow snatched the paper. "It is evil, this paper. It must be destroyed!" Angrily, he ripped the paper and threw it to the ground. "There will be no more 'writing.' Now I know the Gray Robes. Only evil spirits speak from 'writing.'"

Angrily, Sleeping Crow turned and stomped off. Crooked Arrow followed. After a short distance, they met Duplessis and stopped.

Facing the Frenchman, Crooked Arrow glared at him. Duplessis stared back. At length, Crooked Arrow slowly signed a knife across the throat.

The other Indians began to understand. They too became noticeably indignant and began to press in.

Undaunted, Duplessis, eyes burning with haughty pride, began to taunt his audience. "You backwoods heathens! Do you think you have a moral code? Ha! I'll show you mine. It's in my pants." Thrusting his pelvis forward, he motioned toward his groin.

"What is going on here?" Fr. Ribourde, catching sight of the scene, pushed his way through the cluster. Controlling his anger, he reproached Duplessis, "Do not antagonize our friends. If you have some cause for complaint, let me act as your agent. If not, please leave these people in peace. They have shown us every hospitality. They have not earned your disrespect."

Under the force of the priest's reproach, Duplessis became confused then thought better of further banter, at least while Fr. Ribourde was present.

Several of the Indians tempered their own anger on seeing the priest upbraid Duplessis for his rude behavior.

Only Crooked Arrow continued his hard, implacable staring. He was certain of Duplessis' involvement, and—just as certain—he was determined to see justice.

Duplessis did not wilt under Crooked Arrow's implacable glower, yet he understood the man's purpose.

Placing his hand gently on the Indian's shoulder, Fr. Ribourde stood for a moment, considering Duplessis. The old man was about to speak when Crooked Arrow turned briefly toward him, then abruptly signaled his companions.

In great indignation, the three Indians went to their canoe and crossed the river. Only young Barking Squirrel looked back, intrigued and a little puzzled by the day's experience.

Duplessis, too, left, strolling over to a nearby cluster of workers.

"Well, well, Nika. I am indeed surprised. I did not know you could write," Fr. Ribourde said, watching the canoe.

"Robért taught me. Not much. But enough," Nika said, still concerned with the conflict between Duplessis and Crooked Arrow.

Together they walked to the French still discussing La Salle's message.

". . . And that is not all." Chapelle was speaking. "The ship has been lost. *Griffin* is gone. Probably sunk. La Salle's walking to Montreal. W-w-won't be back for a long time. No pay for us either. He owes us all back pay. And just when are we going to see that?"

"As I expected. Not a bloody *sou*." Duplessis spat on the ground, his narrow face working under some inner tension. "Just wait. Won't none of us make a feather on this venture. I'm for going back to trapping. Up north. Who's for it?"

Fr. Ribourde intervened. "Surely you men are due your fair wages. Do not give up on M. La Salle. He will return. You will be paid. Please be patient. Remember he promised to give you a fair release. If you leave now, without his permission, you will all be considered criminals in Montreal."

A few men murmured under their breath. Fr. Ribourde could not catch their words, but sensed their resentment.

Meanwhile Tonti, Renault, and Boisrondet returned from the fort. The *voyageurs* Messier and Laurant had joined the expedition.

"Fr. Ribourde, I trust you and Fr. Membré will keep these men in hand. We must have no more trouble with our neighbors," Tonti affirmed as his men prepared a canoe.

"The men have become restless," the priest said. "They need work to occupy their idle time."

"We will have plenty enough work in a few days. But we must also impose a stricter discipline." Tonti glanced toward the other workmen ascending the path to Fort Crèvecoeur.

"I am afraid our messengers have more bad news than reported to you. Chapelle has told the men the grimmest version of M. La Salle's fortunes," Fr. Ribourde said and relayed the further details.

"We should not be away longer than four or five days. I want to see exactly what will be needed for constructing the fort," Tonti said grimly. He noticed the others were already in the canoe and waiting. He turned back to the priest, clasped his hand, and said, "Remind the men La Salle's misfortunes are not as great as they seem. The men will be paid when they return to the settlements. I am certain of it. Do your best to maintain peace."

Fr. Ribourde watched as the canoe, gliding on the quiet waters near the shore, headed north. He then slowly climbed the trail to the fort. At the precipice, he looked once more at Lake Pimitou. The canoeists were out of sight.

The sun was setting, and the wind had shifted around to the east. Expecting rain, Fr. Ribourde decided to retire to the cabin he shared with the other priest. As he entered the compound, he noticed that the assembled woodcutters, carpenters, and the blacksmith were involved in a heated argument. Duplessis seemed to be leading the discussion.

"It's useless!" Duplessis was saying. "We shall never be paid. It is one excuse after another. We shall never see this *Fleuve Colbert*, either. The Iroquois will be gorged with French soup before La Salle returns."

Fr. Membré was just coming out of the priests' cabin when he noticed Ribourde. The two immediately sized up the situation and marched over to quell the brewing discontent.

"Why should you care about your pay now? There is nothing here to spend it on," the older priest barked as he approached.

"Both Tonti and La Salle have guaranteed you will receive your wages when you return to Montreal," Fr. Membré spoke slowly, holding onto his words.

The old priest shivered. Pulling at his jacket, he felt an increasing chill in the air. It wouldn't be long before the first raindrops, and he had wanted to gather firewood before dark.

"We agreed to explore the *Fleuve Colbert*," Duplessis insisted. "Instead we are holed up, treated like prisoners. We have nothing to do, nowhere to go. And these ignorant Indians, they don't know the first thing about having a good time."

Fr. Membré attempted to reason with the men, "When you hired on for this expedition—"

"Do not remind me of what I hired on to do," Duplessis cut in. "I have—we have—all given our fair share of work. What do you say *Mes Amis?* Are we being treated fairly? Or not?"

Several grumbled, a few restlessly shifting from one foot to the other, but none directly answered the priests.

"You will have to wait a bit longer," Fr. Membré countered.

"Nonsense! We are tired of waiting," Duplessis burst forth, pushing hard against the man.

Fr. Membré stumbled backward, and fell, striking his head against the base of the portable forge.

"Hey! That is no way to treat a priest," Martin cried, staring wild-eyed at Duplessis. "Are you mad?"

"Come on, men!" Duplessis yelled excitedly. "Let's take our wages in trade. Help yourselves to the tools and equipment. They're worth more than a *sou* in Montreal!"

Energized, the men began running around the compound, seizing items of value, destroying others. Several ransacked the storehouse.

Fr. Ribourde helped Fr. Membré to his feet. The man had a gash behind the ear. It was bleeding profusely.

As Ribourde pressed a cloth on the wound, Duplessis faced the priests and snarled, "We are leaving. Now there will be no more broken promises. We will collect more of our wages at Fort Saint Joseph."

"God have mercy on you all," Fr. Membré said. Straightening, he looked with pity at the rampaging workers.

"We do not need your mercy!" Duplessis grabbed a board from one of the huts. Taking a cold charcoal from the forge, he scribbled *Nous sommes tous savages.*

"There!" he said. "Show this to M. Tonti, *le Priss.*"

"U," Fr. Ribourde said, without emphasis.

"What?" Duplessis frowned.

"'U.' *'Sauvage'* is spelled with a 'u'," the priest muttered. He was now supporting Fr. Membré by the shoulders.

"Well, la de da, Smartass. How's this?" Duplessis corrected the sign and flung it, striking the older priest's leg.

"Good for you, Duplessis!" someone roared. "That'll teach him to mind his own business."

Duplessis looked at the priest, puzzled by his lack of reaction. "Do you have no fear?"

"Those who fear God truly have nothing to fear," the priest replied, gritting against the pain in his shin. The old priest looked toward Duplessis, wondering if he understood the irony in his response. "Only those who oppose their own conscience have any need of fear."

"Let's go. C'mon!" Duplessis turned away, watching as the deserters, loaded with food, arms, and tools, filed through the gate.

Immensely satisfied with his coup, Duplessis ran to the head of the column and announced, "Follow me. I know where we may 'borrow' some canoes. We have more work—at Fort Saint Joseph!"

As darkness settled over the stockade, Fr. Ribourde noted the first wet drops beginning to fall. Using torches, the two priests began to survey the damage. Most of the living quarters had been destroyed—doors removed, window frames and fireplace mantels burned, roofs breached. What equipment could not be taken had been strewn about.

The two priests returned to their cabin just as the rain began in earnest. "At least we are not lacking in firewood," Fr. Ribourde suggested, pointing to the smashed furniture. Fr. Membré stretched out on his bedding, still holding a compress to his wound. Fr. Ribourde started a fire, then began repairing the cabin. "I am truly sorry this had to happen," he said.

"True, true. But maybe we are better off without such help. I saw this coming. Duplessis, for example, was never trustworthy. Tell him two words, hear three lies." Fr. Membré lay back, looking up at the fresh holes in the ceiling.

"He may be correct on one point, though. 'We are all savages!' he says. There is an element of truth in that." Fr. Ribourde said. "Would to heaven that were not so."

"Which would you rather have? A world full of saints? Or sinners?"

Fr. Ribourde looked at the young priest, but did not respond.

* * *

Four days later, Tonti returned. Walking slowly around the desolate Fort Crèvecoeur, he examined each item destroyed. Besides the two priests, four workmen remained. Much of the worst damage to the buildings had been repaired, if only through makeshift means.

"What has kept you alive?" Tonti asked as he absorbed the history of mutiny.

"The Indians brought us buffalo meat and corn," Fr. Ribourde replied. "We have no tools except for a few hatchets and knives, and the portable forge."

Grimly Tonti heard the priests' report. "It grieves me that you have been treated so poorly. I had underestimated these men. I did not expect a rebellion."

Tonti shook his head and sat down. After he studied the floor for a moment, he announced, "Well then, here we are. This is all that remains of M. La Salle's enterprise. We have so little to offer. But tomorrow—tomorrow, we begin again!"

Chapter 9

Iron Hand

"Magnificent!" Henri de Tonti beamed, sweeping an arm broadly across the panorama before him, encouraging his colleagues to share his delight in the grandeur of the Illinois River valley. Having just arrived with his men from Fort Crèvecoeur, Tonti had insisted on rushing them to the top of the chimney rock. Rising abruptly from the water's edge, the promontory yielded an excellent view, the high plateau of Starved Rock standing one hundred and twenty five feet above the river. Tonti inhaled deeply the pleasant summer aromas gently rising from the forest canopy.

Looking to the east, Tonti marveled at the silvery surface of the broad river; across the valley, Buffalo Ridge marked the far boundary of Kaskaskia. Between the river and the ridge, some seven hundred lodges nestled among the trees. Many of the inhabitants could be seen going about their daily affairs, several variously occupied on Plum Island, slightly down river from Tonti's observation point.

"This town has no palisades for defense—its inhabitants appear too confident of their safety," Tonti wondered aloud. "They have known for a year the Iroquois may attack, yet they have not fortified their position."

155

"Perhaps they have become too dependent upon the French. There may be as many as ten thousand souls there, but it is much like their winter village—they have no fear of attack, they have lived in peace for a long time." Fr. Membré replied.

"For now that is true. The upper river is empty. But soon it will be crowded with Iroquois," Nika said calmly, but pointedly, looking all the while toward the east, as if expecting momentarily the appearance of enemy war canoes. Turning to the priest, he said, "The reason the Illinois people have not fortified their town is that would be a sign of weakness. They are showing they do not fear the Iroquois; they do not fear death."

Tonti reflected for a moment, then remembering his commission, said, "Of course. But we must do what we can. We must build our fort." Eyeing the nearly flat summit, he began pacing off the periphery, carefully skirting the few trees on the summit.

"Yes," he said as he finished. "There's space enough here for a storehouse, several huts, and a palisade."

"This fort would appear impregnable," Fr. Membré said, peering over the precipice. He dropped a small stone over the side, timing its fall to the river below.

"And so it shall be. But it is the fleur-de-lis that will provide the greatest protection," Tonti said, walking over to the priest's side. "How are you with an axe? Since we are now rather short-handed, can you priests help with the work?"

"But of course!" Fr. Ribourde roared from some twenty paces away. He was standing under a sweetgum tree, one of the few trees growing atop the rock. He ambled over to Tonti. "I enjoy a good day's labor. What trees do you want felled?"

"Those down there," Tonti pointed. "We need a clear field around the base of the rock. A few armed men below protected by fire from above can control the river. This is an ideal location."

Within a few days the small team had built a rudimentary enclosure, wooden stairs and ladders to ease the climb to the top, and inside the fort, two mat dwellings. In one of the huts, the two priests slept apart while in the other lived Tonti, Nika, L'Esperance, Renault, and Boisrondet. Occasional visitors from the town came to observe the progress being made. A few were amused by the French habit of building forts in high, seemingly out of the way places.

* * *

Late one summer afternoon, Tonti returned from the town and announced, "Indians report an Iroquois war party is on the move. A large force has been sighted south of Lake Erie."

"And what news of La Salle? He has been gone nearly six months. Has anyone seen him? Are there any reports of his whereabouts?" Fr. Membré fidgeted with his rosary.

"Not a word," Tonti said with some disgust. "Some local braves suspect he never intended to return. I was treated very rudely this morning; they insist the desertion of our workmen is another sign the French mean to betray them. If La Salle does not soon appear, we may have more reason to fear the Illinois than the Iroquois."

"If help does not come, can these people fight the Iroquois?" Fr. Ribourde asked.

"I believe the Illinois could raise perhaps 1,200 warriors." Tonti said gazing along the expansive river. "But they have no guns."

"Without guns, do they have a hope of defeating the Iroquois?" The old priest looked with wonder at the town on the far shore.

"Say your prayers, Father. We will need every assistance, and that in a very short time." Tonti said joylessly.

Fr. Ribourde jerked around with a sudden realization. "Nika has gone to find La Salle. He is somewhere on the upper Illinois by now. If there is a war party in the area, he may be in trouble."

Tonti winced, but did not respond. Four men and two priests—all that remained after a year's endeavor—could be swallowed by this indifferent wilderness without trace. The clouds of war, he thought, like a bad storm, were forming in the east.

* * *

Days later, on a warm afternoon in early September, a lookout spotted a canoe with a single occupant coming hurriedly down river. "It's a Shawnee," the man cried out. "It's Nika!"

The sentinel alerted the fort. Tonti, the priests, and a few others descended quickly to the river. As they came to the waterside, they saw Nika working the canoe toward a landing.

"Iroquois canoes. I count 500 braves. Many Miami warriors, also, are with them," Nika shouted in French.

"How much time?" Tonti had become grave. He clenched his fist, the muscles in his jaws working continually. "And you saw no sign of La Salle? No sign at all?"

Nika looked at Tonti, but said nothing. Tonti saw the bitterness in his eyes and did not press the issue.

"How long? For God's sake, man, how much time do we have?" Renault burst out. He had his knife in his hand.

Nika looked at the man and smirked, "Time? What do you mean? Time doesn't matter now. We are all dead. Do you not understand?" For Nika, it was not a question of defeatism or fatalism, it was simple judgment. Death in combat was in fact something he had expected since boyhood. He had

had a vision dream, long ago, foretelling his death by tomahawk. He stood ready to meet his ineluctable fate.

Now, at last, he would have an opportunity to avenge the deaths of his parents.

"No, this is not true," Tonti insisted. "We are not helpless. We will meet this threat. Let us find Chief Chassagoac. We will organize a defense."

Tonti and Nika canoed across the river to the town. Alarm was already spreading. Runners were coursing the area. Some warriors were preparing their weapons. A few scouts went up the river to follow-up on Nika's report. Although the day was drawing toward evening, cooking fires were extinguished; men began fasting as they prepared for battle.

Tonti and Nika made their way through the town, seeking the principal chief. As they went, Nika spoke with several Indians, finding the level of alarm had increased steadily. Many people were trying to find their relatives and some were offering their help. Food parcels were prepared for the old, women, and children, who were being organized for evacuation.

Angry warriors confronted Tonti and Nika, sometimes grabbing them roughly. "It is true, Frenchman, La Salle has betrayed the Illinois. He is not coming. He is a spy for the Iroquois. You lied to us." The two, suddenly prisoners of an angry mob, were brought back to the riverside.

Thousands of evacuees emerged from the town and from the woods. Some readied their canoes while others were already afloat.

Elizabeth and her mother, Dawn Bird, with Milkweed, and other children came through the jostling throng. She looked at Nika, then Tonti, but did not speak. Tonti, seeing the fear on her face, could offer no comfort, the commotion around him drowning all sanity. He watched as the women and children silently got into their canoe and joined the haphazard flotilla on its twilight journey to far safety.

Tonti watched helplessly as several Indians brought the portable forge from the town and, in a spiteful rage, heaved it into the river. It was the one item of significance that the French mutineers had neglected. Tonti had had it brought to the Indian town as a last symbol of French support.

Increasing anger was directed toward the erstwhile allies. Tomahawks and knives waved menacingly. Demands for French scalps were heard. Across the river, the priests and workmen scampered for refuge in the aerie fort.

Even when jostled, Nika stood quietly, ignoring the rude treatment, his thoughts focused on the coming conflict. He expected to die, but in combat with his sworn enemy, Limping Wolf. He did not find much dignity nor glory in dying a prisoner at the hands of his ally, the Illinois.

In response to a messenger, the Indians hustled Tonti and Nika back to the center of the town. There, near the council fire stood the chiefs, Nicanope and his brother Chassagoac. Seeming confusion reigned as warriors raced about on various errands. Some men had already shorn their hair in the fashion for war; others were decorated in war paint with the symbols of their personal medicine. On their faces and bodies were drawn the totems of their courage, their invincibility, their humanity.

The council drum's insistent chant, inviting braves to the war dance around the blazing fire, imposed its own order into the chaos. Gradually, the drum's call brought organization as more and more braves joined in the ritual, prepared to fulfill the supreme purpose of their manhood.

Squatting nearby, an old man, who had refused to leave, sang his death song, satisfied he had had a good life. Throughout the night, the Illinois warriors sharpened their weapons and their courage. The Confederacy tribes were already represented: the Tamaroa, the Cahokian, Kaskaskian, Illinois, Michigamea, Peorias, and the Moingwena; other tribes would join soon—runners had gone out to allied villages and towns, to the Weas, Piankashaws, Miamis, and Vermillions.

Toward noon on the following day scouts returned with further reports. The Iroquois leader had been spotted. He was wearing a black hat and a dark coat—surely a French Black robe! Again, angry braves confronted Tonti and Nika, demanding their blood.

"No! No! No!" Tonti insisted. "La Salle would never side with the Iroquois! Let me speak with Chassagoac."

Pushing through the knot of warriors, Chief Chassagoac confronted Tonti. The chief, full of anger, ignored the Italian's protestations.

Tonti, however, continued to protest, "The hat and coat are not Jesuit. That man is not a Black Robe. The Iroquois have stolen French clothing."

Angry hands grabbed at Tonti, pulling him around, but he continued his struggle to be heard.

Finally, black anger clouding his face, Chassagoac motioned for quiet. "Speak!" he commanded. "What do you have to say to me?"

"I promise you, M. La Salle would not go back on his word. The Illinois are as precious to him as children to a father. He will not abandon you. There is some reason for his delay." Tonti spoke with hopeless desperation.

Chassagoac surveyed his council. Most remained skeptical.

"I will prove La Salle's faith. My men and I will fight alongside the Illinois. You will have French allies," Tonti continued to insist. "This I know for certain—our great father in Montreal considers the Illinois his special friends."

"Bring your men from the fort. We have weapons for them." Chassagoac ordered.

The French offer to participate in the defense of the town dampened the ire of the more moderate, but Crooked Arrow and others refused to be mollified.

"The Shawnee remains hostage. He is La Salle's agent. If things are not as you claim, he is the first to die." Chassagoac signaled and Barking Squirrel and Sleeping Crow bound Nika securely to a tree.

Frustrated at the loss of an opportunity for vengeance, Nika nevertheless accepted his status as hostage.

Tonti looked at Nika, but said nothing, for he had heard that Limping Wolf was one of the war leaders of the Iroquois band. Tonti was satisfied there could be no negotiation, no peace were Nika present on the field.

Distant gunfire erupted, the sound of muskets echoed among the trees. A few Iroquois warriors had appeared on the north bluffs, firing toward the town. From the sounds of the shooting, Chassagoac surmised that the few Illinois scouts there were slowly falling back.

Tonti pleaded with the chief, "Let me negotiate. We can avoid a fight. This war is not necessary. Let me present the French position. The Iroquois chiefs must be told France will defend the Illinois Nation."

Tonti hoped the attackers were unaware of the French presence and allegiance with the Illinois. If so, he felt he had a chance to avert the conflict. It was only a slim chance; Tonti understood full well that it was his only chance.

For some time, the council debated the circumstances, listening attentively as many warriors expressed a sense of betrayal, a distrust of the French. Chassagoac considered the arguments. After reflection, he said to Tonti, "Take the calumet. Talk with the Iroquois. We shall not war while you are in council with them."

Chassagoac looked around the circle of assembled chiefs, engaging each in turn. None offered objection. He then presented Tonti with the ceremonial pipe, bedecked with the colored feathers and symbols of good faith and fortune, and said, "Go! Bring us peace. If you can."

* * *

"Fr. Membré, come with me," Tonti called to the priest. "We are to be a peace embassy to the Iroquois."

From the crowd, the Flemish priest came slowly forward, uncertain of the peace prospects. Together he and the Italian began marching grimly toward the Iroquois camp.

"You have not yet learned to speak the Indian language," Fr. Membré said as they walked. "How do you expect to convince the Iroquois of peace?"

Holding high the calumet, Tonti anxiously surveyed the enemy ahead. "No, I don't speak the Indian language—Look, they see us. They are allowing us to advance, no shooting—I hope there is an Indian, perhaps a prisoner, who understands French."

"You hope!" Fr. Membré ejaculated. "Here we are marching to the very gates of Hell and all you have is a hope someone there speaks French!" Fr. Membré shook his head. "Suddenly, I have this great urge to piss!"

"Should you use such vulgarity?" Tonti glanced defensively at the priest.

"It does not matter, neither the language nor the action would do much to express how I feel at this moment," the priest replied dryly.

"Besides, what choice do we have? If we do nothing, the Illinois will skin us." Tonti laughed hollowly.

The Fleming looked at Tonti in amazement. "Are all Italians as crazy as you?"

"No, there are no others, I assure you, I am the only one." Tonti half-smiled at the suggestion. In spite of the banter, Tonti kept his narrowed eyes fixed firmly on the howling crowd before them.

Occasional bullets zinged overhead, arrows whizzed through the air, some striking the ground in front of them.

"They are only testing us," Tonti reassured the priest.

"You know that asking an Iroquois war party to talk peace is as futile as asking the devil to pray," Fr. Membré said, feeling entirely out of place, walking across an open field between two armies bent on war.

"Very well, then, if we must, today, we shall teach the devil to pray," Tonti said, smiling unconvincingly.

"The Illinois are brothers of the French," Tonti yelled to the Iroquois. "They are protected by Onontio, our father in Canada."

On hearing the Mohawk name for the Canadian Governor, Limping Wolf became instantly angry. The French aegis stood as frustration to his ambition for battle glory; it must be removed. He fired his musket, aiming just above Tonti's head.

A warrior wearing the hair roach and symbols of the Onandaga ran forward howling his war cry. He rushed at Tonti and instantly stabbed him in the ribs.

Immediately Tonti smashed his left, gloved hand against the man's skull. The Indian, the side of his face a bloody pulp, went tumbling backward, limp as a mannequin. Collapsing onto a knee from his own pain, Tonti watched the man writhing in the grass, moaning in agony.

A second Indian, a Cayuga, ran up and grabbed Tonti's hair, jerking him to his feet. In a single motion, Tonti rose, spinning around while raising his metal hand. With great force he continued the action, thudding his hand against the assailant's skull, the Indian's knees buckling as he too collapsed in a heap.

Bending over to ease the sharp pain in his side, Tonti ran his fingers over his blouse, feeling the fresh blood oozing from his wound. Slowly, deliberately, he rose to his feet, angrily surveying the yelling, gesturing Indians. Defiantly he drew his blood-dripped finger across his forehead, making three crimson lines, beneath each eye a vertical mark. Wincing with pain, he drew his knife and in spite of his agony, pointed it toward those before him, yelling in Sicilian, "Come on, you devils, it is time to pray!"

Abruptly, Moves-the-Clouds, a Seneca chief, pushed through the crowding warriors and shouted, "Stop!" He looked around, asserting his authority, then commanded, "Do not harm this man! His ears are not pierced. He is not Illinois!"

"Frenchman!" he snapped, addressing Tonti. "You wear the beads and clothes of the Illinois people. But we see you are French; we do not war on the French!"

Tonti's anger waned as he understood the general sense of the chief's actions. Glancing to one side, Tonti saw several braves rudely handling Father Membré. Still clutching the calumet, the priest struggled to remain with Tonti but was nevertheless forced to return to the Illinois. Tonti instantly concluded the release of the priest was a signal that his own fate was sealed, the chief's intervention merely a ruse.

At that moment, Swims-like-Beaver, another Seneca, and Limping Wolf rushed up to Tonti, pinning his arms and tying them behind his back. They were about to drag him off to torture when Moves-the-Clouds again prevailed.

"This man is French! *To-do-dä'-ho* has ordered us not to harm the French!"

Acknowledging the injunction of Tangled, the Iroquois chief sachem, the two reluctantly released their prisoner, Swims-like-Beaver giving Tonti a final, angry shove. Snarling warriors angrily shook their weapons, yelling nevertheless for Tonti's life. With much effort, Moves-the-Clouds regained control, calling for someone to come forward and apply a plaster to Tonti's wound.

In the midst of the mob, Tonti was not visible to the watching Illinois. Limping Wolf, realizing this, hoisted Tonti's skin hat on the end of his musket. The Illinois, understanding this as a sign that Tonti was dead, immediately resumed their battle positions and began scattered shooting.

Sporadic firing erupted from both sides and began to intensify.

Tonti was kneeling on the ground, his hands still bound. There was an angry discussion in progress, his fate still undecided.

Limping Wolf repeatedly pulled at Tonti's hair, ready to scalp him on the slightest pretext, as the vehement debate continued.

A Mohawk of the Deer clan, naked except for moccasins and war paint, came running to report seeing several French among the Illinois. Understanding the general content of the report, Tonti yelled out, "French! There are sixty armed French with the Illinois."

Yellow Snake, kicking dirt at Tonti, snarled, "Burn him! He lies! Burn him!"

"The Illinois have over a thousand warriors. La Salle has armed them. You cannot defeat them," Tonti responded, pleased his words were having an effect.

"We have seen! The Illinois have no guns!" Yellow Snake growled, kicking more dirt in Tonti's face.

"La Salle is not here." Intensely angry, Limping Wolf pressed his knife against Tonti's throat. "It is time for the Illinois to die. You die too. All die!"

"No! La Salle is a friend. Untie the prisoner." Moves-the-Clouds came forward and stood by Tonti. To Tonti he said, "Go quickly. We send you back to the Illinois."

Throwing hate-filled looks at Tonti, Limping Wolf, followed by other angry warriors, stalked off.

Moves-the-Clouds placed a bead necklace over Tonti's head. "This gift shows the Iroquois are also the children of Onontio, our father in Canada. Go, make peace for us and the Illinois."

Tonti, still bleeding from the wound in his side, stumbled toward the Illinois. As he walked, he tried to fathom the sincerity of the Iroquois. He felt manipulated and used, but hoped he had bought time for the Illinois. He was relieved to see Fathers Ribourde and Membré running to escort him.

"We are blessed with a miracle!" Father Ribourde burst out as he steadied Tonti. "We prayed hard for your safety. But in truth, we never expected the Iroquois would spare you. This is truly miraculous!"

Fr. Membré looked Tonti over, appraising his wounds. "I think you will yet live to a ripe old age. You don't seem to be damaged beyond repair. Have you considered trying some peaceful pursuit, say managing an orchard in the settlements?"

Tonti looked at the priest and smiled. Wiping the blood and sweat from his face with his sleeve, Tonti replied, "No, and I think you know me better, my good Padre. Where is Chief Chassagoac? I must speak with him immediately."

"He is waiting," Fr. Ribourde said, pointing. "The Illinois have resolved to fight. They are prepared."

Fr. Ribourde winced. Then looking toward the ridge, he saw nothing, neither activity nor Indians. But he knew the defenses there were being set.

"Old man, how long do you propose to live?" Realizing he had just escaped death, Tonti felt a sudden, delayed gush of elation, a false sense of well being.

Uncomprehending, the priest stared at Tonti. *Good God!* He thought, *I hope the man does not think he has become invincible.*

"Chief!" Tonti called out as he and the priests approached the council that, however, remained unresponsive. "The Iroquois have asked for negotiations. Surely you will talk with them."

Chassagoac watched sternly as the emissaries approached. The council too silently greeted the priest and Tonti. Nika, still bound to a nearby tree, stood under guard.

Tonti offered the beads given him as a token of peaceful intent. "It is, as Nika suggested, a private war party. These are mostly young warriors on a raid to prove their courage and gain glory for themselves. Their war chief is not of the noble ranks—in fact not one of the Iroquois sachems is present."

"Yes, we will talk." Chassagoac bit off the words, brushing aside the beads. "While they talk, they spy on us, on our defenses. They are fortifying their position. After the talks, when their fort is ready, they will attack."

"The Iroquois have many guns, British muskets," Tonti said, emphasizing the obvious. "They have fewer warriors than the Illinois. For your own sakes, I think you should retreat. The Iroquois have come a great distance. They cannot go farther and still return to their homes before the first snows."

"The Iroquois care not for snows or home fires. They want blood, our blood. If we move, that will not make conditions better for us. We do not want any delay. We will fight now."

Raising his hand as a signal, Chassagoac motioned and two young braves came forward with a medicine man. "Take our friend, see to his wound. He needs rest."

Swift Fox and Sleeping Crow escorted Tonti away from the council. Tonti was surprised that he did not at first recognize these men in their war costume.

Sleeping Crow's shaven head sported a single scalp lock above one ear, black lightning bolts flashed on each cheek, while his shoulders and upper chest were painted red.

Swift Fox, too, had shaved his head. His face was marked with the red and blue symbols of his personal medicine. White hailstones cascaded over his black torso.

Together the two braves helped Tonti limp to a shady spot under a tall sycamore. He collapsed onto a bed of cedar boughs.

The medicine man, wearing a fox skin that covered his head, its tail hanging down his back, applied a paste of mud and yarrow over the wound. He also gave Tonti bits of willow bark to chew. Then he began to dance around the patient. Chanting and shaking a turtle shell rattle, the medicine man chased off the evil spirits Tonti brought from the enemy camp.

Tonti inhaled deeply, enjoying the pleasant, moist river air wafting across the dank earth, then passed into a welcome unconsciousness.

* * *

"My, my, what a dreamer," Fr. Ribourde chided as Tonti fought off the last drowsy remnants of sleep.

Tonti gradually regained a sitting position but was feeling, however, unusually stiff. But the pain from the knife wound had greatly diminished, the medicine man's poultice having dried into a hard scale.

"You have slept nearly a whole day." Fr. Ribourde grinned.

With a start, Tonti half-rose when a stab of pain caused him to collapse again. Moaning and rocking back and forth, he managed to ask, "What is happening with the peace talks? I do not hear war chants or drums."

"They are still negotiating. But the Iroquois fortification is just about finished," Fr. Membré replied with an unmistakable hint of disgust.

"And where is LaSalle? Any word of his whereabouts?" Tonti lay back, easing the pain in his crampy limbs.

"We only know he left Ft. Saint Joseph for Montreal. There has been no other word since May. No word on *Griffin*, either. For sure, the ship is lost," Fr. Ribourde said, biting his lower lip. He gazed vacantly at the upper river, beyond the Iroquois encampment, but drew no hope from its empty surface.

"Nika is free! Chief Chassagoac released him when you returned." Fr. Membré announced, abruptly recalling yesterday's events. "The Illinois saw that you risked your life for them; you have convinced them there is no treachery on the part of the French. But they are puzzled by La Salle's absence. They believe some misfortune may have occurred."

"I am Italian. Why does everyone confuse me with the French?" Tonti blustered, half in jest.

"If I am not mistaken, the Iroquois identified you as *Illiniwek*, not so long ago." Fr. Membré chuckled.

"Perhaps you care to explain that difference to an Iroquois war party." Fr. Ribourde said in mock seriousness. "I can see the response that would arouse! 'Do you want to die?' or 'Do you want to die painfully?' That is the only choice they would give you. Perhaps, for their own amusement, they might offer a third choice. But that is not worth mentioning—eh?"

Tonti rolled his eyes and smiled nonchalantly.

The Flemish priest considered Tonti for a moment. "You seem to have had much joy in your life. Do you take everything so lightheartedly? Do you not know fear?"

"Of course, but don't judge by appearances," Tonti replied. "If you show fear, you frighten yourself. There is no doubt on this. But courage! Courage carries you over many obstacles."

"Well, that's true enough," Fr. Ribourde agreed, but wondered whether Tonti's behavior exhibited courage, audacity, or rashness—or for that matter, whether such distinction was even relevant.

"But how does one keep the inner fears from showing? From affecting your actions?" As he spoke, Fr. Membré noticed several Iroquois messengers approaching.

Tonti also had caught sight of the Iroquois. "It is the other way around. I cannot understand how one surrenders to base fear. Look, these warriors understand this all too well."

"Yes, I know what you mean. What do you think the Iroquois are up to now?" Fr. Membré's glance had followed the direction of the messengers. Shortly, they, Nika, and several Illinois came over to Tonti.

"They have requested a powwow with both of you," Nika said, indicating Tonti and the younger priest.

"Do you have an idea as to what they want?" Tonti responded. "Is this a prelude to peace?"

"No, they have guaranteed safety only for you and Fr. Membré. That much, but no more." Nika said, looking aside at his Iroquois escort.

Tonti studied the inscrutable faces of the envoys. "Very well, we shall see what they offer."

Silently, Tonti, Fr. Membré, and the two escorts walked along the river to the waiting Iroquois council. Near the embankment, several war chiefs were arranged in a circle of solemn warriors.

"Tonti and the Gray Robe are welcome!" Moves-the-Clouds exclaimed. "We have heard your words of peace. We have talked many days with the Illinois. You have seen this. We now make presents to you, Tonti." Raising an arm in signal, the chief paused. Six beaver skin pouches were brought forward.

Limping Wolf and Yellow Snake were standing nearby, unmistakable insolence crowding their expressions.

"Here are beaver skins for *Onontio*, our father in Canada. Take these to him," Moves-the-Clouds said, pointing to the first two gifts. "Tell him the Iroquois, too, are his children. We want peace with the French."

As the third packet was opened, Moves-the-Clouds continued, indicating which of the herbs and roots were to be applied directly to the injury, which to be taken internally. "This medicine is for your wound."

"This skin has oil for your arms and legs. It is very good for muscles tired and sore from travel. Use this oil in the evening when you camp. You will sleep well—"

"You are asking us to leave?" Tonti broke in.

The chief stared back for a moment, obviously offended. Among Indians, an interruption is extremely rude behavior.

Limping Wolf and Yellow Snake also reacted to Tonti's impatience. Stiffly the three Indians exchanged glances, silently agreeing that this foreigner's lack of etiquette reflected an inferior culture.

In a dignified and solemn manner, Moves-the-Clouds resumed his presentation of the final skins. With a grand gesture, raising his arm toward the sky, he declared, "The sun is bright; the day is yet long. It is good weather for the French."

"He means is that it is good weather for travel," Fr. Membré said, shocked at the rebuff. "He means for us to leave the Illinois country."

"The French must go! All French must leave this area and return to your Fort Frontenac." Clasping an arm across his chest, the Chief turned slowly

166

to the warriors on either side. Understanding that the message to the French had been delivered, they began to crowd forward, a restless murmur persisting.

"Go now, French. Go back to Canada. Give our message to *Onontio*. Tell him, we will not eat his children, the Illinois."

Tonti cried out. "No, it is you who must leave the Illinois country."

Insistent voices burst out; angry warriors surrounded the visitors, pushing and shoving Tonti and Membré from the council.

"You have lived once. Tomorrow you go to Onontio. We cannot offer you safety beyond that. I have done all I can for you," Chief Moves-the-Clouds called out, turned, and disappeared among the warriors.

"That was not the most intelligent thing you could have said, telling the Iroquois they must leave," Fr. Membré reproached Tonti as they returned.

"Perhaps. But did I have a choice? What do you say?"

"It is clear we certainly have no choices now." Fr. Membré left Tonti to find Nika, Fr. Ribourde, and the others. All converged at the Illinois chiefs council.

"I am not surprised. They have not attacked because the French are here," Chief Chassagoac said when informed of the Iroquois position. "You must go now. Return to you settlements. Do not look back."

"And you, you must retreat! The Iroquois are sure to attack. You are at a serious disadvantage," Tonti pleaded.

"No! We stay and we fight. This is our country; our ancestors died here. We will not betray them. Do not talk to us again on this. We will give you a canoe and some food. Tomorrow, be gone!"

* * *

That evening the few remaining members of La Salle's first journey of exploration to the Mississippi prepared to withdraw from the territory of the Illinois Nation.

Tonti spent a long night of restless anxiety and soul-searching. In the morning, he felt there was no alternate course, no escape for Chassagoac's people. In sullen silence the Italian, Flemish, Shawnee, and French voyagers set off for Montreal. As the seven paddled their canoe upriver, impassive Iroquois braves lined the bank, watching the sorry display.

For most of two days, no one was moved to speak. Even the water seeping into the canoe was ignored.

After a time, Fr. Ribourde mentioned the obvious. "This canoe has a bad leak. We can't go much farther if this is not repaired."

"The Kankakee is not far. We'll stop here to repair the canoe," Tonti said and ordered the men to various tasks. "We have a few hours of daylight remaining. I hope we can make a good start in the morning."

After the canoe was brought ashore, Nika began scrounging tinder and small pieces of dead wood for a cook fire. Boisrondet and Renault gathered pine pitch for the canoe. Tonti arranged fire stones while the priests readied the kettle for cooking.

"I am not certain," Fr. Membré said, as he skewered a small roast. He winced as the pulled the pit through. "I think this is dog."

"Oh, no!" exclaimed Renault, working nearby. "I have never eaten dog before. I think I may be sick."

"Too bad. You should be happy the Illinois gave us anything. This is probably the best they had to offer," Nika said, looking coldly at the man. "Do you want to be sick? Or would you prefer to go back and die with them?"

Sullen and silent, Renault concentrated on making pitch. He felt a knot gradually tightening in his stomach.

As the meat was cooking, and since his immediate chores were finished, Fr. Ribourde announced, to no one in particular, "I shall go off to say my office. I must thank the Lord for all He has given us, and for our deliverance. I must say, even though I do not understand why, at this moment, I feel amazingly happy, truly as happy as I can ever recall."

"Maybe it's a sign of age," Boisrondet offered. "Maybe something happens when you live to be over sixty."

Fr. Ribourde looked at the young man. "Etienne, my son, may you have a long life. You must learn first hand what life is, when 'you're over sixty,' as you say."

Tonti watched as the old man strolled toward the solitude of a nearby copse, carrying his habitual breviary. Since he had met the Fleming, Tonti had never seen the priest cross or angry. He was sincerely devout, anxious to gain converts, yet remained always pleasant and patient. Yet in spite of the ordeal of the past several days, the priest appeared truly elated.

"How are the repairs coming?" Tonti walked over to inspect the canoe.

"Not too well." Boisrondet looked up, dismayed at a lack of success. "It's not just the seams. The bark is old and dry and the lashing holes are stretching. This canoe is not repairable."

"Very well, then," Tonti said. "If that is the case, destroy the canoe. And leave no trace of our presence here. We don't want to leave evidence we are travelling on foot."

The men covered the pitch pit, broke the canoe, and placed small pieces in the fire, a few at a time. They then sat down for their meager meal.

"Where is Fr. Ribourde? He's been praying for a long while," Tonti said as he suddenly realized the priest had over-stayed his absence.

"Nika, would you look for him? The old man may have fallen asleep." Tonti felt more than a little concern, knowing the priest usually did not remain absent for long.

Nika, too, had sensed that something was amiss. Brandishing his tomahawk, he walked cautiously toward the area where the priest had gone. Silently, he entered the woods, treading lightly on the floor of pine needles. A strong sensation of being observed caused him to pause. Tingling with apprehension, Nika warily watched and listened. After a few moments, he resumed his search.

Slowly advancing, he checked each tree, shrub, rock, and shadow. As a hunter stalking game, Nika moved noiselessly from one concealment to another. Listening, he heard nothing. Ominously, there were no bird sounds. He had seen no tracks, but was certain there had been several human visitors in the area. Since they had concealed their presence, Nika knew they were hostile.

Seeing an opening ahead, Nika diligently surveyed the surrounding trees. He felt confident an ambush was unlikely, but in looking across the glade, he at last spotted the prostate, motionless body of the priest.

With a rush of sadness and anger, Nika walked toward the corpse. The man had been tomahawked and scalped, the distinctive bright red top of the head visible from a distance.

Reverently, Nika guarded the body, searching the surroundings for sight or sound of the assassins. Satisfied he was now alone, he holstered his tomahawk, then knelt beside the priest. Grimly, bringing an arm over his neck, Nika rose, and walking slowly, half-carried the slain priest back toward the encampment.

As Nika emerged from the woods, others instantly recognized the situation and came running. Tonti and Renault relieved Nika of his load and together brought the priest's body to the riverside.

Silently, the men laid the corpse on the ground, closed the priest's eyes for the last time, and washed his face. Soon Boisrondet and L'Esperance had dug a grave and moved the body to it.

Renault placed a small cloth over the dead man's face and crossed the priest's hands on his stomach, over his breviary.

"Who did this?" Tonti asked. "Was this the work of the Iroquois?"

"No, not the Iroquois. I think it is a small band. They are strangers in this area," Nika said quietly. "I think they have gone farther. They are no longer here."

Fr. Membré assembled the somber men around the grave. With difficulty, he began his eulogy. "It is a sad, terribly sad day for us. We are unable to help our friends, and one of our own has been taken from us. It is a coincidence, dreadful, but perhaps also telling, that Fr. Ribourde should meet his end here. For he takes his rest here, along the route to the new Indian territories blazed by Marquette, Jolliet, and La Salle. Certainly there will be other missionaries to follow.

"I doubt not but that Fr. Ribourde would be among the first to seek mercy, even forgiveness, for his murderers. He dedicated—and forfeited—

his life to bring true peace to the Indians. I remember that he always spoke of unity among tribes and nations as a way of strength."

Raising his arm, Fr. Membré made the sign of the cross over the dead priest. "Oh Lord, we pray You, accept the soul of your most humble servant. May he rest in Your peace, amen."

Tonti then threw a handful of dirt into the grave and Boisrondet finished the burial.

"We must go on now," Boisrondet said, looking at the late evening sky. A breeze kicked gently at the tops of the pines. "We may not be safe here."

"Go? Where? Do you think we will arrive somewhere? We have no canoe, little food, and few weapons." Tonti exploded. "La Salle is missing; we do not know what has happened to him. His ship is sunk. Duplessis and his men are somewhere ahead, possibly waiting in ambush. Fort Saint Joseph is probably destroyed. Fr. Hennepin's party is overdue in the Sioux lands. And those bloodthirsty Iroquois will soon return along this route. We have *nowhere* to go!"

Abruptly Tonti stomped off, fuming. The men watched him, despair overtaking their grief. After some moments, Tonti, glancing in their direction, noticed their abject despondency and came back to them.

"I am sorry I spoke like that just now." Readjusting his hat, Tonti wiped his brow with his sleeve. "We shall go north. The Potawatami are friendly. We will find help and shelter among their villages."

Boisrondet tightened his jacket against the chill evening air, Renault stood still, pondering the previous outburst, and L'Esperance patiently waited.

"We must find La Salle, he needs our help. Remember that he would say 'Don't quit, don't give up.'" Tonti declared, "Neither shall we!"

"Help La Salle! Now I am convinced—you are crazy," Fr. Membré cried out in disbelief.

Tonti looked at the priest, but did not respond. Instead, he proclaimed with gusto, "We will go north! And we shall arrive! To Green Bay! Let us march!"

Tonti turned and, setting the pace, bravely led the band on what he felt was a pathetic if not futile quest to find La Salle.

Chapter 10

Illinois Moon

Since the French had gone from Kaskaskia, the days had been long with tension. The *Hodenosaunee* had not begun their war on the Illinois. They instead continued to weary the resolve of their opponents with fruitless negotiations. At night, the river breeze carried the war songs and drumbeats far beyond the improvised fort of the Iroquois.

Against the dull red-orange glow of the council fire, Chief Chassagoac stood immobile, defiantly facing the distant enemy. Resolutely holding the shaft of his war lance in one hand, and in the other, the medicine pouch of a principal war chief of the Illinois, he wore a crimson scarf on his neck as his only badge of office. Only the scarlet-tipped feathers of his war lance stirred, gently rocking on the evening air.

"They will come," Chief Chassagoac declared to the Illinois war council. "In a day, maybe two, they will attack. They will try to pass us on the ridge or on the river. If they succeed, they will encircle us. Chief Nicanope, take your best men to the ridge. You are in charge of our most important defense.

"Chief Omawaha, guard the river with your braves. Let no man pass. Even a few of their warriors behind us could cause great damage. A small number may even go down river, to attack our wives and children. The safety of our families is in your hands.

"It is important that both flanks hold. The enemy will try to cause us to weaken one in favor of the other. If we do this we will be defeated. You both must defend your areas at all costs. My warriors will hold the center."

Chief Chassagoac paused, waiting for comment. In contrast with the dark war paint of the chief, the upright tip of his lance gleamed brightly bloodthirsty. The council comprised the red-scarved war chiefs of the Peoria, Kaskaskia, Tamaroa, Cahokia, Michigamea, and Moingwena tribes of the Illinois Confederacy; warriors from the neighboring Vermilion, Wea, Piankashaw tribes; and a few Miami and Kickapoo braves. All remained silent.

Burdened with a sense of his responsibilities, Chief Chassagoac continued, "The day is drawing to a close. I will stand here, at the council fire. This will be my post. Do what you can to help our braves. Capture guns and powder when you can. Our men will fight bravely; many will die.

"Let none of the enemy wounded survive. The Iroquois deserve to die; they have vowed to exterminate the Illinois! Make them pay dearly for our blood. Death to the Iroquois!" In fiery anger he thrust his war lance into the earth.

As the assembly broke up, many warriors went off to continue their spiritual and martial preparations. Standing by his embedded lance, Chief Chassagoac held his stance till all were gone, then pulled it from the ground and began a somber survey of the prepared defenses along the eastern boundary of the town.

* * *

In the morning, in the stillness of a pre-dawn grayness, a fog rose from the river, drifting around and through the trees. From atop Buffalo Ridge, only the occasional tops of sycamores and poplars could be seen floating on the cottony mist. Yet the overcast and the deep morning quiet were cause for alarm. From behind an abatis defense work, Nicanope sensed rather than saw Iroquois phantoms darting among the rhododendron. Straining to confirm his suspicions, he saw nothing; listening, he heard only the morning bird songs. With dismay he realized the dew dripping from the trees deadened the forest litter, aiding the enemy. Looking quizzically at a sentinel lodged aloft, he made a sign, *Do you see anything?*

The lookout waved his arm, signifying *Nothing in sight.* From beyond the rhododendrons, several gunshots punctured the tranquility of the morning. In a semi-instant, a dull splat announced the death of the sentry, his crumpled body tumbling from its perch.

Immediately general shooting erupted, accompanied by screams and yells. War whoops intermingled, resounding along the length of Buffalo Ridge. White gun smoke billowed in the still air, hanging over the Iroquois positions. Blindly, they continued firing, using general sighting. The Illinois replied with arrow barrages. In a rush, the Wea, Moingwena, and Tamaroa warriors under Chief Nicanope charged forward engaging their opponents with war clubs, tomahawks, and lances.

A Wea warrior, turned momentarily by the blow of an Oneida war club, felt a thump on his back. Curious, he looked down and saw a bloody arrowhead protruding near his left nipple. Confused, he sensed only the warm surge of blood in his throat as his knees buckled and all consciousness evaporated.

Rushing through the mass of grappling, twisting forms, Swift Fox dodged among the single combats, seeking an opponent. Seeing a scalplock approaching through the brush, he surprised the Cayuga. The force of the collision knocked both to the ground. Yellow Snake recovered instantly, but managed to inflict only a minor wound. Smarting, Swift Fox drew back to strike a fatal blow, but Yellow Snake rolled aside. Scrambling, Swift Fox jumped onto Yellow Snake, the two braves rolling to the rim of the bluff.

Breaking away, Yellow Snake jumped to his feet. Just as quickly, Swift Fox rose and lunged with his knife. Yellow Snake dodged. Falling, Swift Fox pulled his opponent across him, but there was only emptiness below. Uttering a spiteful whoop, Yellow Snake clung to his opponent as the two spun over the cliff. Together they fell, inseparable, bouncing from the cliff face, shredding branches as they plummeted through the hemlock below.

From his stand at the council fire, Chief Chassagoac intently monitored the battle noises. Standing with his ready lance, the chief stood unmoving as one scout after another came to report. Yelling battle reports and other messages, runners incessantly crisscrossed Kaskaskia, informing the reserves of the battle's progress. To the steady rhythm of the tribal drums, the waiting warriors sang their chants of war and courage. Through all this, Chassagoac tracked the battle on the ridge as well as the skirmishing which had broken out to his front. He shuddered once as a rising breeze, stirring the cool morning freshness, began to lift the river mists.

"We are killing the Iroquois to our front!" Barking Squirrel enthused as he came rushing to report. The young warrior, barely seventeen, was eager to return to the fight.

"Be cautious! The Iroquois are not using many muskets there. We must learn why," Chassagoac said, continuing to mark the battle sounds. "Go back and warn the others."

Barking Squirrel left, returning in an hour. "I have killed one!" He said proudly, breathless yet breathing the faint smell of vomit. "I have seen several dead Iroquois. We will be victorious!"

"Tell me, what do you see? Are these experienced men you are fighting?" Chassagoac looked sternly at the brave. "What clan are they?"

"This one, he came rushing at me. He must have been at least ten years older. He swung his war club but I got behind him. I plunged my knife into his back. He collapsed at my feet. He was still alive when I scalped him"

"Then you became ill?" Chassagoac asked, compassionately.

"Yes," Barking Squirrel replied, surprised at the chief's insight. "Very ill."

"It is not natural to kill a human being, even one that deserves to die. You did not become ill when you killed your first buffalo," the chief observed.

Barking Squirrel did not respond, still breathing deeply, recovering from his exertions.

"And what else did you notice about the man you killed?"

"Snipe clan. He had the *tawistawis* totem. But there was something odd. He had blood on his lips, before I knifed him."

"Of course! Do you not know of the lung disease?" Chief Chassagoac studied the expanse between him and the enemy. "Many Iroquois have gotten this sickness from the English settlers."

"Others we killed had the rotten face."

"Good for you! Now do you see what is happening? The ones with lung disease are dying already. The scarface comes from the white man, too. They call it small pox. No Indian with the rotten face wants to live. To die in war is the only means they have to bring honor to their lives. There is little victory in killing those who want to die."

"I must return. We shall easily defeat these Iroquois."

"No, you will not defeat them. Soon they will begin to fall back. Do not pursue. It is a trap! They have given you weak and sick braves to make you feel victorious. If you follow their retreat, you will meet the *anowara* and the *okwari*. The Turtle and the Bear clans, these are their best fighters. Make them come to you. Use your defenses to slow them. Then you will kill many."

As Barking Squirrel returned to the battle, Chief Chassagoac continued his stationkeeping. The battle sounds on the ridge had moved farther to the west, signifying a slow retreat by the Illinois. The sporadic gunfire of probing raids continued to the front.

Chief Chassagoac surmised that as long as the Iroquois were making progress on the ridge, they would not launch a major attack elsewhere, especially along the river. Nevertheless, he sent a runner to Omawaha.

The report came back. "Chief Omawaha has ready warriors on the island and scouts on the opposite bank. He says he has seen no Iroquois canoes. Scouts in the French fort detected no crossings before the fog came in. Chief Omawaha is confident all Iroquois are on this side of the river."

"Good!" Chassagoac was about to say more when he noticed a sharp increase in musket fire to his front. Checking himself, he directed the runner to reply to Omawaha, "Tell Chief Omawaha to prepare to retreat. The

Iroquois are pressing down the ridge and now are increasing their attacks to our front. I am troubled that so far there has been no attack in his area. It is a bad sign."

Even as the messenger came to Plum Island, Iroquois war canoes were racing down the river on the far side. A short distance below the island point, the raiders turned toward the low embankment.

As the first Iroquois craft reached shore, some Moingwena and Peoria warriors, reckless with the excitement of battle, rushed to meet the threat. As the courageous defenders advanced with their stone-edged weapons, Iroquois muskets told an appalling tale, spreading gruesome and mutilated testimony with their awesome voice.

Surviving the curtain of shot, a few of the defenders broke through and engaged those still in the boats. An Onandaga, rising to meet a rushing Moingwena, was instead knocked sideways into the river. With a yell, the Moingwena leaped upon the thrashing brave, stabbing him beneath the arm. As the Illinois prepared to deliver the coup de grace, a second Onandaga crushed his skull with a war club.

The Iroquois continued fighting from the beachhead. With devastating musket fire the invaders carved a growing niche from the ranks of the defenders. The wounded and dying soon littered the area.

Broken canoes and a few bodies were floating from the island.

In the fighting before Kaskaskia, the Iroquois continued to probe for weak points in the defenses. Occasional openings allowed small squads to race into the Illinois rear, creating panic and chaos.

The Fight at Kaskaskia

Throughout the day, Chief Chassagoac countered such incursions, parceling out his reserves, containing, and then eliminating each foray. As the size of his force dwindled, throughout the town the number of wounded, dying, and killed increased. These had been retrieved from the battlefield, to protect them from certain profanation.

The Illinois could not long absorb such punishment as the Iroquois were inflicting. Chief Chassagoac realized the Iroquois were dangerously near to forcing a major rupture. Reluctantly he concluded retreat was the only tactic now available.

By mid-afternoon, Chief Chassagoac summoned runners for his orders. "We must move the tribal fire. We are leaving our town to the enemy," he announced. "Tell the chiefs to prepare to leave. We go now to our winter village."

Chief Chassagoac's force continued to defend the town for another hour as the warriors from the ridge passed through to the river, launched their canoes, and began their flight to safety. Other canoes could be seen escaping from Plum Island. The fighting to the front had become intense. It was time for the last defenders to withdraw.

Chief Chassagoac again called runners. "The wind is from our back. Tell our braves to start fires in the direction of the Iroquois. This should stall the enemy while we withdraw."

"But some of our braves will be trapped," Barking Squirrel protested.

For a long moment Chief Chassagoac was silent. Then he looked away from the messenger and said gravely, "Then let them die bravely."

Unwilling or unable to comprehend, Barking Squirrel hesitated, turned slowly, then went off to deliver his grisly command.

"Fire the lodges!" The chief commanded as his forward defenders came rushing back. "We have done all we can do here. We must retreat!"

Warriors scattered, throwing firebrands, igniting the rush mat coverings as they went. Grass and green pine boughs were thrown onto the burning dwellings, creating a thick pall of blinding smoke.

As his braves filtered through the town, and others were launching their canoes, Chassagoac, standing by the riverbank, looked up to survey the bright orange sky. To the west, beyond the burning town, an ominous gray cloud stretched long fingers across the red face of the evening sun; to the east, reflecting on the silvery river, an amber moon hung swollen, just over the horizon. As this paling moon waned to its normal size, the last of the Illinois braves pushed their canoes into the river.

Chassagoac then joined the convoy of the defeated.

Limping Wolf, Gray Eyes, and Ghost Deer were the first of the Iroquois warriors to enter the burning town. Running through the dense smoke, they desperately sought the enemy. The three emerged into the clear air by the river. With burning eyes and lungs filled with smoke, they stood gasping at the water's edge. Gray Eyes was the first to see the Illinois canoes.

"Ho-wen-no'-yäke! Ho-wen-no'-yäke!" he yelled, brandishing his empty musket.

Ghost Deer and Limping Wolf both fired, but with the distance, it was a futile effort.

Enraged that their quarry was escaping, the three ran back into the town, looking for stragglers and wounded. Other Iroquois appeared and disappeared into the swirling smoke. Several dead Illinois lay scattered among the burning lodges. Some had been tomahawked or lanced. One had many arrows in his body. Several shooting victims had huge exit wounds from musket shot.

Ghost Deer kicked one bloody body that had few obvious wounds. The Cahokian brave jumped to his feet and began running for his life. Ghost Deer threw his war club, striking the man in the back before he had managed ten paces. Yelling fiercely, Ghost Deer ran over and with his hatchet beheaded the dying warrior. Raising the man's head on a stake, Ghost Deer yelled with glee, making a short victory chant over his latest trophy.

Limping Wolf found an injured Peoria. Full of contempt, he gouged the man's eyes with his thumbs then angrily pushed him into a burning lodge. For a few minutes, the blind man stumbled about inside, screaming, colliding with the burning walls. Showers of sparks on the outside marked the victim's progress. Abruptly, the fiery roof collapsed. The pile of burning mats convulsed once or twice, and then movement ceased.

Stomping and waving his war club, Limping Wolf sang his victory song and danced with delight around the funeral pyre of the Peoria.

Ghost Deer discovered the tribal burial field. With a boast, he summoned the others.

Limping Wolf was ecstatic. He had attacked the living; he had punished the wounded. Now he could war against the most vulnerable of the Illinois—the spirits of their ancestors. In frenzy, he led the graveyard assault, unearthing skeletal remains, scattering bones, destroying the funeral medicine pouches, and stealing items of value. Weapons intended for the use of the departed, he ruined. To his satisfaction, he imagined the great turmoil and anguish he was creating in the spirit world.

The living could only die. But this desecration would bring only eternal sadness to the deceased. The casualties of this war included not only the inhabitants of Kaskaskia, but previous generations as well. There had never been a form of warfare more utterly complete than this, and Limping Wolf knew the Iroquois were its master.

Along the riverbank the severed heads of fallen Illinois warriors were impaled on stakes and displayed as victory trophies.

Twilight became night. Triumphant Iroquois warriors gathered around their tribal fires burning throughout the town. During the night, war drums throbbed their songs of blood lust encouraging the warriors, who danced until delirious, ignoring their exhaustion.

A war council was called. Bear, Turtle, and Deer clan members made long speeches urging continued war on the Illinois.

Standing for attention, Limping Wolf sneered. "The Illinois deserve to die. We must kill more of these cowards. Remember too, they have killed some of our brothers. We must seek vengeance. Let none live!"

An Onandaga, Moves-the-Clouds, rose to speak. He was a large, burly man much respected for his courage. "We have killed enough. We must go home now. There is not much time left for a last hunt before the snows come.

"We have killed many Illinois. We cannot kill all; there are too many. But they have tasted Iroquois war and now respect us. We must care for our own families before the cold of winter closes our long houses."

Ghost Deer pleaded for the young warriors who had not had a full share of combat. "Some of our braves have not yet bloodied their tomahawks. If we turn back now, these will be without honor. We have come this far, let us continue to kill the Illinois. Let all here fear the Iroquois!"

Swims-like-Beaver, a lithe Seneca spoke. "Limping Wolf has said we have lost some of our warriors. He is correct. We need to replace them. We have no prisoners. We cannot return to the families of the fallen without captives to soften their grief. We must fight again."

Contempt spiked with revenge drove the bloodlust to a redoubled intensity. The war chiefs resolved to continue.

* * *

Under a full and brilliant moon, the Illinois warriors paddled briskly down the quiet river, to their winter camp, nearly seventy miles away. Themselves so many black spots on the silvery waters, the disconsolate survivors glided under the shadows of the overhanging trees. For hours the trek continued, the flotilla was strung out for miles. The sullen braves pondered in silent uncertainty the prospects of pursuit, the safety of their families and of the tribe. At length, a low mist gathered on the river, comforting because it denied any immediate threat from a pursuing enemy.

In the last hours of the night the first escaping warriors finally passed beneath the welcome heights at the narrows of *Lake Pimitou*. The moon had already set, leaving an inky blackness. A few miles farther lay the winter camp, but an uncommon orange glow illuminated the riverside. From the distance, it gave the appearance of a great, incandescent worm lining the shore. As the lead canoes approached, the worm resolved itself into a multitude of torches. Along the shore, were hundreds, perhaps a thousand, women—ghostly beneath their torches—keeping silent, hopeful vigils.

As Plenty Fish came along the embankment, he observed the expectant, worried faces of the women. Most were searching for their spouses; some were seeking their sons. Plenty Fish noticed someone who seemed to be looking at him with interest. In the same instant that he recognized Elizabeth, she smiled. Puzzled, Plenty Fish turned to see her better but in that instant she vanished.

As the haggard braves disembarked, some were quickly reunited, while others searched the crowd for some time before finding their spouses. With an increasing insistence, many women began asking after the absent warriors. They received only vague and indefinite answers except in a few cases, the terrible truth. Sobbing and occasional shrieks marked the spreading anguish.

Some of the wounded were lifted from the canoes and carried ashore as well as circumstances would permit. On the grassy embankment, these were made comfortable and some treatment was begun.

The vigil by the lake continued for hours but only a few additional canoes came. By dawn, the last of the stragglers had arrived and the number of torches had noticeably dwindled.

Gray day bared a mournful camp. By the waterside, a few women still kept their watch not yet certain—or convinced—of their widowhood. In the early light, the inscrutable waters surrendered no clues. Others, in the early grasp of grief, sat stupefied while some paced aimlessly about. A few women had already manifested their state of mourning by cutting their hair and blackening their faces with ashes.

Of the 10,000 inhabitants of Kaskaskia, at least half were in the winter camp, others had gone farther down river, or else had scattered overland.

Chief Chassagoac called a council and ordered the immediate evacuation of all but able warriors. "We must send our families farther for safety. All braves too wounded to fight will go with the women and children; they cannot help us here. We must hurry. The sun will be high before all these people are on the water."

With a sense of urgency but no panic, the people began crowding the canoe parks, slowly draining the village as the growing flotilla filled the waterway. Satisfied that the withdrawal was proceeding with appropriate speed, Chief Chassagoac returned to the council to discuss plans for the coming fight.

Since early dawn, warriors of the Illinois and allied tribes had cut shrubs, trees, and branches, building a defense of obstacles and ambuscades for the coming battle. They expected to meet the Iroquois assault along the lakefront and river embankment at the foot of *Lake Pimitou*. Even though exhausted, the men labored as though each effort was an Illinois life saved, or an Iroquois killed.

Across the river were Fort Crèvecoeur and the hulk of La Salle's ship, both useless and abandoned. No smoke came from the palisaded enclosure on top of the bluffs; no activity signaled human occupation. The bare hull sat swollen on the ways, smelling of freshly milled oak and pine. The empty fort and the abandoned ship offering yet poignant reminders of promises of assistance.

As the council concluded its discussions, Chief Chassagoac announced his intention to inspect the area, especially to ensure that the last of the families had gone.

Walking among the lodges, Chief Chassagoac came upon an elderly Indian.

"Old man, why are you still here?" The chief asked.

"I want to fight the Iroquois," the man replied, his gray head held proudly back.

"Our women and children need you," Chief Chassagoac said, appraising the missing teeth and the slack muscles bespeaking frailty, not glory. "They are defenseless. You must help them. Put on your war paint and hope that you frighten the enemy. You are too old to fight."

Breaking into a broad, nearly toothless grin, the old man slurred, "I will not die of fright. I have lived a good life. It is time to die."

Chief Chassagoac studied the man, then placing his hand on his shoulder, said kindly, "Good, then protect our wives and children. The last canoes are leaving. Go, defend our families."

Gazing wistfully upriver, the old man turned, then shuffled reluctantly toward the landing.

Morning passed quietly over the area, silent save only the sounds of the work of defense construction. Lookouts on the heights, mostly Peoria scouts, watching the upper lake saw no movement there, no hint of approaching danger. Towards noon Chief Chassagoac again called a council of the war chiefs.

Struggling with his anxiety and the desire to carry the battle to the enemy, he said, "It is a sad day for us and it is not over. My heart is heavy. We have already lost many sons and brothers. But we must not rest. They are coming; it will not be long now.

"The Iroquois thought that we would die like rabbits or run like dogs. We did neither. Now they know we fight as men. We have been wounded. But we have hurt them as well.

"Some of our brothers, the Miami, have betrayed us and fight against us with the Iroquois. We shall never forgive them; they are worse than the Rattlesnakes!"

"Canoes! War canoes. They are coming!" Barking Squirrel came running to the council, creating an alarm. "Smoke signals! From the heights. Look!"

"How far are they and how many?" Chief Chassagoac asked, studying the smoke in the distance. Turning to Chief Omawaha he concluded, "Twenty boats, perhaps three hundred warriors. Is Plenty Fish ready?"

"Yes, his men are hidden on the far side of the lake," Omawaha replied. Then turning to Chassagoac, he exclaimed, "This cannot be the full Iroquois force. There must be two war parties. We have scouts, on both sides of the lake. Nothing has been reported. Where is the second?"

Chief Chassagoac gravely pondered the question. Several of the confederacy chiefs—Cahokian, Kaskaskian, Moingwena, Illinois, Tamaroas, and Peorias—had offered opinions. Most argued against retreat, notwithstanding a possible Iroquois trap.

Chief Chassagoac considered their counsel, then said, "Enough! We will stand here. If the Iroquois want more Illinois blood, they will pay dearly. We will show the Iroquois there are no Illinois cowards. We do not fear them or their guns. If we die, we die with honor!"

The Iroquois war fleet at that time was energetically entering the narrows of *Lake Pimitou*. To the accompaniment of a fresh fall breeze, the waters danced with an enthusiastic chop. Decorated with victory totems and medicine designs, the war canoes cast off silvery white wavelets as they furrowed the surface of the lake. On a short stake above their high prows, the canoes carried grim trophies of yesterday's battle—the heads of Illinois braves.

Onward came these canoes, their paddlers raising a strong, unceasing rhythm, adding to the speed of the current, the force of the wind, onward they came into the narrows. A few miles ahead lay the second Illinois town. The tattooed and painted men, wearing scalp roaches and little else, driven by some fiendish animus, quickened their headlong rush. From a low chant, the Iroquois raised their voices, now howling, urging each other to a faster pace as the thrill of battle welled within.

Like some animal rousing itself, the heights dominating the northwestern shore came alive with excited activity. With whoops and yells the Indians there fired volleys of arrows down onto the passing canoes. Braving the barrage with impunity, many Iroquois brandished their tomahawks, yelling defiance at the defenders.

From the spit of land jutting from the opposite shore, Illinois warriors pulled their elm bark canoes from the marsh grasses and ran, sliding and falling, into the water. This new wave of defenders swiftly converged on the flank and rear of the Iroquois fleet. As the leading Illinois canoes came into range, Iroquois gunners began quick firing, at first ineffectively.

The Iroquois quickly discovered they had a slight tactical disadvantage. Their large birch bark war canoes, built to hold fifteen or more men, were difficult to maneuver against the smaller Illinois vessels. Like a swarm of water bugs, the small Illinois boats darted and turned, ever seeking an opening as they came crashing to close quarters.

One Peoria brave, leaping onto an Iroquois crew, was quickly wrestled to the floor and hacked to death by Cayugas and an Oneida. Holding high the trophy scalp, the Oneida stood to crow his victory. Instantly, an arrow entered his skull, just below the ear. In a twinkling, he went from stunned surprise to a total loss of consciousness, dead before his collapsing body entered the lake.

An Illinois canoe rammed an Onandaga, splitting its birchbark covering, and swamping the larger boat. Brandishing his tomahawk, the Mohawk Limping Wolf, leaped into the smaller boat, swinging at the first opponent. Plenty Fish countered this strike with his war club, returning a blow that should have been fatal. Nevertheless Limping Wolf fell onto the gunwale, capsizing the canoe.

Swimming beneath the surface, Limping Wolf felt his side, finding a large wound and several broken ribs. Coming up, he took a deep breath and quickly dove under again as a second Illinois canoe came into the melee. When this canoe was nearly overhead, Limping Wolf lunged upward, and grabbed the edge of the boat, pulling it over. Holding on with one hand, he swung his hatchet at the nearest Indian. He missed, his aim thrown off by the extreme pain in his side.

Readying a second strike, Limping Wolf experienced a knock on the head, followed immediately by pain and weakness. Sinking limply, he released the enemy craft.

Meanwhile Plenty Fish had surfaced farther away, amid a flotsam of broken canoes, paddles, and a few bodies. As he drifted, he saw two Moingwena dugouts, heavily manned, approaching. As Plenty Fish watched, one of the unsinkable boats rammed a previously damaged war canoe. Cayugas and Senecas grappled and fought for their lives, pulling their opponents into the churning waters even as their own canoe sank beneath them.

Unable to assist in this fight, Plenty Fish noticed a nearby derelict occupied solely by a Kaskaskian. Swimming over, he found two dead braves inside—the lone survivor incapacitated. Pulling the corpses overboard, Plenty Fish clambered onto the boat. Lying low on the bow, he used his hands to propel the craft.

A nearby Mohawk canoe's occupants were engaged on the opposite side by Illinois canoes. As Plenty Fish's derelict brushed up against the Mohawk craft, Plenty Fish reached over, grabbed the scalplock of the nearest man, and with his knife, ripped his throat. With a loud, protesting gargle, the dying Indian shook violently, then collapsed into his boat. His Seneca neighbor sprung up, and slashed wildly with his knife as he turned, deeply gashing Plenty Fish's arm. A Peoria arrow struck the Seneca from the rear, penetrated beneath a rib, pierced a lung, and severed the aorta, killing him instantly.

Plenty Fish, only a few feet from the man, watched as the Seneca's expression changed from anger to astonishment, then to pain as the already dead warrior's body tumbled into the lake.

At that moment an Iroquois swimmer grabbed the side of Plenty Fish's boat, jerking the canoe backward. Quickly finding a loose tomahawk in the bottom of his canoe, Plenty Fish struck a grazing blow off the man's head. Stunned, yet with his mouth agape, the man released his grip, slowly sinking beneath a billowing cloud of blood.

Looking around, Plenty Fish saw two pirogues crowding several enemy canoes. On the farther side of the engagement several Iroquois canoes stood apart, undamaged, and yet unable to close with the Illinois. Two or three men in each were concentrating musket fire on the dugouts. Although the range was not ideal, they had already killed several of the Moingwena.

Struggling to guide his broken canoe, Barking Squirrel yelled, "Plenty Fish, give me a hand!" As the two canoes joined, Barking Squirrel began to transfer weapons and paddles.

Plenty Fish was kneeling, helping Barking Squirrel into his canoe when the noise of an angry wasp caught his attention. He was being shot at. Looking around, he quickly picked out an Onieda hastily reloading.

At once Plenty Fish was staring down the barrel as the shooter took direct aim. In a flash, it was all over. The musket exploded, the fire searing the Oneida's face.

As he watched the man writhe in blind agony, Plenty Fish abruptly felt a strong, pulling sensation in his abdomen, followed immediately with searing pain as an arrow passed through him. It had penetrated his intestines, exiting just above the pelvis.

Grabbing a bow, Plenty Fish attempted to shoot an arrow but found he had little strength in his wounded arm. Handing the bow to Barking Squirrel, he bawled, "Shoot those with guns!"

Taking a cluster of arrows from the quiver, Barking Squirrel stood up amid the whizzing musket balls and arrows and, in rapid fire, loosed several arrows on a high, arcing trajectory. Hardly had Barking Squirrel loosed his fifth arrow than a musket ball slammed into his left shoulder, knocking him over, dumping both Plenty Fish and the semiconscious Kaskaskian into the lake.

Coming to the surface, Plenty Fish recognized a wounded Iroquois nearby. Limping Wolf saw the attacker and retrieved his knife from its scabbard. Plenty Fish warded off the first blow with his good arm while with his foot, he kicked hard at the enemy's stomach. Limping Wolf doubled over from the blow, disappearing beneath the water. Plenty Fish followed and finding him, grabbed his knife arm. Limping Wolf likewise grabbed Plenty Fish and, locked together, the two turned and twisted beneath the waters.

Fighting to surface for air, Limping Wolf was about to breach when Plenty Fish jerked him down, raising himself as a consequence. Gaining only a small gulp of air, Plenty Fish realized he had won. Looking down, he saw that Limping Wolf also knew now the battle was over.

With a vicious grimace, the Mohawk pulled his arm free. But in that same movement, Plenty Fish spun around, locking his good arm on the man's throat.

With one last, frantic effort Limping Wolf tried to stab Plenty Fish, but no longer had sufficient strength. His lungs exploding, he sucked in a large volume of water, then relaxed, releasing his knife as the searing pain in his side faded and he became blissfully suspended in some dark void, all pain and concern evaporating.

Surfacing, Plenty Fish took several large gasps of air and began to survey the battle area. It was littered with the flotsam of broken, smashed canoes, and not a few bodies. Barking Squirrel and the Kaskaskian brave were not to be found.

Yelling and shouting in the distance and occasional shooting signaled the last of the combats. Not far off Plenty Fish spied a pirogue. As he attempted to swim he realized how exhausted he was, how painful his wounds. Half-floating, using mostly kicking movements, he slowly approached the drifting hulk. An Indian, sprawled facedown over the gunwale stared at Plenty Fish with an expression that seemed mocking derision. Only when he came near did Plenty Fish notice that there was a bullet hole above one eye and that the entire rear of the man's skull was missing. As he swam around the dugout, he found all aboard were dead.

With his good arm, Plenty Fish managed to pull himself into the wooden canoe. Intending to rest just for a moment, Plenty Fish cleared a space among the bodies, stretched out as best he could, then closed his eyes.

* * *

With a jolt, the pirogue slammed into the riverbank. Plenty Fish stiffly rose on one arm, gradually coming to the realization he had fallen asleep and the canoe had drifted across the lake into the Illinois River.

"Here's one that's alive!" someone was yelling in Illinois.

"We are happy to see you," said another warrior.

"Few came back from the lake."

"Many are dead."

"What about the Iroquois?" Plenty Fish asked, trying to focus his clouded mind, his body aching, and his wounds painful. The battle had long ceased. Plenty Fish had slept for at least an hour, perhaps longer, he discovered.

"Some died; many escaped," a youth reported while he and several others helped Plenty Fish scramble ashore.

Looking back toward the lake, Plenty Fish noticed several Illinois canoes picking through the flotsam, looking for the surviving wounded. He watched without emotion as an Indian tomahawked a man in the water—a wounded Iroquois. It wasn't a single blow to the head. The man in the canoe held the victim by the arm, hacking at the skull until it was obliterated. Then the body with its pink, fleshy pulp was released to the current.

Exhausted, Plenty Fish wished only to lie down and rest. Settled against a beached canoe, he gazed over the lake that was slowly regaining its former grandeur as the currents and the wind swept away the disfigurement of battle.

To his left, Plenty Fish noted the cluster of war chiefs intently looking to the northeast, over the lake. Following their line of sight, Plenty Fish saw the distant, portentous pall of smoke, pointing its accusing finger toward the heights occupied by the Peoria scouting party.

From the length of the smoke column, Plenty Fish surmised this attack had occurred nearly an hour ago. Distressed by the realization the Iroquois could now be on the heights, Plenty Fish wondered what actions the chiefs would take. Only then did he notice they were watching a fast-approaching canoe.

Impatient, Sleeping Crow leaped from his boat, sending it adrift as he splashed ashore, anxious to deliver his disastrous report. Standing before the chiefs, he spent a few moments recovering from his exertions, breathing deeply.

"Speak," Chief Chassagoac sternly commanded, bracing for the worst. "Tell us, how did the Iroquois come to the heights? How many are there? And what has happened to my scouts?"

"The Miamis . . . led the attack . . .

"They came up the back way . . . the gully route . . .

"Only we knew this way," Sleeping Crow said, panting. "During the canoe fight . . . the first Iroquois appeared behind us . . .

"They shot some of our braves. Then set the grass afire . . .

"Forced us to the cliffs—like buffalo!

"A few of our braves were captured. . . . It didn't matter. The Iroquois threw everyone over . . .

"I alone escaped. I climbed down the hidden path. I found a canoe . . . and came here."

Chief Chassagoac, beside himself with anger, turned to his chiefs. "Nicanope, hurry to Kickapoo Creek. That is where the traitorous Miamis are bringing their new friends.

"Omawaha, take as many warriors as you need. Go help Nicanope. Attack from above the ravine. We do not have much time." Chief Chassagoac spoke bitterly. Realizing their failure could expose his flank, he added, "I will move my defenses below the mouth of the Kickapoo."

"Nicanope, do your best to protect your men. Our men do not yet know how to fight against the Iroquois. For us it is a mark of courage to touch a live enemy or take his weapon in battle. These Rattlesnakes are murderers. They kill the wounded; they do not want prisoners," Chief Omawaha exclaimed.

"On Plum Island, I watched my men charge, only to be slaughtered. Our weapons of stone and bone are of little effect against their iron hatchets and muskets. The Iroquois have learned a new kind of warfare from the white man. The white man fights only to kill. The more he kills, the greater his glory. This is not the Indian way. On the island, many died because we do not understand the white man's way of war. We do not fight against Indians but against something far worse, we fight against evil."

In spite of his agitation, Nicanope considered Omawaha's remarks. Exchanging glances with Chassagoac, he signaled his men to follow him and ran toward the enemy.

Nicanope's men raced up Kickapoo Creek, into the canyon it follows before crossing the flats to the Illinois River. On the narrow bank they hastily erected a makeshift abatis. Their right was protected by high bluffs, the left by the creek, and before them a narrow defile.

The initial attack down Kickapoo Creek stalled against Nicanope's barrier. The Iroquois began a series of probing attacks, using maneuver and firepower to provoke an opening.

Meanwhile Chief Omawaha with his warriors dashed obliquely to the northwest, over the ridge, in an attempt to come to the top of the narrows. He hoped to attack the rear of the Iroquois force, to box them in the canyon, to compel the enemy to fight where the musket would prove less useful.

Coming over the ridge with a band of Onandaga warriors, Moves-the-Clouds immediately realized the danger, and igniting a firebrand, torched the dry buffalo grass ahead of Omawaha's force. The breeze from the plains carried the blaze toward the Illinois; the phalanx of sizzling flame and suffocating smoke screened the movements of the raiders.

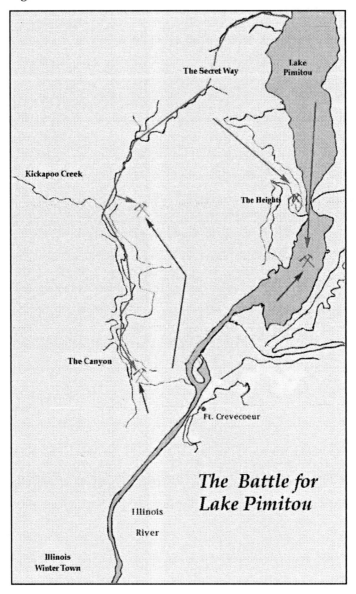

The Battle for
Lake Pimitou

Isolated, irregular pockets fought for survival as Omawaha's advance was checked. Onandagas joined now by Mohawk warriors leapt through the walls of fire, assailing the confused detachments. Exposed, Omawaha's force now fought to regain the defense barrier.

A grassfire was started down the canyon, coming onto Chief Nicanope's position, igniting the abatis. The freshly cut, green brush produced an immense, billowing white cloud. From his place near the river, Plenty Fish watched as the Illinois positions disappeared beneath the smoke.

Choking and disoriented, some of Nicanope's men attempted to escape through the flames, blinded and in pain, only to be hacked down by preying Iroquois. Like phantasms, the enemy came rushing through the smoke, attacking, killing, and disappearing once again.

Singly, or in small numbers, the trapped Illinois warriors escaped one fate only to meet another. One Moingwena, his skin blistered and his loincloth burning yet managed to trade his life for that of a Mohawk.

Leading a small band of Illinois, Wea, and Piankashaw Indians, Sleeping Crow attempted to rescue Omawaha's force. Loosing a barrage of arrows toward a cluster of Oneida and Seneca warriors, Sleeping Crow cast his bow aside and plunged into the enemy flank, smashing the skull of the first opponent with his tomahawk, dodging a slashing move, counterstriking, killing the second.

Sleeping Crow's vision was uncommonly acute, minute details discernible, the flow of time unusually slow. Yet he remained keenly aware of the all-round situation. Breathing deeply, he was dancing. It was a new, unknown rhythm. His body was graceful, coordinated in every move, whether erect, swooping low, spinning about, avoiding blows, slicing with the knife in his hand, swinging the tomahawk. All thought, all emotion dissipated; only the instant was real; there was no future, no past, no hate nor fear; there was simply an ecstatic blend of strength, movement, and skill.

Spinning aside as an Iroquois lance glanced off his shoulder, Sleeping Crow smashed the enemy's arm, and reeling, disemboweled another. Then with a great blow with his tomahawk, he severed the head of a third. Pausing, he looked around and saw that the fight was receding. He wanted to pursue the enemy but felt a need to rest.

Only then did Sleeping Crow realize that there was intense pain and wetness on his shoulder, that there were other wounds on his back and thigh. Noticing his nakedness, he sat down. Smiling because he was wearing only one moccasin, he laughed to himself, feeling giddy. Glancing about the area, he saw many bodies, many of which seemed merely to be sleeping although marked with gruesome wounds. Feeling warm all over, with increasing soreness and several smarting wounds, Sleeping Crow lay down on his stomach, near a fallen enemy. Looking at the Onandaga, Sleeping Crow was amused by his expression—eyes wide open, tongue protruding as though seeking to lick the beetle crawling past the end of his nose. Laughing at the silly spectacle, Sleeping Crow lapsed into a deep sleep.

Later, a passing Mohawk ensured that Sleeping Crow would sleep forever.

* * *

"Our men are the bravest, but that is not enough! We cannot hold much longer," Chief Chassagoac announced to the war council. "We have slowed the enemy on Kickapoo Creek. But we must again retreat. We will defend the riverfront so we can rescue our braves. Burn the grasses. Alert all warriors. We must move quickly."

Beneath the gathering smoke of the new fires, hundreds of Illinois braves fought their way to the canoe park to begin their second, long day's journey south.

* * *

The first of the Iroquois war canoes were descending the lower section of *Lake Pimitou* as the last of the defenders escaped. Hugging the shoreline to preclude detection by the enemy, the flotilla came cautiously toward the mouth of the lake. Although an ominous-looking fleet in the distance, many of the thirty or so canoes were empty, riding along on tethers. A caretaker crew that had guarded the canoes was now slowly bringing them to the battle area.

Meanwhile at the mouth of Kickapoo Creek, Gray Eyes and Ghost Deer, finding that the retreating Illinois had destroyed or disabled their surplus canoes, rushed to the lakeshore seeking their own vessels. Frustrated that their boats were still many minutes away, and impatient to pursue the enemy, they began cruising the waterfront seeking opportunities to vent their outrage at having again fallen short of total victory.

Seeing some native dwellings as well as La Salle's works on the opposite shore, the two braves swam the chill river. Ascending the bluffs to Fort Crèvecoeur, they rampaged through those neglected buildings but found little of value.

Like ants on a honeycomb, a growing number of braves swarmed over the hulk of La Salle's ship. Using whatever means they could, the warriors removed everything made of iron, even pulling some of the nails from the frame.

"It is evening; we will camp here tonight," one of the Iroquois war chiefs said, summoning chiefs and braves. Gathered beneath the shadow of La Salle's vessel, the war council again convened.

One of the Turtle clan, a Seneca, addressed the council.

"Ghost Deer speaks," he said, asking for a hearing. "Our fathers have fought and destroyed many tribes and nations. The Eries. The Tobaccos. The Neutrals. Even the once great Hurons! These are no more. Let their countless and abandoned graves bring fear to our enemies!

"Many who would trade with the French now know there is no safety in distance. *Hodenosaunee* warriors have traveled far, to the great lakes and beyond. Many there fear our might. We have punished the *Adawes*. The *Illiniwek* have tasted our iron. But they have not suffered enough! We must scourge them so that all tribes know the pain that comes from dealing with the impudent French."

Moves-the-Clouds rose to speak. "Twice the enemy has escaped. If we destroy their canoes, we will defeat the *Illiniwek*. But how can we attack their canoes? They are protected and hidden downriver. If we send a small war party, it will be seen."

"There is a way," Swims-like-Beaver said, standing to be recognized. "The Seneca can slip past a watchful enemy. Swims-like-Beaver will prevent their escape."

Silence fell as the council members became thoughtful. An Oneida chief regarded Swims-like-Beaver for a few moments, then asked, "You mean to do this alone? You can attack their canoes without assistance?"

"It is the only way. One brave can pass their guards unnoticed. Only one is needed to smash their boats. I can do this."

"Swims-like-Beaver is truly brave," the Oneida chief observed, then added, "but you will surely die."

"No! They do not guard their boats with their best warriors. I shall live. But if I do not, tell the young women of my deeds," Swims-like-Beaver said proudly. "Let them remember me and sing songs of my brave acts."

A murmur passed through the assembled group. A few nodded admiring approvals, for this could well be an outstanding act of courage of this war, and there were already many such acts to boast of.

"I must prepare now. The Illinois canoes will be destroyed before you attack," Swims-like-Beaver promised then left the council to dance for a while with the other braves.

Into the night the braves sang their war chants, reenacted fights previously won, and fought imaginary foes, providing earnest testimony of their individual valor.

* * *

Once again, but later than the evening before, the bright, full moon had risen. By this time even the hindmost Illinois canoes were at least forty miles down river, gliding on its silvery, moonlit surface. Beckoning brightly over the plains, the moon ever guided them to the limits of their territory, to the limits of their endurance, to the limits of their existence. Ahead, the final camp lay on a long, narrow peninsula just before the Illinois and Mississippi Rivers joined.

Here were waiting the families of the braves.

Russell Breighner

Chapter 11

Quiet Waters

Before dawn the war fleet of the Iroquois and their Miami allies began its swift course down the morning-misty river, seeking the enemy. The warriors smugly assumed the twice-beaten Illinois would not, indeed could not, attempt an ambush; the angels of death were supremely confident of final victory.

After roughly ten hours the warriors came upon one of the advance canoes returning from its probing mission. The scouts reported that the Illinois camp had been located, about an hour ahead, and that Swims-like-Beaver had begun his operation.

Hiding their canoes, Iroquois and Miami warriors checked their hand weapons, muskets, powder, and shot as they prepared for the assault.

Having found a suitable site on the river, Swims-like-Beaver prepared for his one-man raid. First he gathered a few reeds, checked his knife and tomahawk, then tied his war club to his back and removed his moccasins and breechclout. Except for his weapons and war paint, he was naked.

A drifting tree had grounded nearby in shoal water. With some difficulty he used a piece of driftwood to lever the trunk into the stream. When the log was again afloat, Swims-like-Beaver used his feet to propel it farther into the main current. Slowly as the old tree moved away from the shallows, it began to respond to the pull of the river.

When the log came to mid-stream, Swims-like-Beaver ceased kicking and slipped under the water. Breathing through the reeds, he remained hidden near the roots.

Safely beyond the Illinois lookouts, Swims-like-Beaver swam to the riverbank, untied his war club, and settled near a tree to rest and to listen. His hatred generated a sense of satisfaction since his efforts would surely bring death to many. He arrogantly dismissed any thought but that he himself would kill numerous braves. Today the Illinois Confederacy would end. And he, Swims-like-Beaver, would have a glorious share in that triumph.

Swims-like-Beaver had not erred in his estimate of the Illinois dispositions. Discovering the trail to the Illinois canoe park, he advanced cautiously, but was nevertheless disappointed in finding it unguarded. All canoes had been placed inverted on the ground, some covered with branches and foliage. Using his knife, he stealthily slit several, leaving huge gashes in the hulls. Impatient with his slow progress, he began smashing boats with his war club, disdainful of the racket. He was astonished he could make so much noise and yet no one challenged him.

He had destroyed a fair number of canoes when he heard the sudden swish of an arrow passing overhead. Before he could recoil, a second crashed into his knee. With a howl, he reeled, stumbled and, falling onto a canoe, slid to the ground. The pain was insufferable. Swims-like-Beaver tried but could not remove the arrow. At best he was able to break off the shaft, the arrowhead remaining embedded in the joint.

His leg was useless, inflexible. Using his war club as a crutch, Swims-like-Beaver pulled himself around until he was sitting against the canoe, facing the direction of the enemy who had wounded him. Swims-like-Beaver briefly considered using his knife to pry out the arrowhead when a motion in the tall grass caught his attention.

Three Illinois boys—Buffalo Calf, Muskrat, and Milkweed—cautiously edged forward, angry yet curious. The apparent canoe guard, each was armed with bow and arrow. Swims-like-Beaver sensed their goal to master an enemy exceeded their experience.

Frustrated by his immobility and chagrined by the absence of a worthy opponent, Swims-like-Beaver began yelling fierce war cries, attempting to intimidate the boys.

Not certain of the extent of damage to the enemy, the three maintained a wary distance. Although it was obvious the clamorous Iroquois must be finished off, none yet dared attempt the deathblow.

Confident of the timidity of these canoe guards, Swims-like-Beaver readied his tomahawk. As the boys circled their wounded prey, Swims-like-Beaver waited for an opportunity, but not for long.

Muskrat, passing behind a sycamore, did not see the Seneca's sudden motion. As he stepped into the open, the whirling tomahawk thudded into his head, killing him instantly.

Overcoming his inertia, Buffalo Calf summoned his courage, loosing an arrow toward the hideous monster. Shot in the throat, the Indian immediately slumped over, seeming dead. Relieved of tension and elated, Buffalo Calf exulted over his victory.

Curious at last to examine his victim, Buffalo Calf approached Swims-like-Beaver, prepared to cut off the scalp lock. As he pulled the head back from the bloody chest, he was stunned to see Swims-like-Beaver's clear eyes focused on his own, the enemy's face contorted with anger and pain. Surprised, the boy froze. In a flash, Swims-like-Beaver grabbed the boy, pulling him off his feet. Gargling a grotesque war whoop, Swims-like-Beaver brought his knife around, swiftly slicing the boy's throat. Together they died, their hearts freely pumping out the last of their lifeblood.

Thoroughly shaken by the events he had just witnessed, the third boy, Milkweed, collapsed to his knees, convulsing with dry heaves. After a few moments, he slowly rose onto his unstable legs. Wiping tears from his eyes, he abandoned his post, at first with hesitation, but with increasing distance, running more swiftly until he came at last to the Indian camp. There he collapsed again, sprawling on the ground, feeling great wretchedness, overtaken with a deep revulsion.

Recognizing the boy as one of those sent to guard the canoes, Nicanope came over and asked, "What is this? Why are you here? Are you ill? Tell me, what is the matter?"

"An Iroquois . . . killed . . . my friends . . . ," Milkweed stammered. He rose to his feet and stood there shivering and weak. "Muskrat and Buffalo Calf. They're dead."

"What Iroquois! Are the enemies among our canoes?" Nicanope was extremely vexed by the news and impatient at the boy's incoherence.

"Only one. We killed him!" The boy spun around, again convulsing.

"Rest, brave one. You have done well." Helping the boy sit, Nicanope signaled some nearby women to come and care for him. Nicanope then ran off to inform Chief Chassagoac of the situation.

"An Iroquois warrior has destroyed many Tamaroa canoes. Our guards killed him," Nicanope announced to the war council. "Perhaps the Iroquois have not attacked for a reason. The Rattlesnakes have set a trap for us."

"How many Iroquois?" Chief Chassagoac turned, a look of concern on his haggard face.

"Only one," Nicanope said. "I have sent a few braves to make sure remaining canoes are safe."

"Our people must leave!" Chief Chassagoac was feeling distraught after two days and nights of combat and flight. The camp was crowded with thousands of refugees as well as one or two hundred wounded braves. "Tell the women to take our children. Go now to our friends on the *misi-sipi*. Take our families to safety!"

Plenty Fish had overheard the conversation between the chiefs. He was sitting at the base of a broad willow in a bivouac area for the wounded

One warrior, suffering with a deeply embedded musket ball, although moaning, was otherwise uncomplaining. A slippery elm splint had been inserted to keep the wound channel open, allowing suppuration eventually to bring out the bullet.

A woman sucked dry the wound of another brave before applying a plaster of mud and white pine needles over his injury.

A third man had a badly lacerated throat and chest; blood and a clear liquid oozed from his wounds. It was difficult to tell whether this brave would continue his already improbable survival.

Another—the top of his head a bright red mass—incredibly, had survived being scalped.

Making their way to the canoe parks, many people came thronging around the injured men. From out of the crowd Elizabeth suddenly appeared. She was standing beside Plenty Fish, when, surprised, he looked up and saw her. He had not seen her since the French had left Kaskaskia. His joy at seeing her was tempered with concern that she was still in danger.

"Would you like to have your wounds treated?" she asked in a pleasant, impersonal manner. Then without waiting for an answer, she knelt beside him and opened her kit. She had been nursing other patients and had a selection of medicines with her.

With a tea made from crushed buttercup roots she cleansed the gash on his arm and the arrow wounds on his body. She then closed the wounds, covering them with green leaves. She bound the arm with strips of pine bark.

"Shouldn't you be leaving with your mother?" Plenty Fish asked as she finished. "I wonder why you have not already gone. It is dangerous here."

"It is still early," Elizabeth replied, reassuring him with a wan smile. She smeared a mud paste over the leaves covering his body wounds and began rubbing a raccoon fat balm on his bruised shoulder muscles. "There are so many now crowding the riverbank. It is just a matter of being patient. We will be all right. Mother is collecting our things. Soon we shall be safely away. Shouldn't you be leaving with the other wounded?"

"No, I may be able to help here," Plenty Fish said, wincing as a sudden pain shot through his body. "I can see that it is not easy for you to leave."

"No," she replied, pausing to look into his eyes. Then finishing the treatment, Elizabeth continued, "It is not easy. We are leaving our homeland. Perhaps forever."

"Do you know where you will go?" Plenty Fish touched her hand as she rewound her medicine pouch. Firmly but gently he clasped her hand in his.

Hesitating while she considered the man before her, Elizabeth relaxed, then said, "Mother has friends among the Missouri tribes. We will go there."

"I will come for you," Plenty Fish said quietly, "and I will bring you back to your homeland."

Elizabeth sat back on her heels, disconcerted by the man's directness, yet encouraged by his confidence and courage.

"The Iroquois will attack shortly. You will not be here then?" she asked, almost in a whisper.

"This war will soon be finished," Plenty Fish said. "I will find you. We shall go where there is no war, where the water quietly flows."

Fighting to remain outwardly composed, Elizabeth rose to her feet. "I must go to my mother now. I think it is time to leave," she said, looking deeply into his eyes.

After a moment, Elizabeth turned and with a self-conscious awkwardness, walked slowly to her mother's lodge. Overcome with bittersweet emotions, Elizabeth could not resolve the conflicting sensations now tearing at her.

A zinging noise like the sound of an angry wasp caught Plenty Fish's attention. As he regained his sense of location, he realized the 'wasps' were musket balls flying past. The Iroquois had begun their attack and were not far away. Despite the reluctance of his stiff and aching body, Plenty Fish moved to safety on the lee side of the willow.

Nearby Chief Chassagoac was conferring with several war chiefs when a runner came to report heavy pressure on the west flank. Hardly had this report been made when a second runner came in. Iroquois attacks from the north were causing many casualties there.

"Are our lines holding?" Chief Chassagoac asked, deeply perplexed. "Tell our men they must hold. We have few reserves. We cannot send reinforcements; we must protect our escape."

Freshly wounded braves appeared at the edge of the clearing, some stumbling, others helping their comrades limp to safety.

"The enemy is making breakthroughs in our main defense!" Another runner, a grazing wound on his side, came to report. "The men are losing spirit. We cannot hold there much longer. . . . Several areas are already in danger of being overrun."

"The Iroquois fights in the white man's way. In war, Indians delight in acts of courage; the Iroquois delights only in acts of killing. The Iroquois has taken not only the white man's weapons, but also the white man's hatred of life!" Chief Chassagoac intently studied each of his chiefs in turn.

After a moment of reflection, Nicanope shook his head, adding grimly, "The Iroquois did not come to count coup against the Illinois. They want only our blood."

"When will this murder cease?" Chief Chassagoac cried out. Brandishing his war lance, he yelled, "The Iroquois have killed so many of our people. Yet they do not stop. What have we done to deserve this?

"Why have the Iroquois come to the Illinois lands? . . . Do they want our beaver furs? Our buffalo robes? . . . No! . . . Do they want our land? . . . No, they do not! . . . Do they want our tribute? . . . No, again no! . . . They want only our blood!" Chief Chassagoac raged in great distress.

"Who has made the Iroquois so angry they should come so far to kill so many? . . . It is the English! . . . They are jealous of the French . . ." Shaking furiously, Chief Chassagoac cried out, "Is this why we must die?

"Now I know why Jesus Christ came to the white man and not to the Indian! . . . The white man is evil! . . . The Iroquois come to do the white man's evil . . ." Chief Chassagoac said in anguish, "Leave my people in peace! . . . Let my people live!"

As, limp with exhaustion, Chief Chassagoac stomped off to perform his final offices in the defense of his people, Plenty Fish saw the first deserters running from the fight. Their spirit obviously broken, they were now increasing the crowded confusion in the camp. Wide-eyed with fear, uncertain as to their destination, these men hurried along, some wobbly-legged, looking neither back nor to the side, as if half expecting the enemy to appear from any quarter.

Pulling himself upright and bracing against the tree, Plenty Fish attempted to stem the rout. "Why the rush?" he yelled at the nearest brave. "We can hold the Iroquois. Why are you men not fighting? Where are your weapons?"

One brave stared at Plenty Fish but kept moving. He soon disappeared. A second stopped, but said nothing.

Plenty Fish spoke to the man directly. Under an insistent questioning, the man finally mumbled something to the effect that many Iroquois were behind the Illinois position, destroying the canoes.

Recognizing the poison affecting these men, Plenty Fish yelled, "No! There are no Iroquois among the canoes. There was one, but he is dead. There is no need for fear on this account. Take my word on it."

Plenty Fish could see his words were having an effect. Some of the men, recovering from their panic, began to feel a shame that soon yielded to certain anger. Plenty Fish had stopped one small group., but as these men were regaining their courage, more came running. The rumor of a large Iroquois raid on the canoes had become a disabling distortion, hopelessly weakening the defense.

Nicanope hurried into the wounded bivouac. He quickly noted the worst cases had already evacuated. Calling to Plenty Fish, he said, "The Tamaroas have declared they will fight like rooted oaks: They will die, but they will not move! Those who escape will owe much to these braves . . . . It is time to leave. . . In many areas, the Iroquois are breaking our defenses . . . . There is little time. Those who can—To the boats!"

Checking his knife and hatchet, Plenty Fish headed toward the canoe park, expecting he knew not what.

As he passed beyond the village, Plenty Fish saw further signs of defeat. Several Iroquois warriors had raced among the lodges, shooting, knifing, or clubbing women, children and older people as they went. A bloody surge marked the crumbling of the defenses.

The thrill of victory had only increased the attacker's appetite for blood. Firebrands were thrown onto thatched lodges and the emerging survivors ruthlessly slaughtered. Small children had been impaled, then left hanging high on lances planted in the ground. Plenty Fish saw that the breakthrough was quickly becoming a rout.

* * *

Seeking enemy braves, the Iroquois had discovered a new foe. One Oneida, racing past a lodge was suddenly doubled over. A woman, springing from concealment, had cleaved his mid-section with a war-club. Another woman ambushed a second warrior, splitting his skull with a tomahawk.

Some of the women used organized tactics. They would trap a solitary brave, finish him, and then move to another covert position. The collecting number of Iroquois bodies, though few, became a warning to others that a danger existed. Becoming more cautious in their foray, the Iroquois began searching in teams, probing, checking, and looking for ambuscades.

One woman, flushed from her concealment, attacked the nearest warrior but was knocked from her feet and run through with a lance. Another woman, cornered by several braves, sliced the side of an Onandaga's jaw with her tomahawk, smashed the ribs of a Cayuga, and turning, struck a Mohawk before being grabbed from behind, an arm around her throat, a hand seizing her weapon. Off balance, she was disarmed and captured.

Grinning at his prisoner, the man yelled at the other warriors, "Manly women! These women fight like men. Let us see if they are really brave. Let them taste Iroquois torture. Then we shall see! AIEEEEE!" he whooped and threw the woman to the ground.

* * *

Elizabeth was inside their lodge, helping her mother, Dawn Bird, prepare for departure when the first Iroquois came shrieking into their area. Taking a large stone from the fire pit, Elizabeth stood just inside the entrance and waited. A Mohawk stuck his head through the opening, hesitating as his eyes adjusted to the darkness. In that instant Elizabeth smashed his skull. Taking his knife, she dragged the body clear of the doorway.

Checking that no other enemies were near, Elizabeth signaled her mother and the two exited the lodge, running toward the canoe area. Hardly had she gone ten paces when her mother suddenly gasped and collapsed. An arrow had caught her from behind, striking squarely between the shoulders. Dawn Bird died instantly, quietly.

Elizabeth stared at her mother, lying on one side, her knees drawn up, her face showing only surprise, one hand tightly clutching a tuft of grass. Waves of nausea, grief, and anger came in turn as Elizabeth struggled to regain her self-control. But she could not. A Seneca came bounding across the open area, his war-yelp piercing Elizabeth's soul. As she faced her attacker, her numbed mind saw the up-raised war club as something impersonal, not a threat; looking into the warrior's face, she saw only hateful ugliness. The man's eyes were fixed on her, his tense face a mask of concentrated fury, his red war paint and black tattoos adding a gruesome emphasis.

In mid-swing, inexplicably the man's arm went limp, his war club flying harmlessly away. His expression changed to puzzlement as his knees buckled. Looking down at the collapsed warrior, Elizabeth saw the iron hatchet buried in his chest. His final, unintelligible words, mumbled in agony, were encapsulated in a gargled, bloody froth.

Puzzled, Elizabeth turned to see Plenty Fish running toward her. "Come!" he called. "We must find the canoes. Other Iroquois will soon be here. We must hurry!"

Grabbing her by the arm, Plenty Fish pulled Elizabeth away, she, for a while, looking back at her mother's form. Together they passed through some concealing brush. Emerging near the river, they surprised a lone Cayuga brave. Plenty Fish jumped him, grappled for his weapon, and wrestled him to the ground. Struggling to break free, the Cayuga tried rolling to one side, kicking violently. Elizabeth rushed up, saw an opportunity, and struck fiercely with her Iroquois knife. The knife plunged through bladder, the tip imbedding itself in the pelvic bone.

The sudden, intense pain immediately ended the Cayuga's resistance. Plenty Fish stood over the writhing, howling warrior, unsheathed his own knife and prepared to deliver the coup de grace. However, his would-be act of mercy was forestalled.

Three Iroquois warriors came barreling through the tall grass, one knocking Plenty Fish to the ground. Another went to aid the injured Cayuga, pulling the knife from his wound. But this did little to lessen the man's torment.

"Iron! This man has an iron knife. He is a friend of the French!" The Onandaga displayed the blade for all to see. Turning to Elizabeth he exclaimed, "Look! She wears the cross of the Gray Robes. These two must receive special treatment."

The Iroquois quickly bound Plenty Fish and Elizabeth to stakes near the riverbank. A parade of several hundred women prisoners was brought in; many were tied to nearby trees. Plenty Fish knew then that the war was lost.

"When their braves vanished into the tall grass, these women fought like men. Now we shall test their courage!" Laughing ironically, the Onandaga rudely jabbed one with the butt of his war club. "Now they shall learn to respect the Iroquois."

The sky was turning a dark blue-gray as dusk settled. While scattered sounds of battle echoed faint and far, the Iroquois readied their victory celebration. Around a fire built near the captives, warriors came whooping and taunting the prisoners. Several hundred Iroquois and Miami braves, still intoxicated with battlelust, gathered for the ritual of courage.

Yelling fearsome cries of victory and vengeance, dancing braves wound their way among the prisoners, demonstrating with mocking gestures the coming fate of the vanquished.

A cluster of Bear clan warriors took special delight in provoking Plenty Fish, poking him roughly and screaming insults in his face.

After a period, a Mohawk went behind the tree, and taking Plenty Fish's bound hand, began gnawing his fingernails. He chewed until he had loosened the nail, then, clenching it in his teeth, jerked it free, until one by one, several of Plenty Fish's fingers became throbbing, bloody stumps. Returning insult for injury, Plenty Fish yelled back at his tormentors, masking his agony with defiance. He could only watch helplessly as two warriors approached Elizabeth. While an Oneida glowered in her face, a Seneca, taking one of her tied hands, spread it flat against the tree behind her. Using his knife, he brutally severed a joint. Holding it before her eyes, he mocked her courage. "Now you will beg for your life! Beg for Iroquois mercy!"

In spite the pain and derision, Elizabeth felt only disgust. Overcome with a momentary weakness, she nearly collapsed. In defiance she spit into the Seneca's face.

Waving a firebrand in front of Plenty Fish, another Mohawk taunted him. "Do you fear this fire? You will learn. Watch the warrior's dance of fire!"

Crouched over and waving the burning wood over his head, the brave stomped around in a circle before Plenty Fish. As he swirled the flaming torch, sparks rained down upon his back. Indifferent to the pain, he only yelled the louder, continuing his dance.

"See? These sparks are delightful! Now we shall entertain you!" Yelling his war cry, the Mohawk thrust the burning torch into Plenty Fish's crotch. Plenty Fish jerked his head and screamed.

"Illinois! Ask for a quick death. It is the Iroquois who have you. Do you wish for an easy death?" One of the Onondagas insolently screamed over Plenty Fish's tortured wailing.

"I do not ask for Iroquois mercy," Plenty Fish yelled back at his tormentor.

The Onandaga laughed derisively. From behind, a second caressed Plenty Fish's wounded arm. The latter began working a fire-sharpened shaft into the back of the arm at the elbow. Slowly pushing the wood toward the wrist, the man stomped with delight as his victim recoiled with each twist and turn.

Pleased that Plenty Fish and Elizabeth were proving worthy, the tormentors moved on to other prisoners. For some time screams could be heard as the women each in turn underwent some personal torture.

Elizabeth strained to see what was happening.

"Don't look!" commanded Plenty Fish. "It is better that you do not see what they are doing. If the Iroquois know you are watching, they will only punish the others more. Do not make your friends suffer. It will be hard enough for us. Don't let the Iroquois break your spirit!"

Elizabeth stood there, consumed with the pain of her amputation, trying not to heed the sudden shrieks marking the progress of the torture of the manly women. Turning toward Plenty Fish, she called, "Remember your promise! Let us meet at the place of quiet waters. We shall find peace there, together."

"Sing your song, Elizabeth," Plenty Fish encouraged her. "Sing of your youth. Sing of your happy times. Sing, Elizabeth!"

Elizabeth began to chant, *"When I was a young girl, the boys would chase after me. I was happy in those days, not long ago. Not long ago, I was free. This was my happy time."*

An Iroquois who understood the Illinois tongue snarled, "You recall the fun days, huh? Let me help you remember!"

Plenty Fish saw the man wield his knife, then saw the small bit of flesh as he cast it over his shoulder. The Iroquois laughed at her agony.

Straining against her bonds until they cut deeper, Elizabeth continued her chant, tears streaming down her cheeks.

"Illinois, you like her singing? It is not right you should only listen. You must dance to her song."

Plenty Fish was freed from his tree. The Iroquois then tied hanks of dry grass around his legs. Elated with anticipation, they cheered as these torches blazed. As Plenty Fish hopped about, trying to extinguish his flaming leggings, the Iroquois howled even louder, doubling over with amusement.

Plenty Fish yelled to Elizabeth, "Sing your song! Do not mind what they are doing to me. Sing of your family!"

Again, after an effort, Elizabeth began to sing, *"My father was kind to me. He was a great hunter. My mother . . . ."* She stopped, overcome with grief.

Elizabeth looked away as the Iroquois prepared a new torment.

Two hatchets attached by the handles to a hoop were heated in the fire. Then this necklace was placed over Plenty Fish's head, one hatchet hanging in front, the other behind. Spinning round, he attempted to swing the searing scourges away from his body. Bucking back and forth, Plenty Fish recoiled from the pain in his chest only to receive further, searing pain between his shoulders. Yelling and dancing in this grotesque manner, he produced yet further entertainment for the taunting Iroquois. Finally, the hatchets cooled and Plenty Fish stood, trembling from his ordeal, his legs weak to the point of collapse.

Leaving Plenty Fish to recover, the tormentors returned to Elizabeth. Plenty Fish could only see the man's back as he drew his knife and moved it across her face. Offended by her responses to his mocking leers, the Iroquois had blinded her.

Gazing at her wounds, Plenty Fish began weeping.

Seeing these tears, an Oneida exclaimed, "He is weak. See, he fears our treatment!"

"No, I do not fear the least spit from you dogs!" Plenty Fish shot back. "I am crying for my friend.

"Sing, Elizabeth!" Plenty Fish, exhausted and in great thirst, hoarsely yelled, "Sing! Sing, Elizabeth, for our people!"

"Along the silver waters, in the forests of the land, lives a great people, a kind people. Our people, noble and free—" she chanted, barely raising her voice.

A Seneca interrupted. "Your people die! We have killed many, and we will kill many more. The Iroquois will soon eat your hearts!"

"No! It is the Iroquois who are dead. You eat only the shit that comes from the ass of the English dogs!" Elizabeth hissed.

"This woman does not know how to control her tongue!" The Seneca, rolling his eyes in exaggerated, mock indignation, yelled to his comrades. "She must learn to respect the Iroquois!"

Plenty Fish saw the man's angry motion and heard his taunting call, "Sing now, Illinois! We are waiting for your song!"

Plenty Fish could hear only a muffled, gurgling sound. As he looked at her in her pitiful state, he was moved by her courage.

"Iroquois! You can not defeat her," he called. "She has seen you sons of dogs for what you are. Her song will still be heard long after the snows have covered your frozen graves."

Abruptly, scattered shooting erupted beyond the firelight. A large number of Miami warriors came running, chased by howling Iroquois. One Miami brave was knocked to the ground near Elizabeth. Immediately several Mohawk warriors jumped on the prostrate man and hacked him to death. Nearby, other warriors died in a similar manner, the area soon becoming strewn with dead and dying Miami braves.

A muffled sound from Elizabeth caught Plenty Fish's attention. Answering her question, he said, "It's the Miamis. The Iroquois are killing their allies, the ones who betrayed us. It is fitting!"

Elizabeth nodded, making some guttural sound of approval. Contemptuous of her unyielding resistance, an Oneida angrily pulled his knife ready to disfigure her further.

Realizing this signaled immediate death, for the Iroquois do not tolerate those with mutilated faces to live, Plenty Fish cried out, "Elizabeth, you are not alone! My heart beats for you. Your song is always with me!"

Before she could respond, a second Oneida drove a lance through Elizabeth's chest, killing her instantly. Quickly he cut out her heart. Holding it high before Plenty Fish, he yelled triumphantly, "Now she has no songs to sing! You will hear her no more forever!"

Trembling against his bonds, Plenty Fish cried hoarsely, "Beside the restful waters, Elizabeth, wait! I will find you there!"

"Friend of the French! Be calm! You must see the others die," a Cayuga answered. "We want you to stay with us for a while. We have special treats for *les Amis*."

"Hungry?" another sneered. "We have prepared something for you to eat."

An Indian came forward with a bowl of dark soup. It was an Iroquois custom to nourish their victims to extend their endurance. Prolonging the victim's suffering increased the entertainment while further testing endurance. "Here, let our guest try this."

Managing a mouthful, Plenty Fish remained defiant. In spite of his suffering, he felt a sense of superiority in mastering himself and his enemies.

Meanwhile, several Iroquois went among the surviving women prisoners, slaughtering them. The rite of courage was drawing to a close.

"So? How is it? Do you find this tasty?" Holding the bowl close to Plenty Fish, the Iroquois smiled sarcastically.

Between gasps, Plenty Fish took a few small sips from the proffered ladle. The warm, thick broth coursed down his throat, but did little to alleviate his thirst. "Water, give me water. I need water."

"In a while, we will give you water. Do you want more food now, Illinois?" the Iroquois smirked.

"A little," Plenty Fish winced from pain as he sipped again. "What is this? It is somehow different."

"It is our specialty. It is a porridge of child's brains!" The Iroquois grinned broadly, then burst out laughing.

Plenty Fish convulsed and strained against his bonds. Spitting, he tried to expel the taste but his mouth was soon dry again.

With feigned amazement, the Cayuga turned toward his comrades, "Our guest does not approve of our gruel!"

"He seems about to throw up," another guffawed. "Maybe he has been out in the sun too long today. He does seem tired."

"We should help him rest," said another.

"Yes," said the Cayuga. "We will help him cleanse his system."

The four helped Plenty Fish limp to a sapling.

Plenty Fish stood there overwhelmed with pain, yet resigned and hoping for a quick end.

More warriors gathered round, many grinning in anticipation.

"My brothers! Why have you come here? Who has sent you to kill the Illinois?" Plenty Fish called out hoarsely. "You are doing this evil for the white man. It is the English settlers, the *Bostonais*, who are using you."

Plenty Fish paused to moisten his mouth, then resumed, "The English want us dead only because we are friends of the French—the French who treat us with dignity and respect. There is no quarrel between the Illinois and the Iroquois. We have lived here in peace and we have done you no harm."

"The Illinois wish to trade with the French. The fate of the Illinois will be the same as the fate of the Eries and the Neutrals! Consider this—we offered them membership in our League, but they refused," an Onandaga replied. "They chose to die. Now they are no more."

"Our trade does not harm the Iroquois. Your terms have nothing to do with trade," Plenty Fish shot back. "There are many beaver lakes in your lands. The Rattlesnakes do not need our furs, you want only our blood."

Amused and nodding encouragement, several called out, "You are a good speaker. Tell us more, Illinois!"

"It was not always this way. Before the white man gave you weapons and gave you enemies, the *Ho-de'-no-sau-nee* lived in peace in his own lands. Since the white man came, you have killed whole peoples. You have spilled water on many of your brothers' council fires." Plenty Fish halted, his voice hoarse and his mouth dry. "It is you who have given away your honor and your freedom."

A tattooed Oneida, wearing a red deer hair roach, offered water, which Plenty Fish drank slowly, savoring each drop before swallowing.

"My Brothers! The *Bostonais* will become great in numbers. Then they will call you 'savage' for what you do here now, but they are the real savage. They treat you and all Indians with contempt. They will take your muskets so that you cannot hunt. In the winter your people will starve. They will place you under their law and put you in their jails where there is no dignity for the Indian. They will hang you with a rope, a death that has no glory for the Indian. They will take your hunting lands, they will tell you where to build your lodges, where to farm, where to hunt. In the end, the white man will laugh in your face for he has made you savage, he has made you worthless."

"Yes, we are the white man's savage," one of the Cayugas replied, mocking Plenty Fish. "But now it is time for you to die, *Illiniwek!*"

Thankful that his end was near, Plenty Fish began to chant his death song. *"Thank You, O Great Spirit, for my life. My enemies have cut me, they have burned me, they have given me every insult. I have not flinched, I have not asked for mercy, I have not bowed. I have not betrayed my family, my tribe, or my Nation. Before my foes I die with honor.*

"Maker of All Things! Guide my spirit that I may not wander forever restless. Bring me to Elizabeth that our spirits may be together."

Impelled by the mob to take some action, the Cayuga drew his knife and holding it high, displayed it to all, slowly turning as he did so. Satisfied that he had sufficiently aroused the anticipation of the crowd, he faced Plenty Fish.

Plenty Fish looked toward the black sky above, the red glow of the fire reflecting from the branches of a nearby sycamore. As he chanted his death song, he sensed, more than saw, the Iroquois making a long, slow motion with the knife. In spite of the general weakness engulfing him, Plenty Fish continued his fading chant. Laughing, rude faces danced inches from his, yelling and mocking.

The endless pain at last swirled into a distant, dull eddy that carried away the last of his sensitivities. Barely able to stand, Plenty Fish could only mumble as his tormentors attempted vainly to drain his final reservoir of courage.

At the point when he felt he could no longer endure, Plenty Fish became aware of an inexplicable new light bathing him. Becoming peaceful and joyous, even more elated than he could remember, he looked above the trees. There, in an empty sky, hung the large and brilliant Illinois moon.

* * *

Not far away a snapping twig heralded the approach of deer to the water's edge. Two does and a fawn approached cautiously, seeking to quench their thirst. The first, the largest, took a small sip, then raised its head, alarmed by the faint smell of smoke. After a moment the deer resumed drinking, the normal stillness of the night having returned, the water surface resplendently silver in the expansive moonlight.

And quietly flows the river.

About the Author

The author recently retired with over 30 years service as a military intelligence analyst, having been involved in intelligence and military issues at the national level. He performed threat assessments for major weapons system acquisitions, such as the first cruise missiles, the advanced tactical fighter (F-22 Raptor), and the advanced medium range air-to-air missile. He also served with the Strategic Defense Initiative Organization. Although these activities emphasized technical arenas, they brought into focus the need to know and understand the cultural and historical backgrounds of our allies and enemies. While reading Francis Parkman's *La Salle and the Discovery of the Great West*, the author was struck with the need to write a novel on this subject.

Printed in the United States
1176700006B/73-153